# THE
# JACARANDA
# LETTERS

Sylvia Howe

i

For my family – Glyn, Tom, and Harry –
for their encouragement,
and for leaving me with no more excuses

# GLOSSARY

| | |
|---|---|
| *Almirah* | wardrobe |
| *Burra peg* | large alcoholic drink, usually whisky |
| *Chai* | tea |
| *Chota peg* | small alcoholic drink, usually whisky |
| *Chowkidar* | watchman |
| *Dhobi* | laundry man |
| *Dhoti* | male garment, consisting of a piece of material tied around the waist and extending to cover most of the legs |
| *Dosa* | a type of pancake made from fermented batter |
| *Dukaan* | shop |
| *Durzi* | tailor |
| *Juldi* | quickly |
| *Kurta* | a loose shirt falling either just above or somewhere below the knees of the wearer, traditionally worn by men |
| *Lunghi* | also known as a sarong, is a traditional garment worn around the waist |
| *Machan* | tree platform from which to watch for and shoot animals |
| *Mahout* | person who works with and rides an elephant |
| *Mali* | gardener |
| *Murram* | a form of laterite (a clayey material) used for road surfaces |
| *Nan* | Indian bread |
| *Nappit* | barber |
| *Nimbu pani* | cold drink of fresh lime juice, water and sugar |
| *Nullah* | drain |
| *Pais* | coin |
| *Sadhu* | religious ascetic, or holy person |

| | |
|---|---|
| *Shalwar khameez* | loose pantaloons or trousers, wide at the top with a drawstring, and narrow at the ankle with a long shirt or tunic |
| *Syce* | groom |
| *Tonga* | two-wheeled carriage drawn by one or two horses |

# ENGLAND 2005

# Chapter One

The wooden box was not exactly hidden, just tucked out of sight at the back of the drawer. Julia felt for its corners, pulling it out carefully. Its domed lid with brass hinges scraped along the wood as she took it out, but its clasp flew up at a light press on the lock.

Inside was a bundle of folded paper, curling at the edges. She breathed in camphor, dust, and the passing of time.

The string holding it all together fell off at a tug and revealed letters, some written on thin air mail paper, in pale blue envelopes with striped edges, some on aerogrammes addressed to Mrs Arthur Kirkwood. The handwriting was bold, the ink dark blue, hardly faded.

Julia smoothed one out carefully on the flat surface of the desk.

At the top she read a printed copperplate address:

*Jacaranda Lodge*
*Cantonments*
*Ranpur*
*India*
*June 1946*

The signature told her these letters were from her grandmother's sister, Helen. Someone Julia had never met. She'd heard her parents mention Helen only rarely, and with something approaching – what? Slight embarrassment? Guilt, even? She'd had a few letters from her, sent when she was only just able to read. She'd replied in carefully shaped copperplate, encouraged by her mother, who told her that her great-aunt was living alone, with her dog Deena, very far away, on the other side of

India. One day a package had arrived: a small trinket box with a silver lid. She still had it.

*My dear sister Kate*, she read, and stopped, letting the past whisper through the decades...

*My dear sister Kate,*

*Thank you for your letter, which I read with some concern.*

*I'm so sorry to hear that your relationship with Arthur is strained since he has come back from the war. At least it was only two years. I feel sure that your suspicions aren't true. From what I remember of Arthur, he's an honourable man – someone who would keep to a promise – in your case, the marriage vow.*

*He has been away for a few years, and it couldn't have been any fun at all in the jungles of Burma. It will, I'm sure, take him a little time to re-accustom himself to peacetime, and to you. And if something intimate happened there – can you not give him the benefit of the doubt? It was a long way away; he must have missed you very much and I don't see that taking comfort – if it was offered – is so reprehensible. Not as reprehensible as it would be in a little place like Ranpore. Forgive me if that sounds as if I'm raking up the past. I'm not. But I'd advise you, if you feel like taking my advice, to keep your fears to yourself. Apple carts can so easily be upset. I know I've no first-hand experience of marriage but I've noticed that most survive the greatest difficulties, and even grow stronger – as long as any problems are kept private. It is so beastly and humiliating to be the main subject of discussion at the Club.*

*Men can sometimes be a little disloyal – although they don't see it like that, of course. Exploitative even – I hear from nearly every woman at some point that they feel that they do all the work, and their husbands get the benefit, without taking the trouble to show their appreciation. I sympathise, although the other argument also holds – the men work and earn the money, and so it is a sort of business arrangement. Rather like the British in India, I realise, as I write this. India gives a great deal, and we take it, and I'm not sure we are very gracious about it. I'm not going to be boring and revolutionary – I'm not brave enough for that, and can't face all the arguments, but it is just an observation.*

*I can't help noticing that British men – the ones fresh from the boat, anyhow – have a way of treating their wives rather like they treat Indians. They can't help it – many are neither cultured nor educated, and need to feel they deserve all the bowing and scraping they get from the people they control, so they puff themselves up, and put their own needs very high up the list! The bowing and scraping is often new to them, and, although pleasant, it must be a bit disconcerting at first. They do get used to it pretty quickly of course, and then they start ordering most people about (except their superiors, who order everyone about!).*

*It seems to me that it is best to allow a little slack and try not to mind if people are a little self-absorbed. We are all guilty of it sometimes, and it is not particularly attractive. Nor is resentment, an emotion I've worked hard to quell. Sometimes I feel rather cheerful at the success of my efforts, but shadows lie in wait, and catch me out when I least expect it.*

*How is the heat where you are? Still cool in lower Assam, I should think. Not here in Ranpore, alas. It is getting very hot and the humidity is rising – quite the worst time of the year. Mother, as she ages, gets tired and cross more quickly in the heat, and I'm afraid I'm less patient than I could be. Still, Cassandra is a delightful friend and we are enjoying the dry season together on our bicycles. Mother is enjoying the Bridge tournaments at the Club, trouncing all-comers and proving her remarkable recall. She only forgets what she finds convenient, a skill I very much admire.*

*I'm sure you and Arthur will find a happy equilibrium – as time passes relationships evolve, and I read somewhere that we can't change other people, only ourselves. More philosophy, so I had better draw this note to a close before you screw it up and aim it at the waste-paper basket. At least Arthur isn't a "temporary gent", embarrassing you by trying to show how superior he is to even the educated locals! That remains, at present, one of my bugbears. As if a pompous, ill-educated little sahib with less breeding or kindness than Sudham, the bearer, deserves his high estate simply because he attended some dreary little public school in Sussex. Forgive me. I rant.*

*I look forward to your next letter, and in the meantime I send you my love. The men are returning to their families from their regiments. Some are not. Things have changed – for good – although Ranpore still feels pretty much like the backwater it has always been.*

*We all grow older, some grow wiser, some just grow. Like the garden, which at the moment dry but still flourishing as the* mali *wields his hosepipe, and the water is pumped up from the well. The rainy season is coming, so we try to fill the house with flowers. It makes me happy, although Mother thinks it extravagant unless we have guests. So we have guests – tonight, Cassandra and the Cunninghams. The* dramatis personae *don't change.*

*With love,*

*Helen*

# Chapter Two

"Have you seen the *Daily Mail* today, Julia?"

The voice on the telephone had been sympathetic, but interested.

"No. Why?"

"It's Freddie. He seems to have... well, there's a big photograph of him draped over a girl who could pass for his daughter. She's ... er, not wearing a lot."

Julia looked at a photograph of her younger self with a wide smile and beautifully-cut hair. She took a deep breath.

"Thanks for telling me, Tasha. I'd better get off to the newsagent!"

She grabbed her handbag and her coat. Checked she had her keys.

Mr Ahmed's shop on the corner of the street was open as always. He looked at her sympathetically, but took her money without a word. She dropped the tabloid into her bag and left with a smile. He was a nice man, Mr Ahmed, considerably nicer than many of his customers. Glossy well-kept women, like she'd become. Manes of hair that moved as one swishy block, faces smooth and clear, painted by a master to look as if they were strangers to foundation, primer, blush, highlighter, fixing powder...

She, like them, worked hard to keep her bingo wings at bay, going to Bikram Yoga classes wearing Juicy Couture; she had her regular eco-natural facial; she went to Adam Paul in Trevor Square for a weekly blow-dry, more often if there was something special happening. She didn't work, unless you counted an occasional philanthropic shift in the Oxfam shop, and she didn't have children. Not for want of trying, but there you were. Neither she nor Freddie had worried about it – there was always plenty of time.

Perhaps not now, she thought. Freddie had aroused her suspicions before, but had competently explained away a silent telephone call, or an early morning arrival to change and shave before leaving for the office. And she'd chosen to let sleeping dogs lie – in every sense.

"You never need worry, Julia, darling," he would say. "You're stuck with me."

And so far, this seemed to be true. Freddie always turned up, smiling, with a hug, a bunch of flowers, a piece of jewellery if he had been away longer than usual. He had taken her to the Danieli in Venice, to the Four Seasons in New York, for a week in the Caribbean at Montpelier Plantation on Nevis. He loved getting away with things.

Freddie was no longer a Man-to-be-Watched, he was a Man-who-had-Made-It. And a babe magnet, as his friend, Charlie (there was always a Charlie, wasn't there?) would say jovially, reddening when Freddie frowned at him.

A rich property developer. Intelligent, good company, handsome. What not to like? Not at first, second, or third meeting anyway. It took a little longer than that to come up against the flinty self-absorption.

Julia sighed. On the front page of the newspaper, in the bottom left-hand corner, was a photograph of a very beautiful dark-haired girl in a red dress, smiling at the photographer and leaning into her companion. Freddie, looking confident and younger than his forty-five years. His wide smile showed rows of white and even teeth (thanks, discreet and expensive dentist in Beauchamp Place), his hair dark and romantically floppy over his Botox-smooth brow, his bow tie untied, his dinner jacket nonchalantly carried over his shoulder. He knew how to strike a pose, did Freddie, exuding success and charm.

*Hot Property!* cried the headline.

Oh, surely they could do better than that?

*"Freddie Hunstanton and Antonella Morandi. Full story p9."*

Could she bear it? She needed a cup of coffee. She opened the glass door of the little Italian coffee shop, asked for an Americano, and pointed at a couple of *biscotti*. What the hell.

Then she turned to page nine, where the article went into detail about Freddie and the glorious Antonella *"star of* The Song of Sicily, *De Luzzi's new film, shot on that beautiful island, and opening in London in a couple of weeks."* They had been attending some sort of Industrial Awards evening at the Dorchester, and yes, there was a trophy dangling from Freddie's right hand.

Julia took in Antonella's high cheekbones, the lean brown arms, set off with a diamond bracelet on a slim wrist. Her own arms had been like that once, she thought, annoyed with herself for minding. This young woman sparkled, carefree, her eyes on the future. She looked like the other young women who had attached themselves to Freddie. Sukie or Susie or Tiggy. They had been nothing like Julia, which at the time had been a comfort, but now she wondered. Had she become just a wife? A help-meet – awful word, but horribly accurate.

There was a photograph of Freddie on a yacht on a still turquoise sea – the paper had obviously trawled through the archives. Freddie had invited several clients on that trip. It had sounded so great – sailing from island to island in the sunshine, swimming off the boat, looked after by an experienced crew, but it had not worked out that way for her. She'd been sick for a couple of days, which had annoyed him, as she'd taken to her cabin rather than share dry Martinis with guests who might have been fascinating conversationalists, or might, just might, have been there because they were very rich and thinking of buying in the UK.

Freddie, bronzed and dashing, stood elegantly on the deck in the swimming shorts he had bought from Harvey Nicks. She couldn't remember the designer, but it would have been the most popular one at the time. Gucci, probably. Labels mattered to Freddie. Labels and pretty women and everything that hollered High Life, and Success, and Money. Julia wondered where she fitted in.

She folded the newspaper and raised her eyes to watch the well-kept women pass outside, some with pushchairs that probably cost as much as a small car. French was spoken a lot in this bit of South Kensington; the Lycée was just round the corner. At least you could get good coffee. The florist by the tube was doing a sprightly trade; Julia recognised one of the recent bouquets Freddie had brought home for her as an apology for being late.

She closed her eyes, shutting out her husband's face in the paper, and the innuendo in the paragraph beside it. She needed to think. Did she love Freddie now, or had all these humiliations finally done their work? This time it felt worse than ever before. Her eyes pricked, and she took a tissue surreptitiously from her bag. She squeezed her lids together. She wasn't going to let herself cry about a pair of lithe tanned arms.

Freddie had always done whatever he liked. He had never pretended otherwise. She'd let it pass, but today she felt crushed and foolish. He could have been more discreet. The *Daily Mail*! He *must* have known how awful it would be for me to see him draped over someone twenty years younger than me... than *him*, for Christ's sake. The bastard.

The tears were coming. Julia stood up shakily and walked out into the street, narrowly missing the *Big Issue* seller to whom she usually gave a pound. He looked surprised as she clipped past, her heels tapping on the pavement. I must get home, she thought, the words taking on the rhythm of her steps. I must get home, I must get home. She dashed a hand across her eyes, leaving a streak of mascara on the back of it. Soon she was at her front door, her hand shaking as she put the key in the lock.

Slipping a capsule in the Nespresso machine, she made herself a strong black coffee. I can't bear this again and again, she told herself. So what do I do now? I'll go down to Linton, today, this afternoon. I can't hang around here to hear his excuses.

Linton would help. The house had become hers when her mother died and her father had gone into a home three years earlier. She and Freddie went there for weekends occasionally – not as often as she would like.

Freddie enjoyed having "a house in the country". He liked the hidden drive, the large drawing room, the back stairs, the Aga. Whenever Freddie was there, meals were taken in the dining room, at the oval oak table, mellow with years of beeswax, laid with silver and Spode. The green baize door swung shut with a resigned sigh.

But he didn't savour the smell of wood smoke from

the large fire in the drawing room, and the smaller one in the tiny nursery.

"A touch too rustic for me, darling. I love this house, I do really, but it could do with a bit of smartening up. You must see that."

"I don't, actually. It's home. I like it like it is."

"There's space, I give you that. But it would be much better if we got some people to slosh some Farrow & Ball about. Don't you think?"

She'd stuck to her guns. His attention would move on quickly enough and give her some breathing space. He might have converted the central heating and Aga to gas, but she'd fought to keep the wood burners in the dining and drawing rooms. One thing was certain. She was not going to be a publicly-cuckolded wife. And she would never, ever, give another party for Freddie's ghastly billionaires.

That decision taken, she felt a lot better.


## Chapter Three

Linton's ochre bricks and mullioned windows looked romantic in the early evening light, the last sloping rays of the sun reflected in some of the small uneven panes.

She parked on the circle of gravel in front of the heavy oak front door, and took the key from the glove box where she always kept it. Freddie would, as always, have lost his. She felt relieved at the thought. She couldn't face the charm offensive. He would turn it all on – it would be so inconvenient to lose her.

She felt the familiar scrunch of small stones under her shoes as she walked up to the front door. It was opened by a grey-haired man, a duster in his hand.

"Julia!"

"Hello Davie," she said, as jauntily as she could

manage. "Is Mivvie about? I'm so sorry I didn't tell you I was coming. It was a bit of a rush all round. Sorry to be a trouble, but I've decided to stay for a few days..." Her voice tailed off.

"It's always a pleasure to see you, Julia."His Welsh accent could be brisk. "And no trouble at all, of course. Myfanwy will be as pleased as I am. Any luggage?"

"A suitcase, badly packed. It may fly open! Otherwise just me."

And that was that.

Davie and Myfanwy had lived at Linton since her parents had bought it. The details were hazy. Davie had been in the war with her father, then in Pakistan with the family, and when things became difficult, the two of them hatched a plan. Mivvie and Davie took care of Linton and whoever was staying there, and in exchange they lived there rent free.

"Keep the burglars away, make sure the roof doesn't fall in, and they're pretty good company, too," her father, Sandy, had said once.

She followed Davie into the kitchen, warmed by the large cream Aga. She saw him slip the *Daily Mail* into a drawer.

Footsteps tripped down the red-tiled corridor outside the kitchen, and the door opened to admit a small woman in an apron, almost a caricature of a housekeeper, except for her very dark hair with one white streak which flopped over her face. She pushed this back as she stepped forward and gave Julia a hug.

"Haven't seen you for a while, Julia. All okay?"

Davie turned away to put the kettle on the Aga. Mivvie, after a brief pause, moved into motherly mode. She missed little.

"Yes, I'm fine," Julia said, although it sounded a bit flat.

"Any news?" Mivvie asked.

Davie coughed gently and went outside to "bring in

some wood for the fire in the drawing room."

"That would be lovely. It *is* a bit chilly in the evenings now. May I have the heating on as well please?"

This had always been a bone of contention with her frugal parents.

"It's a big house, Julia. It doesn't heat itself. And doesn't pay for all that oil either," her mother would say.

"Of course," Mivvie said, smiling. "If we'd known you were coming, we'd have turned it on. Still, it won't take long to warm up. Davie will light the fire and everything will be cosy. You all right, love?"

She looked hard at Julia, who looked back as calmly as she could. She wasn't ready to unburden herself – there were too many loose ends. The phone rang, and Mivvie answered it.

"Linton House, good afternoon. Oh, hello Freddie..."

She looked enquiringly at Julia, who leaned over and took it from her. The door creaked as Mivvie left the room.

"What on earth are you doing?" His voice was sharp. "We have eight people for dinner tonight, remember. Douglas Carlton – it's important. Will you be back?"

She could feel him trying to keep calm, but he spoke louder than he needed.

"No, Freddie. I won't," she said. "I'm staying at Linton for a while. The weekend, at least, probably longer."

Silence.

She waited, surprised she was so calm. In the past she'd confided in a friend or two, voicing her suspicions, sometimes tearfully. This time she just felt cold and slightly sick.

"Now Julia, It's that stupid photograph, isn't it? It means nothing at all. You know the *Mail* – they love a shiny starlet..."

"This is one shiny starlet too many, Freddie. I don't like being the subject of sympathy. The poor little wife..."

"You're not the poor little wife. I need you here, Julia. I've always needed you. I depend on you, you know that. Don't know what I'd do without you. Please don't be like this."

"Like what?"

"So – so unlike you. You sound, well... different."

"I feel different, Freddie."

She squashed the flickers of righteous anger. There was no point. It would probably lead to tears, and tears so far had led to acceptance, to convincing herself that she was overreacting, that it was nothing. One of Freddie's favourite phrases.

"The stupid papers always get it wrong. You know that," he said. "It was nothing. Antonella is beautiful, and they love having photos of girls like her, and I had just won the award so it looked good and newsy too. And I got in plenty about the new development, which was great..."

The chink of profit drowned out any hint of penitence.

She took a deep breath and spoke very clearly.

"Freddie, as I said, I'm staying in Linton for a few days. Then I'll call Tom Farmer – ask his advice, one way or the other."

"This is ridiculous, Julia. There's no need to speak to a solicitor. This is an..."

"An overreaction? Not this time, Freddie. I've had enough."

"I need you, Julia. What do you want me to do? Be around more?"

"Actually, Freddie, that's the last thing I want at the moment. I don't think I want you to be around any more at all. I need to talk to Tom about how to leave without a fuss. I shan't be too demanding, and I know you'll be civilised, too."

Silence.

"Bloody fucking hell, Julia, I can't believe this. You need to think about what you're saying. You..."

"I agree. We both need to think. So, now I'm going to have a glass of wine and watch television. I hope your evening goes well. Bye."

The ting of the receiver landing in its cream cradle was satisfying. Ignoring a butterfly in her stomach, Julia took a bottle of *Gavi* from the fridge and poured herself a large cold glass. She walked slowly through the entrance hall to the drawing room where Davie's lively fire in the wood burner was warming the panelled room. She stretched out on the sofa, and reached for the remote control.

## Chapter Four

It was the first time Julia had felt strong enough to go through her parents' belongings at Linton.

She went up the back stairs to the first-floor landing and opened a dark wooden door to her father's office. It smelled of her childhood: tobacco and paper, blended with that other scent that always fills rooms which have been empty for a while: cold and dusty, with a hint of loneliness.

There were black and white photographs from his school days, a looking glass above the mantel, the picture of Julia as Desdemona in a school play, the heavy cigarette lighter with its green baize base that had fitted in his hand to light each of his sixty a day. She left these alone, to be stored or got rid of. His papers were tidy, his bank statements filed, his few investments in clear folders.

Resenting the unkindness of fate, of old age, Julia looked around and felt a moment's panic. Things had changed when her mother had died. She missed her brown eyes which wrinkled when she smiled. She missed the laughter, the sense of humour, the teasing…

Stop this, she told herself, and opened a drawer.

She found a pile of paper and curling notes, including

one on the top from Freddie. He had worked hard at the son-in-law stuff. Her father had enjoyed discussions about politics, sport, and history over a Scotch or three by the fire after dinner, and Freddie enjoyed feeling part of a family. His own had not been loving, which was probably why he didn't understand what kept families together.

She carried on, her heart heavy, tidying and sorting. Some files she left neatly on the shelves, while she tipped others into a black plastic bin liner that she dragged out on to the landing. Then she moved next door.

Her mother Susannah's room, decorated with Indian miniatures, fabrics, and candlesticks, was very much her own space. The duck-egg blue on the walls had been her favourite colour:

"Keeps it cool, makes my brain work," she used to say.

On the mantel a large silent clock had to be wound weekly, flanked by some brightly painted wooden and *papier maché* Indian gods.

"Touch Ganesh's trunk whenever you pass him, Julia. Makes you rich."

She touched it now, and her finger came away dusty. She opened a window and a light breeze fluttered some papers on the camphor wood desk she remembered from Tindharia. She clicked open the face of the clock and wound it up with a brass key. The immediate ticking made everything seem less ghostly. To its comforting regularity, she could begin her work.

Standing by the window she looked down on the roses and borders – slightly ragged now – which had been her mother's pride and joy, then sat in the chair at the desk. She drew the pile of papers towards her. Many were out of date, so she put them straight into another black plastic sack before turning to the drawers. The one in the centre held pens and pencils, staples and a little stapler. A hole punch, Sellotape, and other bits of stationery Susannah had bought on one of her many trips to W H Smith. A bright red lipstick, lopsided in its tube.

"I love stationery, Julia. Just love it. It is so – full of promise. I'll draw a beautiful sketch with this 6B pencil, perhaps. Probably won't, but I just might. And as for writing paper – mmmm."

In the right-hand drawer there were correspondence cards, white and thick, with an address embossed in the middle at the top: *Mrs Alexander MacCleod, Tindharia Tea Estate* on some, and on others, *Mrs Alexander MacCleod, Linton House, Balcombe, Sussex.* And the post code, which she'd hated. Letter paper, a choice of birthday cards, envelopes. Stamps, a menu from an Indian restaurant, more clear plastic folders. Nothing remarkable, but everything represented a living moment and caught at Julia's throat. She didn't have time for tears now. They would drag the sad little process out, and she wanted more than anything to finish it, clearing the scraps, leaving the memories.

All predictable, not particularly interesting, mostly familiar. Except for this box of folded paper, stored away from casual eyes. Julia folded the letter she'd been reading and put it back into the box. There were plenty more, she could see. She looked forward to reading them, perhaps learning about her grandmother and her great-aunt, decoding undercurrents. She knew bits and pieces about her family, but there were big gaps. It was all part of Susannah and Sandy's Getting-On-With-It manifesto. There was probably not much to tell: middle class, comfortable, a mother's colonial past, a father's tea planting days, ending with a generous pension and a nest egg built up by sending the monthly remittance to the bank.

Picking up the crackly, fragile sheets, she read on, feeling Helen's briskness as she wrote carefully to her sister, several days' train journey away from Ranpore. There was something about her words that seemed rehearsed, holding herself in check. She would probably write about servants and riding and the difficulty of getting the right kind of flour and the weather and the Monsoon Ball. Although interesting historically, these letters would probably be nothing new. Shame. Julia hoped for revelations.

She thought of the times she'd gone to Tindharia Tea Estate to stay with her grandparents. She thought she'd noticed Kate looking odd when Helen was mentioned, or was that just her imagination? Had Arthur really changed the subject every time? These little moments had flickered away so quickly it was hard to tell if they had been there at all. She'd been too young to question any of it then. Her father had taken over the running of Tindharia Tea Estate when Arthur decided to retire with Kate to the guest cottage in the grounds in 1970. He had died five years later, and Kate had swiftly followed him, her life poorer without his vitality.

Julia remembered playing with the servants, and enjoying the loving attentions of Lily, her *ayah*. She saw the grown-ups for meals, and in the evenings after her bath they would play board games and listen to the crackly BBC World Service if they could get it on the radiogram. It was happy and serene.

Then, in 1978, she'd been sent away to school, where her haircut and clothes had needed serious attention to quell the giggles of her classmates. Pamela Phillips, the hockey captain, had laughed when Julia appeared on the pitch in a divided skirt that came down to her knees. Julia had wanted to kill her. And her mother.

"Oh, for goodness sake, Julia," Susannah had said, poring over the school clothing list. "It says 'navy blue divided skirt' as part of your games kit. That's what this is. It'll do perfectly well, and saves us a tenner."

Julia soon discovered that there were divided skirts and divided skirts. And hairdressers and hairdressers, and her father's barber (the *nappit*) didn't cut it. She learnt the differences fast, and soon was indistinguishable from any other Eighties schoolgirl.

While she was at school, her parents began to prepare themselves for leaving Tindharia. Times were changing, and they were too old to change with them. They bought Linton, in Sussex, very like an old colonial house in one of the hill stations where the family had spent their local leave each year. Lots of slightly shabby space. Julia spent a few more holidays at Tindharia, and then it was over. Linton was now the family home.

Julia was too young to regret it much, especially after her eighteenth birthday party had been such a roaring success. Susannah said, wearily: "I suppose one benefit of living here is that nobody can hear the screams."

Julia drew herself back to the present. She'd begun to empty the other drawers, one by one, when the sharp trill of the telephone made her jump.

"Hello?"

"Hello? Susannah?"

A voice, deep but slightly crackly, with an occasional Scottish vowel. Her father.

"Hello, Dad. How are you?"

"Julia. Are you home for the holidays? Oh good. Have you been a good girl?"

*Guid gairl.*

"Mum's not here, Dad. She's ..."

"Oh. She said she would come and see me today. I expect she's on her way. We have people to drinks this evening, so she won't be long. When are you going to come? It would be lovely to see you, too. Come and have a picnic. Bring Major."

Major had been their dog in Pakistan, who had died just before they left the country.

"Mum's not here, Dad. She's – not here."

She stopped. If she told him again that his wife had

died, would it make any difference? Was it not kinder to leave it? He wouldn't remember.

"I expect she's taken the bus and it's been delayed. She'll be with you soon, I should think."

"Oh good. Well, must be getting on. Come with her next time, Julia. It's great you're back."

The phone clicked down firmly. Her father didn't do protracted goodbyes.

Julia suddenly felt completely alone.

The world around her seemed to have stopped. The sounds outside were muffled, the birdsong muted, the clock ticking indifferently. A lump in her throat made her swallow hard, and the great hole in her stomach hurt.

The house felt bleak and chilly for a moment, but shifted again to become the place she remembered. Her memories were comforting, soaked into the blotting paper of the carpet. The sun came out from behind a cloud and threw sharp-edged shadows on the lawn. A blackbird's song was loud and clear. She stood up and breathed deeply. On one of the bookshelves, beside an eighteenth-century china figurine, she noticed a misshapen clay cup with *Mum* cut into it. She closed her eyes. No tears came, and when she opened them nothing had changed.

## Chapter Five

The next morning Julia opened her eyes and looked around the bedroom, enjoying the snug duvet which had replaced the tightly tucked-in blankets and sheets of her youth. Another of Freddie's updates.

Back when she was young, England had always seemed very cold. There had been eiderdowns and hot water bottles for nights when a thin layer of frost spread on the inside of Linton's diamond panes, to melt in the chill morning sunlight and trickle down the glass on to the marble windowsill. She'd had to grit her teeth to make the dash across the carpet to the bathroom. Now the electric blanket had replaced the hottie, and central heating came on at five in the morning.

The bedroom was filled with early sunlight slipping through the gap in the heavy curtains, and the birds were singing outside. She squinted at the clock on her bedside table. A quarter to eight.

She wondered for half a heartbeat what had happened.

There was something she had to do.

Then she remembered.

Freddie. And the starlet.

What now? What would be best?

If she really wanted a divorce, she would have to get moving before she lost her nerve. Stupid. She should have done it last year, or the year before. Freddie wasn't going to change.

"I love you very much, Julia," he had said, one evening in bed. "You keep my feet on the ground. You aren't frightened of people."

"Are you?"

"Sometimes. When it matters. When they've got to be won over. You're so good at that. You know about good behaviour. I'm not sure I do."

It had been unexpected, and it never came again.

Julia brushed her dark curls while she ran water into the enormous green tub which took twenty minutes to fill from the crusty old-fashioned taps. It didn't matter. There was no rush today.

She took her time over breakfast, and then went out into the garden with Lupin, the Evanses' shaggy old setter. The cool air held promise of later warmth. The flowers were beginning to fade, the square pond's cracked fountain was silent. It had stopped working and there had been no real need to get it going again. I might do that, she thought, if I'm going to be here more often.

A robin trilled. The telephone rang, a mechanical echo.

Mivvie appeared at the side door, studiedly neutral.

"Your husband is on the telephone, Julia."

Julia smiled wearily.

"Please tell him I'll call him back when I've had my walk."

Freddie never gave up when he wanted something. She would have to steel herself for an extended siege. But her resolve felt stronger still this morning. A switch had been turned off in her head, and she wasn't going to be tempted to turn it back on.

It would take conviction: Freddie fought dirty. There would be the soft reminders of happy times together. Holidays in the sun, just the two of them, in Greece, the Caribbean, Cape Cod. How her father had enjoyed his company by the fire...

And the solitary nights in, waiting for a phone call, she reminded herself. His weekends "working" in Italy, Sicily, France; his exasperated explanations.

"While I'm here," she said to Mivvie and Davie, "I'll carry on sorting through my parents' stuff. If Freddie rings, please ask him very politely to stop. I'll call him when I'm ready. Now, before I start upstairs, could I have a cup of your delicious coffee, please?"

Davie nodded, keeping his face expressionless. "Of course you can. But it might take a while to go through your parents' offices. There's bound to be all sorts of interesting bits and pieces."

For some reason Julia didn't want to mention the letters she'd found. They were too private, too full of promise to share just yet, even with Davie and Mivvie, the two people she trusted more than anyone. She wondered if they knew about them. Unlikely. Susannah's door had been kept firmly closed, and the Evanses would not have intruded without asking.

Julia finished her coffee, rinsed out her cup and put it

down on the draining board. She suddenly wanted to get back to the letters. It was so intriguing, opening long-folded paper to read – what? Secrets was too strong, but there was something in their tone suggesting hidden layers. Helen seemed dignified and slightly defiant. Perhaps she was being silly, Julia told herself. Just her imagination. She would go on reading and see what else she found. The allusions to Grandpa Arthur were, on the surface, friendly and complimentary, but there was something uncomfortable tucked away in the tightly polite sentences, and she wondered what it could be. Like the first letter she picked up this morning, after leaving Mivvie in the kitchen...

*Jacaranda Lodge*
*Ranpore*
*June 1943*

*Congratulations. A baby girl! How lovely! Susannah Helen Ramage Kirkwood! Thank you for the compliment – I always thought my middle name ugly, but it's flattering that you have added it to Susannah's collection.*

*I was sorry to learn that her entry into the world was a bit of a struggle. From the photographs she's a bouncing baby. I enclose a little something from Mother and me. A cotton blanket. I hope it'll come in useful – we worked long and hard on the crochet, and it'll be light in the heat and warm in the chill.*

*Please do send more photographs. And if you plan to go to Calcutta, let me know and I'll see if I can make the journey. It is not easy at the moment while people are busy joining up, but it should be possible. I expect Arthur's itching to go, and you're hoping he stays... I know I would be.*

*Doris says she'll cover for me at Jacaranda Lodge should I ever wish to go anywhere, as long as it is not for too long. I've never asked her exactly how long this would be!*

*Mother and she tolerate each other; Doris puts up with her assumption of superiority and slight frostiness, putting it down (quite correctly, of course) to Doris's mixed parentage, and Mother has accepted her presence perforce. Familiarity has not bred contempt. Rather it has diluted it, and she has been forced to recognise the good things about my friend.*

*And there's always Cassandra, who has offered to come and stay, too. Mother can't fault her antecedents, but says she's "too clever by half". She's engaged to Cornelius Clandon, did I say? They're perfect for each other, and there is nobody to stand in their way. I envy them a little.*

*He obviously doesn't think her too clever for him: they laugh, they talk, and listen to each other, he has enough money for them to live comfortably together, and he wasn't looking for a bright young thing. I'm not sure he was looking for anyone, which is why this is such a joy to behold.*

*Mother doesn't get much joy from it, as you can imagine. Not that C and C do anything too embarrassing, but they look at each other with affection and the other day they held hands a little longer than they needed to when he was helping her into the tonga! Mother humphed and said it was an unnecessary display. As I say, nothing changes. And I quite like unnecessary displays sometimes. Anything to show real affection, as you may remember.*

*Anyhow – let me know if you're ever nearby, and I'll try to arrange something...*

*Helen xx*

# Chapter Six

Ivy Lodge was a comfortable care home. Julia's father had settled in without fuss, although occasionally there was a querulous demand to call a taxi.

On this unseasonably warm October day, the ivy on the Lodge's red-brick walls was hardly moving. Julia could see a herd of deer through the trees, looking up now and again, but comfortable enough not to shiver and bolt.

She always felt like running away whenever her taxi drove up to this elegant country house, and the guilt she felt was always the same. She scrunched up the gravel to the front door between two pillars, stopped for a second, breathed in quickly and walked in.

"Hello?" she said, smiling at the woman in white behind the desk. "I've come to see Mr MacCleod?"

"Okay. You know where he is... he's chatty today. Feels well, and he'll be very happy you've come."

This was a familiar exchange, but Julia always thought she detected an undercurrent of reproach. She knew she should come more often. Once a week sometimes stretched to once a fortnight. It hurt her to see her father, once strong and solid, reduced to a smaller version of himself.

Her father's room had French windows opening on to a wide lawn that led to terracing and a ha-ha. He was sitting on the terrace with his feet up, enjoying the sunshine.

"Dad? Dad? Hello, It's me, Julia."

He didn't open his eyes.

"Julia."

He turned his head towards her and lifted his eyelids slowly, putting a hand up to shield his face from the glare. He tried to haul himself to his feet, but Julia put her hand on his arm.

"No Dad, don't get up, please. I'm fine. You look so lovely and comfortable, I don't want you to move."

"Call the bearer for a glass of *nimbu pani*," he said firmly.

She didn't say anything, but helped herself from the jug of lemon barley water on the table beside him, taking care to put ice cubes in it from the cream Bakelite ice bucket she remembered from the sideboard at Linton. She handed him his drink and drew up a chair beside him.

"How are you, Dad?"

"Fine. Feeling a bit lazy today. Your mother has gone out to the shops, so I took advantage of her absence to have a bit of a zizz. But I'll have to get up in a bit and mow the lawn."

A pause. A voice came through the open windows of the next-door room – sharp, irritated.

"Oh, mother, don't worry. You'll be happy here..."

"Are *you* happy here, Dad?" Julia couldn't stop herself asking. His pale blue eyes, the iris rimmed with a pale circle, settled on her face, then looked away.

"Can't complain. Food's a bit ropey, but it's fine. I like the hotel we stayed at last year, though – better than this one. But Nice is always warm at this time of year. Have you got a paper for me? Or a book?"

She always brought something. It was a ritual between them, and a sort of comfort for her. Beside his chair was a table with three thrillers on it. Through the tall French windows that led off the terrace into his room she could see that his bed was tidy, covered with a white bedspread crocheted by her great-grandmother. *Labour of Love, 1924* it said, in the centre, surrounded by cherubs. And underneath them, in smaller letters, *From Evangeline*.

"What was Evangeline like, Dad? Did you know her?"

She didn't expect a reply – her father's memory was unpredictable, came and went, and was not always accurate. But today he responded clearly.

"Your great-grandmother? Only met her a couple of times. I went to stay – to meet the family. To have an interview, really. Who was I? My family? My school? My prospects? Kate and Arthur had already given me the third degree, and I'd passed muster, but Evangeline couldn't resist. She's a formidable woman, Evangeline. Tiny. Always wears the same thing – long and black with white lace collars. Hair in a tidy bun, on the top of her head. Must be very hot, but then a lady never shows the heat, she says. I don't know how she does it."

He sighed, and looked across the lawn.

"Her eyes are like a magpie's, almost black; she misses nothing. Are you going to come to the Bridge Night at the Club tomorrow? I do like a game of Bridge, but not if Evangeline is playing. Always bites my head off."

He grinned, showing teeth stained by years of smoking.

Julia tried again.

"And her daughters. Granny Kate I knew a bit. She was quiet and vague, I thought. She married Arthur. Great-aunt Helen wrote to me at school. Did you know? She sent me a little silver and glass box, which she said had been her mother's. That's Evangeline, isn't it?"

"Where?"

He sat up, and looked around.

"No, It's okay, Dad. She isn't here."

"Thank God. I'm scared of Evangeline, don't mind admitting," he said. "Kate was pretty, like your mother, and nobody could say she's faded. Helen – she was the popular one I believe – the one who – well... Some people were a bit nervous of her – her own opinions, clever. "

He frowned, trying to keep track of his memories.

"Evangeline – tricky. Not kind – but don't say I said. You know your great-grandmother – that's what she is, isn't she? She's tricky. I like Arthur, he's a good chap. Good shot. Bit of a social climber though. Needed a suitable wife, and saw that he got one. But he didn't quite come up to scratch with Helen. Or perhaps it was her. Can't remember, but there was something."

Silence again. He looked at his daughter, with a glimmer of his old spirit.

"I know she's dead. Susannah. That's why she doesn't come to see me. I miss her."

He spoke firmly, shoulders back, jaw set, facing the truth, which had seeped into his mind. It wouldn't last, but for now he had to be brave.

"Yes, Dad. I miss her, too. I miss you."

He didn't hear the last three words.

His voice was still firm when he continued: "Arthur married Kate. Left Ranpore, had your mother. Helen didn't come to our wedding. Evangeline may have. Did she?"

He frowned again, and started to shake his head.

"Evangeline – she isn't a kind woman, you know. Selfish. Helen must be lonely – she's such a good cook. I don't really know her. Is she here? Is she coming to see me soon? Where am I?"

Julia could see he was tiring. She stood up.

"Do you want to rest a bit, Dad? Shall I go?"

"No. No, don't go. Your grandparents were very kind to me. Tindharia. Enjoyed that. I loved your mother, you know. Didn't love Kate – boring. Arthur wasn't. Boring, I mean. He should have married Helen. Always thought so. And I wasn't the only one. But Evangeline always got her way."

"You took over Tindharia, didn't you Dad? From Grandpa Arthur?"

"Yes. Tindharia is beautiful. Your mother likes it. Should we go to the UK, do you think? Have we got a house there? We do, I think. Would you like Linton? Is your mother there?"

"I remember people being nice to me at Tindharia, and my *ayah*, and bright colours and weaver birds and hibiscus flowers. I don't remember anything bad about it at all. Rather magical, really. Then things changed. I went to school."

"Your mother and I are coming to your play next week, Julia. Desdemona, you said. Well done!"

Julia smiled. His eyes were beginning to lose their focus.

"Where on earth is your mother? She said she was

coming today," he asked crossly. "I wonder if she's heard from Kate. Arthur's dead, you know. He died when we came back to UK. Bit of a shame really. We got here and he popped his clogs. Where's Susannah?"

The moment had passed. He lay back in his chair, and sighed, his eyes filling with tears. A face put itself around the door, after a crisp knock.

"Ready for supper, are we, Sandy?"

"*We* aren't," he snapped. "I'm waiting for my wife. My daughter's just leaving."

"Okay. Fine. I'll be back in a minute then. Goodbye, Miss MacCleod. Nice to see her again, isn't it, Sandy?"

She closed the door with a click, and Sandy glared at it.

"Patronising cow. Treats me like a child. I like the others much better. They know me. Right then. Off you go. Good of you to drop by. You'll miss your train. Here."

He took a five pound note out of his pocket and gave it to her.

"Don't tell your mother! Off you go. See you at half term!"

He winked. His manner had changed again. It was now brisk and military, a man with things to do. She kissed him, and squeezed his hand, all bones and crinkled skin.

"I'll be back. Next week, Dad, if I can. Look after yourself."

He nodded, and turned his head to look out of the French windows. She hesitated, but for him she was no longer in the room. His thoughts were somewhere else entirely.

# INDIA
# MAY 1937

# Chapter Seven

"Oh my goodness, it's so hot today."

The young woman fanned herself with a handkerchief. "Going outside is terrible. I need to be near a fan at all times."

Her sister laughed. "Not very practical, Kate!"

"Oh come on, Helen. It's ghastly. We're supposed to be used to it, but this year it's so much worse than usual. Isn't it?"

"I'm not entirely sure. You say that every year, I think," Helen said, smiling.

"Ohhh..."

Kate flung herself on a rattan chair, sinking into its chintz cushion and stretching her legs out.

There was no sound on the wide verandah except for the beat of the fan overhead, which moved the thick hot air just a little. The orange and red and dark pink bougainvillea that framed the pillars on either side of the red stone steps stirred slightly, and a bee buzzed between the flowers. A dog barked in the distance and a small bird darted from bush to bush, its tail flicking up and down. On the lawn below them, the *mali* shuffled past, pushing a wooden wheelbarrow. Its wheel squeaked.

"He's probably much less sweaty than we are," Kate grumbled.

"We'd look a bit odd in his loincloth, though. Come on. Cheer up. I'm waiting for the vegetable man and then I'm taking Bodhi's *tonga* into town. Come too?"

"You must be joking. I'm sticking to the cushion just being here. I'm going to stay in my bedroom and read. I can't summon up any energy at all."

As she stood up to leave, Sudham, the bearer, answered the sharp ring of the bell at the gate and let in a small wizened man in a grubby *lunghi*, carrying a rod across his shoulders. From each end hung a basket of breadfruit, cabbage, cauliflower, lettuce, radish, beetroot.

He bowed and spread brightly-coloured vegetables and fruit on the steps of the bungalow. Papaya, guavas, custard apples and wrinkled passion fruit looked tempting.

"Ramdas. How are you today?" asked Helen.

He bent his head and gestured at the spread he had laid at her feet.

"Mmm, this looks good. Wonky..."

Wonky the sweeper and dogsbody who had one leg shorter than the other paused in his work. He leant heavily on his broom and looked at Helen.

"Please tell the cook that Ramdas is here," she told him.

Soon a small round man in a stained white jacket came and chose what he needed. With him came the scent of wood smoke and garlic; Helen and Kate were amazed he never seemed to smell of sweat, despite working in a small room over a kerosene stove and a charcoal fire. When the transaction was finished Ramdas walked away, his baskets swinging lightly on the pole across his shoulders. He closed the gate behind him, its hinges screeching.

"*Memsa'ab* Helen, the *tonga* will be here in ten minutes to take you to the bazaar."

Sudham spoke softly, with a slight inclination of his turbanned head. Evangeline was very particular about the servants' uniforms, and his tall slim figure looked suitably smart in his crisp white *dhoti* and jacket.

Helen sat back in the chair, folding her skirt about her knees. She looked forward to her visits to the shadowy depths of the tailor's workshop, which smelt of talcum powder, starch and newspaper, overlaid with a hint of incense. She liked keeping up with styles that suited her, taking inspiration from the magazines that came out from Europe and sat on the low peg tables at the Club.

In Bond Street she would not be fashionable, but here

in Ranpore she enjoyed her reputation for elegance. Today, her skirt came to just below her knee and her light cream top skimmed her slim hips, in the straight silhouette of the 1920s. Her shining dark hair was plaited and pinned into a coil on each ear, and her lobes were studded with small pearls. Her style was her own, and it suited her.

"My daughters are a credit to me," she often heard her mother tell friends. "They've their own style – very different from each other."

If they knew what was good for them, a listener would fill the pause with a light compliment. "Like their mother," worked well. Or "They've been very well taught." Or, if they were feeling enthusiastic: "You always look so fresh and smart. I don't know how you do it – the material here is usually so dull and the *durzi* needs such close supervision."

It was Helen who was good at the pleat and fold and slip of fabric, and could probably have made the clothes she ordered herself. But why would she? A tailor cost little and saved her the trouble, and – more importantly – it Wasn't Done.

Kate turned back to her sister, after she'd tweaked the flare of her pretty cotton skirt.

"Could you possibly check if my dress is ready?" she asked. "Ahmed said it would be, yesterday, but you know what he's like."

Helen nodded. Indian time did not always tally with European expectations; the tailor sometimes accepted too many commissions and tried to please everyone.

The clip-clop of hooves announced the arrival of Bodhi's *tonga*. He waited, smiling. He was always smiling, and the seats in his wooden cart were clean, covered in white cotton, regularly washed by his patient wife, Roshana.

His chestnut horse was also called Bodhi. It was of

indeterminate age and always wore blinkers.

Helen sank into the fat sofa seat, looking backwards, resting her legs on a support. Her empty basket was on the floor beside her, rustling and rocking slightly as they moved off. She was grateful for the breeze that started to cool her face.

Bodhi hummed a little tune as he drove them down the narrow streets leading to the stalls in the centre of Ranpore's clattering bazaar.

The ride wasn't especially. comfortable – the large wooden wheels with their spokes did not absorb the bumps – but it was convenient. When Helen arrived at the bazaar, she alighted wherever she wished, and always returned to find the *tonga* waiting. Parking, as a concept, was completely unfamiliar to her – it was Bodhi who occupied himself with such things.

She began her familiar walk between the carts and stalls. Terracotta kitchen bowls and tall water filters were laid out, bamboo baskets, fruit and vegetables, kerosene and little lamps, as well as larger hurricane lamps that needed to be pumped to light. One stall had rows and rows of glass bracelets in many colours, rimmed with gold. They were often very small, made to fit the delicate wrists of Indian women. Helen had a faded scar on her hand where one had broken as she'd tried to push it on to her arm, scoring a bloody line down her skin.

She hardly noticed the dust and the dirt. It was as it had always been. At the side of the road piles of filth rotted in the heat. The air was heavy with the stench of discarded vegetation, stagnant water, gutters full of rubbish. Stallholders shouted across the muddy street. *Tongas* and bicycles wove around each other, narrowly missing pedestrians, cows, dogs. Young boys selling hot sweet *chai* poured it steaming into terracotta clay cups. Indian ladies clutched their bright saris around them – turquoise, orange, fuchsia pink, lifting the hems as they picked their way carefully through the market, heads high. A European alighted from another *tonga* in front of a wooden table spread with bolts of cloth, and sent the driver to a butcher's stall. Beef carcasses hung in the open air, buzzing with flies, but he went inside to buy the meat that was kept cool in the fridge.

Suddenly there was a clatter, shouts, and the sound of running feet. A little boy ran past her, followed by a stallholder waving a frying pan, and behind him a group of about twenty people, shaking their fists. The boy bumped into a post, staggered back, and fell against her. His face was blank, but his frightened eyes flickered up and down. The crowd drew closer and as he pushed past her she lost her balance and fell to the ground. A sharp stone cut into the flesh of her knee. Bodhi was beside her at once, tutting and clearing a space. Hands helped her stand unsteadily, holding on to Bodhi's arm. She watched the blood drip out of the cut and stain the fabric of her skirt. Some people turned away, others stared at the unfamiliar sight of an injured white woman in the street; she felt slightly sick.

"Hmmm. It's quite deep," said a male voice. British, with a lilt that echoed the Anglo-Indian accent she was familiar with. "Come over here. Sit down on this chair, and I'll go and get a plaster and some antiseptic. Make sure she's not bothered," he ordered Bodhi, who bowed and stood beside her.

Helen was left, feeling foolish, on a little rickety chair that had been brought from a shop nearby. She hoped the boy had not been caught and beaten. She could not see him anywhere. He was probably hiding, panting and sweating, praying not to be found, hoping to get away with the few *pais* he had pocketed or the mango he had slipped off a pile of fruit.

The stranger was back in a few minutes, with a paper bag of cotton wool and a pink plastic bowl of warm water.

He folded himself into a squat beside her, hitching up his khaki cotton shorts, and dipped a ball of cotton wool into the water to wash away the blood that had almost congealed on her skin. The sharp antiseptic smell of TCP hit her nose and she gasped as the stinging started.

"Sorry. Shows it needs cleaning. It'll be fine."

He gently rubbed away the dirt from the cut, and the water turned pink as he squeezed the cotton wool. Tiny wisps of blood floated beneath the surface as he soaked another ball to wipe the skin.

"Sorry. Bad luck. But you should be okay now."

"Thank you so much. I'm fine, really I am. I was just off balance. It's very kind of you to clean me up. I'll be fine now. No infection."

He threw the water into the dirt and stretched a strip of plaster over the cut.

"These things do sting, don't they?"

"Silly of me to flinch," she said, trying to regain some dignity. "It's gone now. I'll put some iodine on it when I get home."

"That would be best, but until then keep the plaster on to protect it."

Banalities. But the conversation stretched – neither wanted it to end. She thought she knew all the British men in the area, but not this one.

He read her mind.

"I've not been here long. Arrived yesterday, and I'm just looking around and getting my bearings. Arthur Kirkwood."

"Helen Armstrong."

They looked at each other for a moment, and she suddenly felt embarrassed and clumsy. She hoped she'd not looked too ungainly as she fell. Had her skirt rucked up and shown her underwear?

He helped her up from the chair, holding her forearm. His touch was light and cool.

"Well, Miss Armstrong," he said. "Will you be all right now? Are you going straight home?"

"No, I've various things to do. I – my sister... I promised to collect something for her."

"As long as you're sure you're up to it."

"Good heavens, yes. I was clumsy. I could so easily have moved out of the way."

She spoke quickly. The silent moment was full of something she didn't understand; she felt out of her depth.

He smiled. "I'm sorry you were hurt, and glad that I was here to help in a small way. I'm sure we will meet again. It'll be a great pleasure."

She took refuge in formality.

"I'm sure we shall. Until then, Mr Kirkwood..."

She looked around for Bodhi, who shot to her side and put his hand under her elbow to guide her past the crush of people.

"Shall we go back to Cantonments, *Memsa'ab*?"

"No, Bodhi. I need to go to Sew Nicely to collect *Memsa'ab* Kate's parcel. Come on, let's get it done and then I can go home and put my leg up."

Sew Nicely was in the next street but Bodhi insisted on driving her. He stopped outside the shop front, under the name painted in bright blue on a wooden panel, beside a woman's salmon-pink face. Bodhi unfolded the steps for her to descend.

"Careful, *Memsa'ab*."

Her leg had stopped bleeding, but the dressing was rusty brown and the blood had leaked around it. She leaned down and wiped the stain away with her handkerchief.

Ahmed the tailor came out from behind his ancient treadle Singer, and bowed over her hand.

"*Memsa'ab* Helen! Welcome! I've *Memsa'ab* Kate's dress, just here. And is there anything else?"

"Good morning, Ahmed. I've come with some material

I found in the market a while ago – look, it's light cotton, and I think it very smart."

He nodded, feeling the spotted cotton fabric between his thumb and forefinger. Letting go, he went to the back of the shop and brought out a bolt of fabric.

"For you, *Memsa'ab*, I will make a special jacket to go with it. In this material. Is that acceptable? No, no, my gift. You send me so many customers. They see how you dress, and they want to look the same. You're – I'm not sure of the English – a style leader."

They spent a happy half hour talking about clothes, and Helen started to feel normal again, the *Memsa'ab* who ran a house, bought supplies, knew her way about.

The *durzi* understood his customer. He had stitched for her many times and preferred their discussions to the more peremptory ones he had with her mother, who never changed her order for a dark skirt and a white shirt, usually cotton, sometimes silk.

"It will be ready for Friday, *Memsa'ab*. I hope *Memsa'ab* Kate will like her dress. I will alter it if necessary, of course."

"Thank you," said Helen, as Bodhi helped her into his vehicle.

He clicked his tongue and the horse started to pull the *tonga* through the crowds, cows wandering down the dusty road, pie dogs lying asleep in patches of shade.

A flick of the whip, another click, and the carriage increased its speed, raising a low cloud of yellowish dust. The horse's ears were forward, its eyes shaded by blinkers, and with Bodhi's skill they avoided most of the potholes. Dust was now sticking to the bloodstain that had seeped through the dressing on her knee, which began to throb. She remembered the closeness of Arthur Kirkwood, the touch of his hand on her leg. She sighed.

"Everything okay, *Memsa'ab*? Too bumpy?"

Bodhi's hearing was remarkable.

"No, it's fine. I'm fine. Just carry on."

He turned his attention back to the road.

She went over the events of the morning. What was it that was making her feel so – what? Different? Excited? The attention of a polite stranger? A plaster and some TCP – that was all. Hardly worth a heartbeat, but nevertheless... something had changed.

She recalled his hand under her elbow. So what? Just politeness. He would have done it for anyone. But his touch had given her an inkling of a different possibility. Perhaps life didn't have to consist only of trips to the market in the *tonga*, or work at the local school, of dinner in the formality of the dining room, or drinks on the verandah with a book from the Club library.

"*Memsa'ab*. Excuse me, *Memsa'ab*. May I help you descend?"

The world came back into focus. She was home. The black gate still needed a coat of paint to cover the rust, the bougainvillea with its salmon and orangey flowers still frothed over the arch above it.

Sudham was standing there, waiting to carry her packages into the house.

Of course, nothing had changed. Why would it?

## Chapter Eight

Evangeline put her book down on the glass top of the rattan table beside her.

"Good heavens, you're back early!"

"Am I? Oh, I expect it's Bodhi's new horse. It trots along at a clipping pace."

Helen put her handbag on the floor and sat down opposite her mother.

"What have you done to your leg?" asked Kate, looking at the stained plaster that was almost the same colour as her sister's skin.

"I was knocked over by a boy. He'd stolen something, and was running away."

"Oh."

Kate wasn't interested; she wiped her forehead with a little handkerchief trimmed with crocheted lace, and returned to the magazine she was reading. Her mother raised her eyebrows.

"Are you all right? Did you disinfect it immediately?"

"Yes."

"Bodhi is a treasure really, isn't he?" Evangeline said.

Helen hesitated. Now was the moment to say that she'd met Arthur Kirkwood, if only because the arrival of a new person in Ranpore was always worthy of a mention. She swallowed.

"I put TCP on it and then the plaster. I'll dab it with some iodine after my shower."

It was only a tiny omission, but worth it. For the moment, he was hers.

*

The Armstrongs lived in one of the larger bungalows on the Cantonment. The houses had been built a hundred years before to insulate army officers and their families from disease and the Indians. A lively (and untypical) lady diarist recorded that Ranpore had "adopted Bridge in a very big way and society ladies there had become very suburban. It's like a Surrey village dropped into the middle of this enormous wonderful country."

Jacaranda Lodge was neither the grandest house, nor the most humble. It was in the shape of a T – a central verandah with a living and dining room behind, and a long verandah leading off each side. Doors to its six bedrooms opened off these, each with its own bathroom, overlooking a shady garden of about an acre. Nicely precise.

The family used the large central verandah most of the time, except when the monsoon rain beat down so hard it was impossible to avoid getting splashed. Here people sat to write letters, to read, to welcome visitors, to sip a *chota peg* before dinner, and take coffee afterwards.

The monsoon would come in a month or so. Till the rain cooled the air, the temperature seemed to rise every day. Even the occasional puffs of wind were hot, whipping up a fine dust from the road, and setting it down in a thin pale layer on any flat surface, providing steady employment for servants to wipe it away.

Helen worked as a part-time secretary to the Principal at the Methodist High School, and her sister taught reading and Religious Knowledge to the junior children. The work got them out of the house.

Their lives, undeniably comfortable, were slow. There were never any surprises. Nothing happened in Ranpore, a town with a railway station, a ragged market, thousands of unseen Indians, and the Cantonments where the British lived in polite exactitude.

Most people had known the girls from childhood. Helen was admired by many for her stoicism, her knowledge (gathered by reading anything she could get her hands on) and her intelligence. The more conventional women in Ranpore accepted her, but found her too *unusual* to be a close friend. Her often unexpected opinions were disconcerting. She didn't seem to recognise the difference between Anglo-Indians and the British. Her friends came from both camps, and she was at home in either. Very peculiar, said the ladies to each other. And she read the *oddest* books. Not the romances the ladies would exchange, but the ones their husbands ordered from England, and often passed on to her. Helen's tolerance for an exchange of recipes was short.

Although she talked confidently to the men, Helen could never be accused of overstepping the mark. She never flirted, she looked people in the eye, and didn't titter or flutter her eyelashes. Any direct criticism of her made the speaker seem mean-spirited, so the ladies contented themselves with the devout hope that one day Helen would be able to leave Jacaranda Lodge and the ranks of unmarried females.

I don't know how Helen puts up with Evangeline, everyone said. Evangeline doesn't know how lucky she is. And, with feeling: I hope Helen finds someone who deserves her, and manages to have a life of her own. As Kate will.

They were right. Kate was not at all like her sister. She wasn't going to stay in sleepy Ranpore if she could help it. Most people enjoyed her excitable presence, but nobody would count on her practical support. Decorative and flirtatious, she stirred the air of any room she entered. In one mood, she sprayed anger, drama, complaints around her like water from the *mali*'s hosepipe; in another, she was generous with compliments and put herself out to be charming.

*

There is no twilight in the tropics. The sun falls away at six-thirty almost to the minute. The air remains heavy, but the solid wall of heat is gone. This evening, the fans moved the air to cool sticky skin.

"It's so warm," said Kate. "The market was an inferno the other day. You're such a brick to go. I told the *durzi* I wanted the sleeves on my new frock bracelet length. With a bit of white trim to liven it up a bit, otherwise I shall look just like a Sunday School teacher."

"Since you are a Sunday School teacher, Kate, that would only be accurate," said Helen, sitting down on the white chair beside her.

Ice clinked in long cold glasses.

"Ah, *nimbu pani*. Thank you, Sudham. Just put the tray there, will you?"

The bearer inclined his head, and handed each of the women a glass of fresh lime juice, mixed with cold water and sugar. He covered the jug with a circle of white net, trimmed with coloured glass beads to hold it down and keep out the insects. As Helen once said, she preferred her protein cooked.

The fan hummed and a bee buzzed, disappearing inside the purple velvet trumpet of a gloxinia. A fly tried to follow, but Evangeline swiftly despatched it with a sharp flick of a swat. She set the wicker wand down, looking pleased with herself. There was keen competition in the house to see who was the most accurate in the endless battle against flying insects, and she usually won.

Kate finished her drink and stood up.

"What's for supper?" she asked. "Nothing too heavy, I hope. The tennis court was hot stuff today. Like my serves, I'm delighted to say! I'm off for a shower. I won't be long."

"It's a fish mousse, with some lettuce and tomato," Helen called after her. "After Cook's *consommy* – he insisted. He wanted to make some curry and rice, but I knew we wouldn't be able to face it; he's saving it for tomorrow. Just to warn you."

The cook's food reflected his mood, so Helen hoped that he felt cheerful enough today to produce the light meal Kate had asked for. If he had had other ideas about dinner, he could sulk, and the result would then be touch and go. The Armstrongs had taught him many recipes, and some of his cooking was very good. His bread, cakes, jams and chutneys were absolutely delicious, and much in demand at the local charity sales. His garlic and cinnamon soufflé, however, had been less successful, especially when served with peaks of whipped cream.

Helen regularly inspected the kitchen, its walls coated with sooty streaks. Disease was caused by dirt, and ingredients used when they had passed their best. The milk – like the drinking water – had to be boiled and used the same day. The cook wiped his workspace down in anticipation of Helen's visits, but he was not convinced the effort was necessary. His kerosene stove could be as temperamental as he was, but they understood each other.

"I've invited James and Gladys Matthews for supper tomorrow night," said Evangeline. "With their new houseguest, Arthur Kirkwood. Some relation or other. He's Welsh, apparently, and has spent a couple of years in India, I believe. He's staying with them for a couple of weeks. Gladys was rather vague about the relationship, and where he intends to live, but anyhow, it was the least we could do. I only hope we can understand what he says."

Helen gave a tiny gasp. Hell, hell, hell. She smoothed her skirt, keeping her hands steady.

"Mmm."

"I've told the cook that we need food for six. And Sudham knows, too, so he can lay the table appropriately. Will you please check that this is done?"

"Of course, Mother."

Although Evangeline behaved as if she were a wonderful housekeeper, Ranpore had realised long ago that it was Helen who ran the house, paid the bills, smoothed ruffled servant feathers, hired and fired. Kate did very little to help her.

"If you don't mind, Mother, I think I'll take a shower too. Excuse me. I'll just call in on the kitchen to make sure everything is under control!"

Helen walked out carefully, closing the mosquito screen behind the door as she left. She stood very still for a moment in the shadowy drawing room, steeling herself, before walking out to the savagely hot kitchen in an outhouse.

# Chapter Nine

Life in Ranpore revolved around meals, but the following day the heat took away the appetite. The fan struggled to push the heat from one side of the room to the other.

"It's almost too tiring even to eat, isn't it?" Kate said. "I don't think I can manage another thing. Would Deena like some of my ham, Helen?" she whispered, so her mother would not hear.

Helen nodded almost imperceptibly, and Kate put a little of the meat from her sandwich on one side of her plate. The little mongrel looked up at Helen, and waited. Evangeline never fed her from the table, but the dog had learnt that when the old lady had left the room, it was probable that some delicious titbit would come her way. It was not long before Evangeline stood up and placed her starched napkin on the tray.

"Time for a siesta, I think, girls. I hope you will have a rest this afternoon. We have people to dinner."

"As if we didn't know," Kate murmured, as her mother walked away. Helen smiled and passed the piece of meat to her dog, who ate it fastidiously and licked her lips with a long pink tongue.

The sisters finished their lime juice before going to their rooms. Deena followed Helen to her curtained bedroom, cooled by a ceiling fan. She curled up in her basket on the floor under the window and closed her eyes.

Helen lay on her bed in her underwear. Tried to sleep, but couldn't. Her thoughts jostled, thickening into sense, evaporating into muddle. The chutney. The tailor. Arthur Kirkwood. The house. Her mother. Arthur Kirkwood.

As the servants walked down the brick path over the lawn to their quarters, there was a murmur of Hindi outside her window. Everyone slowed down from three till four. It would take another Mutiny to alter the pattern.

She plumped up the pillows and leaned back on them, reaching for her book, a Georgette Heyer from the Club Library. The elegantly-described adventures of Judith Taverner were a diversion until the oil slick of sleep curled around her, and she closed her eyes.

*

Helen enjoyed the Matthewses, and always looked forward to seeing them. Gladys never asked her archly which beau she was thinking of, nor watched Helen out of the corner of her eye when her husband went over to talk to her.

Like Kate, Helen minded the lack of excitement and new faces but she made less fuss, entertained herself by reading, and by recording a great deal in small leather notebooks which she was almost certain nobody had found. She relished words. Her favourites were *somnambulist, jalopy, prestidigitation,* and she added to this list whenever another caught her fancy. She kept these notebooks in a small wooden box under Sudham's bed and the key in her jewel case. They were perfectly safe. Her mother would never look in the servants' quarters. It simply wouldn't occur to her.

Two hours before their guests were expected, Kate looked up when Helen came out on to the verandah, her hair damp about her temples, and loose around her shoulders.

"Thank you for collecting my skirt," Kate said. "I can wear it for our guests."

"Yes. Sudham took it to your room. Have you tried it on yet? It's a nice colour. I like the print and the fullness. I hope it fits."

"Mmmm, not like the last one when one side of the hem was higher than the other."

Helen remembered the fuss.

"I particularly checked. Anyhow, try it on and I can

send it back with Bodhi if you need anything altered."

She spoke matter-of-factly; she wasn't in the mood for a tantrum.

Kate was never happier than with something new to try on, to read or to use. She skipped off and returned to twirl, the crepe fabric flowing out from her hips, and falling down to below her knees.

"Yes. This works. I'm so glad."

Helen admitted to herself that she was relieved to have encountered the helpful Mr Kirkwood alone. If Kate had been there, she wouldn't have had a look in.

She sat still for a moment, considering. She really needed to stop this. It had been a chance encounter. He had picked up a clumsy woman from the dusty ground. He had been polite, friendly and businesslike. Nothing important had happened.

Although it had, of course.

"Oh, Helen," said Kate. "Mother asked me to say that our visitors are going to be a little late this evening. They sent a chit. They're having to wait for this Mr Kirkwood to come back from wherever he's gone, and say it's unlikely they will be here before eight. Can you make sure the cook knows?"

Helen stood up.

"Of course. I'll go and tell him to delay. It's a white curry, so it won't come to any harm. And won't it be nice to have someone new to talk to."

Her voice was light and impersonal. She felt proud of herself.

Kate nodded, indifferent, for the moment.

"I don't know what Mother would do without you. Nobody does. She could manage without *me* quite happily, I think."

It was not the time to discuss Kate's grievance, if it was one. Sometimes she felt badly done by, but it soon passed.

"Perhaps you could make the table look nice," said

Helen. "You're so good at that."

It was placatory, and it worked.

"Okay then. I'll get flowers brought in and we can use the damask table cloths...Can't we, Mother?"

Evangeline came in, carrying a basket and a pair of small scissors.

"Yes, that would be fine. But not okay, Kate, please. You're not an American, although quite honestly, the way you speak sometimes makes you seem so."

"It's 1937, Mother. You saw that film at the Club: *Holiday*, with Cary Grant. You said you liked it. And they said all sorts of things like okay."

Helen waited. This could go either way. Her mother, to her relief, had other things on her mind, and walked down the red semi-circular steps into the garden, calling for the *mali*. A butterfly flicked its wings past her head and landed on a scarlet ixora, drinking deep.

Evangeline disappeared behind a bush, returning with some white hibiscus flowers. They would bleed veins of deep pink into their petals, and by dinner-time they would be at their best.

Kate made the table look pretty, while Helen went to the kitchen and checked that the cook had everything he needed. There was no need. The white curry was scented with cardamom, cinnamon, cumin and all the side dishes were prepared: *nan* bread, *chappatis*, chutneys made from the fruit which hung heavy on the mango, lime and lemon trees in the garden.

## Chapter Ten

"I wonder what he'll be like, this Mr Arthur Kirkwood," Kate said, shortly before their dinner guests arrived. She was stretched out on Helen's bed, leaning against the pile of pillows set against the headboard.

She was always ready before Helen, who usually found something that needed her attention before her clothes did. Kate, in a cloud of *Je Reviens*, looked very pretty, hair curling charmingly, skirt ending in soft folds around her calves.

Helen wore navy and white – smart, crisp, almost a uniform. Her skirt's pleats flattered her and her pearl necklace looked soft and pretty against her clear skin. Evangeline did not encourage her daughters to wear make-up so they never used more than a slick of pink lipstick and some powder. Helen brushed her long dark hair and braided it, turning each plait into an earphone, a circle over her ears.

While they talked, Helen checked her reflection in the pier glass in the corner of the bedroom, more for information than vanity; she was happy with what she saw. She knew that some of the women at school copied her. Tidy and stylish, her appearance would not raise an eyebrow.

"Mr Kirkwood?" she said airily. "Probably short, with a bald patch and a speech impediment. And very baggy trousers."

"Oh, don't. Not everyone is like Mr Prettijohn."

"No," said Helen, with a shudder. "Not everyone is like Mr Prettijohn, but then not everyone had to go to the Club dance with him. My bunions are a direct result of his foxtrot." She put down the silver-backed brush firmly. "And he wouldn't let go of my hand either. I had to shake him off like a mongoose with a cobra."

"A lesson to us all, then. Don't dance with anyone under five foot four, and better still, don't accept any invitation from someone who can't say 'expressly' without spraying the room."

Helen laughed.

"I've got it carved on my heart. Like Calais on Queen Mary's."

Kate looked puzzled, and opened her mouth to ask, but she had no time. There was a soft knock at the door.

"*Memsa'ab* Kate, *Memsa'ab* Helen, Mr Kirkwood is here."

Smoothing down her skirt, Helen looked at her sister and smiled. "That's early. Oh well. Here's hoping for no reminiscences of the lakes of Kashmir, or duck shooting..."

"Or crocodile hunting – 'see this briefcase, Miss Armstrong?'"

"'Shot the thing meself...'"

While Kate hurried off to join her mother on the verandah, Helen held back. She'd suggested that she and Arthur Kirkwood were strangers to each other. This could be awkward; she hoped he was not going to greet her as someone he had already met. If he did, she would have to think of a plausible explanation. The Club would do – a Bridge game, or in the library. Or that his name had slipped her mind.

She took a deep breath and followed Kate out on to the verandah. Evangeline was already there; the rustle of her stiff black skirt echoed the evening chorus of cicadas as she turned.

"Mr Kirkwood, these are my daughters Helen and Kate," she said, at her most gracious.

Helen put out her hand quickly and looked up into his eyes. He smiled reassuringly, which made her feel calmer. Perhaps he wouldn't say anything awkward about their meeting... He had dressed well for dinner – a smart pair of cream trousers, a blue shirt, a dark tie with some kind of crest on it. His hair was still a little damp by his ears and she caught a whiff of cologne.

"How do you do, Mr Kirkwood," she said quietly, noticing to her annoyance that she was a little breathless. "Welcome to Ranpore. We don't often see new people."

"I'm so sorry to be early," he said. "I told Mr and Mrs Matthews I'd meet them here at eight, and decided to walk – it's not far. But I obviously walk faster than I thought!"

"Certainly faster than the horse on Bodhi's *tonga*, that's for sure," said Helen. "He took me to the market this morning. It was very warm by the time I got home."

"Ah yes, I went in to do some shopping today, too. And you're right, it was very hot."

His blue eyes met Helen's. Hers flicked up at his face, looked down and rose again to meet his.

"Mrs Matthews suggested I take the *tonga* this evening," he continued. "But one sits about so much in this country. Though I must admit that Bodhi is very useful, isn't he? Does he only have one horse?"

Helen looked at him, grateful for the small talk.

"Yes. Although this one is a new one. A little younger and livelier than the last! But not much – getting about in Ranpore is never very fast!"

"Mr Kirkwood, I'm not sure if you have had a chance to go to the Club yet?" Evangeline wanted to know. "Have you joined?"

"The Matthews have kindly proposed me," he told her. "I've not been there very often though – my job doesn't leave me very much time."

"Have you been long in India?" Kate asked. She smiled at him, her even teeth white in her lightly tanned face.

"Not quite a year. And only a couple of months in Ranpore."

"Come and sit here, Mr Kirkwood, next to me," commanded Evangeline from a rattan chair. "Here. Draw up this chair."

He obeyed her.

An insect hit the light bulb and fizzled as it died.

"Thank you, Mrs Armstrong. Please call me Arthur."

Sudham produced a tray of glasses, blurred with cold, clinking.

"There's gin and tonic, *nimbu pani*, or Scotch if you prefer...Arthur."

"A gin and tonic would be perfect. Thank you."

He took one, holding the small folded napkin to catch the chilly sweat of the glass, and sipped approvingly.

Helen stayed with her mother, chatting to their visitor, while Kate slipped into the dining room, ostensibly to cast a glance over the preparations but really to rearrange the place cards. She placed the one with Arthur's name next to hers, moving Helen next to Mr Matthews.

There was suddenly a bustle. A small woman with a bright scarf over her shoulders came up the wide verandah steps in a tangle of apology.

"I'm so sorry, Evangeline, Arthur. Thank you, Sudham. Just leave the torch by the door. We meant to be here before Arthur but, as always, there was something. Is it eight o'clock? Oh dear, it's just after. Apologies. Apologies."

Gladys Matthews was always late, and always sorry, but she never managed to change her ways. Everyone in Ranpore was aware of her inability to keep to an arranged time. Sometimes people told her events were taking place half an hour earlier than they were.

Her husband, James, walked in quietly behind her.

Sudham bent over Evangeline to murmur something in her ear. She inclined her head and he melted away.

"I'm told that dinner is served. One of the many blessings of Helen's white curry is that it gets more delicious with keeping. James, Gladys, Arthur. Why don't we go straight in?" she said, and rose from her chair.

Sudham held open the mosquito screen door to allow them all to pass through.

The dining room was filled with a rich scent of frangipani from the waxy blooms in vases on the sideboard. The hibiscus flowers in their low glass containers on the dining table had bled deep pink into their white petals. The heavy cut glass and silver, laid out on thick white damask, twinkled in the candlelight. Thick napkins lay folded at each place, and the old dinner plates were decorated with painted flowers and edged with gold.

"The cutlery has been in our family for many many years," Evangeline would tell people, slowly, in an accent that became a little Scottish as she reminisced, unlike her normal voice which was painstakingly English, pronunciation received carefully, stored and reproduced.

As they took their places at the table Arthur's dark blue eyes met Helen's green ones, with a little smile in them. She started to respond, feeling happy, but remembered their secret. Her expression frosted slightly and she noted his surprise and withdrawal. Oh dear, she thought. I'm not good at this.

But now Kate had decided it was time for her to attract his attention.

"How are you enjoying the delights of Ranpore, Mr Kirkwood?" she asked.

"I've been to the Club with Mr and Mrs Matthews." He bowed slightly in their direction. "It was comfortable, and people were very welcoming."

"We *are* welcoming in Ranpore," she said, smiling brightly. "We welcome *anyone* who will make our humdrum existence more lively."

"I'm not sure I'll be able to make it more lively, but I'm a new face, and I know that has its own interest, for a while. Until familiarity breeds, if not contempt, indifference..."

"I'm sure we will never be indifferent to you, Mr Kirkwood. Especially if you shoot, play Bridge, can dance a little..."

He smiled.

"I can do all that, a little. If that is what's needed, I promise I'll try to oblige. I can have a go at the steps of most of the dances, although please don't expect too much!"

"Off the dances", he said, his voice lilting, definitely Welsh. Helen had expected her mother to be a little lofty about Arthur's accent, but although she'd heard him emphasise the second syllable in "electricity" a little earlier, Evangeline either did not hear, or did not mind.

Conversational tennis, meaning nothing. It may have been, but Kate loved the attention. And he was obviously happy to provide it. Helen remembered her manners and turned to James Matthews on her left.

And so the dinner began. Evangeline listened to everything, checked everything, beckoned to Sudham to fill glasses and pick up napkins. The bearer hovered by the table, in his white *dhoti* and red jacket, smart for dinner. He had learnt everything from Evangeline, a demanding teacher, and never put a foot wrong.

The cook's *consommy* was ladled out carefully, and the curry that followed was light and subtly spiced, the *nan* bread puffy and not cloying, the rice grains separate and fluffy. The chutneys were remarked upon, and the lemon syllabub was perfect.

Arthur was a polite guest, easy to please. He answered all enquiries, and told them about his work as an engineer in Asansol and Calcutta and about his early life in Wales.

He had left to study engineering at the local college; a Welsh scholarship gave him the chance to further his studies at the South Wales and Monmouthshire School of Mines. India meant novelty and excitement, and the opportunity to make his way, earning more than he ever could in Newport. "My father was the local vicar, my grandfather a coal miner. Good, hardworking men."

Helen watched Evangeline's smile, as she inclined her head towards Arthur. It was a lofty gesture, indicating her social superiority, but not dismissal. So far, so good.

"Please don't get me wrong, I love my family – I've four sisters and a brother, all happy and settled in Wales. I miss them, but I wanted to travel. To look out, not in."

After university, he had taken the boat to Bombay, and immediately loved the smells, the crowds, the buildings... the difference.

"It was – fantastic. Then, one day, I took the train to go to an interview for something, I think it was engineering in a factory. I never got there! The railways really caught my imagination – such a wonderful project, so ambitious. I decided to try my luck. I've worked for the railways for two years now, and I can honestly say I've enjoyed nearly every minute of it. I'll not be a railway engineer forever, but I've learnt a great deal. It's time to move on soon. I'm not sure where, but I want to see more of the country and do different things. Don't we all?"

There was a pause. Everyone looked at him, thinking their own thoughts about his last question. His eyes met Helen's. She could have sworn he winked.

They finished their meal, then took coffee on the verandah, where the pungent tang of the mosquito coils mingled with other scents of the night: dust, distant wood smoke, the perfume of the Yesterday, Today and Tomorrow shrub (with flowers that were white for one day, pale lilac the next, a day later a deep mauve), and the heavier scent from the creamy moonflower trumpets.

It was always a toss-up whether the pleasure of sitting outside on the edge of darkness was worth the constant attention of flying insects. Tonight candles were lit on the verandah. This encouraged conversation, and made the insects less insistent than they might have been in brighter light.

The Matthews excused themselves at ten o'clock, and Sudham accompanied them with a torch to light their way out of the garden. The hinges creaked as the gate opened, and they walked carefully out into the silent road.

"Sudham, bring the Caram board, please," Kate said, when the bearer returned. "On the table over there. Thank you. And move those candles closer. That's it."

"Kate, dear, Arthur might not be quite as enthusiastic as you are." Evangeline said. "Do you play, Arthur?"

"A bit. I know the basics: like billiards, but on a board,

using your thumb to flick the counters into pockets at each corner."

"That's right. Everyone plays it here. You need practice, Mr, er...Arthur," said Kate, sitting down on one side of the square table. "Helen, I challenge you to a game. Come on now. Arthur can watch and then when he feels like it he can play."

She tucked her hair behind her ears like a child, and lined up the wooden counters on the painted line in front of her.

Evangeline stood up.

"Arthur, I'm afraid you're going to see an unfortunate side of my daughters now. They show no mercy where Caram is concerned. If you feel up to the battle, I wish you luck! But for now, please forgive me. I'm an early riser. Remember, I've warned you. Be on your guard, and be ruthless!"

Arthur took his place in a Lloyd Loom chair to one side, leaning forward to watch the sisters.

Soon the night was punctuated by the clack and click of counters.

"There. I knew I could get that one in!"

Kate clapped her small hands together.

"You pushed the counter. That's cheating!" Helen protested, looking at her accusingly with her large green eyes.

"My turn. I go again. Ha ha!"

In the end Helen lost the game, and gave Arthur her place; he proved himself clumsier than either of them, to Kate's delight.

"That's it, Arthur," Helen said, as he concentrated on positioning his hand for a particularly difficult shot.

"Don't help him, Helen. I'm sure he has played pool or billiards – this is just the same."

"It is, but we have stronger thumbs and lots more practice. Oh, I say, well done!" as the wooden circle skittered across the board and clicked into a net.

"Humph," said Kate. "Beginner's luck."

It was soon eleven-thirty, and at the end of a game Arthur looked at his watch and got to his feet.

"I'm sorry to break this up, but I must leave you now," he said. "Work tomorrow – and after all this excitement I need to rest." He grinned, and bowed. "Next time, I hope I'll be able to beat at least one of you. I'll have to get in some secret practice."

Helen laughed. "Try Archibald Cunningham. He's the Head of St Xavier's, often to be found at a Club table taking on all comers. I'll look forward to our next encounter!"

Kate smiled. "So shall I. And I hope it'll be soon. You have all the makings of a worthy opponent, but I should tell you I was the Upper School champion." She spoke as if Helen were not in the room.

"It has been a lovely evening," Arthur said. "Thank you so much. Delicious food and delightful company. It's been a while since I've sat on a verandah, drinking good whisky out of cut glass, and I shall go home and sleep well. Goodbye Kate. A pleasure. Helen."

"I'll see you to the gate," Helen said quickly.

Kate waved happily and went inside.

Fireflies flickered, and shadows thrown by the moon darkened their faces once they moved out of the yellow glow thrown by the lamps.

"Thank you," Helen said, softly.

He did not pretend to misunderstand her. He looked up to the house, and opened the gate.

"I must get that hinge oiled," Helen said, feeling awkward.

He turned to her and spoke seriously. "It must feel – hemmed in, living in Ranpore. I'd find it hard not to have privacy, a life of my own. Worse for single women, I should think. Everyone must be watching."

She nodded, the moonlight on her hair catching the slight movement.

"It feels like that sometimes. I don't mind usually, but sometimes, it is..."

"Oppressive. I can see that. I'm glad we met in the market."

There was a pause.

"So am I."

"Is the cut better? It wasn't too nasty, but sometimes these things don't heal."

"No, It's much better. You dealt with it very efficiently – it was hardly life-threatening."

"And there was I thinking I'd performed a great service to a damsel in distress. Oh, well."

She laughed softly, and put out her hand. He held it for a moment.

"You were quite brave, in fact – I know how much TCP stings on grubby cuts! I hope you'll believe me when I tell you that I was delighted to be there, and able to help, if only because it meant we could speak."

She gasped.

She made to take her hand away, but he gave it a gentle squeeze.

"Cigarette?"

"Yes, please," she answered. "Mother doesn't much like me smoking so I make the most of it when she isn't around."

He took two out of a packet of Chesterfields and put them to his lips. His lighter flicked into flame.

"There you are," he said quietly, smiling and passing one of them over to her. "Let's make the most of it together."

"Thank you. Do you have your torch?" she asked, sending out a light cloud of smoke to mix with the scent of dust, vegetation and wood smoke.

"Yes. Here it is, but I shan't need it. It's only about half a mile, and the moon is bright. Unless you have heard of any marauding thugs on the rampage, I'd much prefer to walk without it. Better for thinking."

They smoked in silence, better transposed: standing together, enjoying the closeness of the night. After a while, he took a long draw on his cigarette and threw the butt on the ground, grinding it out with his foot.

"I had better go," he said. "We will meet very soon. I'll make sure of that. And I'll keep our secret."

"The only person who knows is Bodhi," she said, with a snuffle of laughter. "And he's probably better with everybody's secrets than anyone!"

"Goodnight. It has been a pleasure."

And he was gone. Just his shoes crunching on the *murram* road and fading into the night.

Helen stood in the shadows for a few more seconds, listening to the familiar sounds of dogs and human cries from the village outside Cantonments. Her cigarette end glowed and faded. A firefly blinked in the bush to her right, trying to entice a mate. Rather like the single women in Ranpore, she thought, but few of them shone so warmly. She didn't, as a rule; Arthur, however, with his long vowels and lilting cadences, his bright eyes and his obvious appreciation, was different. Handsome blue eyes, dark hair cut short, white teeth in a wide mouth. She thought of his smile, his secret wink, and felt a flutter in her stomach as if the firefly had set it off. Walking up the steps to the verandah she threw the cigarette into a flowerbed. The *mali* would collect it the next day, and squeeze out any unsmoked tobacco for himself. She bent over to blow out one candle, then another. The shadows crept in to take over. Almost silence. She sat back in the thick cushions of a low planter's chair and stretched out her legs. The night sky grew lighter as her eyes adjusted. It was a pity to go to bed, she thought, as she smelt the perfume of the moonflowers, so she took out another cigarette from a small box on the table, and lit it, the flame of the silver table lighter highlighting her features.

Deena, curled up at her feet, looked up.

She'd liked his eyes. And he had understood that she didn't want to talk about their first meeting. No comment, no questions, no telling. What a relief!

Until now nobody had excited her in the slightest. She thought of Alphonse Bertram, the history teacher; the tennis coach, Harry Ambrose, who was almost certainly Anglo-Indian. A touch of the tar brush, Evangeline said – her most damning description, not negotiable. Not that it mattered. They were pleasant, sometimes amusing company, but her heart beat steadily, unstirred.

At the last Club dance, Harry had been amiable and solicitous, but she'd not regretted the end of the evening. She didn't feel guilty. There were plenty of other women who were only too happy to accept an invitation.

But Arthur Kirkwood was different. Tall, alert, without Harry's showy physical vitality or Bertram's slightly preening bookishness.

She smoked, enjoying the lack of company or conversation. When she finished, she threw the butt into the hibiscus.

"Come on Deena, bed time."

The dog looked up and wagged her tail languidly.

"Come on, if you want, or you can stay here to be eaten by a leopard."

The animal stretched, and followed her through the door to her bedroom, her claws tick-ticking on the stone floor. There was a call, magnified in the dark, perhaps a growl, perhaps not. A rustle, the creak of the door closing and the verandah was empty.

# Chapter Eleven

Helen slid off her bicycle, and propped it up outside the Headmistress's office. She took her handbag out of the basket on the handlebars, and smiled at the small girl walking past her to her classroom.

"Hurry up, Yasmina. Quick. You promised you'd stop being late."

The child smiled sheepishly, and quickened her steps.

"Morning, everyone," Helen said cheerily, as she walked down the corridor to her office outside the Head's room. Helen was there to handle the admin, type letters, file documents, but also to prevent Dorothea Cartwright being disturbed by visitors unless they had an appointment, or it was an emergency. She filtered them very well – polite, friendly, but firm.

The shelves around the panelled walls were laden with files of different colours, and black and white photographs of past Principals. In good weather, rays of sunlight streamed in through the windows, highlighting motes of dust that swirled in the air. The building was late Victorian, constructed so light never reached into the corners and the thick walls kept out most of the heat. These days *punkah wallahs* were no longer employed, and fans helped.

A very poor oil painting hung over the fireplace: the founder of the school, Emmeline Hartfield, whose basilisk eyes watched everything with disapproval. The fire was lit only occasionally, when the fog came down. If anything, it made the Founder's gaze even less friendly.

"Should I've worn my ceremonial robe?" Helen had asked the Headmistress one dank day.

"I know. She's a bit depressing, isn't she? But I think if I moved her, there would be an outcry. What does it matter? She knows her place, and so do we."

"I wish the painting was less... er, gloomy. Her mouth is

so rigid, and someone should have told her that purple simply didn't suit her. A nice white, or pale blue. That would have been the thing."

"Or red, to match her eyes."

The two women had worked together for five years, ever since Helen had heard that Dorothea was panicking about her secretary who was going back to the UK. The work was not onerous, but it needed an ordered mind, and Helen's experience of running a house was an excellent qualification.

As was her humour. Helen's predecessor might have been the very model of efficient accuracy, but "when God was handing out the laughter," said Sally Muir, the class mistress of the Lower Fourth, "Annette was somewhere else. Probably filing."

Helen also made great efforts to avoid confrontation. A row, a raised voice, and she would dissolve, simply remove herself.

Sally asked her about this one day. "Don't you care about what people say, Helen? What they say about you, and what they say about other people? You never stick around to find out."

"It's always nice to hear good things about people," Helen answered, diplomatically. "Don't you think so?"

Now this was clever. Of course, Sally didn't think so, and often enjoyed delivering a sting. She called the games teacher, Elaine O'Connor, *Hathi* (Hindi for elephant) because of her large ears. "They help her whizz about the hockey field," Sally would tell the group of women who enjoyed her brand of humour, "but oh my, the cogs grind slowly. No whizzing in the brain department. Don't you agree?"

Helen did agree, privately, and didn't particularly like Elaine, but she chose not to join in the mockery. Groups weren't her kind of thing. She liked to keep her thoughts to herself.

"Good m-morning, Helen."

She looked up.

"Dudley. How are you?"

"Fine, thanks. I wondered if you could p-possibly let me know when Dorothea is free. I'd like to t-talk to her about my c-class."

Helen took out the large leather-bound diary she used for everything – notes, appointments, sometimes a doodle or two. "She's free for fifteen minutes at twenty past three today. Will that do?"

"That would be v-very good. Er...."

Helen tried to look very busy, frowning and turning over the pages in the diary with a pencil in her hand.

"Are you thinking of g-going to the school p-prom?" he asked finally, looking at her with yearning. She took pity on him.

"I haven't decided yet. I may be in Calcutta. I'll let you know if I'm here. Even if we don't go together, we can certainly see each other there."

Dudley pushed his hand through the very straight hair that flopped over his forehead, and took on the expression of a learned cockatoo that had been told it had done very well at spelling.

"Th-that would b-be terrific. I sh-should like that v-very much. I thought you would be b-besieged with offers..."

His gobbling gallantry irritated her, and she felt immediately guilty. She'd been asked by three other teachers, and she'd given them all the same evasive reply.

"I don't think besieged is the word, Dudley. I shall let you know if I decide to go, and it'll probably be at the very last minute."

Teachers were all expected to supervise their girls, who would be quivering with excitement at the prospect of a rare social encounter with the boys from St Xavier's.

"Oh hello, Dudley. Hello, Helen."

Elaine O'Connor – *Hathi* – was for once a welcome distraction.

"Talking about the dance? Oh Lord. I may need some new glasses. Last year I missed some of those children's antics. They're very... er, imaginative, aren't they?"

She summed up the feelings of everyone whose duty it was to lead their charges gently through puberty.

"Sometimes *in parentis* is indeed pretty *loco*, isn't it?" Helen agreed, thanking her stars that it was not her role to separate clumsy couples who danced too enthusiastically together when the music slowed and the lights dimmed. Those who had been lucky enough to be picked for a "smoochy-coo" looked very smug when the lights went up again, while those who had not, tried hard to look as though they had other things to do.

"Who's playing? Alfonso da Souza and his Sizzling Sounds? Good," said Elaine. "No polish, lots of gusto. Suits the occasion. Last year my lot practised like anything to *At the Codfish Ball*. This year it's *Gee, Ain't You Swell*. An improvement, I'd say. You going, Helen?"

"I was just telling Dudley I may be away. But of course if I can I will."

Elaine nodded briskly.

"Right. Here's a note for Dorothea. May I leave it with you? Good. Nothing to worry about. Now, back to the trenches."

Dudley followed her out, and Helen sighed as the door closed behind him. She bent her head and settled back to her typewriter.

"Hello. You free?"

A woman looked around the door, and Helen smiled, delighted. It was Doris Carter-White, the Head of English. She and Helen had shared confidences and birthday parties since they were very small, and Doris had given her a very positive reference.

Doris giggled. "Oh dear, duckie. Dudley gasping all

over the floor as usual? I passed him in the corridor. You really must put him out of his misery."

"It's all right for you. He used to moon at you, too, before you married Henry; I don't have the same get-out clause."

"Oh, do give over. You could crook your finger and most of the men in Ranpore would come running. Several are keeping fit so if you do, they'll be the first to reach you."

They laughed, sharing a long-standing joke.

"Anyhow, when we get to Calcutta at the end of term, we can put all this behind us. Think about it. Shopping – in real shops. Whiteaways. Ice cream sodas. Dancing, in a real nightclub. Comfortable hotel, my family thrilled as always to have you, lots of late-night gossiping. Can't wait!"

"And nor can I. Of course, I still have Mother to deal with but I doubt she'll be much of a problem."

She didn't have to explain. Doris knew that Evangeline would not be encouraging. Wider horizons for her elder daughter were not in her plan. The Carter-Whites, and Doris's parents, were the Enemy, especially as Doris's mother was Indian. But they all agreed that Helen deserved more freedom, and a chance to travel, and they always invited her on their trips.

All Helen had to do was break the news to her mother, and get it over with.

## Chapter Twelve

Helen knocked at her mother's door.

"Come in."

Helen gently opened it.

"Hello, Mother."

Evangeline's forehead creased. "Good morning, Helen. What is it? I'm going over your accounts."

Both knew there was no need. Helen sat down without being asked, a small gesture of rebellion.

A pause, then Helen spoke.

"Doris's mother and father have invited me to accompany them to Calcutta. I'd like to go, and have accepted. I just wanted to tell you that I plan to be away for about ten days."

"Doris's mother and father." The four words dripped with disapproval. "Who else will be there? Doris, I assume. And Henry?"

"They are married, so it is not surprising, is it?"

It was sharper than Helen had meant it to be, and her mother looked at her with a glint in her pale blue eyes, ready to take her on.

Helen moved fast to smooth it over.

"Henry's work as a member of the legislative assembly means that he'll be in Calcutta at the same time. But he'll be working a good deal, which is why Doris has asked me to come."

"The legislative assembly." A pause. "For an Anglo-Indian, Doris has done *very* well for herself."

Helen pressed her lips together. She'd expected nothing less – Evangeline could not mention her friend without a snap of condescension.

"So it's Doris who has asked you to go to Calcutta?" went on Evangeline. "I thought you said her parents had invited you?"

The note of triumph was maddening – Evangeline was licking her lips with delight at being able to insinuate that Helen might be bending the truth.

"Doris has asked me," Helen answered, patiently. "Her parents have confirmed the invitation, and invited me to be their guest. It's half term so I'm free and it all ties in very nicely."

She could see her mother reviewing her own needs quickly. As far as Helen knew there were no plans for dinners or outings, for which her mother would require her attendance and help.

"I was planning..." Her mother said softly, slowly, thinking. "...But Kate can help me. She can't manage the house as well as you, but she has more style."

Which wasn't true and they both knew it; Evangeline had said this sort of thing too often for it to make much impression, and Helen had long ago learnt the skill of using politeness as a deflective weapon. Unlike Kate who, like her mother, preferred drama in the face of contradiction.

"Will they be paying for your accommodation? And where will you be staying? I should not like you to be beholden to them."

"They always stay at the Grand, and they've booked a small room for me. Doris and Henry will, of course, have theirs, and ..."

"The Grand! That family has more money than sense. The Grand. Well, I hope you enjoy it."

There was nothing more to say. As her mother went back to the accounts, Helen left the room, the mesh mosquito door creaking behind her. She never enjoyed these encounters, but she was determined to go. She was an adult, after all.

There had been a time when she hadn't been strong enough to resist her mother's disapproval. But one day, she'd stood her ground, and had come back to Jacaranda Lodge expecting a chilly reception at the very least. Her mother, however, who always enjoyed disconcerting her daughters, had been all smiles when she returned, flinging only an occasional barb into the conversation.

It wasn't just the family's background that made Evangeline bristle. Doris's parents were rich. And they liked being rich. Not for them the Victorian tight-lipped lack of ostentation. They were not extravagant, but they enjoyed comfort: in Calcutta they stayed at the Grand

Hotel, in Bombay at the Taj, and in Delhi at the Imperial.

Edgar Johnson, Doris's father, was a businessman, and quite clearly a very good one. He had been born and educated in England at what Helen's mother delighted in calling "some minor public school" and had come out to make his fortune in the Colonies. He had done so in a short space of time ("probably dishonestly" murmured Evangeline), and had met and married a very beautiful and cultured Indian woman, Roshinara Chowdhury. Their children were Doris and her brother, Anthony.

Doris was a teacher; Anthony, like his father, made money. Pale-skinned and attractive, there was little about them to indicate that they were Anglo-Indian, except for the occasional sing-song intonation, and an omission from the guest lists of dinner parties for visiting dignitaries. Not often, but it could still sting.

Nor did Roshinara's beauty or culture make up for her origins, in the eyes of the British, or her marriage, for the Indians. Indeed, it was just as well for the Johnsons that they were a close and happy family, generous and welcoming, and with little sense of inferiority, however hard Evangeline and her kind worked to make them feel it.

Kate, who didn't expend much energy on examining her convictions, joined her mother in despising Anglo-Indians who said "Hotle" instead of "Hotel", liked doilies, and stuck their little fingers out when picking up a tea cup.

"Doris is nice, isn't she, Helen?" she remarked one day. "She's lucky to be married to Henry. He doesn't seem to mind the way she speaks, and I expect when they've been married for a while she may lose the accent."

The British who came and went noticed it, sometimes imitated it and laughed. Those who were country-bred, itself a social impediment, never did; they worked hard to acquire the clipped accents of the visitors, and distance themselves from the local intonation.

Helen simply didn't care. She was fond of Doris, she spoke in her own, British, accent, but sometimes tried out a singsong intonation just to annoy her family.

"Helen, for goodness sake, you aren't an Anglo. Don't let anyone at the Club hear you say it like that. You know better."

"Sorry, Mother. But sometimes, when you hear someone say it enough, you start saying it the same way. Surely it doesn't matter that much."

Her mother's frown told her how wrong she was, but Evangeline turned away as the bearer came in, and issued an order, taking great care to use pronunciation received from the BBC, and not the local schoolteacher.

Now Helen went to her room and began to pack with a light heart, humming. When Kate let herself in to the room and sat down on her bed, as Helen knew she would, she asked her whether the floral tea dress or the striped one would be better to take to Calcutta.

Her pleasure was infectious.

Kate, although she would have loved to go too, was prevented from minding by her sister's smile, and she said, "Take them both, Nell. I'm sure you'll get a chance to wear them. And if not, so what? But get things copied –I'm sure Mrs Johnson will have a wonderful tailor. She dresses so well, and I'm certain all her stuff doesn't come from England. And there is always Whiteaways. But that's expensive."

"Never mind. I shall go there once or twice. I've saved up a bit."

"Did you know about this in advance, then? I thought it was sprung on you?"

Helen shook her head.

"No, I didn't know about it really, but Doris said a while ago that they planned to go, and asked me if I'd like to join them. She didn't say when, but I've put money away – there isn't much to spend it on here, is  there?"

"You're right! Although I never seem to have much left at the end of the month, but that's because I spend it at the *durzi*, and I like having bits of jewellery made, and I bought my bicycle the other day."

Both girls had been given sturdy but uncomfortable bicycles which they used to get around when it wasn't too hot, or they didn't have much to carry. Bone shakers, Kate called them, so she'd bought a very snappy peacock blue and black one for extra comfort and speed. Its extra comfort was not particularly evident, but the colours more than made up for it, and Kate pushed harder on the pedals to make the point.

"And it's so *boring* here. Mother will make me do the table laying and the flowers and all that, every day, and I won't even have school to distract me. I'll go to the Club, and I'll play tennis, and I'll talk to the girls and to some of the men, and perhaps we will dance a bit. But it's always the same. Although..." Her eyes lit up. "...Although perhaps Arthur Kirkwood will come more often? He's attractive, isn't he, Helen? I did think he was a bit of a dish."

Helen turned and took a dress off its hanger, folding it up carefully. "Yes," she said slowly, as she laid it in the suitcase. "I suppose he is. I expect Mother will invite him round again, and you will have him all to yourself."

She turned back to her *almirah*, and picked out a pretty yellow skirt. Oh well, she thought, don't get your hopes up, my girl. However romantic the farewell in the garden after dinner had been, it probably meant nothing. He'd met Kate now. And Kate thought any handsome man was hers by right. If she decided she wanted someone, she usually got him.

# Chapter Thirteen

The school hall was festooned with streamers and the Upper Sixth had worked wonders with the flower arrangements. There was a smell of perfume and lilies in the air, and the tables were spread with heavy white damask cloths, and laid with white china from the dining room.

The young people trooped in, self-conscious in their dinner jackets and party dresses. The girls touched the flowers in their hair, a boy wiped the front of his black shoes on the back of his trousers. They made their way to tables, checking where they were to sit on the list by the door, which Helen had carefully drawn up after consultation with relevant teachers.

"Do not, under any circumstances, put Dora Martinson next to a boy, just don't. She gets flustered and starts upsetting the plates and bumping into the furniture," was Lauren Da Silva's advice.

"You'll never get Serena Singh off the floor. She'll dance with a broomstick if she isn't asked by anyone, so a bit of introduction may be needed," was carefully noted.

"And you must keep an eye on the three girls of the Upper Fifth – Susie, Elva and Anita. They're right little madams, and love a bit of a snuggle in the dark. Their parents are concerned, but don't know the half of it. Reputations go before them, and we must go behind!"

At seven-thirty on the dot, Dorothea Cartwright stood on the daïs, and made a short speech of welcome. She ended as usual: "Behave yourselves as befits members of these two venerable schools, and above all have a good time. Off you go."

Alfonso da Souza began to play, smiling benignly, shaking his maracas to a samba tune.

Helen sat near Dorothea, and Dudley was not far away,

his eyes following her like a small dog. She wished Kate had also come, but she'd declined.

"You're joking, aren't you, Helen? I don't have to go, you do. And I really can't face it. I'm so sorry."

Helen didn't believe her. She said nothing, but suspected that she was planning a visit to the Club instead, hoping to see Arthur Kirkwood. Her mother would almost certainly go there to play Bridge and this would give Kate an excuse.

Helen had put on a lacy party frock which fitted her without a wrinkle. She pinned a gardenia in her hair, and was amused when she arrived to be presented with another from Dudley.

"Thank you, how pretty. But excuse me – I've to go and do my duty. I'm on the same table as you – so I'll see you in a bit."

"Well done," said Doris, always amused by Helen's attempts at deflecting admirers. "Am I on the table, too?"

"Of course. But Henry?"

"No, the lucky beggar is away. Perfectly good excuse, but I admit to a slight irritation. Dudley's quickstep…"

"Oh, don't. But is it worse than Stephen Bailey's waltz?"

"The clockwork soldier? I wonder. Let's give them points out of ten and compare at the end. There is always Percy Sealey. He dances well."

"Yes, and he's nice too. Married and likes it. Always a plus."

It was a School Prom like every other School Prom. Someone smuggled in a bottle, so the night was punctuated by drunken seventeen-year-old gargling. Girls simpered, and their laughter grew screechier as the evening wore on. Teachers danced with students, students with each other. Dorothea did an enthusiastic samba with Nicholas Armitage, the head boy of St Xavier's, who towered above her proudly.

Cassandra Smallpiece, the new English teacher who

had come out from England to stay with her aunt and uncle in Ranpore, joined in gamely, with, everyone noted, just the right balance of good humour and firmness. She danced with everyone who asked her, once. She exerted herself to talk to all the adults, and the students, always critical, agreed she was a good sort.

Elsa Hartley, the head girl, was asked to waltz by handsome Archibald Cunningham, the Headmaster of St Xavier's, which left her blushing and speechless for at least twenty minutes after he had led her back to her chair.

He asked Cassandra next, and the two made an odd couple, dancing sedately ("no tricky steps please, Archibald. I can keep up, even enjoy it, if you keep it simple"), Archibald's blond head nearly a foot above her neat dark one. Cassandra, though small and dumpy, was not ungraceful, and despite her modest protests, did more than keep up. He led her to her seat after the music had died down, and sat beside her for a few minutes.

"So, Miss Smallpiece. You're the new teacher at the High School. I hope you're looking forward to the next few terms. Are you here for the duration?"

"As far as I can see. I'm keen to start, and to get to know the students and my colleagues."

"They're a good lot. Helen's been showing you the ropes, I think. That will have made things easier for you. Everyone likes her – with good reason. She's a brick. All the things you see, and a good deal you don't. She puts up with rather a lot at home."

Cassandra nodded, and he said no more, but gave her a serious look before his wife came over.

"This must be Cassandra," she said, holding out her hand. "I'm very pleased to meet you. Everyone says that Dorothea is delighted to have you here and that you're going to be a very good thing. I think those words may have been in capitals."

Archibald smiled in agreement, and faded away to

check on his pupils, saying "there's always one!"

At last it was over. The servants cleared the tables, cars and *tongas* came to collect teachers and students, and a silence fell on the hall. Its wooden herringbone floors were scratched a little more, but that could be remedied. The flowers were still pretty in their vases, so they were offered to parents as their children left.

Cassandra was collected in a car belonging to her aunt and uncle Cornwallis, and disappeared in a throaty hum, waving cheerily through the back window.

Helen and Doris left later at about midnight.

"Now, Helen," Doris said, sitting beside her in the *tonga*. "Shall we stop at the Club to see if your sister has collected any other admirers? I believe she planned to go tonight."

Helen turned to look at her, a question in her face.

Doris looked straight back and shrugged. "She said nothing to me," she continued. "But Kate never disappoints."

"No," Helen said. "She doesn't. But let's not. I'm exhausted, and I'm sure I look like a market woman, all sagging hem and drooping hair."

"And if you're going to impress Mr Kirkwood, you had better not look like that, had you?"

Helen said nothing, and Doris smiled. She and her husband, Henry, had come to the conclusion that he would be perfect for Helen.

"The only problem is that Evangeline may not think so," mused Henry. "And I'm not sure Helen has the courage to deal with that."

# LONDON
# 2000

# Chapter Fourteen

"Are you coming back, Julia?"

Julia had absentmindedly picked up the telephone at its first ring, and regretted it instantly.

She sighed. "No Freddie, I'm not. I've spoken to Tom Farmer – he should have been in touch?"

"He bloody has. I told him no chance. Divorce. Bloody hell. Too bloody sudden by half, Julia. Is there someone else?"

That would be the worst thing that could happen to him, Julia realised. He could dole it out, but he couldn't take it; if another man had been involved, Freddie would have lost. Unthinkable.

"No Freddie," she said, wearily. "There is nobody else. This is nothing to do with anyone else – at least not anyone specific. That Antonella woman was just the last straw. I know, I know..."

She interrupted his protestations.

"I know she meant nothing," she said. "I'm quite prepared to believe she was just one of many pretty little girlies in your life, not the first and certainly not the last. We need to settle things, Freddie. I'm going to leave you to enjoy yourself without me. I'll only get cross, or hold you back, and it'll be much more fun for us both if I move out of Onslow Square and start being me again. I'm sure we will meet and probably be friends, in the end, but right now we need to settle things."

"Friends? Christ! Do me a favour. I don't want to be fucking friends. This is ridiculous behaviour, Julia. You're my wife, for fuck's sake. We really do have to settle this, as you say. Once and for all." He paused, and then served his ace. "Have you spoken to your father about this?"

She'd been expecting something like this.

"I could speak to Dad about this for hours, and he

wouldn't remember a word. He has changed a lot since you last saw him, Freddie. What? A year ago? He isn't really here now, so he won't mind – as far as he's concerned I'm still at school, and he may not even recognise you. Sorry. He won't be your ally. He would have been, I expect, but if I told him that I've been quite unhappy for a while, and showed him the paper, he would have understood. He's my father. And, yes, I'm your wife." She paused. "And you, for what it's worth, are my husband. Husbands are supposed to stick around, forsaking all others. That's the bit that matters – to me. I don't want to make a fuss, Freddie, I really don't. I just don't want to be the little woman. Her Indoors."

"Okay Julia, I've got the picture. I apologise. It was crass of me, but it meant nothing. It won't happen again, I promise."

He sounded so sincere.

"Freddie, you know that's impossible. You're in the habit of it. We've changed. You like being rich, and well known, and admired, and fancied, and in the news. I don't. This isn't me."

There was a silence. The birds outside were quiet, listening. The clock on the mantel ticked the seconds away.

"So, what do you want to do?" he asked, eventually.

"I'm going to talk to Tom Farmer about this. I just want enough money, not to rip you off. To be comfortable, not rolling in it. Although I appreciate that that won't be fourpence either."

"Oh no, Julia. Not fourpence. Just a couple of million."

He sounded annoyed. She ignored it, and went on: "The equivalent of half the flat in Onslow Square is quite enough for me, so that will mean it'll have to be sold, I expect. I know you leverage yourself to the hilt, so you won't have much actual cash. Just give me whatever seems fair, which is not something I can really work out yet. If things have to be sold, then I'd like an allowance so I can live. I want to go back to University – a Masters, or a PhD or whatever they will accept me for. Then you're free to carry on with your life, and I won't be a drag for you. No guilt. No mess. I won't interfere, or turn up wanting more or anything like that. We can have lunch every so often..."

And pigs might fly, she thought. He read her thoughts.

"Ha. I know you, Julia. You think you're civilised, but you're less so than you think. We won't have lunch. We won't meet – at least not on purpose. It'll be over. Is that what you want?"

He waited. She felt a bubble pop in her stomach, a tiny gasp.

"Do you know, Freddie, I think it is," she told him. "I need a break. It's been a long time, and I've not been feeling very good about things for a while."

"I don't get it. You've been able to do whatever you wanted. You know that. I've never been mean."

"Dead right, Freddie, you've never been fiscally mean. Ever. I've had to occupy myself with what was available, which wasn't exactly what I wanted, because if I had wanted you to spend more time with me, to be faithful, to –"

Her voice cracked a little, to her irritation.

"Ah. You don't find this as easy as you say you do," Freddy said, triumphantly.

"I've never said it's easy, although I have to admit it's easier than I thought it might be, now it's happened. I didn't want our marriage to end – I thought it was for ever..."

"It could be, Julia, it could be."

"... For ever. But it's too unsettling. It makes me feel – less. That I do the things you need done, and give you the freedom to do what you feel like doing."

"You've never said you minded."

"Oh for God's sake Freddie, do you think I liked it?

Money is lovely, but it isn't everything."

"Don't be pious, Julia. It doesn't suit you. You've always had money and you won't like having less, believe me."

"Freddie, let's see if we can sort it out. Fairly. I don't want to drag this out."

"Let me think about it, Julia."

She'd known he would say that, to keep her uncertain for a while. It was a familiar tactic. "Keep 'em waiting," he would say. "They'll come round."

"I'm not going to change my mind, Freddie. Just as long as you're clear. I don't, repeat don't, want to have to fight this, but I won't be a pushover either."

"Okay. Leave it with me. I'll speak to my people."

*My people.* It grated, but she shrugged it off. So what. The law was the law and she would be comfortable, whatever happened. If the worst came to the worst, she could sell Linton, but it would be a blow.

After he hung up, she dialled a number and watched the steel wheel on the phone revolve slowly back to the stopper each time.

"Hello, Farmer and Forthcombe. How can I help?"

"Tom Farmer please. It's Julia Hunstanton."

## Chapter Fifteen

Julia put the phone down after a long and sobering conversation with her solicitor. It had been uncomfortable, but she felt the rush of freedom humming very softly in her ears, and wanted to savour it, even though life was going to change a great deal – and Freddie could be very difficult about things he didn't like. He didn't like not being in charge.

Still, she'd decided. Things *were* going to change.

And while she waited for the next broadside from Freddie, she had the letters to read, letters from long ago that hinted at a past that kept its secrets. She'd begun to put them into some kind of order, and make notes in an old exercise book. Just to see where they took her. And how astonishing and intriguing they were turning out to be. Like the one she'd just read. A model of polite good wishes from one sister to another, but laden with a restraint which made her wonder.

*Jacaranda Lodge.*
*November 1938*

*Dear Kate*
*You looked very beautiful in your wedding dress the other day, and it was a privilege to be your maid of honour. It was such a masterstroke to put the lilies in the bouquet. The colours really lifted everything.*
*Arthur, of course, looked handsome and dignified. I'm sure you have both made the right choice.*
*I wish you every happiness in your new home in East Bengal. You will both settle in beautifully. It was the right time for you to marry – no gossip! Your wedding dress covered – I was going to say a multitude of sins, but you know what I mean – and mother looked the picture of happy pride.*
*Please be aware that your son or daughter will always have an aunt who may be far away but will be thinking of them, and sending them every good thought across the miles. I shall even write to them sometimes and hope for, but not expect, a reply!*
*Please pass my best to Arthur.*
*With love,*
*Helen*

Julia stared out of the window, inhaling the faint scent of roses and camphor, trying to imagine India in the late 1930s. Odd. No gossip? Why would there have been any? What had Helen known, she wondered? Making a note of the letter's date and its contents, she folded it away.

She pushed her own situation to the back of her mind. It could stay there for a couple of days, and she could enjoy the peace of Linton and some long walks with Lupin, returning tired and muddy to nursery food and the television in front of the fire. It was very quiet at night, and she found going to sleep not as difficult as she'd feared. There had been no calls from Freddie, but she didn't fool herself that he had given up. He was preparing his battle plan, and she would have to have her defences in place.

## Chapter Sixteen

Julia walked through the sunshine along the streets of Notting Hill. She was looking for Number 26 Elgin Crescent. She found it easily – one of a row of tall white houses from the early nineteenth century. Once smart, then shabby, now smart again, although Number 26 would need a coat of paint pretty soon.

Her supervisor, Annie Renwick, had seen the postcard Julia had put up on the SOAS noticeboard:

*Need accurate typing and an orderly mind? I can help.*

"My friend Hari Dhawan needs a sort of Girl Friday," she'd told Julia after one of their monthly meetings. "He's disorganised, but writes brilliantly. He told me the other day that he wants someone with a brain to organise his office and his diary, read his manuscripts, correct grammar and mistakes, and prepare them for the publisher. Bit of typing, bit of reading, bit of admin. That sound your sort of thing?" She looked across at Julia. "Heard of him?"

"Yes."

Of course she'd heard of him. A blend of Vikram Seth and Hanif Kureishi, with bit of something else thrown in – not always successfully, in her opinion. She liked his books, not as much as many others did – including several judges of prestigious international prizes – but enough to have read most of them.

"He can be nice, charming even. But he's demanding; his research is exemplary, hardly ever gets a fact or a date wrong, and I doubt he does it all himself. I'm sure he'll ask you to help him with that too. But he's a bit like me," – a wave towards the disorder around the room – "and that is really what he needs you for. Tidying, filing, sorting, typing, that sort of thing, at least to begin with. Sound okay?"

Julia nodded. "Just the thing. I'm good at that. I'm going through my mother's stuff at the moment, so I'm combat fit. And I could do with an income at the moment – to cover food, books, travel..."

"Then this sounds just the thing. But don't take on too much, will you? You must keep up work on your PhD. He's not mean and will pay you proper money, so you will be able to take on just a day or two. Shall I call him?"

Hari's office occupied the basement of 26 Elgin Crescent, and he told Julia that he lived upstairs on the ground and first floors. Higher still, a separate flat was kept empty for visiting members of his large family. "You'll find it easily," he'd told her on the phone. "Just follow the arrow down to the basement, beside a wooden sign saying OFFICE."

The steps led to a dark green door. The shadows of the iron railings played on the wall, and the sunshine flickered on the gently moving blue-grey leaves of an olive tree in a large terracotta pot.

"So you're Annie's student. Good. Welcome. Coffee?"

"Yes, please."

Julia sat down in response to his waved hand. The chair was lower than she expected so she hit the cushion harder than she meant to.

The complicated machine in the corner, on a very full

filing cabinet, gurgled and spat convincingly. He turned and met her eyes.

"I know. Just like that ad – do you remember? I should be in the other room coughing and spluttering over the instant."

The tension faded a little. His wide smile showed perfect white teeth.

"Have you read any of my books?" he asked, passing a white cup with black coffee in it. "Milk? Sugar? No? Good girl. Saves such a lot of fuss."

"Yes, I have. Nearly all of them. *The Tamarind Shadow* was my first, I think."

"Hmm. I think that was my least successful. A bit too one-sided. *O poor India, in the face of the tyrant's rule.* That sort of thing. But I was young. I can see a few more sides to an argument now."

"I liked *Consider the Lilies.*"

He looked at her, with a flicker of a smile in his narrow face, the colour of milky coffee.

"Really? Lots of people didn't. But I agree. I enjoyed writing that one. But God, it took it out of me. Easily the most demanding, technically and emotionally."

She sipped her coffee and waited.

A few moments passed. Then he put his cup down and said:

"Okay. Consider this. I need someone to organise my life, my filing and my diary, and keep people I don't want to see away. A bit of fielding and the occasional fib – is that going to upset you? No? Good. I don't want everything tidied. If I leave something here," he pointed to a pile of papers, "I do *not* want it moved. I don't want to spend my life searching for something that's been put in its right place. Tidy away, but according to my system, not yours. Believe it or not, I do have one."

His very dark eyes narrowed. "What did you say your thesis is on?"

"I didn't, but perhaps Annie did. Colonial influence on Indian art, with special reference to Uttar Pradesh and Rajasthan."

"And vice versa, I should think."

"And vice versa, as you say."

Another pause. "Why?" he asked suddenly.

"What?"

"Why have you chosen this subject?"

She thought for a moment, and then looked him in the eye.

"Well, because my family has been in India since the eighteenth century. I'm the last one born in India – there isn't anyone else. Because I had a happy childhood, and I love the country. I know my viewpoint is privileged, that I had no real contact with the people..."

"Okay, okay, you sound as if you've had to defend yourself a lot! You don't have to do it with me. I'm not entirely convinced colonialism was completely bad for India, and times change. I'd not want the British back, thank you very much; there's lots not to like, but I don't have a soapbox."

"I'm relieved. I was worried you might find my background – annoying. If you'd been...ratty about it, I'd not have been able to take the job had you offered it to me. I can't help where I come from..."

"No, you can't. That's fine. I'd like to offer it to you, if you'll consider it? Oh, I forgot to check. I assume your typing is good and fast?"

She nodded. "Yes, it is, and I'd be happy to accept; that would be great."

"So it's a deal, then? When can you start?"

They made arrangements for her to have a key, to help him meet his deadlines, and to leave an invoice at the end of each month.

"Fifteen pounds an hour. Two days a week, so let's round it up to a hundred and fifty a week to cover any extra demands I might make on your time." He held up his hands. "No, no, don't look worried, I won't want too much from you, but I'd like you to arrange and accompany me to the Ajmer Book Festival in a couple of months. And that will certainly mean some overtime – setting it up and also spending a few days there. Is that okay? And lunch, of course, if I'm here. I'm a good cook, and I always make too much. Living alone is not good for portion control."

The sun was still warm when Julia left, shaking his cool, dry hand at the door. He didn't grasp hers tightly, as some men did, to show, she thought, how manly they were, and he didn't let it slip out of his hand either.

"Thank you for coming. It was good to meet you. Annie was absolutely right. I think we will work well together. See you next week."

The steps and paving stones radiated the warmth they had absorbed all afternoon. She strolled along, past blocks of flats, shabby bars, and a shop with hanging multicoloured scarves, reggae music pumping out of open upstairs windows, and red buses trundling past.

She felt a wash of relief, and a flutter of excitement. The Book Festival was an added bonus, and it would mean that she could perhaps extend the trip in her own time, and do a bit of family sleuthing. Where was Ajmer? Not too far from Ranpore, she hoped. All things considered, she decided, this was going to be a good thing. And six hundred pounds a month would make the difference between scraping along till Freddie paid her what they had agreed, and managing fairly comfortably. She could even indulge her secret vices – she was often tempted by clothes she loved but did not need, and had been brought up to regard money spent on books as not worth reckoning. Her broad smile made a man half way up a ladder shout, "Thank you, young lady! You've brightened my day!"

*Jacaranda Lodge.*
*January 1939*

*Happy New Year!*
*It was so good to hear about all the places you visited on your honeymoon. How clever of you to combine it with a trip to meet Arthur's new employers.*

*You visited so many of the places you and I have talked about visiting one day. I wonder if I ever will, but your photographs will be the next best thing, I'm sure.*

*Of course I'm happy for you both, but I miss you too. It was such a breath of fresh air to have someone like Arthur around, and I much enjoyed our bicycle rides together to Massacreghat. What a long time ago that seems now.*

*What happens here? Well, mother is as fit as ever, and we live together, as she wishes it, in a mostly harmonious household. She continues to play her Bridge and go to church – why should anything have changed? You have only been away a few months. Dashing gentlemen like Arthur ride in over the horizon only every so often. That sort of thing doesn't happen twice in a decade – not in Ranpore anyhow.*

*No visitors from Britain at present, not even at the Cornwallises, although there is talk of Mrs Cameron's nephew coming out from England for a while, to see if he can make a go of it here. Like Arthur, I suppose, and I can only wish him the same success in finding a wife and a job that suits them both.*

*There is also talk of the war, of course. People here are already knitting and crocheting blankets for the troops, which may or may not get to them, I suppose. It all seems a very long way away, and we are all hoping it'll be soon be over.*

*The roselle jelly I've made is almost as good as the cook's, and I'm struggling with the mali's idea of how to plant flowers. I want to fill the flowerbeds and have no soil showing, but he regards that as a slight on his position. He likes sharp borders and neatly circular brown beds, and plants every so often.*

*Forgive me – this is a dreary letter. I hope you're both enjoying married life, and that your baby is soon to appear. I'm knitting for her or him (so it's a rather charming pale green) and will send you what I've done when I finish. Mother, too, is working away at her needles, and between us we make a happy pair on the verandah after supper, clicking away!*

*I'm now going to submit to the demands of Deena and take her out for her evening constitutional.*

## Chapter Seventeen

The key fitted into the lock in Hari's office door. It took a little wiggling but after a few seconds it turned. Julia hung her denim jacket on a hook and made her way to the kitchen. Hari hadn't come down yet so she ground the beans and switched on the coffee machine; both needed a large pot to get them through the morning.

She picked up the letters on the mat, and put the ones that looked important on his desk in the room next door, in front of a large-screen Apple Mac. The bong that sounded when it booted up was the first note of *It's A Hard Day's Night*. Sometimes Julia hummed the song, but today there was a lot to do. Three chapters to get ready for Hari's next meeting with his editor, and this evening she'd work to catch up on for Annie, who wanted to reassure herself that Julia's thesis was going to plan.

"I hope Hari isn't taking up all your time?" Annie had asked the last time they'd met, looking at Julia with her head on one side.

Julia found the head tilt irritating.

"No. I'm keeping up. I'm not doing much else, mind you, but that's an economical way to live. My only outings, more or less, are to the library and the bank to pay in my cheques from Hari. I enjoy both!"

Annie had smiled. "Be careful. Watch out for the tiny

extra requests. They may mount up without you realising. Do you like him?"

The question took Julia by surprise. "Yes, I do. But we don't talk much. He works in a small room next to where I type, and we only really meet up over the coffee machine."

"Probably wisest. He gets around, does Hari."

"Hello, hello. And how are you today?" said Hari, with his usual brisk wave, walking past Julia's desk to his office. He pushed a heavy lock of hair back off his forehead.

"Fine thanks. Coffee?"

"It's okay. I'll get some in a minute. I just need to sort myself out. Meeting tomorrow, yes? How are you doing on the pages?"

He flicked through the letters on his desk as he spoke, and opened the ones that looked interesting.

"Private View... Book Launch... Opening of a shop... Another Book Launch... Would I speak at a festival...? Do you know, when this lot started coming I was thrilled. Now I couldn't be less interested. Do you want to go to any of these?"

He deposited a small pile of cards in front of her. She'd been there long enough – a month now – for it not to excite her much, either.

"Perhaps. The ones that have free food are always a good idea! Especially if I can take a friend!"

"Oh, poor Julia." He smiled, slightly ironically. "Don't I pay you enough?"

"That is not what I meant. Of course you do. More than enough for what I do."

He enjoyed her embarrassment.

"Oh, shut up." she smiled sheepishly. "But when you were a student, didn't you find that filling the fridge is a) expensive and b) a chore?"

"Well, of course, but luckily the expense was not a problem. My kind parents saw to that. Their brilliant son who had made it to Oxford had to be royally looked after. I was rather well off, actually. Still am, I'm happy to say."

"Well, I'm not," she snapped. "And your stipend is very usefully keeping me off the breadline."

"Your parents, though? You said you were going through your old house. That will help too, surely?"

"My dad's in a home in Richmond, so that needs to be paid for. His cash is covering it luckily – for now, at any rate. Linton is where my parents moved when they came back to this country. It's mine now, but I don't want to sell it. My, er... settlement isn't coming for a bit, so there's a lot to work out."

Stupidly, her eyes filled with tears, and she turned her head away, hoping he wouldn't say something jarring, and preferably nothing sympathetic. She needn't have worried.

"Coffee?" he asked. "I need to get you going, and keep you at the keyboard today."

That was fine. She blinked hard.

"Yes, please."

She turned to the computer and started to type.

He came back into the room carrying two mugs, and sat down beside the desk.

"I know I said you had to get going, but I just wanted to ask. Do you remember anything much about your childhood, your family, in India and Pakistan?"

"Why? Because you need something colonial for people to take against?"

It was uncalled for, and she knew it. He let it pass.

"Not really. I just wanted to know what it was like, being a child in the – what? 1960s?"

"I was born in 1968. Dad didn't want to leave, so we stayed on, but eventually it was clear that it was not going to be the right place for our family any more. They bought Linton to come back to, and packed up completely in 1984."

"So you don't remember much?"

"There are family stories that I may or may not have been there for. It doesn't really matter – I've heard them so often that I feel as if I had been. And I remember things like the *nappit*, my father's barber, turning up to give us all a haircut. He trimmed my mother's hair and hacked mine into a terrible pudding basin shape. I hated it. There are some photos of me looking as if I want to bite someone."

"Yes, I've seen that expression."

She looked up to see him smiling at her.

She stuck her tongue out at him. "If you want any more authentic titbits from a quasi-colonial childhood, you will have to stop teasing me. Members of the ruling race don't have a sense of humour, you must know that!"

"Indeed. I'll remember, *Memsa'ab*."

"I can't be of much help, really. My mum would have been just the person. My dad, too, but he's pretty muddled now and doesn't know if he's Arthur or Martha half the time."

Hari opened his mouth, and closed it again. "Okay, I'll leave you in peace."

She wondered if she should tell him about her discovery at Linton. She was working steadily through the pile of faded pages. Some were just about the day-to-day goings-on in a stiflingly polite middle-class society, with all its social events and mores, but a few were more revealing about her great-aunt's state of mind. And there was something else, too, which Julia had not yet been able to pinpoint. Tiny hints about another life, unexplained. Mentions of people Julia had never heard of. She wished, not for the first time, that she had Kate's replies to read as well, but she would have to make do with just one side of the story, and then do a bit of detective work when she got to Ranpur. It had been Ranpore in the colonial days, but, like Kolkata, Kanpur, Mumbai, it had been Indianised since then.

*Jacaranda Lodge*
*1965*

*Well, we are settled in our happy ménage à quatre. I'm delighted to say that we all get on famously. Henry is often away, and dear. J.J. keeps Doris and me company. I'm never away, but I spend time peacefully in what the servants grandly call Old Memsa'ab's Wing!*

*I've a little verandah and I fill it – with help from the malis – with pots of bougainvillaea, begonia, cosmos, portulaca, plumbago. It is quite a riot of shape and scent and colour. Wonky comes and sweeps each afternoon; I find the swish of his broom soothing. It lulls me to sleep under my fan in my room when I retire there after lunch.*

*The cook is training his son or nephew, or whoever he has chosen – I'm told he's a family member but who knows? He has produced some delicious curries except for one that set my palate on fire and made me gasp for breath, and his dhal is quite something. Also, his lemon pudding. As you can tell, I'm being well fed and therefore I've also to tell you that I become a little rounder each year.*

*I've not been exercising, I admit, but. J.J. is very lively! I get breathless, so my walks are shorter these days. And I stopped cycling a couple of years ago after I almost ran over the water man. It'll be a long time before I forget the look of horror on his face as he set down his water barrels and took to his heels. It makes me laugh, for which I shall probably go to hell, but my excuse is lack of coordination, not lack of concern.*

# Chapter Eighteen

After an hour of deciphering Hari's spidery writing in the margins and lines of his manuscript and incorporating the changes on to the computer, Julia took a break, with a cup of strong coffee. The window was open and the warm air, laced with petrol and London summer dust, moved around the room, flicking over a page here, stroking the corner of a desk, shifting a strand of hair off her forehead.

Although Julia had decided to leave the letters from Jacaranda Lodge at her flat, she'd not been able to resist bringing a few of them to the office to read when she'd a moment. There were so many of them, talking of the weather, the dog, the food, the parties, the dinners, the changes after Independence. Helen wrote fluently, in detail, as if they were her diary.

Julia was enjoying her own growing insight into the life of her great-aunt, and caught by the shadows of regret flitting through all the letters. Helen was affectionate, and almost militantly restrained. It rang false.

She took out a crumpled page of light blue paper and was spreading it out carefully on the desk when Hari came in.

"Ha! So this is what I pay you for, is it?"

She looked up guiltily. She'd not been expecting him for an hour or two, and was not ready to explain what she was doing.

"Oh, don't look so silly. You deserve a break! What are you reading?"

She put the paper down, and placed her hand on it protectively.

"It's okay. I'm not going to tear it out of your hand." He looked irritated.

"I was taking ten minutes. I came in at half past eight and I've to see Annie this afternoon. It's...it's...one of my great-aunt's letters."

She spoke reluctantly, not wishing to release the words into the air of the twenty-first century.

They hung there. He grinned.

"Ahhh. Just to be clear, Julia, I don't need you to explain how you spend your time. I don't care if you work under water as long as you feed me your continuous stream of corrected copy. And also, it is absolutely up to you what you read in your breaks, although, of course, I'm curious."

She moved her hand involuntarily, and he frowned.

"I'm not going to steal them, you know. Show me when... if... you want to."

He went through to his desk, and sat down, taking up some pages that she'd printed out from the pile in his in-tray.

She looked at the piece of paper in her hand.

"Hari?"

He raised his eyes slowly from what he was reading. Making her wait.

"Oh, for God's sake, stop pretending. You're as interested in these letters as I am."

"Positively bursting with curiosity, my dear. But as I said, you decide."

"She spent all her life in Ranpore. Ranpur to you. It's been changed since Helen's time. She died in 1975 – not long ago, and I never knew."

She took the letter to him.

He read it in silence.

"She's definitely holding something back, isn't she?" said Julia. "She asks for photographs – her sister is hardly keeping her in the loop. Her mother sounds a burden... And her mother's opinions about Indians can't have gone down very well."

Hari folded the letter, with its browning edges and sharp creases. "I agree. Fascinating. I'd have liked to meet her."

Julia nodded. "She wrote to me when I was at school. I wish I'd written back more often. But..."

"But you were a small girl, far from home, trying to settle down, and distracted by so many things around you. We all regret not keeping up with people in our past. Don't beat yourself up about it. Helen chose her life."

"Ah, but did she? Why was she stuck with Evangeline, getting older and crosser? What is the life she alludes to? Why did Kate get married and not her? She was the older sister. Dad said the other day that she was elegant, clever, intelligent. Is that not marriage material?"

"I'm not sure. In the 1930s men were still in charge. They wanted biddable wives. Good housekeepers."

"From what I can gather I don't think Kate was any good at that side of things at all. I certainly don't remember her showing any interest in anything to do with the house. When she visited Tindharia, after Dad took over, she didn't bring any knitting, she didn't talk about recipes or anything at all like that. Dad said Helen was the competent one. She ran the house for Evangeline, certainly."

Hari looked at her quickly, and then away again. She didn't notice, staring at the envelope in her hand.

"Did Helen choose her life?" she continued. "Why was she left alone in the end? Or was she?"

"I expect it is all there. You need to do some digging. Is there anyone in Ranpur you can talk to?"

Julia shrugged. "I don't know who's living in the house now. Or even if it's still there. Perhaps I should write and see what turns up. I need to go to India for my thesis anyway, so after the Festival would be the perfect time to do some research, to check if there are any pictures in museums or collections."

"I always enjoy the Ajmer Book Festival – helps my sales a treat, and it's nice to be treated like a celeb. If I spent a few days in Ranpur with you after it, I think I could be of some use, couldn't I?"

He looked at her and grinned. She looked back, with a slight frown. "As we agreed, I'll do all the organisation at the Festival and I'll stay around for the time you're there, if you'd like me to..."

He nodded slowly.

"...But coming with me to do my family detective work?" she went on. "I'm not sure. It's a very colonial story. A very small one. Why on earth would you be interested? There'll be lots that has nothing to do with –"

"Doesn't matter. I'm not a hidebound anti-imperialist. For God's sake, Julia, give me some credit. But it'd be interesting, and if you'd permit me to accompany you for a couple of days – only a couple of days – I think we'd enjoy it."

Julia continued to look doubtful.

"No strings attached. Nothing. I won't use anything in a novel if you don't want me to. Cross my heart and hope to die."

"I'm not sure that works if you're Hindu. You should probably promise on Shiva, or whatever."

"Okay. I'll promise on Shiva and Vishnu and all the rest. My own *ishvara* is Saraswati. She's the goddess of knowledge. Music, arts and science. I think if we had her blessing, if *you* had it, then it would help your quest."

She smiled now. "Quest" sounded exciting. "You make it sound very swashbuckling. I don't think Helen's story qualifies, but – well, okay. It would be nice to have you along for a bit." She paused. "Should I take an *ishvara*, too – Hindu or not? It's always good to have a bit of help from your own deity."

"Well, in that case, why not go the whole hog and take Parvati. The goddess of power. She gives energy to everything – without her, we'd be nothing. She does have a dark side, though, but we don't need to bother ourselves about that. You must know all this anyway. You can't do a PhD on Indian art without taking on a lot of information about our gods."

This was true. Julia had spent a lot of time learning about the complications of the Hindu religion. The gods and goddesses and all their manifestations were fascinating, but when she'd been told that there were more than three hundred million of them, she had given up after the main ones and a few of their offshoots. Nevertheless, having their blessing on her project seemed like a good idea. She would certainly need help to find out what had happened in Ranpore half a century ago.

More than ever Julia wanted to know more about the great-aunt she'd never met, whose independence of thought glimmered in the letters, despite her apparently dutiful submission. Had she loved? Had she been able to enjoy her life? Had something else been going on, something that gave her the strength to put up with her mother's meannesses? And, possibly, her sister's betrayal?

*Jacaranda Lodge*
*June 1944*

*Dear Kate,*

*Today I'm feeling – what? Grumpy. Annoyed with Mother's demands. And when this happens, the past reminds me of what I could have had. I can't allow myself the luxury of wallowing in what might have been. It just doesn't help.*

*I wish I had a life of my own. Not at the beck and call of an imperious old woman, whose grip on social niceties jangles my nerves. I'm sick of her pointless snobbery. Her nasty little jibes at Doris and the Anglo-Indians, whom she calls chi-chis. What a disgusting word. She plays Bridge like a demon, but instead of using her undoubtedly excellent brain for a happier purpose, she directs everything at keeping up appearances. She's almost sycophantic to Leonora Cornwallis with her big house, and rich husband, and polished motor, but treats dear Cassandra with superiority, even though she's Leonora's niece. She isn't able to compete with Leonora but she works hard on what she calls "putting our best foot forward." Why bother? We won't ever starve, but we don't have Leonora's money to spend on large parties at the Club. If I hear anything more about the dinner service or the crystal glasses or – whatever – I shall scream!*

*My friends – those very same chi-chis – are my greatest comfort. Sometimes I've thought that perhaps I could marry to get out of this house. It would have to be someone from Ranpore, as I can't really leave Mother alone. But it all seems too much of an effort now. There was a chance a few years ago, but I was too frightened to argue. When I remember that, it makes me think so much less of myself, and wish I had stood my ground. But I didn't.*

*One blessing is that I do not have anyone I shall miss if anything happens to them in this horrible war. Of course I'll mind if my friends don't return, but there is nobody in my family except Arthur who has joined up, and he's yours, not mine. There is someone – a tiny chance, but I've been a spinster for a very long time, and my presence is requested at dinner each evening.*

*I wish I were braver.*

# Chapter Nineteen

Sandy MacCleod's old eyes were cloudy, no longer the bright blue that had narrowed as he looked out from his house on the hill in Tindharia. He remembered his little daughter, Julia, turning somersaults on the lawn in her knickers as the monsoon rain rattled down from the thick dark clouds overhead. She was laughing, her baby teeth uneven, her lips wide in her pointed face. Her mouth was too big for her, but she would grow into it, said Susannah. Susannah. Was she here? No, he thought not. She'd left him alone in this great big house, with little people in white coats coming in every few hours to ask if he needed anything. Yes, of course I do. To be thirty again, happy in my work, living in a beautiful place full of extremes. Extremes kept you alive. Susannah was extreme – either very happy or in a bloody awful mood. Julia wasn't extreme, but she didn't say everything she was feeling. Not like her mother. Perhaps because of her mother. Would she visit today? Hadn't the mousey nurse said something about Julia coming? Or was that yesterday? Or last week? Always questions, no bloody answers.

Kate had never answered questions either, when Susannah wanted to know what Helen was like, when Helen had sent her presents for her birthday.

"I've never met Aunt Helen," the little girl would say. "Why not?"

"Aunt Helen lives far away," Kate would answer. "She is old now, and she writes letters because she can't come and see you."

"But why can't I see her? You come and visit, Granny Kate."

"It's easy for Grandpa and me to come and see you all. We live much nearer than Aunt Helen."

"But what does she do all day?" Julia always asked.

"She stays in Ranpore," Kate would say. "She looked after our mother, your great-grandmother, but she died the year you were born. Now Helen lives alone, with her dog, Deena."

It was all so long ago. Sandy sat back in his armchair and closed his eyes.

"Dad, Dad, It's me, Julia."

"Good lord, so it is. I thought of you today. Or was it yesterday?"

"Doesn't matter, as long as you think of me sometimes."

"Oh I do. I do. And I think of your mother, too. She's dead isn't she?"

Julia nodded.

"Thought so." He paused. "I miss her. I think. I miss you, too, when you aren't here. But I think of India, and I remember you and your mother, and your grandmother and grandfather – bombastic chap he was. Big man. Tall. Strutted about a bit. He was intelligent, don't get me wrong. But..."

Julia waited, but he gestured to the chair next to him.

"In a minute one of those bods will be along and we can ask them for tea. Would you like that?"

"It's four o'clock, Dad. That would be nice."

"And a custard cream. You like those. Is that chap here?"

"What chap, Dad?"

"Rory. Rufus. Rupert. Some ghastly name like that. Short chap. Actor."

"No, Dad. That finished years ago. Before I married Freddie"

"Good. Never liked him. Too full of himself by half."

"Nor did I, in the end."

She squeezed his hand gently, feeling his signet ring loose on his little finger.

They sat together in silence for a few minutes. Sandy had his wits about him today. A good time to ask about India.

The tea came. She poured his into one of the china cups. He liked it strong, with only a little milk, poured in last. Most planters did, she thought. Her mother too – she said it let you taste the flavour.

He took a sip, and looked at her over the rim, before putting it down carefully with a little clink.

"Fairly disgusting." He smiled.

"Dad?"

"Hmmm?"

"I'm thinking of going to Ranpur – Ranpore. I need to do some work, and I'd like to see where Helen and Granny Kate lived."

"Evangeline."

She waited. She heard disapproval in the word, delivered flatly.

"Evangeline?"

He looked at her and grinned. His leathery cheeks creased as his thin lips stretched to show his teeth.

"She's a piece of work. She came to our wedding. I couldn't decide if she liked me. So flipping aloof. Watching. Saying very little. Helen looks after her, without a word of complaint – is she coming to see me? Oh no, she died. Didn't she? Or did she? I like Helen."

"Lots of people seem to. Why did she stay on in Ranpore?"

"Nowhere else to go. Had a bit of money, I think, but was born there, lived there, died there. People did that then. Wasn't part of the fishing fleet. Although there were plenty of people who wanted to marry her – apart from...well, lots of people. But she wouldn't accept them. Not while Evangeline was alive. I don't know the details. Only met her a couple of times. I liked her. Came to our wedding – her mother had died by then. She was elegant, good looking. We're going to see her, when we go up to Lucknow. Have you got my passport? They said it would need renewing. Probably."

He thought for a little. "Kate left. Helen's still there. Duty, you see. Kate got Arthur."

He looked at her blankly.

"We talked once, Arthur and I. One night, after a few *burra pegs*. We didn't go into details, but I got the impression there had been something. Wasn't sure. He was a bit of a show-off, your grandfather, and whisky does things to show-offs. I thought he regretted marrying Kate in some ways, but it did him well as far as promotion and so on was concerned. He needed a suitable wife but..."

Julia waited.

"His voice changed a bit when he spoke about Helen," her father continued. "Couldn't put my finger on it, but it was warmer, and then he changed the subject. I didn't press him, of course."

Of course not. And now there was nobody else to press. Nobody who remembered.

"Arthur was bored of Kate, I think. She'd been pretty,

and she'd been spoilt, so what she wanted she usually got. Lots of men around her. She liked that. Furious when Helen and Arthur – "

He leaned over and picked up an empty glass. Julia poured some water into it.

"It's a long time ago, Julia. Time passes. We get old." He sighed. Then looked at her with a twinkle. "Evangeline can't stand Helen's friends. Too *chi-chi* by half, she thinks. Let the side down. Awful snob, did I say? But Helen likes them. No side to her. I've always wondered – well – if she might... Is that Susannah?"

"No, Dad. It's not. It's only me."

His eyes flickered over her shoulder as if he didn't believe her, then he sighed deeply and shut them. Soon he was asleep. She stood up, and looked down at the old man. What had he wondered? What might Helen have done?

She would go to her great-aunt's house in Ranpur, and lay the ghost of her curiosity. It might help her learn where she belonged. A child of Empire, always connected to her past? Or a modern English woman for whom London was reality, and India a pleasant childhood memory? Perhaps Helen's spirit would still be in the shadows, a silhouette against the sun.

*Jacaranda Lodge*
*1963*

*Mother is not well. She has weakened quite fast over the last couple of months and the doctor says she'll not be with us much longer. I wonder if you would be able to come and say goodbye to her? She asks for you, and for Arthur, although she speaks of him as if he's not your husband but mine. Not surprisingly I find this awkward!*

*Her mind is going, and of course I put her right each time she does it. The time for that sort of thing is very much in the past, and the part she played in yours and Arthur's connection was a powerful one, parting the waters rather like Moses. At present, she looks a little like Moses, too, if that prophet had long grey hair and a bit of a beard!*

*I hope you're happy, Kate. I thought for a while that I should have put up more of a fight, but I think everything has turned out for the best. I didn't think it would. I thought I'd never forgive either of you. But time passes.*

*I, of course, do not feel any anger about little Susannah and your family, just sad sometimes, especially as we don't see each other. Distance rather than disinclination, I know, but still...*

*Mother needs looking after. There isn't anyone else to do it. Even though the servants could manage perfectly well, she wouldn't like it. She's difficult, and it is my duty. I've had to accept that. It is easy for other people to say that I should leave her to her own devices, and make some sort of other life for myself, but it's not easy. She wants me around all the time, so I only get a chance to see my friends occasionally, when she's sleeping! And as for a relationship with a man – pigs might fly. Sometimes I hear the beating of their wings, but that, too, is discouraged these days.*

*I wonder if I'll ever have the courage to tell her the truth – what I really think and feel... It might lay a few ghosts.*

*Forgive the snivelling of a crotchety spinster. I'm not feeling very cheerful today. If you can fly out here – I know it is a lot to ask – it would make mother very happy. If not, I'll pass her your love. I'm sure she'll understand.*

# INDIA

# NOVEMBER 1937

# Chapter Twenty

Helen stood on the platform at Calcutta's Sealdah station with the world rushing around her, clattering, shouting, pushing, jostling. The whoosh of steam and clanking of couplings from trains coming and going filled the hot air, adding to the humidity which made her hair stick to her forehead in damp curls. Beside her, Doris was neat in red and white stripes, her little feet in shiny red shoes.

Doris's mother and father were organising porters and taxis and, for once, Helen was happy to let it all happen around her without feeling she was expected to do something useful.

A scrawny boy with old eyes heaved her leather case on to a rolled-up pad on his head. He turned slowly to look at her, inviting her to follow him. Which she did, her heels clacking on the dirty concrete, the sound weaving its way through the tapestry of noise, louder when there was a tiny lull, then drowned out as the decibels rose.

India was always noisy and Helen was used to it. Nevertheless, it had been exciting to alight from Bodhi's clunky carriage in front of the terracotta towers of Ranpore Station, with its creamy cupolas and latticed balconies. The rosettes and arches were a nod to the subcontinent, but the splendour of the curlicues inside, the coolness away from the blasting sun, the marble floors, the mosaics – all emphasised Victorian pomp and circumstance. *Paan* sellers shouted, scrawny men sold sweet *chai* in clay cups, designed to be thrown away after one use. Whenever a train came in or was about to leave, waves of travellers rushed towards the doors. Trains in India mostly ran on time, so there was no allowance for any delay.

But Sealdah Station was bigger and busier than Ranpore's, and though it sounded and smelt the same it was more crowded, far busier, noisier and more overwhelming. Sooner than she'd expected, Henry and his father had three phaetons waiting for them, leather seats padded with bright cushions, and filled with their luggage. Helen gave her boy porter a few *pais*, and he bowed quickly before running off to find another load.

"The Grand Hotel, Chowringhee," Henry told the first driver, who clicked his tongue and flicked his whip to make his horse move forward. The other two phaetons followed briskly.

Doris smiled. She enjoyed bringing Helen away from her family and watching her relax. After a few days she lost the wariness in her eyes. Not subject to rule by guilt, Doris would never have accepted Mrs Armstrong's tyranny, or the tight social strictures she imposed on her friend. She knew that she and her family – no matter how rich, cultured, elegant, or pale-skinned – would never be accepted by Evangeline Armstrong and her cronies, by Kate or by most other Europeans. But Helen was different and Doris loved her for it.

Of course, Henry's marriage to Doris had been a surprise to everyone. London-born, educated at Rugby, he had been considered quite a catch. Everyone in Ranpore expected him to set up home with a pretty, suitable wife. Plenty of families in Ranpore had eligible daughters who could make his life comfortable and give him some healthy children.

But Henry had deflected the caps set at him and had done exactly what he wanted – quite charmingly. He had fallen in love with neat, witty Doris, with her bright brown eyes and a fashion sense she shared with her great friend Helen. And he'd married her. The wedding had been one of the most beautiful the Ranpore Club had seen for years, and Helen had accepted with delight Doris's invitation to be her Maid of Honour. The flowers had been breathtaking, the food delicious, the music at the evening party of the highest quality. Ranpore had had a ball, despite itself.

Evangeline was unforgiving.

"Vulgar extravagance!" she'd remarked. "I suppose they think they've made it now, those Johnsons. Well, they'll soon find out that it takes more than deep pockets and an expensive wedding dress to do that!"

"Here we are," said Henry, turning towards Doris and Helen. The carriage in front had stopped outside the Grand Hotel, and Roshinara Johnson was being helped down, her little foot resting on the step that had been let down to help her. Her husband eased his tall and portly frame out behind her, and hotel staff came hurrying out to collect their cases. The Johnsons and the Carter-Wrights were well known here, and Helen was recognised as their regular guest.

"*Sala'am Memsa'ab*," said one, inclining his head with its plumed turban. "*Sala'am*, Johnson *Sahib*."

They walked under the splendidly-pillared portico, and into the Reception, cool, lofty and very grand indeed. A carpeted corridor led towards the bedrooms. It was flanked by cages holding plump white fantailed pigeons which purred and cooed as people passed.

Their bedrooms were on the third floor, reached by a wide dark staircase. The Johnsons had their customary suite, the Carter-Wrights a double room, and Helen had her own, with – luxury of luxuries – an en-suite bathroom.

The Grand in Calcutta had started life as Mrs Monte's Boarding House at 13, Chowringhee Street. Now it was owned by Armenian Arathoon Steven, who had turned it into a smart three-storey hotel with 500 rooms. Mr Johnson had it from his contacts at the Tollygunge Club that Mohan Singh Oberoi was interested in buying, and word had it that Steven might be interested in taking him up on his offer.

"It might be the best thing," Edgar Johnson said, under

his breath, over tea in the lounge. "Steven has other interests, and ever since his Everest Hotel in Darjeeling burnt down, he has not been concentrating on hospitality and tourism. Oberoi knows what he's doing and I'm sure he'll make a go of it."

"Oh well," his wife said cheerfully. "As long as they keep the same staff, we'll keep coming here. It's so nice to be looked after by people who know us."

That evening Helen dressed with more care than usual. She put on a silk shift dress of the palest creamy yellow, and clasped a citrine and silver necklace around her neck. The pale amber gold of the stones made her skin glow, and her dark eyes gleam.

"You'll do," she told her reflection, and turned to put on a pair of low-heeled cream leather shoes with a strap across the instep. They would have been out of fashion in England, but not here; she liked wearing them.

Several purring pigeons watched the tall Englishwoman with smooth, shining dark hair walk slowly past their cages and fanned out their tail feathers in appreciation.

"Helen, look who's here," cried Roshinara Johnson when she saw her come into the room. "Isn't this a nice surprise?"

A tall man stood up from one of the white wicker chairs.

"Hello, Miss Armstrong. I hope it is."

Arthur Kirkwood held out his hand, and she shook it lightly, trying not to blush.

"Helen, please. Of course it is – how nice to see you again. Are you staying in the hotel?"

"No," he shook his head and remained standing till she'd settled herself comfortably. "I'm in the Great Eastern, just down the road. They know me there and I've been going for a year or so – whenever I'm in Calcutta."

"We stayed there once when there was a conference or

something here, and there wasn't a room. Mother wasn't too pleased, but in fact it was comfortable, as you say," said Doris.

"It gives the Grand a bit of competition, which is a good thing," pronounced Edgar Johnson, always the businessman.

The talk was light – of people and places, and what to do the next day as Edgar was working and Henry involved with the Legislative Assembly.

"I could hire a carriage to take us around the City, if that would please you?" offered Arthur. "I could drop you at Whiteaways while I've a meeting just round the corner, and then we could have lunch somewhere? How about we go to Firpo's? The stairs are a bit of a climb, but the food is good."

"Mmmm," said Doris, "especially the vanilla ice cream with hot chocolate sauce. What a good idea!"

Helen nodded. She had often been taken to the well-known restaurant and it had never disappointed. It was said that the steak there was real beef, and not the usual chewy buffalo served elsewhere.

The shadows had fallen, the cicadas were chirping. The servants had moved unobtrusively about, closing shutters, drawing curtains and lighting lamps. Tables in the bar were illuminated by small oil lamps that threw long shadows over the dark furniture and the high rooms were cooled by many overhead fans.

"*Memsa'ab*," murmured the waiter in Roshinara's ear. "Your table is ready."

She looked around at her companions and stood up.

"Why don't you join us, Arthur? With Henry off at some meeting, you can make up our numbers. Oh, good. So why don't we go through to the dining room?"

Dinner was quite delicious. The curries were subtly and carefully spiced, according to individual preference. Helen liked hers lightly flavoured, others, notably Edgar, preferred their chilli administered with a heavier hand.

"Shall we take the ladies down to the Nightclub, eh, Arthur?" he asked jovially, when the last pudding plate was removed. "Would you like that, ladies? Henry said he would join us; his dinner was due to finish about ten. I'll make sure the waiter tells him where we are."

He turned and beckoned a waiter over.

"A table in Bentleys for us all, please. Oh, not you, Roshinara? Are you sure I can't lead you around the floor?" He smiled into his wife's eyes, but she gathered the silken folds of her crimson silk sari about her and shook her head.

"Not for me. I'm tired, and longing for cool sheets! You all go off and cut a rug. Shake a leg. Whatever you call it. Enjoy yourselves, and tell me all about it over breakfast tomorrow."

The nightclub was dark, the music jazzy. The singer, Eloise Ryan, was well known on the nightclub circuit. In a skin-tight black velvet dress, on a small dais, she sang into a chunky microphone. Her rich contralto vowels curled around the words of *Mean to Me* as they walked in.

Helen accepted Arthur's invitation to dance.

They moved smoothly around the floor, his hand light in the middle of her back, steering her around the other couples. They said nothing for a while, and Helen allowed herself to enjoy the pleasure of dancing with someone who knew what he was doing, instead of having to steel herself to ignore the flat-footedness of most of her usual partners

"You dance beautifully," said Arthur quietly, in her ear.

"So do you."

"Where did you learn? I didn't think Ranpore was a good training ground. The men I've met there so far don't look to me as if they'd be skilled in the arts of Terpsichore."

Helen's heart jumped. She smiled into his eyes, and

saw a reflected gleam of appreciation.

"Do you know, nobody in my life has ever said Terpsichore to me," she said.

"Well, now I have. I did wonder if I should, if you would think it pretentious, and write me off as a tedious little show-off."

"Should I?"

"Well, tedious or not is up to you, but I did think that you wouldn't need a translation, and since I left university, I've missed that."

"University. How lucky you are. I wish... but I don't expect women are encouraged to attend, are they?"

"Some do. But I don't think they're awarded degrees, so probably not worth the effort."

"I would so like to go, to try. But as you say, it's out of the question."

"Not just too far?"

"Too far, too expensive, too unsuitable. You've met my mother."

They said no more. Soon the music came to its sultry end, and he led her to her seat. Henry was sitting with them now, his legs stretched out before him under the low table. He looked relieved to be off duty. A glass of whisky was brought to his elbow on a tray, a thick damask napkin beside it to catch the condensation that clouded the glass. He offered Helen and Arthur a cigarette. They each took one, leaning forward for Henry to light them before settling back and exhaling in big smoky sighs.

They stayed until each of the men had danced with Helen and Doris, who also knew her way around the dance floor. Edgar was business-like, accurate, enjoying the music but without a shred of lyricism. He didn't enjoy the sensation of moving with the music, as Arthur did.

Henry enjoyed it more, but was less proficient. Not for him Edgar's complicated steps, so there was less need for his partner to concentrate in order to keep up.

"Arthur's a good chap, isn't he?" he said to Helen. "I like him. Educated. Interesting. A good thing he started looking for his new life in Ranpore, or he might have been snapped up somewhere else."

"You're right. He – I like him too."

They talked of other things after that. Henry seemed content, and led her to her seat when the song was over.

As Helen took off her necklace in her bedroom, a gift from her father for her eighteenth birthday, she felt – what, she asked herself? Well, happy. Lighter, too, with butterflies floating languidly about in her stomach, in Terpsichorean fashion. She smiled. Terpsichore. The muse of dance. She added the word to the others in her notebook, and wrote a paragraph about her evening. The last word she scribbled was "hope".

Then she folded up her memory, a fragile butterfly wing, and tucked it away in a secret part of her mind.

## Chapter Twenty-one

The sound of the horse's hooves died away as Helen went to kiss her mother, writing a letter in her accustomed place at the table on the verandah.

"Hello, mother. How are you?"

Evangeline put down her pen and looked up. She patted her neat grey bun, and turned her face with its pale, smooth skin slowly towards her daughter.

"Hello, Helen."

She allowed her daughter to place a kiss on her powdered cheek. She smelled, as always, of Houbigant's *Lily of the Valley*.

"In time for lunch. I've told Sudham to serve some mulligatawny soup on the verandah. I hope you don't mind. I know you have been in smarter surroundings, but you're home now."

Helen ignored the nasty little jab. She'd prepared herself for her mother's displeasure, which would take a day or two to simmer down. Both her daughters were accustomed to her jibes whenever she felt they might have been having a better time than her, or that they might find life at Jacaranda Lodge less than stimulating. It didn't matter. The week in Calcutta had been worth it.

"I wonder – could you possibly have a chat to the *mali* this afternoon – after tea perhaps? He's poking the soil and looking about him aimlessly in the veg patch and it is clear he doesn't know what to plant where. Also, the bleeding hibiscus needs looking at. There seem to be fewer flowers."

It was not a request.

"Of course. I'll just go to my room to freshen up before lunch," Helen told Evangeline, and moved off immediately, forestalling another request.

She checked her appearance in the oval dressing table mirror and tried to smile. A hibiscus, its white petals streaked with red veins, was reflected beside her tired face.

The house felt heavy and stagnant. Everything in its place. The Victorian console table outside her room stood dark and serious on its patch of red floor. She knew that underneath it the stone would be as shiny as everywhere else, polished by the sweeper. The ornaments – a green glass bowl, a photograph of her father and mother in a silver frame – were picked up daily, dusted, and replaced exactly. There was a light smell of polish in the air, mingling with dust, and an occasional waft from the lilies on the verandah.

Her bedspread had been washed and spread out again – it smelt fresh – and her flowery curtains hung straight and still in front of the mosquito screens on the windows. She listened. Birdsong. A call to prayer from far away, over the wall at the bottom of the garden. Recently, Evangeline had ordered broken glass pieces to be set in concrete on the top of it, to dissuade any "unwelcome visitors" as she put it. But even she had no jurisdiction over what happened outside her property.

"That Gandhi person is stirring up trouble. And Indians follow his lead. Lord Linlithgow will have his hands full. Mark my words, things are going to change, and not for the better for people like us," she said one morning. "He's giving a lot of interviews to the press, and they're causing a real kerfuffle. It'll build. Just watch."

The Cantonments at Ranpore seemed far away from any "kerfuffle", but Evangeline was right, Helen thought. She didn't want trouble. Of course not. But the predictions of gloom and imminent war were insistent and the news disquieting.

She knew there had been bloodshed in tranquil Ranpore during the Mutiny, nearly a century before. The town had been right in the middle of the action, and the memories of a bloody siege in 1857 were kept alive by nicknames such as Massacreghat, which people used without thinking where it had come from. Nowadays it was a quiet area, a popular place for rhesus monkeys shamelessly thieving from unwary picnickers. The river flowed calmly past until the Monsoon, when it rose dramatically and threatened to burst its banks. Which did cause a sort of "kerfuffle": people flocked there to see the water swell and thrash and roar.

"Helen, Helen, are you there?"

Kate rushed in and sat on the bed. "It's so nice to have you back. You're lucky to have been asked to Calcutta. Nobody asks *me* anywhere like that. It's soooo boring here. Except for that lovely Arthur Kirkwood. We've been to the Club a couple of times while you have been away – tennis, and then Bridge with Mother. He plays Bridge rather well, and even she was impressed. He partnered her for a bit, and she couldn't fault his game plan, which, do admit, is pretty rare. She tried though!"

Kate giggled.

"She tried to say that he was taking a bit of a long time, which was rubbish of course, and then he trumped the next three tricks and won the rubber for them. He's very popular now with Mrs Matthews and Mrs Cannon and their husbands. They've been waiting for ages for someone who isn't scared of Mother!"

"He handles her very well, doesn't he? And it helps that he has very good manners so she can't be offended!"

"Oh yes, he said he'd seen you in Calcutta. Lucky, lucky you. Did you spend time together?"

"No, not really. He wasn't there very long."

Helen didn't mention anything about the nightclub and Terpsichore. That was private, a secret, something for her to think about in the still of the night...

"He's dreamy. Don't you think? Handsome, tall, quite funny. Not many of those around in Ranpore."

"Mmmm?" Helen brushed her hair hard. "Sorry. What did you say?"

"I was talking about Arthur Kirkwood, but you don't seem interested. I hope he'll be at the Club Dance. "

There was a gentle knock on the door, for which Helen was grateful.

"Lunch, *Memsa'ab* Helen, *Memsa'ab* Kate."

"Okay Sudham. We're on our way. I'm hungry," Helen said, winding up her plaited hair into her usual style over each of her ears. "Breakfast was a long time ago. We had it on the train – and dinner the night before, and lunch and breakfast! The Grand sent us off with a hamper. All fun and picnicky to begin with, but by the end it was all a bit stale! *Chai* at the stations kept us going!"

As usual the plates were set out in the formal manner Evangeline insisted on for every meal. Starched white napkins were folded on the side plates, and a butter knife placed on top. A tureen of soup was brought to the table, and held beside each person, who used the silver ladle to pour themselves an aromatic bowl. Bread and *chappattis* were in their baskets, curls of butter in a little domed dish, and a bowl of fruit bright and tempting in the centre. Sudham filled water glasses, replaced the jug on the sideboard, and retreated to stand beside it, watching to see when someone might need a refill.

Mulligatawny soup was one of the cook's specialities. He made it thick and spicy, without being either too hot or cloying. The girls loved it, and Helen suspected her mother might be making a conciliatory gesture. Or not...

"Well, was Calcutta interesting? What did you do there? Were the Johnsons well?"

Evangeline buttered a piece of bread and raised a spoon to her mouth, looking over the top of it at her elder daughter.

"It was all very nice," Helen replied. It would not be a good idea to over-enthuse. "The Johnsons were generous and friendly, and it was lovely to stay in the Grand, which is just the same as it always is. We went shopping, went to church, to the Tollygunge Club, to watch the racing. I brought you each a present. I hope you like it."

Evangeline's expression did not change, but Kate clapped her hands together.

"Lovely! How lovely! I love presents. Do go and get them, Helen!"

Her mother frowned.

"Helen must finish her meal. We can have them over coffee. I don't think it is necessary for her to leave the table while we are eating. Come on, finish up. I'd like my afternoon sleep. We delayed lunch for your arrival, Helen."

Kate met Helen's eye, and looked down quickly, her expression a blend of triumph and understanding.

"I expect Kate has told you that we shall all be going to the ball at the Club on Saturday, Helen. There will be plenty of partners there for you both, but I shall not be dancing. Bridge will be set up in one of the rooms, and there will be plenty of players. Including Mr Kirkwood. He proved himself rather skillful the other night. We enjoyed our evening."

"Oh, Mother," cried Kate. "I hope he'll enjoy being *my* partner, but not at Bridge. I want to dance with him. It'll be such a pleasant change from Dudley and Denzil and Percy, and..."

"...Roland, and Geoffrey, and..."

Helen took up the refrain.

"Oh, excuse me, Miss Armstrong. Did I step on your toes? These new dances from England – they're not so easy to learn, are they?"

"It's a foxtrot, Dudley, not a tango, do keep up!"

"Oh, I'm so sorry, Kate. I misinterpreted the rhythm. Is that better?"

Even Evangeline laughed, before standing up.

"I think we are agreed that there is less sophistication, less glamour, in Ranpore than in other racier places," she said blandly. "Such as Calcutta, for instance."

The girls said nothing, ignoring the gleam in Evangeline's pale blue eyes.

"I'm going to my room. I shall be there for a couple of hours. And then, perhaps, we can have a walk about the garden in the cooler air, Helen, so you can see what I mean about the vegetables."

"Of course, Mother," Helen said to her mother's back.

"Oh God, how long is she going to go on about Calcutta?" asked Kate, grimacing.

"She does it every time. She'll get over it, especially when she wants me to do something. Like the vegetable garden. I think I'll go and have a quick look at it now, in fact, and talk to the *mali*."

Helen walked across the verandah and down the dark red steps to the garden. Usually she was able to navigate Evangeline's nastier moods, letting them pass. This time however, she felt acutely uncomfortable. Every dig made her feel guilty. What for, she asked herself? She'd done nothing wrong. As she walked slowly towards the vegetable garden the *mali* caught her eye and looked worried. Realising he thought her frown was directed at him, she smiled. He gave a tiny twitch of the lips and a little bow, incongruously dignified for someone wearing a grubby loincloth and torn red shirt.

## Chapter Twenty-two

Helen and Kate were good riders. The *syce*, Kumar, took care of their horses, Blue Moon and Sunny, and kept their coats shining and supple.

Kate was enthusiastic rather than graceful, but she was completely fearless. She nearly always won the paper chases, galloping along with her curls flying out under her riding hat.

Helen's style was more elegant. She rode for the pleasure of it, rather than the speed. She worked on sitting properly, heels down, heavy in the saddle, moving with the horse. Kate looked more glamorous, her cheeks glowing, her eyes shining, but she was not interested in any relationship with her animal.

Each week, the sisters were invited by the Cornwallises and other friends to join them on a picnic after an energetic gallop along the grassy rides of the Ranpore hills. Evangeline was quite happy with this arrangement – it was an acceptable pastime among people of whom she heartily approved.

The Cornwallises' niece, Cassandra, was always there, of course, her short sturdy body firmly astride a pony whose long face held an expression of benign doggedness that mirrored hers. She'd by now been in Ranpore a couple of months. She was always good humoured, taking even an occasional tumble in her stride. Her hair was neatly tucked under her hat in a hairnet, and she wore her usual sensible tweed.

Somehow her presence made an event cheerful; although her bright brown eyes missed nothing, she was never waspish or unkind, and always discreet. Helen and she'd become friends, recognising in each other an acceptance of what could not be changed but could, nevertheless, be enjoyed. Cassandra was braver, Helen more elegant. Both laughed. Their bond had developed into a trust that allowed an exchange of opinions, and confidences that neither shared with others.

Henry Cornwallis, Leonora's younger son, was a clipping rider, and he and Helen would enjoy breaking away from their slower companions for a good gallop on a straight stretch. Kate of course was far out in front, usually followed by young men. Blue Moon's ears pricked up every time they came over the final ridge, with a wide slope swooping away below. He needed no urging to pick up speed and rush to his nosebag and gulp from a water trough.

The rides started at sunrise, and ended wherever a picnic breakfast had been laid out on immaculate linen on the grass. This was no sandwiches-and-hard-boiled-eggs affair, but a spread of kedgeree and bacon and eggs, produced in an improvised kitchen operated by Majid, the Cornwallises' ancient bearer and his juniors, out of sight of the guests. Leonora rode her large hack, Humphrey, the short distance between her gothic mansion, Auchterlony, and the picnic site. And there she greeted her guests, sitting on her cushioned chair, holding a bone-china teacup.

"Honestly," Kate said one day as she sat on a cushion with her legs stretched out, "we may find it hard to get supplies, but my goodness, the stuff we do get, we know how to use! This is absolutely delicious, Mrs Cornwallis. Can't think of anything I like better – Majid's fresh bread and butter at my favourite time of the day. Mmmmm."

Nobody disagreed. The barbets were just starting to repeat their harsh trills, adding their song to the snuffling and snorting of the horses. Conversation subsided as the sun rose higher in the sky and the air became warmer – it was time to move on and ride back under the trees before the earth began to bake.

Not long after their last riding picnic. Helen offered to take a note from her mother up to Leonora Cornwallis. She did so with such alacrity that Evangeline looked at her suspiciously. Helen smiled back as calmly as she could, and asked Sudham to have Bodhi bring his *tonga* round in half an hour.

"Thank you, Helen. That would be most helpful. I've asked Leonora and Cedric to join us for dinner in a week or so. She has been so kind as to invite you and your sister to ride with them – I want to thank her, and anyhow, I enjoy her company."

Helen nodded. "I do, too, in small doses though. You have much more to talk about. I find her a little... grand, for me. I always think I might have a droopy hem or something on my nose when I'm with her."

"Hmmm."

Evangeline wasn't in the mood for light chatter, especially as Leonora's hauteur was something that Evangeline liked to cultivate for herself.

Helen left her mother to write her letters and went to her room to tidy up. Soon she was in Bodhi's *tonga*, moving along at a brisk trot. Little curls blew haphazardly about her head, and she pushed some of them back behind her ears. It was rather charming. Unlike her expression; there was something clearly bothering her. Bodhi took one look and apart from a little bow and a "*Sala'am*", kept silent as they went along. When the gates of Auchterlony creaked open, Helen composed herself and smoothed her skirt, skipping down before Bodhi could come to help her.

"Please wait here for a moment. If *Memsa'ab* is at home, I'll wave and you may go. Come back for me in one hour."

Her tone was unusually curt.

"Is *Memsa'ab* Cornwallis here?" she asked the turbanned bearer who answered the door. Before he had a chance to reply, Cassandra appeared.

"How lovely to see you, Helen. Come in, come in. I was just about to have a glass of cold juice. Would you like some?"

Helen gave her the envelope from her mother.

"Well, I'm delighted you decided to act as post woman, instead of sending Bodhi. Come, sit here. Are you going to the Johnson's dinner? They kindly extended their invitation to Leonora and Cedric to include me..."

"How do you do it, Cassandra?" Helen interrupted bitterly. "How do you put up with all the silly invitations to sillier evenings? You've lived in England, you have a brain. How can you seem so happy about a dinner in Ranpore?"

Cassandra turned in her chair to look carefully at Helen.

"Now, what's happened? This isn't like you. You're usually so..."

"So calm and useful and reliable! I know. I'm invaluable to my mother, I believe. I'm to have no feelings, never to leave Ranpore, or at least not until my mother decides to allow me. I've just been to Calcutta, Cassandra, and I enjoyed myself. I felt free, neither pitied by people as a spinster, nor frowned upon for having an opinion of my own. But I was with Anglo-Indians, so that of course wasn't Quite So, was it? Not according to my mother."

"And Arthur Kirkwood? Wasn't he there too?"

Cassandra's face was unchallenging.

"Yes, that's right. And Arthur Kirkwood. Who is very English and therefore very acceptable in Ranpore society of course, but – oh dear, Cassandra, I'm not at all sure what I'm going to do."

A canary flycatcher chirruped sweetly in the jasmine-scented air.

"I'm so *sick* of being expected to live at a reduced pace, in my mother's shadow. Kate, now, she's allowed to flirt and dance and play with people's hearts, but let me leave for a few days to have some fun, and oh dear, returning is like crossing the Antarctic. Mother freezes me out until she thinks I've learnt my lesson."

Cassandra looked sympathetic.

"I do understand," she said. "I'm very used to being the extra young lady at social gatherings. I was my father's hostess for some time after my mother died, until he married again; his wife stepped neatly into my shoes and I – er – found myself no longer necessary. So I took myself here, and I'll stay as long as my cousin will have me. I'm still a novelty, and I may be able to establish myself better here than at home. I have to be pragmatic about this. I don't have the luxury of independent means, and not much time to waste."

"I'm sure you will be married, should you want to be," Helen said, feeling uncomfortable at her friend's situation, so much more precarious than her own. "I was delighted to see you so in demand at the school dance."

Cassandra nodded. She'd made no secret to Helen that she was in India as part of the Fishing Fleet, an uncomplimentary name for single women who came out from Britain to find a husband. Without one, their future was bleak.

"So, is Arthur Kirkwood in the running?" she asked abruptly.

The question was a simple one, and Helen answered her at once.

"I would – I mean, I think so, but Kate is going to launch an assault on him and my mother seems to be encouraging her. Not that she needs to – what Kate wants, Kate usually gets."

"Your mother doesn't realise that you may want to marry? To have a family? To leave home?"

"Oh yes, she realises it all right. But over her dead body, quite literally. She wants me around, to make sure that nothing changes, and everything runs as smoothly as it always has. That's been my role till now. Fair enough, I suppose. Kate is not a natural housekeeper."

Cassandra smiled.

"Indeed not. But she's pretty and amusing, although anybody who wants a companion as well as a mother for his children would be bored fairly quickly."

Helen nodded, and then looked guilty.

"We both know Kate will fade," Cassandra said. "Happens to us all. The only answer is to make oneself a little more interesting. If I don't get married, I'll at least be good company – to anyone who cares to find out. But men go by looks – at least initially."

She realised this sounded bitter, so she softened it with a smile.

"I'm reasonable company, I think," said Helen. "Well, to some people anyhow. Oh Cassandra, what I mean is…Arthur and I talked about interesting things. About – *real* stuff. I haven't done that for such a time. It made me – happy. Really happy."

"That's always to be encouraged."

"Arthur likes me, I know that. Nothing's been said, but I think if I could, we could, we would… but I honestly don't know if I can face the fight."

Cassandra sighed.

"Helen, you *have* to," she said firmly. "Don't be feeble. I've *seen* him looking at you at the Club. He seeks you out. He doesn't look up when Kate appears, but when he hears your voice, he becomes – more alert. If you feel something too, then for heaven's sake! Do something. Don't let him think you aren't interested in him. He's stood up to your mother, he's mad about you, but he's ambitious and needs a wife, and he isn't going to hang around. Don't shilly-shally around. Men aren't interested in complications. And Arthur Kirkwood really doesn't strike me as the languishing kind!"

Helen looked back at her gloomily. Cassandra put her hand on her arm.

"Helen, think!" she said. "If he gives up, if he decides that you don't want him and Kate does, then what are you going to do? Your mother is not here for ever. There'll come a time when you're alone in Jacaranda Lodge and wishing that you'd been braver."

Helen knew she was right, but the thought of the battle made her queasy.

"Come on, don't look like that," Cassandra said briskly. "It's in your hands. You can do it. You just have to decide. If not Arthur Kirkwood, then someone else. Your mother will always try to stop you. You know that. But you *can't* let her. And you can't let Kate win this time. It matters too much. "

Helen looked at her bleakly. Her stomach clenched with despair, and she felt ashamed at her cowardice. And wondered if she would have the strength to overcome it.

## Chapter Twenty-three

In the tropics, darkness falls like a theatre curtain.

The dusk, if it can be called that, begins to creep in at about six-thirty in the evening, just as people are getting out of their baths before dinner. There is half an hour of twilight, before darkness is tucked in for the night, when pale colours are luminous. People call this owl light, and in India it is particularly beautiful. This evening, the lilies shone out of the dark spikes of their leaves, the cicadas struck up their crackling overture, and the sound of music from inside the white colonnaded Club building trickled out into the dusk.

The Club Dances were Ranpore's social landmarks. The ballroom was decorated and the bar manager polished the optics behind the Long Bar to a sparkle to prepare them for heavy use.

The Ranpore Club was proudly known as "one of India's top elite Clubs" by its members and, more grudgingly, by those who had not been allowed to join.

Members had to be upstanding members of society. A title never went amiss, and failing that a Director or proprietor of a respected company stood an excellent chance of being admitted. Three Indians had been knighted in the fifty years since its founding, and as such were admitted as extraordinary members. They did not often attend, finding the atmosphere stiflingly rigid.

The Armstrongs had been members for many years. The girls had been coming to play tennis, to swim, or to watch cricket, rugby or football matches somewhere on its twenty-four acres for as long as they could remember. The staff had picked them up when they tripped, and cleaned their grazes and wiped their tears when they fell off a pony or slipped on the side of the pool.

The Dance after the rains was always fancy dress. A sort of celebration of the passing of the incessant downpour and the heavy, inescapable smell of damp. People worked hard on their costumes, which were kept secret wherever possible.

Evangeline never dressed up, but Leonora always did – as plumply upholstered as an armchair; Queen Elizabeth I one year, Victoria the next, or, memorably, as Boadicea. Any costume that grandly covered her curves and gave her jewellery an outing.

On the night of the dance the horse drawing the *tonga* carrying all three Armstrongs clip-clopped along the Club's driveway and up to the entrance. The younger women were helped down by Bodhi, and waited for their mother on the marble steps. As always, Evangeline took her time.

"I need to go to the loo," Kate whispered to her sister, who hid a smile.

Evangeline descended carefully, gathering her skirts around her in a heavy rustle, and pressed a rupee into Bodhi's hand.

"Girls."

She climbed the steps slowly, grandly, and they followed her, feeling slightly foolish. They were not very late, but as always, Evangeline preferred not to enter until she thought there would be plenty of people there already.

Inside, the large room was full of chatter and laughter.

Gladys Matthews came up and leant forward to kiss Evangeline, who allowed her half a second's contact with her palely-powdered cheek, before turning it regally away. Helen, mortified at Gladys's crestfallen look, stepped in and kissed her, smiling warmly as Evangeline walked away, her small feet in black leather shoes tapping on the honey-coloured herringbone parquet.

Kate appeared with a lean young man with oiled hair and a hopeful expression. He wore flannels and a cravat tucked into the neck of his shirt and had the look of a youthful otter.

"Hello, Teddy," Helen said. "Are you taking Kate off to cut a rug?"

He smiled, a little timidly. "If she'll let me. I've managed to book her for the foxtrot. You have to be quick, you know."

He remembered his manners.

"Perhaps I might ask you, too, Helen? Are you free for a dance later on?"

"Of course, Teddy, that would be lovely. Ask me after supper."

Another, deeper, voice spoke at her elbow.

"I shall ask you before, if I may."

She turned sharply and her heart missed a beat, but her voice was very steady as she answered: "Of course, Arthur. Teddy, I shall be ready for you – nice and limbered up!"

She smiled at the youth, who wasn't listening by now, but looking devotedly at her sister.

"Oh, all right, Teddy. If I can fit you in I will," Kate said to him. "We already have the foxtrot booked. If there's another chance, ask me, and let's see if the tune is a good one." And then, when she saw Arthur, her tone changed. "Arthur. How lovely to see you. We didn't know you were coming. What a treat. We ladies welcome a new partner who dances as well as you do."

Her voice had turned from citrus to honey, and Teddy looked as if he were going to cry.

"I didn't know myself," Arthur replied. "But I was able to get away, which is just as well. It was a busy few days."

Kate's no fool, thought Helen nervously. She knows something's going on. She opened her handbag and took out a small fan which she used energetically to cool her flushed cheeks.

Cassandra was watching, too, her eyes as sharp as Kate's, but her expression gentler. Her presence made Helen feel less fluttery, although her heart was beating fast.

"Misses Armstrong," Arthur said, cheerily. "I hope you will both honour me by accepting an invitation to the waltz! Or whatever pleases you..."

Kate didn't waste a moment. She threw him the smile she kept for her favourites – never known to fail – and slipped her hand through the crook of his elbow before he knew what was happening.

"I would love to," she cooed, and steered him towards the dance floor.

For once, Kate's triumph was hollow; Helen knew that there really was no competition. Arthur had come to see her. She was sure of it. But rather than stand uncomfortably at the edge of the floor she accepted a halting invitation from Dudley, who appeared from nowhere. He swung her proudly onto the floor, and she tried hard not to mind the crunching of her toes. After Dudley it was Archibald Cunningham's turn, the headmaster from St Xavier's who, unusually, could dance and talk at the same time.

"It was a pleasure to see you at the school dance, Helen. I thought it went very well."

"Yes. I was relieved that there wasn't too much mess to clear up."

"Mmmm. Not like last year!"

They both laughed at the memory of the broken window, and the words sprayed in weedkiller on to the front lawn: Ranpore Stinks.

"Hardly witty, but accurate!" she said, and he laughed.

As the music came to an end, Cunningham led Helen back to the table where Evangeline and Kate were sipping cold drinks with a group of their friends.

"Mrs Armstrong. Kate. Good evening," said Cunningham. "Helen and I've had a very lively time of it. But I think we all need to rest a little now, before supper! Thank you, Helen, that was delightful."

As Cunningham moved off to his own table, Arthur Kirkwood appeared. "May I join you?" he asked, with a short bow to Evangeline. With a tight little smile Evangeline inclined her head, and as he pulled up a chair the turbanned staff in their maroon jackets started serving dinner.

Conversation grew louder, almost drowning out Alfonso da Souza's band. Leonora Cornwallis grandly called the winner of the raffle, who was the stationmaster's wife. She beamed as she collected a side of beef.

"Not very appealing," murmured Helen. "She seems happy enough, but I'd have preferred something jollier!"

Evangeline frowned at her, and she smiled back

sweetly. It was risky, and she might pay for it later, but she was feeling heedless. Usually she was cool, quiet, in control. Tonight she felt giddy, happy, admired. It was heady stuff.

Arthur worked hard to make himself agreeable to everyone, complimenting the women and joining in hearty conversations about politics with the men at the bar.

Eventually, he came over to stand beside Helen.

"Enough of all this. I've worked extremely hard to be pleasant and charming to all and sundry. My social duty. Now I think I deserve a reward." He bowed gallantly to Helen. "You owe me a dance."

She nodded, and stood up. He took her hand and led her to the floor, just as a waltz was starting. They danced for a while without speaking, enjoying moving together. Her head came up to his nose, so he had to bend a little to talk to her.

"You smell wonderful."

"Thank you. Mitsouko."

"I thought so."

"Are you showing off your knowledge of perfume, or of other women?"

"Other women haven't worn it like you do."

"Oh, don't talk such drivel, Arthur. You're very good at flirting. I don't know how you have the energy."

"It's rather fun. I like it. I like making women feel special. Especially you."

She looked up at him, wondering what to say, and how to say it.

"I'm not very good at this sort of thing," she managed at last. "Rather clumsy, in fact. Kate's much better at it than I am."

He looked at her seriously.

"That's true. She's used to being flattered and followed about, but the people who follow her are callow youths.

I'm not a callow youth, and although I can toss a flirtatious comment as far as the next man, I prefer to talk to you."

Helen felt his arm tighten a little behind her back and, tentatively, she rested her head on his shoulder.

"That's the ticket," he told her, softly. "How can I show you how much I want to hold you if you stand ten feet away?"

"Hardly ten feet. But I get the point."

The waltz came to an end, a sprightly samba started up, and they had no choice but to move apart. When it finished, they were both slightly out of breath.

"I think we should sit the next one out," she said.

"To my great regret, I fear you're right," he answered. "We can't have people talking, can we?"

But it was too late. Their closeness, the way they had danced, their evident enjoyment of each other's company had been noticed. Doris was smiling a secret, contented smile but Evangeline's didn't reach her eyes. Other women, wives and daughters, looked at Helen in surprise. She'd had her chances, God knew, but she hadn't taken them up. And now here was Mr Kirkwood... what a turn up for the books he was. She'd even blushed while they were dancing. She was usually so composed, so self-possessed; it was comforting to see her behaving in a more *womanly* way.

And all the while Kate flirted harder than ever, laughing, twirling round the dance floor, teeth sparkling, eyes flashing... Interesting. Some of the ladies exchanged looks. For the first time anyone could remember it looked as though Kate was being pipped to the post by her sister, although she was working hard to show how little she cared, surrounded by the usual cluster of admirers. But not the one she wanted.

For now, none of this mattered to Helen. She turned her attention to other dance partners, treating them more patiently than she usually did. But all the time she held the thought of Arthur close, the memory of his voice, the warmth in his eyes as he looked down at her. Yes, she did feel special, and she liked it very much.

## Chapter Twenty-four

"Goodnight, Mother. Goodnight, Kate. I'm exhausted. See you tomorrow."

Helen hurried to her bedroom. She undressed, looking in the pier glass at her tall, slim body which she'd never shown to any man.

Her mother's training had seen to that. Sex was never referred to, and when she'd needed an explanation – for the changes that happened when she was thirteen, for instance – her mother raised her eyes to the ceiling and spoke in a flat monotone.

"Oh, for goodness sake, Helen," she'd said when her daughter, embarrassed, showed her the bloodstains. "It's going to be like this each month, for many years, so you had better get used to it. Happens to us all. It means that you can now have a baby. Here, take these."

She'd pushed some unwieldy pads at her daughter, and some tape.

"Stick them into your knickers when you...when it happens, and as soon as they're wet through, fold them up and put them into a bucket. I'll get one put in your bathroom. They need to be burnt. Wonky will see to it..."

"Wonky?"

Helen had been aghast that something so private would be seen by the sweeper.

"He's an untouchable. That's what they do. Oh, stop making such a fuss. Anyone would think you were the only person in the world to have to do this."

The facts of life had emerged in a biology class, with some additions from Janet Perkins, who seemed to know a lot more than anyone else. Helen did not enquire how or why, but filed it away in her head and made sure she never mentioned it to her mother.

Brushing her hair with hard, sweeping strokes, she wondered now what it would be like to be naked with a man; and wondered, too, if she would ever find out. She put down the silver-backed brush, and thought again about Arthur, the smell of him in her arms, the feel of his stubble on her forehead as she leant her face against his shoulder. It had all seemed so natural.

She'd never felt like laying her head on the tweediness of Dudley, or the cravat and cotton of Archibald Cunningham. But she wanted to feel Arthur's arms around her again, and to hear his voice close to her ear. He had murmured her name as the last dance had drawn to an end, and she'd felt, in that moment, that life was perfect. With head held high, she'd allowed herself to be led back to her mother, who was standing up by the Club entrance looking impatient. The dance was over. It was time to go home.

"Goodbye, Mrs Armstrong," Arthur had said, charmingly neutral.

Helen looked down, making a business of finding her handbag, and putting her stole around her shoulders. Kate had been delivered earlier by some handsome gentleman, and was waiting on the front steps, tapping her black patent shoes.

There would be trouble tomorrow, Helen was certain. But as she lay down under her white linen sheet, in her cotton nightdress, she felt happier than she could ever remember.

# Chapter Twenty-five

Breakfast was a quiet meal. Kate was monosyllabic, Helen silent, Evangeline cool as she poured coffee from the silver pot with its fat belly and curling wooden handle.

Nobody mentioned the dance until Evangeline said: "The Club knows how to put on a dance, doesn't it? I don't dance anymore, of course, but both of you seemed to have had a good time on the floor."

Kate met Helen's eyes.

"Yes," she almost snapped. "It was fun, but I'd certainly have enjoyed myself as much as Helen if I had been partnered by the best dancer in the room. And for nearly every dance. It was embarrassing, Helen. You made a real spectacle of yourself. Men don't like women throwing themselves at them."

Helen took a sip of coffee.

"I didn't monopolise him," she said steadily. "I danced with whoever asked me, and I've the bruises to prove it."

Kate opened her mouth, but help came from an unexpected quarter.

"Kate, Helen is a very good dancer, and she has indeed had to suffer any number of clumsy partners over the years. Mr Kirkwood obviously realised that there were very few women there who could keep up with him."

Helen said nothing, surprised.

"I would have danced with him," said Kate with a pout. "I can dance just as well as Helen can."

"Kate, that is simply not true," Evangeline said calmly, ignoring Kate's glare. "You're good at many things – your prowess on the tennis court is much admired but Helen has a grace you lack. Mr Kirkwood spent time with you the other evening. In fact I thought he gave you a lot of attention. Manners wouldn't have allowed him to repeat that last night. So do stop making such a fuss. It doesn't suit you. You look like the *dhobi's* donkey. Or a particularly disgruntled camel."

Laughing, Evangeline rang the bell for Sudham.

"Now I've some letters to write this morning, so if you wouldn't mind checking what provisions we need with the cook, Helen, perhaps you and your sister might go to the market and buy them? And I'd be grateful if you could stop at the bank. It's the first of the month."

Helen went to the kitchen and did what she'd been asked. She hoped Kate wouldn't want to come, as usual, but when the *tonga* arrived, she saw that she was not going to be allowed to get away so lightly. Her sister appeared with a basket, and climbed in beside her.

They moved off slowly, and Helen spoke immediately.

"Look, Kate, let's not argue. It's so undignified. I had a lovely time last night. I really enjoyed the dancing, and I saw that you were, as always, spoilt for choice with your partners. So please, don't be cross."

"Something must have happened in Calcutta. He could hardly take his eyes off you."

"You told me that you had been at the Club with him while I was away, so I could say that you've spent much more time with him than I have. But honestly, it's because he's a new face. Once he's been here for a while, we'll all take him for granted."

Her words seemed to soothe Kate, and it wasn't long before they were chatting about this and that as if nothing had happened, bumping along the *murram* road in Bodhi's *tonga*. A thin film of dust settled on their clothes. A herd of goats blocking the road bleated plaintively, and Bodhi shouted at the herdsboy to get them out of the way.

An hour later, their shopping at an end, Helen and Kate were standing together at a stall loaded with watermelons when they heard a familiar voice behind them.

"Why, if it isn't the Misses Armstrong. And how are

you both? I must say, last night's dance was terrific, wasn't it? I so enjoyed myself. And how lucky I was to have the pair of you to dance with."

Kate opened her mouth to say something, and promptly shut it – any comment about his preference for her sister, she realised, would only sound petulant. Instead she decided to do what she did best – to sparkle. She smiled and asked intelligent questions, and paid the closest attention to his answers in a way that she knew always flattered her male listeners.

And Arthur responded, Helen noticed, just like any other man.

Except... Except for one brief, thrilling moment when he leaned between them to buy three slices of watermelon. She could have sworn that he caught her eye and lowered one eyelid so quickly it was over in a flash. And that wink, if wink it was, made all the difference. Her sister could sparkle as much as she liked, but Helen knew that Kate would never win him away from her.

When they'd finished the watermelons, and as he helped them into the *tonga*, Kate invited him to join them that afternoon for tea.

"Terrific," she said, when he accepted. "Helen's scones are delicious and I'm quite good at pouring! See you about four o'clock!"

"I'll be there. Thank you. As long as your mother won't mind."

Helen left it to Kate to deny this, although she wasn't entirely convinced her sister was right. Evangeline could be tricky if she'd not been consulted. But an invitation was an invitation, and Arthur Kirkwood had accepted it.

# Chapter Twenty-six

The tea table was laid with Helen's scones, a cake, and napkins crisp enough to delight Evangeline at her most demanding. This happened every day at four o'clock, although today the sisters made more effort, pretending they weren't trying.

Arthur arrived, tea was poured from the silver pot into pretty bone china cups that sat sweetly in their saucers, and curls of steam rose into the air. Sunlight dappled the garden through the leaves of the trees. The verandah offered its usual shade and cool, its corners crowded with pots of richly-flowering bougainvillea.

The conversation was lighthearted and inconsequential, the way Evangeline preferred it.

"There is talk for tea," she liked to say, "and talk for dinner. The two are very different."

And so she smiled, and Helen poured, and Kate passed plates, while Arthur appeared comfortable and at ease. Yes, he did like Ranpore. Yes, he thought he would stay for a while, although his contract was ending in four months' time and he would need to look elsewhere. Yes, he would be at the Club at the end of the week, and would look forward to seeing them all there.

After an hour of this, Helen began to wish it was all over. She wanted the house quiet again, the quivering undercurrents of anticipation and misinterpretation no longer humming like electric wires. Soon, to her relief, Arthur folded his napkin, placed it beside his plate on the lace tablecloth, and stood up to take his leave.

"Thank you so much for a very pleasant afternoon. Mrs Armstrong. Your daughters' cooking does you proud. I'm sure they must have learnt it from you. I look forward to seeing you all soon, but I must get back home. I've a report to finish."

Kate smiled gaily and offered her hand, Evangeline inclined her head, and Helen followed him down the verandah steps to the tree where he had left his bicycle.

"It was good to see you, Helen."

His tone was different. She said nothing. He took the handlebars of his rusty black machine, and drew it towards him.

"If you would like it," he began, "I should be very pleased if you would join me on a picnic."

"A picnic! When?"

"I thought Sunday, after church? I know you go to All Souls. I don't, but I can pick you up afterwards."

She could think of nothing, not even her sister's inevitable displeasure, to make her refuse. But...

"I shall provide all the food and drink – don't look so surprised. I've moved into my own small quarters, a guest cottage in fact, and I've taken on a cook cum bearer. He comes with excellent references and is itching to show me what he can do. For fun, and for appearances' sake," he added, "I've asked four other people to join us. Graham Carter and his wife, Catherine; Tony Wilson – you know him I think? And your friend Marjorie Morris; she's his cousin."

She liked Marjorie, who often made up a tennis four with her and Kate at the Club. But still Helen hesitated.

"Do come. How else can we spend any time together without everyone in Ranpore watching us?"

The *mali* opened the gate to let him out, and Helen raised a hand to shade her face from the sun. He was right. How else could they manage it? And if there was any gossip, she decided, well, so be it.

She nodded.

"Oh, that's wonderful," he said, with a broad smile. And then, out of the blue, "we need to spend a bit of time together. Or we'll never know if we can bear to spend more?"

He swung a khaki-trousered leg over the saddle and was off with a scrunch of rubber, cycling down the *murram*, waving as he went.

"See you at the church on Sunday," he called, over his shoulder. "I'll be waiting for you when you come out."

## Chapter Twenty-seven

The last hymn faded away. Carmen, the organist, in one of her brightly-printed dresses, liked to finish with a flourish. Her hands danced over the keys, a ring flashing in a shaft of slanting sunshine.

All Souls Cathedral was high and cool, its whitewashed walls covered in brass and marble memorials to the British of Ranpore. Helen liked coming here. It was quiet and peaceful, a very long way from the heat and the dust and the flies. During the day, light fell in bright pools on the heavy dark pews.

A loud organ trill ended with a crescendo. The quiet took its place again, as the final notes rose up into the cathedral's rafters and people got to their feet. Helen sat for a moment, looking at the flowers so charmingly arranged by one of the ladies on the Flower Rota, and watched an altar boy in scarlet skirt and white surplice snuff out the candles.

"Come on Helen," Evangeline interrupted her thoughts. "People will wonder what on earth is the matter. Kate is already at the door. Mr Kirkwood will wonder what on earth has happened to you. He'll think you don't want to go on this picnic."

The last two words were dropped into the sentence like sugar lumps into a cup of tea. Plop... plop. Evangeline had said nothing when Helen had told her she would not be in for *tiffin*. Kate had not been there, but by the time Helen reached the door, it was clear she knew what was happening. Her tight smile didn't reach her eyes and she turned away as her sister approached.

Arthur seemed not to notice the chill, and if he did, appeared not to care. He was swinging two motorcycle helmets; when Helen appeared, he held one out to her.

"Helen. How are you? The others are waiting. Let's go. I've sent Choni ahead to set up an awning by the water, so we won't boil. Did you bring your bathers?"

Helen had, but she was not convinced swimming was a good idea.

"No, don't look like that," he told her, as he put her bag into the space behind the seat of the side-car. "I wouldn't be so silly as to suggest the river. Apart from meeting a crocodile, I don't want to die of some complicated disease carried in the water. No, there's a pool, fed by fresh running water, which isn't near any village, so it's safe. I promise. Here, put this on."

Three motorcycles rattled into life. Helen settled behind Arthur, while Marjorie clutched Tony's waist, looking a lot less comfortable than Catherine, at home on the back of her husband's Triumph Scorpion, which buzzed along cheerfully. Nobody could have said they whizzed, or roared, or raced, but they went at speeds Bodhi's *tonga* could only dream of, hitting thirty miles an hour, inching up to forty for a short space of time, until the potholes reduced it to ten.

After fifteen minutes or so, they turned into a field, and carefully negotiated a narrow mud road through bamboos into a wooded area that eventually stopped in a clearing. Choni had been busy. He had hung a canvas awning over some branches, with wooden poles to hold it up. Folding chairs were set underneath it, and a picnic rug was spread out on the ground beside a fold-up table laid with a blue and white gingham cloth, plates, glasses and cutlery. Some way away a fire was burning, its smoke fending off the insects. A chicken was cooking, and some kebabs on sticks. The scent of charcoal, meat and spices mingled with the smell of vegetation.

The men turned off the rumble of their machines, and they all enjoyed the shadows under the trees and the babble of the water.

"This is absolutely delightful." Marjorie's soft voice cut through the thick air, and Arthur smiled, pleased.

"Shall we have a swim?" he asked.

Without waiting for an answer he disappeared behind a makeshift curtain, and Tony joined him. The two women looked doubtfully at the water, which was surprisingly clear. Helen put her hand into it.

"It's lovely and cool. Oh well, if I become a croc's dinner, Choni can inform my family. I doubt it'll hurt much..."

Marjorie, still looking doubtful, nodded, and when the men came out in their scratchy woollen trunks, she followed Helen to change.

"The mud at the edges is a bit sticky. Your feet sink in! I'd keep your shoes on if I were you," advised Tony.

Helen tried without, but the feeling of the mud seeping through her toes was disconcerting, so she followed his advice.

"Honestly, girls, there's nothing horrible here." Tony was being encouraging. "Don't hesitate. No reason to stay hot and sticky a moment longer than you need to."

Helen walked purposefully into the water and struck out with her steady breaststroke into the middle of the pool. Marjorie was less intrepid, and preferred to stay in the shallows for a while, splashing herself with water. Soon, though, she was tempted to dive in, and a smile spread over her face.

They splashed and swam and trod water and talked until the smell of food was impossible to resist, and they climbed out carefully to dry themselves on the shore.

Choni brought large towels – "Honestly Arthur, you've

thought of everything!" – and it was not long before they were dressed and sitting around the table, the women drinking barley water, the men beer. A kettle was on the coals to make coffee or tea for later, and a bottle of milk, wrapped in a cloth, hung in the water from a string connected to a tree stump nearby.

Babblers clicked and chittered and whistled, and Helen put her head back to look at the leaves overhead and the patches of blue sky.

"I've not felt as contented as this for a long time. Thank you, Arthur."

He smiled at her. "You have been so generously hospitable to me since I arrived in Ranpore, it's the least I can do. Marjorie, another glass of barley water? Or a cup of something hot?"

Later, as they walked through the trees, looking for birds, Arthur asked Helen seriously: "I hope this is not going to be a problem for you? When you get home?"

She didn't pretend to misunderstand.

"I'm twenty-six years old, Arthur. Almost an old maid. I doubt if anyone will even notice I've gone."

"Oh really? Not even Kate? "

She couldn't deny it. Kate would be cross, and she wasn't sure her mother would be good humoured about it either. Evangeline had always been cool with any man who showed a serious interest in Helen.

She put such thoughts firmly out of her mind.

"That's my girl," Arthur said, noticing her tiny shake of her head. "Forget about them. They're lucky to have you. Don't think I – and most of Ranpore – don't know how much you do in your house, for your mother and sister."

She wasn't used to being complimented, and looked away.

"I'm right, aren't I? I don't mean to be rude, but your mother leaves the real management of the house to you, doesn't she? She relies on you a very great deal."

Helen said nothing. A few minutes passed.

"Have you ever thought about leaving Ranpore. Going somewhere else?"

"Why? What could I do? It isn't easy to just pack up and go."

"It would be if you were married."

"Yes, then it would be possible. But..."

"But? You're a beautiful young woman in your twenties and if anyone could persuade you to marry them, he'd be a lucky man. You're intelligent, amusing, you dance like an angel..."

He stepped towards her, and she involuntarily stepped back, and almost fell over a small log. A lizard scuttled under the dead leaves, and she clutched Arthur's arm. He drew her towards him, and she blushed.

Silence. Nothing but the sound of the trees and the insects around them.

She took a deep breath.

"Arthur, I'm not good at all this. I think you're saying that you – like me? That is really flattering, of course it is..."

"But? There's a 'But' there somewhere. What is it?"

"Oh, for heaven's sake," she snapped.

"Sorry," he said quickly. "I've said the wrong thing. I didn't mean to annoy you. I thought you'd like knowing how terrific I think you are. And that I wondered if, well, if you might consider a proposal. I'm going to leave Ranpore, Helen, and I'd like to leave with a wife beside me. Not just any wife (there are plenty of those) but someone I – someone like you. Oh, for heaven's sake, not someone *like* you. You. I've thought of nobody else since we met in Calcutta. I thought you understood, and hoped you might feel the same?"

Helen sat down on a tree trunk. Part of her was disconnected from the scene, watching from above or beside or behind a tree. This Helen wondered why she was making such a meal of it. It had been what she'd been hoping for, although she'd not imagined this moment very clearly. There was always a hazy barrier, a mesh of disbelief, a mist of unreality. But this was real enough. Arthur looked down at her, his face expectant. Expecting the answer Yes. He usually got what he wanted, she realised.

Her voice came out thinner than she wished, and the other Helen sneered.

"Calcutta was wonderful. And I've thought of you, and I'd like to consider your proposal, as you put it. But leaving Ranpore, and my mother, and my sister..."

"I know it won't be easy to tell them. But surely you want to? I've – you seemed to be..."

"Oh yes," she interrupted him. "Of course I want to. I'd love to marry you, to make a life together, to have a family. But Kate's the one my mother, everyone, expects to do this. Not me."

She paused. He stood still, his expression serious. He ran the fingers of his right hand through his short dark hair and squinted into the distance.

"I'm sorry. It's just that I've had a long time to understand what her expectations are. We've never discussed them, of course, but she's made it quite clear that she...that I...that Kate..."

He brought his dark blue eyes back to her face.

"Your mother can't make you do anything, Helen. You can make your own decisions. I don't want Kate. I want *you*. I've got a good job, and will get another. Money won't be a problem. We can go somewhere like a tea estate – Assam, perhaps, or the Nilgiris. I've been told about an engineer's job going at an estate called Tindharia. I could become an assistant manager, then a manager. It's a nice life; well-paid, travel and education covered for our children. We could be happy. Wouldn't you like to start again, with me?"

He moved towards her, and she allowed him to take her shoulders and raise her to her feet. She knew he wanted to kiss her, and felt her cheeks colour. She was not practised at kissing. She knew Kate allowed her young men to be affectionate sometimes, but she'd never done so.

"I..."

She raised her head to his and closed her eyes.

"Oh, there you are, you two."

Arthur let his arms drop.

"Yes, Tony, here we are. I was trying to find a hoopoe to show Helen. I heard its call, and wanted to see if it was visible."

This was a perfectly acceptable reason for the two of them to be standing quietly together in the forest. Nearly everyone who came out to India was sucked into an appreciation of the natural world. It was impossible to avoid it. It did not explain why Arthur had been holding Helen's upper arms and looking very seriously into her eyes, but the others accepted the explanation. They knew Arthur was keen on Helen, and they hoped that this would give her a chance for the life she deserved, far from the demands of Evangeline.

The six of them walked back together to the picnic site. Choni had laid the table with tea things, and presented a lemon sponge cake with a flourish.

"I'll be mother," said Arthur, and poured out the tea into six white enamel mugs. "Forgive the bone china, but it travels well. Milk? Sugar?"

The cake was delicious, light and sweet. The smoke from the fire kept the insects to a minimum. They talked softly, not wishing to disturb the sounds around them.

Helen sat back in her chair, which wobbled a little as one leg sank into a softer piece of ground. She closed her eyes and smiled. The birds sang in the trees above and the dappled sun warmed her. She relished the peace and the company. Nothing was expected of her here. There would not be a request, a look askance, a servant hovering to ask instruction.

This is how it could feel if I accepted Arthur's proposal, she thought. In charge of my life for a change. Not the Helen Mother wants: biddable, organised, never making a fuss. Mother has made it quite clear that if I marry anyone, it has to be someone she knows, someone in Ranpore. She must never be inconvenienced.

But I don't want to be stuck here. I want to move away, I want to be with someone I love, who excites me. I want to leave Ranpore as Mrs Arthur Kirkwood – she lingered over the name in her mind.

She felt butterflies of excitement, but also of fear. This was a fantasy that could never happen. But it could, surely? Here was her chance. An offer was on the table, waiting for her to take it. So what's stopping me, she asked herself. Her heart beat hard behind her ribs at the thought of telling her mother; she felt sick with dread. To accept, to leave Ranpore with Arthur, to marry, to marry before Kate... The task seemed enormous, impossible.

"You will stay here, of course, Helen. To look after me."

Evangeline could have been sitting beside her.

"You cannot leave me alone here, in my old age. You're not someone who cares for excitement, to travel. No, we will do very well together here, in Ranpore."

Was this true? Was she really just someone who preferred a quiet life? Didn't she care for excitement at all? Oh yes! Yes, she did. She longed for the excitement of a new life with a husband who loved her, a new home, a new family.

Oh yes, she cared for that idea very much indeed.

# INDIA
# 2006

# Chapter Twenty-eight

Julia had been dreading her arrival. Indian airports, she remembered, were chaos. She steeled herself for the crush, the shouts and the general disorder as people pushed and shoved their cases through customs and passport control.

To her amazement everything had changed. There was glass and marble, advertisements on moving displays, lots of space, smooth luggage carousels with people standing fairly patiently beside them waiting for their cases. Still an occasional push and a shout, but the porters were ranged tidily outside in the arrivals lounge, waiting for a chance to earn the specified sum of ten rupees for a suitcase. Last time, Julia had been pushed aside by an over-enthusiastic arrival rushing to greet a parent, and had bruised her knee. This time she walked steadily with Hari beside her. There was no doubt his presence helped a great deal. He moved through the crowds with patrician ease.

"Stay beside me," he told her.

"Yes, *Sahib*," she answered, pulling her forelock.

He grinned. "Glad you know your place. Now, I've to go into the India Passport queue, and you have to go into the one for foreigners. I can't tell you how nice that is, after standing at Heathrow for hours watching you lot being nodded through."

"Serves you right. You were probably smuggling diamonds in your sponge bag."

"I wish!"

They were soon wheeling their cases beside them on the other side of Customs – "like leading a pair of Alsatians," Julia murmured. "I feel like telling them to sit!"

The taxis, yellow and black Ambassadors among sleeker Japanese cars, waited outside the automatic doors, their drivers standing beside them and looking keen.

"It's got to be an Ambassador," Julia cried. "I love them. I want one of my own."

Hari raised his eyes to heaven and spoke quietly to a man standing at the head of what bore little resemblance to a queue.

"At least we'll have one with air-conditioning," said Hari firmly.

"Okay. No problem with that, but I'm not going to take one of those huge white Toyota things."

They slid across the back seat, and Hari spoke swiftly to the driver, who nodded and moved off, ignoring the blare of a horn from a car behind. Hari spoke again, and the twanging of the music on his radio was turned off.

"That's a bit mean," Julia said. "I didn't mind it."

"Well, I did. Just because I'm in India I don't have to listen to jimcrack music when I'm paying."

It could hardly be said that they travelled in silence. The speed increased as the road became a motorway, and they sped along in a glorious game of dodgem cars, in and out, in front of and behind other cars, whipping in, taking another chance to overtake. Lorries, piled too high with goods, people, animals, jounced past each other. Bright capital letters on the back and sides of larger vehicles declared NO HORNING or HORNING, depending on the driver's preference. The horning was incessant, whatever the instructions. A family of four sat together on a small moped, the man driving, the wife facing backwards with a baby on her lap and a little girl squeezed in between her parents. The smell of cows, excrement, spices, petrol leaked into the car, even through closed windows streaked with the dust that swirled up and landed on everything, blurring edges with a pale film. Julia was flung from one side of the back seat against Hari on the other as the driver overtook a car and a strolling bull in front of him, and almost collided with an oncoming bus. She was not yet used to India, so she gasped at every near miss and clung on to the handle above the window so it hurt her palm. Hari smoothed his cream linen trousers as she righted herself after yet another zigzag.

The black and yellow Ambassador shot off the straight fast road into the city proper, narrowly missing a deep pothole. A horse, its saddle and bridle decorated with ribbons, bells and brass clip-clopped to a wedding, and the three-wheeler *tuk-tuks* hung with garlands of paper flowers nipped in and out of the traffic like angry wasps.

Suddenly Julia relaxed. This always happened. India became familiar, and she was no longer in a state of panic, expecting disaster. She began to enjoy the smells, the organised disorder, the glimpses of green spaces and larger houses.

They drove past a park on one side of the road, with a stained white stone wall, and a settlement on the pavement on the other, where families squatted over their cooking and eating, and lived under corrugated iron roofs or plastic sheeting. To Hari's disgust, she lowered the window to drop some coins into the hand of a dirty little girl carrying a baby on her hip.

"Pointless, you know. She'll have to give it to someone else."

"I know. I know. I'll get hardened, but she was so thin and hopeless."

"Like millions of others like her," he said, flatly. "Save it. You can give it to my family's charity if you like. We've set one up to supply water to villages, so any contribution is welcome."

She remembered that Karma was important to a Hindu. People were philanthropic in one way or another to help smooth their path to their next incarnation.

Hari had refused to stay at the Anjan Palace where the Festival took place every year.

"Too crowded, no decent wine, and some of the rooms are grim."

"Some, on the other hand, are absolutely lovely. Are you sure?" Julia had asked, disappointed.

"Yes."

So she'd booked the Ajmer Palace, with which, she felt, she could hardly go wrong. Maharajah glamorous, with swooping curtains and marble and mirrors and rose petals and soft-footed staff. Even Hari could find nothing to criticise.

Their rooms on the fifth floor were next to each other, each with a balcony overlooking the gardens and a bit of the dark blue swimming pool. Even up here she could smell sweet blasts of scent from the flowers beside the smooth trimmed lawns. She looked around her high-ceilinged room, with its whispering air-conditioner and wide, welcoming bed. The sheets were crisp thick cotton, smooth to the touch, cool to the skin. She grinned to herself – better not get too used to this!

"Thank you," she said to the young man who had carried her suitcase in after her, and pressed a note into his hand. He bowed slightly and was gone, his feet soundless on the marble floor.

Julia had a quick shower, changed into a light blue linen dress and let herself out into the wide corridor. It was a relief to be out of her crumpled travelling clothes. The lift smelt of roses, and it took her down swiftly and silently to the ground floor. She walked out through the lobby on to a verandah. The air was hot and heavy, the orange bell flowers of the climber on the trellis plump against its dusty greenery.

She sat on a dark wooden armchair, sinking into thick cushions. At her shoulder appeared the same young man who had carried her case.

"I'd like a *nimbu pani*, please," she told him.

The same bow.

"Cold lime juice," he said, in an accent that held only a trace of the Indian lilt. "Of course. Would you like ice?"

He saw her hesitate.

"We boil all our water, of course."

She nodded. "That would be lovely."

Soon a small silver tray was placed carefully on the low table in front of her, with a jug full of pale green liquid, clinking with ice; rivulets trickled down it, and she resisted an urge to put her hand around it and wipe her forehead with the cold water. She sighed happily and helped herself to a glass.

Hari appeared, looking cool and comfortable and very much at home. He had changed into Indian clothes: a simple dark blue *kurta*, the ubiquitous collarless cotton tunic, and loose black linen trousers – half way between pyjamas and the western style.

"Well, what are your plans?" he asked, sitting down and leaning against the fat cushion at his back. "It's what? Four o'clock now. Shall we have this delicious drink, and then go to the – what's it called? The Anjan Palace Hotel and see what they've in store for me tomorrow?"

She nodded, taking another sip.

"We can check where and when you should be there, and see who else is speaking in case you want to go to any of the other presentations."

"I doubt it. I cannot imagine why on earth anyone comes and listens to a writer bang on about his work. *No* idea why they bother to come to these things, but it is all the celebrity stuff..."

"...Which you love, so don't give me that. And celebrity sells – means you can pay the rates at the Ajmer and still have enough for a business-class flight home!"

He paused, and looked at her.

"You know me so well, Julia. And do you know, I rather like it! I can't think of anyone else who has challenged me quite so often, but hey, that's okay."

"You can sack me when we get back home to the UK. I'm off duty from tomorrow, so you're on your own. Well, not quite on your own – with me for a bit, but not as my boss, anyhow."

"Got it. You don't have to go on about it. Anyone would think you were longing to be free!"

"Not free, but longing to get going. I'm sure there's all sorts of stuff to be discovered – hope so, anyway."

"So do I. For your sake."

His tone was unusually gentle and his smile made colour come into her face. He stood up, extended his hand to her, and pulled her gently to her feet.

"We need a taxi. Come on, madam. To work. My public awaits."

*The Ajmer Literature Festival – Come and Soak up the Literature of the World* proclaimed the sign over the entrance of the Amjan Palace Hotel. One look at Hari's face made Julia heartily thankful that she'd trusted her instincts and not booked a room here.

He walked beside her through the lobby, following the signs to the Conference Room. A large table had rows of badges for the delegates, the speakers, the guests.

Julia saw Hari relax as he scanned them, and spotted some familiar names. He even smiled as he pinned on his badge, inclining his handsome head graciously to the pretty girl who offered it to him.

Julia sat down on a small chair against the wall, and watched Hari become the Gracious Author. He listened and smiled, and stopped and listened some more, and said something that made people laugh and nod and gather round him. She saw his name prominently on the front of the programme lying on every surface and realised for the first time how famous he was in his own country and elsewhere. The audience was international – she heard Hindi, French, German, a smattering of Eastern European.

"Right, come on."

Hari caught her elbow, and led her firmly to the door.

"I've made our excuses. We have to be back here at

9.30 tomorrow, so let's go. We can have a lovely hour to ourselves, before dinner and an early bed. What do you say?"

"Does it matter?"

"No, but I'm still on my charm offensive."

Which extended to the commissary at the entrance. A wide smile.

"Taxi please."

And that was that. They were driven swiftly to the Ajmer Palace, gleaming cream and white in the evening sunlight, and agreed to meet in an hour in the bar.

As the door of her room closed behind her, Julia looked at her watch. Six o'clock. It would be dark in less than an hour. She turned on the taps of the enormous bath, and while it was running, spread a pair of white linen trousers and a pale turquoise shirt on the bed. The sheet had been turned down, and a frangipani flower laid on the smooth white pillowcase.

She looked forward to dinner, and admitted to herself that she was happy to be with Hari. Tomorrow would be busy, but then her investigations could begin in earnest.

*Jacaranda Lodge*
*22 December 1964*

*Mother died last night. Closing on eighty she had aged pretty well – mostly, I like to think, because I have looked after her as she expected. She got what she wanted – a comfortable, well-ordered existence. And despite the war, and that "silly Mr Gandhi", she managed to ignore anything inconvenient and maintain the comforts she's always enjoyed.*

*A week ago, however, she asked me a question which she has avoided for the last thirty years. She wanted to know if I was happy.*

*Well, you can imagine. I have spent most of the last thirty odd years working hard not to mind being an unpaid spinster housekeeper, and this question was, to say the least, unexpected.*

*I am not a saint, Kate, you know that. I seethe with resentment if I allow myself to do so. But never mind that, no point in complaining now; I should have been braver all those years ago, and had the courage to defy Mother. But I did not, and I've not said anything – ever. But she asked me.*

*I suddenly realised I could not let her die not knowing what she has done. All the feelings I have kept locked away washed over me like the Hoogli in flood.*

*So – I told her the truth, Kate. I had to. I told her that I have been angry with her every single day, that I despise her snobbishness and her inflexibility, and above all that I despise myself for being such a bloody coward and letting her rule my life.*

*I also told her something that I haven't told even you, and I'm not sure I shall. Things happen when we least expect them to, and a few years ago, when I had resigned myself to dreary, unchanging Ranpore, my life changed, and everything became brighter. Mother wasn't exactly delighted by what I told her, but as I pointed out, it would never have happened if she had allowed me to marry Arthur and leave Ranpore.*

*I did spend years alone, lonely, unloved, despite the attentions of Percy and Dudley and Alphonse Bertram. Remember them? You should – you flirted with them, and then discarded them all when a bigger prize appeared. But remember, Kate, remember, he loved me first.*

# Chapter Twenty-nine

The driver, Mohan, was waiting when Julia and Hari walked down the sweeping stone steps of the Ajmer Palace. They climbed into the back of his shining Ambassador car, and slid open the white nylon curtains his wife had made to shade his passengers.

"Where are we going?" Hari asked Julia. "The Ashwara

Lounge? In Kanchpur? Not far?"

"No, not far, *Sahib*," said Mohan, overhearing. "But I can make other suggestion?"

He drove slowly, making a few enthusiastic attempts to get them to change their minds.

"My family's restaurant is very good. Only just around the corner – ten minutes drive. You will eat like Maharajahs. Meat, vegetarian, all fine."

"No thank you, Mohan. Another time perhaps. Today we would like to go to the Ashwara Lounge," Hari said firmly.

Soon they were on the pavement outside a brightly-lit building in the centre of Kanchpur, with a pretty terrace overlooking the river. The lights of boats were reflected in the water below. From inside came the sound of a sitar, playing softly.

"Oh God," said Hari. "I knew we should have eaten at the hotel. At least there was no atmospheric music."

"Yes, there bloody was. In the Chandni Lounge. I don't see the problem, frankly. And it's hard to avoid, so let's not complain," said Julia, and walked in ahead of him to ask the *maitre d'* for a table. Hari followed reluctantly.

"You'll be sorry," was all he said, as the plangent chords continued over the gentle mutter of talk.

A plump waiter with a plumed orange turban led them to a table outside.

"Mind the bloody mozzies," grumbled Hari, slapping his neck theatrically.

Julia slipped him a tube of insect repellent.

"Here. You may not want to use it because it's very effective, and then you won't be able to moan about the insects."

His eyes narrowed mischievously and he smiled.

"I'm sure I can find *something* to moan about. No, seriously, this is fine. We can hardly hear Rostropovic inside, and you can hear me when I say that I'm really grateful for your efforts so far on this trip. Comfortable hotel, easy flight, no problems. – yet! And…" He held up his hands as she began to say something. "No, no, hang on. My turn – I just wanted to say that you look lovely this evening. That colour really suits you."

She said nothing, surprised by his compliment.

"Don't reply. You don't have to," he said, quietly. "I mean it. Now, what shall we eat?"

Suddenly the menu seemed too complicated.

"Oh, choose for me, please. Nothing too spicy, but nothing too creamy and bland either. Just delicious. And a cold beer, please."

He ordered. Dishes came quickly, and were spread out on the little heaters on the tablecloth. He was quick to point out that one dish was too dry, another had too much sauce, until she frowned at him across the table. He stopped talking and raised his eyebrows.

She smiled.

"Hari! Do shut up. It's a lovely warm moonlit night. We are looking out over a river in Kanchpur. Tomorrow, in Ajmer, you will be feted and bowed over like the Nabob you are. I'm just a tourist and this food is fine for me. Even the sitar is fine – atmospheric, charming. I don't have your delicate palate, but right now who cares? Another time, you can take me somewhere that serves the sort of food you enjoy, and I shall enjoy it too, but right now let's just thank Heaven that we are here and not on the Kings Road or Notting Hill Gate."

"But I like the Kings Road. And Notting Hill."

He stopped and almost giggled.

"That's better," she said. "Would you like a bit more of this, whatever it is. And some *nan*? Rice?"

"Okay, you win. I won't moan any more. Pass the *nan*, and then let me know when I'm expected tomorrow."

"You know very well – your talk is at ten, peak time, and so you should get there about nine-thirty. At the latest.

I've arranged for your books to be delivered, so prepare yourself for signings. That is, of course, if anyone wants to buy any."

"Oh, they will. Just watch. I don't think you've really understood what a bigwig I am here. I've tried to show you by being as grand as a famous author should be, but you simply don't get it. I've been waiting for a change in your manner – a bit of humility. But alas, so far..."

She ignored him and continued.

"Mohan is primed and ready, and I don't think he has too many relations with restaurants in Ajmer," she said. "We'll eat and drink in the hotel in any case. There's too much going on to do much else. It is going to be a packed day. I did suggest we stayed one more night but..."

She frowned, thinking about all the arrangements and hoping she'd covered everything.

"God, no," he said, raising his hands. "No more discussions and bowing and being sweet to the public, and explaining exactly what I meant by paragraph three on page sixty-two. It'll be fine. I'll sing for my supper, and you'll deal with all the other stuff, and then we'll pack up, and move on."

They finished their meal, discussing the presentation he had prepared, and the finer points of administration. Hari was amusing, focused. He moved his chair next to hers, their heads bent over the notebook she was using, and she could smell a light lemony fragrance on his skin.

"That's a lovely scent you're wearing," he said. "I've noticed it before. What is it?"

That his thoughts ran alongside hers should not have surprised her, but it did.

"Mitsouko. I've worn it for years. But..."

"What's the problem?" he asked. "Presumably you wear scent so that people can smell it? I do."

She nodded. Their eyes met, and his were laughing.

"Right," he said briskly. "We have established that we

155

like each other's scent. Good. And we have also decided on what is happening tomorrow. Now, Julia, I'd like to pay the bill (with a little extra for Ravi Shankar over there) and go back to our lovely quiet hotel. I think we deserve a drink on my balcony – or yours, if you prefer."

He turned to the waiter who was hovering nearby, and soon they were in Mohan's taxi. There was a slight awkwardness in the air, as if something was about to happen. She felt slightly breathless, and annoyed with herself. There was no doubt the atmosphere had changed, but so what? It didn't mean anything, so there was no reason to feel uncomfortable.

Soon they were sitting on the balcony of his suite, a bowl of nuts on the low table between them, and a bottle of chilled white wine in a cooler. Lights in the gardens below flickered in the warm, soft shadows, and the tables on the terrace were busy with guests and waiters. Occasionally a murmur was carried past them on the night air. She enjoyed being cocooned in comfortable luxury, and sipped her wine. Neither of them spoke. A distant car horn sounded, muffled by the trees – not even the grandeur of the Ajmer Palace could quite obliterate the real world that bustled about on the other side of its high white walls.

"This *is* a pleasure." Hari's deep voice interrupted the silence.

Julia nodded. "Mmmm. Delicious wine, a lovely starry night, peace and quiet. I feel very spoiled."

"Well, that's a nice change. It's usually me who gets accused of that. Not that I feel all that spoiled at the moment."

She looked at him, surprised.

"No, no, don't tell me off. I've something to say."

Julia waited obediently, and watched as Hari poured some wine into her glass. As she put out her hand, he reached to take it. She felt breathless again, and concentrated on the dry coolness of his palm.

"This is ridiculous," he began. "Don't tell me that you don't sense that something has changed."

"No, I do. But it's the night and the wine, and – well, all this. It gets under a girl's skin."

He paused.

"I've no idea how to go on. It's not a familiar feeling. I'm not usually clumsy with women, but right now, I feel a bit – well, awkward and uncomfortable. I just wanted to point out – if it's all right with you – that I feel something is different between us."

He paused. Julia looked at him, taking in his creamy brown skin, his long dark lashes, his shiny hair with its heavy fringe, almost black. She didn't speak.

"Thank you," he said. "That's one of the things I like about you. You aren't flighty and flirtatious, and don't pretend that nothing's happening." The three words hung in the air. "You have noticed, haven't you? Let's not make a meal of this. I think we both feel something for each other that's not the same as before. Yes, of course, the night and the wine and all that helps, but I've been aware of it for a couple of days. I like your smile and your skin and the clothes you're wearing, and you make me laugh, and you tease me, and – well, all I can say is, although I do like your clothes, I've spent some time thinking about you with them off."

Julia's heart was beating very fast now. She felt the world stand still, and her attention was drawn to a leaf from the creeper that climbed up past the balcony. It moved gently, almost lasciviously, like a stroking finger.

She looked away and focused on his face, feeling shy. He drew her slowly to her feet. She could sense that he, too, was uncertain, his breath coming faster than normal.

His eyes, for once, were entirely free of teasing or distance. He lowered his head and they kissed, slowly and tentatively, and then more urgently. Some minutes later he led her through the French windows, across the sitting room and opened the door to his bedroom. The bed, like hers, had been turned down, and they sat on it together, kissing again. A bedside light threw a creamy pool of light on the cool thick sheets and plump pillows. They lay back, her head on his shoulder, his hand caressing her neck and hair. The room smelled lightly of jasmine flowers, and the air-conditioning had made it deliciously cool. Their shoes lay on the floor, kicked off.

Hari looked down.

"Do you think this is a good idea? I don't want you to feel awkward."

"Probably not," she said, swinging her feet to the ground. "But I don't much care. Let me go to the bathroom. I will be back in a moment. Do please bring in the wine from the balcony – I think I might need a drink."

He looked at the closing door of the bathroom.

No, he thought, probably not the best idea. But on the other hand, why not? It was what he wanted. And what Julia wanted, too. Tonight had begun well; there was no reason for it to end badly. He put the bottle and glasses on the bedside table, and lay back on the pillows until the bathroom door opened and Julia appeared in one of the towelling robes that hung on the back of the door.

"You look lovely," he said. "Come here. Here's a glass of wine, to pass the time till I get back."

Dropping the robe to the floor, she climbed in under the sheet, drawing it up to her chin. As she sat up to take a sip, she caught sight of her reflection, at an angle in the dressing table mirror. Was that a double chin? She raised her face as she put down the glass and the bathroom door opened.

"Hello," he said, untying the cord at the waist of his dressing gown and letting it fall. She inhaled to steady the beating of her heart.

Naked, he slipped in beside her, touching her shoulder

and drawing her towards him to kiss her, very gently. He smelt of shaving foam and toothpaste. This is it, she thought, closing her eyes and putting a hand up to his cheek. No going back now.

## Chapter Thirty

Early the next morning Julia opened her eyes and listened to the rhythm of someone else's breath beside her. She looked over to see a sleeping Hari, his hand under his cheek and his dark hair rumpled on the white cotton pillowcase. It was half past six.

He opened his eyes and smiled at her.

"I must go and get dressed," she whispered. "No, don't stop me, I've got to go back to my room. I'll take a peep out of the door and slip down the corridor."

"And you think the hotel staff won't spot you? In your dreams, my dear. Forget about them. Forget about what we have to do today. It can wait."

He pulled her down gently and brushed a curl of hair from her forehead.

"You look exactly as I had expected. Younger. Entirely sweet. Much less classy Miss Efficiency, much more approachable. And now my dear, I want to approach you some more."

After a very pleasant half an hour, she slipped quietly out of bed, and picked up the dressing gown she'd dropped on the floor, sliding her arms into the sleeves as she walked quietly to the bathroom to collect the clothes she'd left there the night before.

Hari rolled over to look at her and rested on his elbow.

"What a pity. Do you really have to go? We've got plenty of time..."

"Yes I do. It's nearly seven thirty. I *have* to have a shower and get dressed, and I want something to eat."

"You always want something to eat, I've noticed. Especially at important moments. Okay, okay, off you go. I'll see you downstairs when I've got myself together. Please order me a glass of orange and a strong coffee. I'm sure your stomach will encourage you to get there before me."

She let herself in to her room, barefoot, enjoying the feel of carpet between her toes, and the cool marble of the bathroom floor. The shower was hot and reviving. She dressed carefully for the festival, in a white linen dress with short sleeves and a softly flaring skirt that moved fluidly as she walked. She knew it suited her, and as she put on some make-up in the brightly-lit bathroom mirror, she felt good.

Her stomach rumbled gently as she brushed her damp hair. Hari was right. Breakfast would be welcome. She slipped on a pair of moonstone earrings and pushed her feet into her red Birkenstock sandals. Ready for anything, she thought, as she closed the door behind her on its oiled hinges and walked towards the staircase.

The dining room smelled of freshly-baked bread and bacon and eggs. She sat down at a small round table set for two and asked for coffee. At the buffet she helped herself to crispy bacon from chafing dishes and ordered two poached eggs on toast from the cook in an impressive chef's hat. They were delivered to the table with a cafetière just as Hari was pulling out a chair to join her.

"Good idea. I'll have the same," he said as he sat down. "Do I have to get it myself?"

"That's the general idea of a buffet," Julia said, with her mouth full. "I'd avoid the toast though – it's the usual flobby synthetic variety. A *chapatti* would be nicer."

"Hmmm. We've never got bread right in this country – at least not the kind you lot like. Hang on a moment. I'll be back." He was, five minutes later, with a full plate.

They concentrated on their breakfasts, saying little; the

clinking of plates in the background merged with the murmur of morning conversation in the big room.

She leaned over to pick up the handbag at her feet when she finished. Hari drank his cup of black coffee and replaced it on its saucer with a clink before standing up beside her. It all felt completely normal, and she returned his smile.

"Come on. Taxi's waiting. Let's get going. My public awaits," he said. "And then we can get down to the real business of why we are here. First, us, and then your aunt. It's exciting!"

## Chapter Thirty-one

Hari was very much a main attraction at the Festival, and as always he handled the attention with an air of gracious entitlement which pleased everyone. He gave his talk, invited questions, then answered them politely and comprehensively.

His book, *Heroes*, was welcomed, discussed, bought and reviewed in the local papers, and by the BBC and other foreign media. The Amjan Palace buzzed. There was some controversy, a lot of gossip, and plenty of food and drink.

The organiser, Shireen Majid, was effusive, delighted by one of her star guests. "You must please return next year, Mr Dhawan. I'm sure *Heroes* will soon be out in paperback, and you will be working on another...? Come and tell us all about it. Everyone would be so pleased to see you. It's been a privilege to have you."

"A privilege to have you," Julia said, under her breath, as they walked out to Mohan's car.

"No," Hari said, grinning. "I think that is what I should say to you, don't you think?"

She had not expected it, and her face flamed. He grinned some more, and then turned to wave goodbye through the back windscreen of the Ambassador.

"Phew. That was fun, but the kind of fun I can only cope with in small doses," he said, closing his eyes and resting his head on the back of the seat.

By now Julia had recovered her composure.

"You loved it, you peacock!" she teased, and then, quickly, said: "You were terrific. Your book is great and it really was a thrill for me to see how well it was received. Well done! Although I suppose you must be used to this sort of thing."

"Not really. Last time I hadn't finished a new book, and my old one was yesterday's news. I had a little celebrity, a hangover from the success of *Consider the Lilies*, but I was much further to the back of the schedule. This time was much more of a celebration." He sighed. "Now, of course, it's back to the grindstone. The publisher will put me to work, on the promotion trail, so I'm going to need a few days in Ranpur to prepare. Because after that, my dear, we aren't going to have any time off for a good few months. That is, if you'll carry on working for me. Especially after..."

"It's fine. Of course I will, for now." She spoke quickly. "Last night was great but..."

"Mmmm." He touched her hair, and slipped a strand behind her ear.

"It *was* great," she said, "but we have lots to do, and lots to think about. And I want to concentrate on Helen and Ranpur and what we're going to find out." She realised she was nervous and happy – she enjoyed being with Hari, alone and with his adoring public. The excitement of the night before was still there between them; when he touched her arm, her heart jumped, and she felt her cheeks redden when he looked at her.

"All this celebrity! It is exciting, but I am sure it eats at one's principles," she said, trying to make her voice matter of fact.

He laughed.

"Yes, I can hear it nibbling away. But I love the fuss. You know that!"

"I do. And you deserve it, but don't start throwing your weight about with me in Ranpur, or I'll put you on the first plane out. I don't mind being the respectful assistant in Ajmer but when it's just us, I am not going to bow and scrape. Don't get too used to it!"

"Please do try to be a bit nicer to me, Julia. It's not all that difficult – you didn't have much trouble last night, did you?"

She made a face at him. He grinned.

"You're so easy to tease. Come on, let's get to the airport, and have a jolly good lunch before we get on the plane."

They flew down to Delhi, and then caught the express train to Ranpur, while Mohan went on ahead to meet them at the other end.

"You see," she explained to Hari, "I want to put myself in Helen's shoes. She wouldn't have had a car, or taken a plane very often, if ever, and I want to arrive in Ranpur by train like her. I've seen photographs of it – it is a wonderful colonial palace, and it will feel great. Believe me, it will. So for now, please let's mix our experiences. This is my bit of the trip, and you're here because you asked. If you don't like it..."

He raised a hand. "Okay okay, I promise, Miss. Stop lecturing me. I'll behave. So long as I can sink into a comfy chair in an air-conditioned bar at the end of a gruelling day, I'll take everything else on the chin. I don't do that for anyone, as my mother will tell you. But anything for a quiet life..."

# Chapter Thirty-two

Julia awoke in her own room the day after their arrival in Ranpur, feeling as if she'd eaten a coconut husk. Her mouth was dry, scratchy and stale, and her head was heavy.

She'd been expecting a stomach upset at some point, but not so quickly. What had she eaten or drunk the night before? *Nimbu panis* and a cold beer, with a curry, overlooking the river. Something had attacked her digestion very quickly. She struggled down to breakfast, but the smell of cooking made her want to be sick. Concerned at the sheen of sweat on her top lip, Hari stood up.

"You look terrible. Come, let me get you back to bed."

He led her upstairs, and opened the door of his room.

"Stay here for a moment in the cool while I speak to the chambermaid to get your room done. Kick off your shoes and lie down – here, on my bed. I'll be back in a moment."

She nodded weakly, and darted to the bathroom before he'd even left the room. After an unpleasant interlude, she lay back on the bed and closed her eyes, sweating, grateful for the cool air on her body. In what seemed a minute or two Hari was back.

"It's ready. Come on. Can you walk?"

She sat up and started to shiver.

"No, you're very wobbly. Here, put your arm round my shoulder. I'll carry you."

She tried to tell him she was fine, but it took all her concentration not to be sick. He laid her carefully on her bed, covering her with her duvet.

"No, don't fuss. You can take your dress off later. Just rest. These things are appalling but usually they don't last very..."

But she wasn't listening. She flung back the duvet, and stumbled shakily to the bathroom, slamming the door behind her. When she emerged he had gone, and she got thankfully back into bed. This was the pattern of the night: waves of sweaty heat followed by shivering, punctuated with dashes to the bathroom. She could do little else but lie with her eyes closed, waiting for the next onslaught. Eventually, she slipped into fitful sleep.

When she awoke, the room was shadowy, the curtains drawn. She felt weak, but no longer feverish or desperate for the bathroom. She swung her feet on to the floor and sat up gingerly. So far so good.

There was a gentle knock at the door.

"Come in."

"Oh good. You're up. I've been in a couple of times to check on you – dead to the world. And snoring! Oh my goodness. Still, forewarned is forearmed."

She gave him a weak smile and accepted a glass of water. She took a small sip.

"That's better. You're probably pretty dehydrated," he said. "There's no urgent need for you to get up. It's three o'clock in the afternoon. Stay in bed until you feel better. I'll be up to see you in a few hours and if you're feeling like it, you can have something to eat. Don't get too excited – nothing but white rice and if you're very good, I might let you have a banana."

She sighed, and lay back. Yesterday she'd been itching to get going, but this afternoon the prospect of bouncing around in the back seat of Mohan's Ambassador made her feel queasy. She closed her eyes.

When she opened them, the sound of the day had changed. She sat up, and realised that she felt much better. After a shower, she dressed, splashed her face with cold water and applied some make-up. She went downstairs and walked through the bar to the verandah.

Hari was reading *The Times of India*, and drinking a

glass of something cold, with ice and lemon. She sank into a chair opposite him, and he looked up with a slight frown.

"Hello. Poor you. Are you feeling stronger? You need to be careful now – no risks."

Julia looked at his drink yearningly, but thought better of it.

"I know you're right," she said. "A cup of weak tea, please."

"That should be fine. Don't be too enthusiastic. A bowl of white rice will work wonders if you are very hungry. Shall I get you a banana?"

She pulled a face, and took the newspaper he offered her. It was full of all the articles that would appear in any Sunday paper, but with an Indian slant – the recipes were curries full of spicy ideas, young women had written to Mama Begum on the problem pages about their arranged marriages, and there was a profile of a fabric designer called Ananda Singh. Fashion pages were bright with colour, and the clothes in the photographs were both Western and Indian, with accompanying lists of where to buy them. She felt tired just looking. Later, she would take a trip to FabIndia, the store selling clothes and household fabrics that was found in many Indian towns. In the heat, nothing was more comfortable than loose cotton drawstring trousers under a tunic – a *shalwar kameez*, in a bright colour that would look gaudy in the cold grey light of Russell Square in October, but absolutely appropriate in the sharp sunlight here. That was for another day. At the moment, she was going nowhere.

Julia folded the paper as a banana was placed in front of her, and she peeled it slowly.

"Well?" asked Hari, putting down his paper. "Tomorrow? Are you up to anything in particular?"

"I thought we could ask Mohan to take us around. Sitting in the back seat won't harm. I need air-con, that's all. And lots of water," she added, asking the waiter to bring her another bottle.

A guide book lay on the table, and Hari opened it at a map of the city.

"Here's Cantonments. What number did you say?"

"85A. Jacaranda Lodge."

Julia was quiet, looking at the plan in front of her. She'd thought, initially, that her first visit to her great-aunt's house should be on her own, but now, suddenly, she felt nervous.

"I think I'd like you to come with me. Would you mind? Once I've found Jacaranda Lodge, I need to lift up the stones and look underneath them. To see what's been hidden and if there's anything left. And to feel if I am a part of all this or not."

"Can't you tell that yet?"

"No, not really. I love being here, and it's all very familiar. But it's not the same as belonging. People can love places and visit them a lot, but they're always visitors. I'm not sure what I'm going to feel."

He was silent.

"That's it!" she said.

"What?" He looked at her, surprised.

"That's how I want you to be, when we get there. Nice and quiet. Now, can you manage that, or is it going to be too much for you?"

He grinned and flicked her with her napkin. "Forgive me. My mother would be horrified, but when you speak like that you remind me of her."

"Well, thank you very much. I'm not only your employee..."

"No, you're off duty now." He paused. "And your position has – shall we say – changed somewhat."

She smiled.

"Off duty here, an employee in London, a lover, and now I'm your mother, too. Oh God. I'll try not to mind that she's old enough to be mine."

They sat on the verandah, talking. About films and books and about family; Hari told her something about his childhood in India and England. She listened as he sat back in his chair, looking over the lawn, his words accompanied by the sound of hissing water from a staccato sprinkler, the barking of a distant dog, a crying baby, a coughing moped, a braying donkey. A wagtail hopped across the grass searching for insects.

A little later they were sitting in the back of the white Ambassador, an efficient air-con doing its job, and Mohan driving carefully, as requested, down the dusty tarmac towards Ranpur. He would have driven backwards had Hari requested it, and took great pains to follow his instructions to the letter.

Julia looked out of the window at the green paddy fields they drove past. The rice crop was knee high and everywhere small figures were tending it. Little breeze-block or wooden huts stood on the corners of the emerald rectangles, a woman crouched over a pot on a fire, curls of smoke rising into a sky that by now was a hard bright blue. Vans and pickups, painted in faded colours, carried too many passengers, clinging on tightly. Here a bright scarf fluttered in the breeze, over there a white *dhoti* stood out from brown and grey and dull pink, faded by washing and beatings on the rocks of a riverbank.

Julia suddenly had a memory of the *dhobi*, the wiry little man who came to her parents' bungalow with large wicker baskets slung across his donkey's back. It was his job to collect their dirty clothes and wash them at the river. His scrawny turkey legs poked out of his tucked-up *lunghi* as he perched on the bank, rhythmically beating the clothes on a smooth wet rock. She had felt like an intruder as he slapped the sudsy fabric down again and again, his wrinkled face matching his prune-shrivelled hands. Suddenly he had looked over his shoulder at her and smiled. Embarrassed, she'd skipped away. When she looked back, he had turned back to his work, and carried on as if she had never been there.

"Are you still with us?" asked Hari. "You seem a million miles away."

Julia turned her head, blinked.

"I'm sorry. Yes, I was... I was dreaming... remembering something."

Hari frowned at her.

"I was just asking what you want to do when we get there? To your great-aunt's house?"

For some reason her eyes filled with tears.

"I'm not sure. I want to see it, I want to be there, but I have... well, no idea at all what to expect."

Suddenly unexpected tears blurred everything and slid down her cheek.

"Sorry," she said, looking away out of the window. Mohan's horn blared as he swung the car round a stationary bullock cart.

The noise made Julia jump, and even Hari looked up sharply. The moped family didn't turn a hair, and Mohan grinned at Julia in his mirror.

"Stupid people, *Memsa'ab*. No idea of Highway Code," he said, jamming his hand on the horn again as he looped past a speeding lorry painted green and red and yellow, its flatbed load of stone and marble slabs swaying dangerously.

She nodded weakly.

"Look, Julia, let's just play it by ear," Hari was saying. "I'll come with you, we'll introduce ourselves, and then let's see. I can hang back. I can be there for moral support."

She nodded.

"But I can also make myself scarce," he added.

She nodded again, and looked at her watch.

"How much longer, Mohan?"

"Nearly there, *Memsa'ab*. Don't worry. We will be arriving soon and in one piece. Five minutes. Maybe less."

And five minutes later they passed a faded wooden sign, painted white with chipped black lettering, declaring "Welcome to Cantonments." Then another – painted red this time, dusty but more recently erected – with an arrow pointing to the right.

The houses on both sides of the street they turned into were large, set behind high walls with broken glass pressed into cement to deter intruders. Uniformed men in khaki uniforms were sitting inside small sentry boxes at some of the gates. One or two were chatting to each other, or walking up and down.

"Not the most interesting work," Julia remarked.

"No, but necessary. Sometimes people get hungry, and jealous."

Julia sat silently, her head full of questions, memories, half-remembered snippets of her parents' conversations.

This was the country she came from. Or was it? What connection did she have with this place? Just a romantic one, from the blue remembered hills of her childhood, when everything was gentle and possible and taken care of? Or was India deeper in her soul? She'd the oddest feeling that she was home, but again, did she know why? The smells, of course. And the language, the faces, the rattle of lorries and the crowing of cocks were all familiar, but there was something else. She felt she understood Helen, understood how closely connected she was to Ranpore. She'd decided to stay, to look after her mother, to do what she saw as her duty. That was the bit Julia found hardest to come to terms with. Her father had described Evangeline as demanding and difficult, yet Helen had chosen to stay with her until she died. From what Julia could work out from the letters she had read, there had been something between Arthur and Helen. So why had he married Kate? There was a great deal to find out, she thought, and now she was here, she was going to do her best to get to the truth.

Hari slipped his arm around her shoulders. He dropped a kiss on her head, catching Mohan's eyes in the driver's mirror. Mohan looked away, the back of his neck rigid with discretion.

"Don't look so worried. This is exciting," Hari said.

Julia nodded slowly.

"Yes it is. But I feel nervous too. I've so many questions and actually very little to go on. Nothing specific, anyhow. Maybe Helen stayed because she decided that Arthur wasn't her cup of tea? Maybe she wanted the comforts of home rather than leaving to start again somewhere else. But that doesn't feel right. Not from the little I've heard about her, and not from the tone of the letters..."

They said nothing as they drove past the large houses hidden behind their gates and walls. Some had been modernised, others were shabby and crumbling, and a few were as neat and well kept as they must have been eighty years ago. Gardens were bright with lantana, yellow mimosa, and hibiscus, shaded by the branches of old mango and lychee trees.

"Stop here a moment, Mohan, please," Julia said suddenly, winding down her window and pushing back the nylon curtain.

The *maidan* stretched out before them, and the car came to a standstill at its edge. A cow wandered past with arrogant aimlessness, the grass stretching away from them scorched and browned by the sun, the dusty air reeking of burnt charcoal, cow dung and cooking.

Hari looked at the view distastefully.

"Let's walk a bit," said Julia.

"What? Now? Here?" he asked.

"This is Massacreghat, isn't it, Mohan?"

"Yes Memsa'ab. Massacreghat. The massacre – during the Rebellion. The British call it Mutiny. Many people die here."

"Come on then, Hari."

171

Hari gave her a chilly look, and opened the car door. They walked into the middle of what was little more than a singed field dotted with palm trees sloping down to a stretch of muddy brown river. Scavenging pie dogs looked for scraps, and women in cheap coarse saris walked with their children. One little boy sat down in the earth, screwed up his small face and began to scream, more for something to do than because anything was wrong. His mother pulled him up by one arm, and he hung lopsided beside her, still screaming.

"I have to say, Hari," Julia spoke at last. "Indian children can be absolute little horrors. They're so indulged."

"Hmmm. I liked it," he answered, with a grin. "I was a boy, you see, and my *ayah* and my mother took great care not to upset me."

"Surely they didn't allow you such silly tantrums?"

"They did a bit. But then, you'll be happy to know, I was packed off to school in England, where I soon realised that tantrums didn't cut the mustard so I -"

Julia wasn't listening. She interrupted him, her eyes on the parkland before her. "This is where Helen and Kate would have come for picnics, on their bicycles. Perhaps with Arthur, too. Oh, I wish I knew more about their lives. "

"Well, you're going to their house tomorrow, are you not?" asked Hari. He frowned. "So let's go and have a *drink*. I'm boiling. This is neither useful nor ornamental, as my mother would say."

Mohan was listening to the radio with the sound up high when they got back to the car. An Indian pop song playing at full volume.

"Oh God, this is *Teri Umar*. It's from a Bollywood film. *Awara Baap*. My sister loves it," grumbled Hari. "She plays it all the bloody time. Even after my mother told her Kishore Kumar was her pin-up, too!"

"Kishore Kumar. *Atch'a Sa'ab*, Kishore Kumar," grinned Mohan. "Very good. You like this, *Memsa'ab*?"

"Mmm. Yes, thank you, Mohan. It's a bit different from the songs I listen to, though."

After she and Hari had slid into the back seat, Mohan rolled up the windows, turned the music down, and waited to be told where to go.

Hari spoke to him in Hindi, and a short while later they were sitting by the river on the terrace of the Mandragora, a very westernised hotel.

"This is your true habitat, isn't it?" teased Julia.

"And why ever not? Any fool can be uncomfortable. I get hot just like anyone else. I live in England, remember."

She sipped a cold Coke, with a slice of lemon, but no ice. Hari had been firm. "I'm not allowing you to be reckless again, posh hotel or not."

He had ordered a black coffee, firmly specifying NOT Nescafe, and a cafetière had been placed in front on him.

"Right," he said, sitting back in his chair and looking at her.

"Right what?"

"Right – what are your plans now? We've trailed about dull expanses of *maidan*, you've had time to examine the lavatories of our hotel in some detail, we've located Cantonments. All well and good. So when are you going to take the bull – sacred cow – by the horns?"

Julia looked at him, and her eyes, to her embarrassment, again filled with tears. She dashed them away, blinking hard.

"Here," he said.

She took the white handkerchief he was offering.

"Thank you." She paused. "It's just... I don't really know how to describe it... It's just... I feel extraordinary. Really odd. All I wanted was a quick look. But I feel the echoes of everything ringing away inside me. The roads, the noise, the smells, the food, the way people walk, what they say, how they say it... It's almost as though I've only been away for a couple of years."

"But you've visited since your childhood?"

"Of course. But I never felt like this, all nerve-ends twitching, antenna on receive... I almost feel I belong. That England was the break, and now I'm back. As if Helen is welcoming me home. Is that stupid?"

She swallowed, and her bottom lip quivered.

"Depends where you're coming from. I think, perhaps, you should go for a little walk on your own. Take your time. I'll wait here."

He said it firmly, almost an order, meeting her eyes. "Off you go. Enjoy yourself. There's only one first time."

## Chapter Thirty-three

After a tiny hovering hesitation Julia got to her feet and left the terrace. The sun was climbing in the brownish sky, and the traffic rumbled loudly. She almost wished herself back in the car.

Straightening her shoulders, she walked along the pitted road around the *maidan,* stepping around potholes and avoiding piles of rubbish. The sun was heavy on her shoulders, somehow comforting, wrapping around her. She reached a crossroads; the *maidan* was on her right, and straight ahead were the shops and market. An occasional *tuk-tuk* went past as she stood for a minute or two, looking around. One of them slowed down past her, its driver gesturing to the back seat. She shook her head, and he accelerated away.

This was the market where Helen would have shopped. Julia tried to remember if there were any photographs of her in the albums her mother had shown her as a child. She thought of the few words her father had used to describe Helen – elegant, understated, much-liked.

And he had said that Arthur's voice had changed when he spoke of her.

Was this just a simple little story of self sacrifice? Of duty? Not completely, she decided – she knew there was something else. Why did Arthur accept Kate as a substitute? Susannah had arrived very quickly, but that was normal then; babies were what marriage was for. Had he married Kate because he really preferred her to her sister? Or because her mother had told him to? Or was there another reason? Whatever, once the decision had been made, it would have been very difficult to go back on his word, or hers. It would have shocked everyone, and Evangeline would not have tolerated the disgrace.

Julia's family was not given to extravagant gestures. She couldn't remember a single instance of excessive demonstration, from her parents or her grandparents. They assumed that their pride in her achievements, or their appreciation of a piece of music or a beautiful view, was taken as read – "mmmmh" was high praise, or "that's it!" Showing off was not encouraged: the gruff phrase "Steady the Buffs" was very familiar to her. Arthur her grandfather and her father Sandy had both used it to quell any unnecessary enthusiasm or attention seeking.

Julia felt desperate to know more about Helen. Hints, vague memories, perhaps an old photograph – that was all she had to go on. She needed to find someone who might be able to help her pull back the curtain that hid – what? The reason why Helen, popular, attractive Helen, had ended her days alone in Ranpore. Who would remember?

Julia's light cotton dress was sticking to her back as she walked, past the shadowy interiors of shops, and the brightly-coloured spices or gilt and plastic jewellery spread out on pavement stalls. Saris in soft slippery silk brightened windows, and mannequins wore filigree-embroidered *shalwar khameez*.

It was organised commerce, amidst organised hubbub:

beggars, taxi drivers, mopeds bouncing over uneven roads, ramshackle vehicles clattering past. A little further along the road there was a turning to the right; it led to peeling green gates that opened on to a small park. Julia followed a chattering group of school girls, trying to imagine being a little girl again, walking with her mother past tidy flower beds waving the dusty orange flags of canna lilies.

She crossed the lawn, passing a lake with painted rowing boats bobbing on it, waiting to be hired. At weekends fathers probably rowed their families out on the water but today the boats were empty, moored next to each other, rocking a little. Julia could hear echoes from her past: the distant clink of teacups, a clunk of a croquet ball, the deep twang of a ball spinning off a wooden racquet. Everyone she encountered, mostly women, smiled as they passed. Everything was friendly, low key, and she drank it all in.

As she let herself out of the gate on the other side of the park, the noise began again. She walked slowly, looking around her, enjoying the energy, the colour, the sharp smells. She avoided a car on one side, sidestepped a dog turd, almost bumped into a bicycle. She felt completely at home. The noise, the music, the driving – it was all normal. The ghost of Helen seemed to take her elbow, guiding her around a hole in the pavement, warding off collisions, happy she was here.

At home. She stood still. At home. Was that it? Was it just a romantic fantasy or was it really something to consider? Why did Helen not come to grow old in the comfort of England? She'd had the chance, Julia knew. Her mother had asked her to come and live at Linton with them, but she'd kindly and gently refused. She gave the weather as an excuse, but it was unconvincing. She'd died quietly in Ranpore, leaving only a bequest to the Evadne Littlewood Home for Anglo-Indian Gentlewomen and a stack of old letters that needed reading between the lines.

After about an hour Julia realised she had no idea where she was. She sat down on a dusty bench, with a rusty iron frame marked with a heavy VR, a legacy of *Victoria Regina*, Empress of India. A dog immediately came and sniffed around her, hoping for some food.

"Sorry, mate," she said softly. "Nothing for you. No treats."

"If you feed him, he'll only hang around. Like beggars," said a man who had been dusting down the seat beside her so he could sit down.

Julia nodded, and kept her bag on her lap.

"Are you just visiting?" he asked her.

"Sort of. Looking around. My family came from here a long time ago, before Independence."

"And you wanted to see it for yourself. Well, that's more than most people do. They stick to the palaces and temples." He paused, seemed to take her measure, and then held out a hand.

"Ajitabh Dalal," he said, "originally from Bombay. People call me Ajit. I work at the university here."

They shook hands and Julia smiled. She suddenly realised that this was what she wanted. To meet people randomly, outside the kind of sanitised environments that Hari preferred.

"I came to see for myself, as you say. I'm hardly slumming it, but I wanted to walk about a bit, on my own."

"Grubby. Can be dangerous, too, for tourists, although I see that, sensibly, you have nothing on show to tempt a passing thief. So what do you think of Ranpur? Is it what you expected?"

Julia thought for a moment or two. Was it?

"It is, I think. I'm trying to decide whether to stay a little longer. I'm not sure."

She turned to look at him, and saw that his eyes had settled on a small family group on the other side of the road. Two little boys were running around their parents' legs and everybody was laughing. For some reason Julia felt sad for a moment, and sighed.

"That's a big sigh," he said, watching the family. "Is the decision so very difficult? Can you not stay? Is there a complication? Sorry – do you mind these questions?"

She realised she didn't at all, and looked down, gathering her thoughts.

"There are complications, I suppose. There always are, aren't there? But not insuperable, if I..."

She hesitated.

"If you really want to. Is that it? Well, why not just leave it for a day or so. Things work out best when they're left alone, I find. Here, take my card," he said, holding out a small white rectangle. "If you do decide to stay, be in touch. I think we may enjoy a coffee together one of these days."

She took the small white rectangle, and looked into his almost black eyes.

"If you're not hurting anyone else, you must do whatever feels right to you," he continued. His expression was neutral, and his tone very mild. "Don't let anyone else confuse you – bamboozle, isn't that the word? Bamboozle. Just see how *you* feel, and then you will know."

She watched him as he stood up and extended his right hand. She shook it, and they smiled at each other.

"I must be off," he said, suddenly brisk. "Lots to do. I hope your decision – whatever it may be – makes you happy."

And he was gone. She sat for another five minutes, and everything seemed clear. She would stay, probably another week, and let Hari return home alone. He wouldn't like it, but that was his problem. And if he wanted to be difficult about it, she would have to call his bluff. She didn't want to lose him, but she had to start as she meant to go on. For once she would do what she wanted to do. That was why she'd left Freddie and she was never going back to being the tolerant little woman once again. If Hari minded she would deal with it; her ex-husband had taught her that it wouldn't be the end of the world.

Julia looked at her watch. She needed to get back. Her sense of direction told her that the Mandragora was not far away, but rather than risk getting lost, she hailed a *tuk-tuk*. She'd been right. A left turn, a right turn, a roundabout, and a straight stretch of road brought her back to the hotel in less than ten minutes. On the terrace she found Hari reading contentedly, drinking a glass of some cold clear liquid with lots of ice, his iPhone beside him,.

"That looks wonderful," she said, pulling up a chair and sitting back in thankfully. "My feet are tired, my head hurts, I'm hot and sweaty, and I could really do with a cold drink! I'll have a *nimbu pani*, with lots of ice. And a glass of cold water too."

Hari looked at the dust on Julia's hair and face, and smiled.

"Good walk? Your feet are filthy, your face is streaked with dust, but you look – refreshed. I hope you feel better."

She nodded.

"I'm glad," he said quietly, and returned to his book.

*Jacaranda Lodge.*
*25 August 1975*

*Dear Mr and Mrs MacCleod*
*I am writing to let you know that Helen Armstrong died last night, peacefully in her bed a little after midnight. She had not been well for about ten days.*
*My husband, Henry, and I, and our adopted son, J.J., were all by her bedside, and I can tell you that her end was untroubled. She said goodbye, and slipped away.*
*She asked me to send her love to you and to Julia and to pass on her regret that she had never met her great-niece, to whom she*

*has bequeathed the necklace enclosed with this letter. She also expressed a hope that Julia would be able, one day, to come to Ranpur and see where one side of her family had spent so many decades. I pass this on, in the spirit in which she meant it.*

*Helen will be much missed. She was discreet, understanding and had a warm and generous heart, and a bright and quick intelligence.*

*We laughed together, sometimes wept together, and I'm proud to have known her. She had some sadnesses in her life, and it is to her very great credit that she overcame them with grace; this enabled her to live calmly, at rest with her conscience. She ended her days among those who loved her very much.*

*She had looked after your grandmother sympathetically and with care, and showed very little resentment – something I would have found very difficult to do. Her life after Evangeline died turned out to be deservedly happy, and we will all remember her with love and great affection.*

*With best wishes and sympathy,*

*Doris Carter-White*

## Chapter Thirty-four

The peanut seller on the corner, sitting on his chipped wooden stool, smiled at Julia, showing red-stained teeth.

"Jacaranda Lodge?" she asked him.

He looked back at her without changing expression.

"The house. It was Mrs Armstrong's. Jacaranda Lodge. Jacaranda Lodge?" she repeated, without much expectation of a response.

He raised a hand, pointed to the right and nodded enthusiastically, pleased to be able to help.

"Armstrong, Armstrong. *Atcha*. Yes, yes. Armstrong. This way. *Atcha*. Not far."

She put a five rupee note into his cup, and took a folded newspaper cone of peanuts. He nodded again, delighted, as she turned to follow his directions.

The houses now were a little larger. Their garden walls were high and dusty branches hung motionless over them into the street, their leaves streaked brown and grey. Nothing moved. A pie dog came into view, hopping along on three legs. Shadows were lengthening in the afternoon sun. It was four o'clock. Tea time.

Some of the houses had numbers, some names, but in no real order. Baffled, Julia stood under a *neem* tree and felt the perspiration trickle off her forehead, beading at her temples and running down the middle of her back. After a few minutes, a gate opened. A small woman in a very white uniform, obviously a servant, closed it with a click and stepped out into the road.

"Excuse me," Julia called.

The woman stopped and looked at her calmly.

"Yes, *Memsa'ab*?"

"I'm looking for Jacaranda Lodge. It used to be Mrs Armstrong's house. Do you...?"

"This way. I'm going past it. Come with me."

They walked together in silence. There were butterflies in Julia's stomach again, although she steeled herself for disappointment. What more could she hope to find out about her great-aunt Helen, a colonial spinster who had lived with her dog and her mother in one of these large respectable houses?

"Here. Jacaranda Lodge. Armstrong."

The small woman gestured to a black gate between two white pillars.

"Thank you."

She hesitated outside the gate as the woman walked away. Straightening her shoulders, she pressed a round brass button and heard a bell ring inside. Some moments later, the gate was opened a little. A face looked through the gap.

"Hello," she said, smiling.

The face disappeared, although the gate remained ajar. She heard the whisper of bare feet going up stone steps, on to a verandah, she supposed. The creak of a mosquito screen, the sound of voices.

Julia pushed the gate open a little further and let herself in. She bent to go under a mass of salmon-coloured bougainvillaea, skirted a large hibiscus bush, and looked up in front of her. She'd been right – the steps led up to a wide verandah. The air was quiet, warm, punctuated with a bird's song. A *mali*, on his haunches, digging away with a rusty trowel at the roots of dark pink cosmos, sat back on his heels to look at her, then turned back to his work.

She heard the sound of leather slippers on the stone and a tall man wearing a *kurta* and loose trousers appeared He was about her age, she guessed, with a pale brown skin and delicate features. His eyes were dark and he had something of Hari's perfectly-turned-out imperturbability.

"Hello," she said again. "I'm Julia MacCleod. I... My great-aunt used to live here and I wondered..."

She smiled hopefully, feeling foolish.

"Helen Armstrong?" The man stood back, and made a gesture of welcome, palms spread. "Please, do come in." The voice was deep, with a slight Indian inflection.

Disconcerted, Julia walked past a small fountain that splashed gently into a circular pond, and came up the steps. Everything was neat, well-kept, freshly-painted and tidy. There was a timelessness about it, as though the plants were the ones her great-aunt had planted years ago, as if the same birds were singing, and as if this elegant man had always been in the house. And how did he know she was Helen's great-niece?

Her image of the house and its occupants had not included this. "That's very kind," she said. "I don't want to disturb you. I..."

"I always stop work at around this time. Come. Please sit down."

Julia lowered herself into a rattan armchair, painted white, and sank back into its bright red seat covers. She adjusted the white crocheted cushion at her back.

The man sat down, watching her, and smiled. As if he knew something she did not. She began to feel more uncomfortable.

"That cushion was made by Evangeline Armstrong," he said, and paused. "My grandmother. Your great-grandmother. I'm J.J. Carter-Wright. Christened Joy. Your great-aunt Helen's son."

He met her eyes with a flicker of – what? A smile? Embarrassment?

For a moment Julia's mind went blank. An empty blackness. His words meant nothing to her, as if he was speaking a language she had never heard before. She frowned, tried to say something, but nothing came. Then, hardly more than a whisper: "Your grandmother?"

He looked at her and nodded slowly.

"I knew you were in London, and I've always wanted to contact you but..." He shrugged. "I wasn't sure what to say. Or what you would feel about – all this..."

"All this." She frowned. "All this? This house, do you mean?"

"The crocheted cushion. The bougainvillea your great-aunt tended till she died. The gravestones at the bottom of the garden, all saying Deena. Different dates, different dogs. Deena..."

He snapped his fingers. A small black mongrel stood up, wagging its tail. Julia looked down, grateful for the distraction. Her thoughts were still tumbling over one another.

"My apologies," he said, watching her expression. "This must be quite a shock for you. At least *I* knew you existed. I'd always hoped we would meet, one day, but I wasn't sure how to go about it. Would you like something to drink? Tea? A coffee?"

"A coffee would be lovely," Julia said, and the bearer, who had come onto the verandah, bowed and walked away as slowly and silently as he had entered, his straight back speaking volumes. J.J. smiled at Julia.

"Shireet is bursting with curiosity. This will be all over the servants' quarters in ten minutes, and Cantonments will be humming with it in an hour."

Julia said nothing. Deena sniffed gently at her toes, then looked at her master. She stretched out at Julia's feet, offering up her stomach to be tickled. Julia obliged.

"She doesn't do that to everyone, believe me. I expect she recognises a family resemblance. You look a little like my mother, you know."

"Do I? I never met your mother," Julia told him. "I can see from the family photographs that she and my grandmother Kate sometimes had the same expression. But Helen was taller, with darker hair, wasn't she? More like me than her sister."

"I never met your grandmother. I doubt very much she knew of my existence."

Julia was silent for a moment, not sure what to say. It was true. Kate would never have been told about J.J. and nobody else in the family had known about him either.

"It's all right," he said. "Don't look so worried. It was never a problem. Not here. Helen was very happy, with me and with her friends, my adoptive parents, Doris and Henry Carter-Wright. We all lived here, together. I had a very happy childhood."

Julia frowned.

"But who *was* your father? After Arthur Kirkwood, my grandfather, left Ranpore with Helen's sister Kate, I thought she...that Helen...that she died alone here in this house."

"Ah. I wasn't thinking. I should explain. My father was Prakash Sultanpuri, an Indian poet, artist and musician. He met Helen here when he came to give a concert at the

Methodist School, invited by the Headmistress. They fell in love, and had a long relationship. Her friends among the Anglo-Indian community worked hard to keep it a secret from the British. It would have not gone down at all well!"

He gave a short laugh. Julia let his words sink in slowly. So this was Helen's secret. What had she said in her letter? *"Things happen when you least expect them to."* Everything was beginning to make sense. She would not have expected to fall in love with an Indian, and certainly not to have a child outside Ranpore's stifling British society. Jacaranda Lodge had kept her secret close, and so had her friends.

"It does seem so – unnecessary, doesn't it?" she said eventually. "That she had to say nothing about her life. It must have been very difficult to make sure nobody knew about it."

"It was, but it was unavoidable. Imagine the gossip, the disapproval! How my father would have been treated? An *Indian*. Unapologetically Indian, and unapologetically having an affair with Miss Helen Armstrong of Cantonments, Ranpore. "

She nodded.

"I know. Helen writes about the boredom of her life all the time, in her earlier letters. How nothing ever happened. But something changes a few years before Evangeline died. That was when you were born, wasn't it?"

"I was ten when she died. I think my mother was very sorry that she was never able to introduce me to her, but there was absolutely no question of that. We never mentioned it."

"Not until she asked if Helen was happy."

J.J. raised an eyebrow.

"In one of her letters, Helen says Evangeline asked her if she had been happy. That's when I think something snapped in Helen. Evangeline died knowing the truth, which must have been a great relief for her daughter, mustn't it? After all that bullying and hiding and heartbreak she was able to wipe the slate clean."

It was J.J.'s turn to consider new information. After she stopped speaking, he sat quietly for some moments, then stood up and went inside the house, returning with a leather-bound Bible.

"Here. I think she would have liked you to have this. She always said it was for the family. And you're the only family I've left. As far as I know."

"Your father?"

"He died some years ago. Before Helen did. I was glad I was able to be with her here, for the last years of her life."

A wave of regret washed over Julia.

"I'm glad she had you here. I've always felt she must have been lonely in Ranpur once her mother died and her sister – my grandmother Kate – went away. I'm happy to meet you. I mean it. Delighted. It makes things feel, somehow, balanced."

"Are you?" he asked. "Really? You must be the only Englishwoman in Ranpore who has ever responded in this way."

"I'm very surprised, of course, but happy that Helen didn't have a lonely life. I had imagined her looking after her tyrant of a mother and then being on her own, never having been loved, never having had a family. I'm delighted I'm wrong. And that this house has stayed in the family – our family.'

He inclined his head, still cautious.

"Yes, the house is mine. Helen and my father never married. That would have been a step too far, even for Helen, but she lived here, and he visited as the guest of the Carter-Wrights. He was well-known, particularly among the Indian intelligentsia. Dorothea Cartwright was very fond of Helen, and like many of Helen's friends, she felt very angry at her mother on her behalf."

"Was your father never accepted by the British?"

He smiled, and shook his head.

"I don't think you understand what life was like then. I'm not sure I do, either, but my father told me about it once, about a visit to the Club, as Dorothea's guest. He refused to go there again. An overreaction, of course, but very like him. I remember him getting very irritated at silly things that Helen let pass – comments, behaviour, what was called The Right Way. She just got on with it, rather enjoying her double life, I suspect!"

"Ah, I see. I think. I've her letters. Some of the things she writes – and doesn't write – have puzzled me. But now ...''

Julia picked up the small cup of dark coffee that had been placed beside her and took a sip.

J.J. looked at her seriously.

"When I heard you were in Ranpur, I was worried you might have come to claim an inheritance of some kind. That we would fall out before we had even met," he said.

"I never thought of owning this house. I wanted to see what had happened to it. I understand she sold it to Henry and Doris Carter-White so...?"

"They let her live here – did you know that?"

She nodded. "She'd her own rooms, didn't she? That was the deal?'

"Yes. My father visited, and as they were all friends it was not difficult."

"But I don't understand..."

"...why I inherited it? Well Doris and Henry couldn't have children, to their great sadness, and so they adopted me when I was born. Partly to stop tongues wagging and partly to make it easy to pass it to me. Henry was an excellent businessman, and resented paying any tax he didn't have to!"

"But your father must have minded? Did he not want to be involved in bringing you up?"

J.J. smiled.

"My father was the most charming man, and the most selfish. His work was more important than anything else. He was delighted to have a son, he loved Helen very much, but he never wanted to live with her, and he never wanted the duties of fatherhood."

They sat quietly together, drinking their coffee, getting used to each other's existence, both a little wary, but beginning to relax.

"This house is just as I imagined it," Julia told him, looking around her. "My parents didn't talk much about it, and I know everyone thought that Helen was pretty special, but nobody mentioned anything much about her private life, her relationships..."

"I'm quite sure your family knew nothing about me or my father and Helen. Helen's friends were very discreet."

"I'm sure you're right. But my grandmother, Helen's sister, surely knew – guessed – something?"

He shook his head slowly.

"Very unlikely. Kate and Helen didn't see each other very much after your mother was born. And you've found no letter telling Kate about my father, or me, have you?"

"No. There's nothing. What did your father's family think?"

He grinned. "My father was used to getting exactly what he wanted. His mother had indulged him from the moment he was born. Like a great many Indian boys – and men."

Julia laughed.

"I wonder how the relationship began," she said. "I suppose Helen felt since she'd lost Arthur, the man she loved, she'd little to lose."

"He was a handsome man, my father, and great fun when he wanted to be," J.J. explained. "Bit of an attention seeker. A talented artist and poet, no doubt about that, and he loved doing the unexpected. He'd have relished having Helen as his – what – girlfriend? Partner? Not sure what to call it. Lover?"

"Lover sounds about right. I doubt she'd have had a child with someone she didn't care for," Julia said. Her great-aunt was prepared to fly in the face of convention, but she must have loved Prakash very much to have the courage to do so. And she must have learnt a great deal since she had lost Arthur Kirkwood, not least to keep her own counsel.

"Are you here to do some detective work, then?" J.J. asked. "How can I help? I remember my mother well, of course, and I knew Doris and Henry. They supported her completely, and worked hard to keep wagging tongues still. Difficult in Ranpur – Ranpore back then."

"I just wanted to find out more about Helen, to meet people who knew her, to learn more about her life out here in India. There are some letters from Helen to Grandma Kate which intrigued me, and I decided to follow them up."

"Happy to help. How long are you here?"

"I think I'll go back to London in a few days," Julia told him. "But I haven't decided yet."

"I wouldn't have thought you'd find out anything very much in that time. Why not extend? Or come back? Either way, why not stay here? Helen's wing's empty."

Julia didn't answer. It was all moving very fast.

"Thank you," she said. "May I think about it? I'm here with a friend who needs to get back to England. I had planned to return with him, but I've yet to decide what is the best thing for me to do."

They sat together, not speaking. Julia listened to the distant sounds of the afternoon, and watched the *mali* digging. J.J. was restful company. Very different to Hari, she thought. She drained her coffee cup and set it down with a clink.

"I think I had better be off," she said at last. "I'd very much like to see you again, if only to let you know what

I've decided to do. I – er – I wonder if you would like to have dinner with us tomorrow. I'm here with my boss, in fact – Hari Dhawan, the writer?"

"I've read his books. And enjoyed them," J.J. said, smiling. "Yes, that would be lovely. But why not come here instead? I have a dinner planned. Guests are invited for eight, so if you came at seven o'clock I can show you some photographs, if you would like to see them."

"Of course. I'd love to. Thank you. I accept with pleasure. Tomorrow – about seven then?"

"Perfect. It's been a real pleasure to meet you. My driver is waiting to take you to your hotel now, if you wish."

She could hear the sound of an engine outside the gate.

"Thank you. That *is* kind. I'll see you later."

She walked down the polished red steps to the gate, which Sireet was holding open. A bird flew up out of a hibiscus bush as she passed, and a dragonfly settled on a water lily pad on the small pond.

## Chapter Thirty-five

Julia did not mention her meeting with J.J. to Hari immediately. It was too complicated, too much of a surprise, and she wanted to think about what had happened.

She checked Helen's letters when she returned to her room. There was one she had set aside to read again. Helen had not sent it, as if her courage had failed her.

*...Then I met someone. He was in the middle of a group of admirers, but I was introduced, we talked, we laughed and everything seemed a little brighter.*

*That was the first time: he was not often in Ranpore (who is, after all, if they've somewhere else to go?) but when he was, we met and had dinner together at the Carter-Whites. We grew closer. It has been important to keep it secret, and I'm grateful for the love and support of my friends who saw that I did not again become the subject of Club gossip and Cantonment pity.*

*I was unmarried, and I loved him, and he loved me, in his way. I had to accept what he offered and he always kept his word. He died six years ago, and I miss him every single day.*

*I know this will be unexpected news, and I hope it doesn't shock you. Mother was completely silent after I told her all this, poor old girl. It may, in fact, have hastened her to her grave, although I hope not. I don't imagine so – she was tougher than any of us gave her credit for! I gave her your love also and told her that everything had worked out well for all of us, in the end.*

*Since Mother's death I'm a woman of property but only briefly. I'm selling Jacaranda Lodge to the Carter-Whites, who have agreed to let me live in a wing of it for as long as I need to.*

*I have to prepare myself for a comfortable – but not moribund – retirement. I've spent too long behaving well. I'll become less careful as I get older! An eccentric English lady who does what she likes, at last!*

Well done, Helen, thought Julia. She'd done what she liked, at last. And had J.J. to show for it. She smiled, enjoying the thought of Evangeline's reaction to her secret. Helen would have needed all her Anglo-Indian friends to make sure Ranpore colonial society never found out about her scandalous relationship, leaving her in peace to enjoy herself.

That evening, she put it to the back of her mind, and concentrated on Hari. They enjoyed a lovely dinner together, and drank a little too much, followed by what Hari, his mouth full of toothbrush the next morning, called "a night of unbridled passion."

Julia pulled a face at him in the mirror.

"I suppose." She grinned. "Unbridled is a bit too *Fanny*

*Hill* for me. Anyway, I'm off. I want to have a shower and get ready. See you downstairs for breakfast in twenty?"

She kissed the back of his neck and avoided his arm as he tried to pull her towards him.

"Ugh. I don't want a toothpaste kiss. Order me coffee if you're there before me."

After another quiet breakfast together, Julia and Hari climbed into Mohan's Ambassador, waiting as always by the pillared entrance to the hotel. He was smoking a companionable *bidi* with a uniformed hotel porter; he quickly flicked it away before bounding over to open the car door.

"Right, Mohan," said Julia, firmly, taking charge. "Today we want to see Ranpore, I mean Ranpur. We want to visit the Methodist School, the club, the market. Can you take us around, and wait for us? And where is a good place to have lunch? I'd like a cool room which serves delicious *dosas* and cold coffee. Is that possible?"

He grinned. "Very possible, *Memsa'ab*. Very possible. My friend..."

"That would be fine, Mohan," interjected Hari crisply. "First, we'd like to see the school. Let's go! *Juldi*."

She couldn't help laughing. It was true. Mohan could never resist inviting his passengers to meet this uncle or that nephew, most of whom, of course entirely coincidentally, owned a restaurant or a shop selling decorated *papier maché* ornaments and boxes, jewellery, clothes, carpets – all designed to part foreigners from their cash.

Their trip began by visiting the places Helen would have been familiar with. First, the red-brick Methodist High School beside the Cathedral.

The school buildings were a slightly shabby Victorian Gothic, the windows curlicued and edged with white paint recently applied with a slapdash hand that left flecks on to the bricks around them.

They went to Reception, and introduced themselves to the lady behind the desk.

"Helen Armstrong?" she said, slightly puzzled. "I think she used to work for the Headmistress – Dorothea Cartwright. Mrs Cartwright has retired. She has a flat in the Evadne Littlewood Home. Do you know where that is?"

"No, but my driver will. May I take a look inside the Head's office? Is the Head's secretary in there?"

"Not at the moment. She's at lunch." A pause, a glance at Hari, then a decision. "But please, do go on in."

Julia opened the heavy wooden door with its carved sign: HEADMISTRESS. A large anteroom was lined with files and images of past Principals. Emmeline Hartfield glared down from one of the walls.

A vase of fresh red and white flowers stood in the centre of a low table on a breathtakingly ugly red carpet. Bookcases were full, filing cabinets had neat labels, and a desk was covered with paperwork, pens and a large blotter. The Headmistress used a fountain pen.

Julia worked hard to see the place through Helen's eyes, before leaving the Head's office and walking thoughtfully down the corridors, pressing herself back against the walls to let chattering children pass.

Next she asked Mohan to take them to the Club. This was white and imposing, its neatly clipped flowerbeds thick with canna lilies and cosmos, and humming with the buzz of bees.

There were only a few people there at this time of day. Some were reading newspapers, others coming out of the changing rooms, a couple were signing up for what looked like a Bridge tournament.

"It could be the 1930s," she whispered to Hari. A Club servant approached.

"Excuse me, *Sahib*," he said, softly. "Are you members?"

"No, I'm afraid we're not," he said, "but we wondered if

we could possibly have a look around. We won't stay long. We..."

Julia interrupted.

"I'm the great-niece of one of your late members. I'm here just to, well, to see where she lived. It would be really kind of you to allow us to have a look around and perhaps to have lunch here?"

It suddenly mattered a great deal to her to be allowed to spend a little time in the Club.

The man bowed.

"Please wait here, Memsa'ab, Sahib. I will ask."

Five minutes later, a man in a white jacket appeared.

"I understand you're the relative of one of our old members?"

Julia nodded. "Helen Armstrong. She lived at Jacaranda Lodge, Cantonments. All the Armstrong family were members. I think before your time?"

He smiled.

"Well, not quite. I've been working here since I was twenty – in 1972 – and my father was the Manager here before me. A family business, you might say," he said, all dignified politeness. "And I do remember Miss Helen Armstrong. She was a little elderly when I arrived, and she died a few years after I started. A kind, polite lady."

He paused.

"Why don't you have a drink at the bar, as our guests of course, and I'll see what I can dig up. Would that be helpful?"

They took him at his word, and ordered gin and tonics. Faded black and white photographs of men and women on horseback, in perfect riding clothes, looked down at them. A group of tennis players, Indian and white, smiled at the camera, racquets in hand, names on a brass plaque.

"Cheers," said Hari, clinking his glass on hers. "This is grander than grand, innit? But he'll find something, don't worry."

Eventually, the Manager reappeared, holding some photocopied pages.

"I've found these... Membership records – nothing exciting but they confirm Miss Armstrong was a member here until she died in – let me see...1975. And as the relative of one of our longest standing members, please allow me to invite you to lunch. It's a very traditional menu – curry, of course – but there is European food, too."

Hari made a face at Julia behind the manager's back as they followed him to a small table in the dining room. She frowned at him. The room was huge, and only two other tables were occupied. A water jug was placed carefully on the thick white damask by an ancient waiter in a white uniform with a club badge on his turban.

He brought their order – roast chicken, beans and roast potatoes – on plates decorated with a small gold crest.

"This is perfectly okay," said Hari, surprised.

"The roast potatoes are delicious," agreed Julia, with her mouth full. "After all the curry, it's a pleasant change. And rather better for my tummy."

Pudding was ice cream and fruit salad, again served with the ceremony of a state banquet, under the chilly gaze of long-dead members. On one wall was a tiger skin, and in the corner an elephant foot supported a table.

"Very un-PC," said Julia, quietly, "but isn't this extraordinary? So little must have changed."

It seemed right to speak softly in this large shadowy room. Silver cups and trophies were ranged in glass cabinets, and the names of past presidents were painted in gold on big wooden boards. The herringbone parquet floors were covered by Persian carpets and a ray of sunlight spotlit a tiger skin under a window. Helen would have felt completely at home.

After their lunch Julia decided to visit the Evadne Littlewood Home. This turned out to be another Victorian

Gothic mansion, with a thatched roof, leaded window panes and acres of shiny wooden floor. Were it not for the beating of ceiling fans, the exotic bird calls and luxuriant vegetation, it could easily have been Ivy Lodge in Richmond.

Like Julia's father, Dorothea Cartwright's room overlooked the gardens. She was a neat old lady, whose large brown eyes and high cheekbones still showed traces of beauty. Her back was straight, her movements precise, even though her hand shook slightly as she pushed her softly waving grey hair from her face. In a gently authoritative voice, clear and without any tremor, she asked a hovering servant for tea and biscuits. In a few minutes they were placed on a small table beside her.

"So, my dear," she said to Julia. "I understand you want to talk about Helen Armstrong. Your great-aunt, I believe. Well, you'll find that there are many people here who'll be only too happy to share their memories of her. She was greatly admired for her dignity and her kindness. I was happy to call her my friend."

Silence again.

"Mrs Cartwright..." Julia began.

"Do call me Dorothea," she said with a smile. Then, narrowing her eyes, she added "you know, you really do remind me of Helen. You have the same look behind your eyes. A potential for unhappiness."

She took a sip of her tea, saucer in one hand, cup in the other.

"You see, dear Helen always put her duty first. Laudable, of course, but a mistake. When it came to Arthur Kirkwood, she should have fought harder."

Dorothea put the teacup and saucer back on the table.

"It turned out all right in the end, of course. But...well, what happened afterwards was all rather...unconventional, shall we say?"

"What was Arthur Kirkwood like, Dorothea?"

"If you'll forgive my saying so, he was a very selfish man. Ambitious. Intelligent. And handsome. Handsome, intelligent, energetic young men did not often come to Ranpore in the 1930s. So of course he was a catch. Your aunt was an attractive young woman from a good family. Even if she hadn't been slim and pretty, Arthur Kirkwood would still have found her appealing. Although I believe he did fall in love with her. And she with him."

She took another sip from her cup and went on.

"He was used to getting what he wanted. When Evangeline put difficulties in their way, and Helen was out of the picture, he moved on to replace her with your grandmother very smoothly. Helen became past history very fast. I have to say I liked him before his marriage, and a lot less after it. Not that it mattered. He and Kate were soon off to another life entirely."

"Leaving Aunt Helen here."

"As you say, leaving Helen here, to look after her demanding and rather unpleasant mother. Forgive me, Julia. I can be more tactful if you prefer, but I think you're here because you want to know the truth."

Julia nodded firmly. "I found these letters, you see," she explained. "Letters from Helen to Kate – my grandmother. They're dignified, affectionate but they actually say very little. Dutiful, if you like. But with a vein of – resentment is too strong. Frustration, perhaps? And, I suspect, there's a great deal not mentioned."

"I wouldn't be at all surprised. Evangeline ordered Helen about like a servant. She demanded her presence until she died, and never admitted what she'd done. In effect, she ruined Helen's life. Although, I'm very glad to say, not completely."

Dorothea's eyes stayed on Julia's face. She waited.

"I went to Jacaranda Lodge yesterday," Julia told her.

"I see. That must have been - illuminating."

A raised eyebrow.

"It was. I don't think any of my family knew."

"And why should they?" Dorothea snapped. "Did they come and see her? No. The Carter-Whites supported her – she lived in her own wing, discreetly, comfortably. When she found love, they worked hard to keep her safe from the prying disapproval of her compatriots."

She paused, looking out over the lawn. Her eyes had the same lack of focus that Sandy MacCleod's had had in Ivy Lodge as he remembered the past.

"It was a dreary little society, you know, back then. Nothing ever happened. That's why Arthur was such a bright spark, and of course one of the reasons Kate wanted him."

"One of the reasons?"

Dorothea frowned.

"Kate was very like Arthur in some ways. She was used to being admired and allowed to do what she wanted. Always the centre of attention, especially with men. So when Arthur directed his interest to Helen instead of her, she couldn't bear it. She had to win. She did – aided by her mother – but I don't think their marriage was particularly happy. Helen expressed her concern to me a few times. To be honest, I found it hard to care."

Dorothea poured some more tea, and sat back wearily in her chair.

"As a matter of fact I introduced Prakash to your great-aunt. He was quite something, you know. Aristocratic, undisciplined, very handsome. A poet, a painter, a charmer. He was related to my mother – who was Indian, as I'm sure you guessed."

Julia nodded. Dorothea looked at her directly, and then gave a little squeeze of her lips.

"No, it doesn't matter to your generation, does it, but oh my, it certainly did to mine," she said, her voice studiedly neutral. "I was a good headmistress. I behaved well, and kept my place. No encroachment. My skin is not dark, my accent not *chi-chi*. I passed muster, but only up to a point. Evangeline never ever invited me to her more intimate dinners, for instance. Not that that was a great loss, but it shows how things were."

Julia nodded. "I knew – of course I knew from things my parents said, and my grandparents when I was small. A – well – a sort of amused disdain. "

"We don't eat children, you know," Dorothea said coolly. The heat was heavy in the little room. It slid between the china figurines on the mantel, settling around the inlaid teak side table, curling around its tooled legs. She waited.

Dorothea turned her slightly milky eyes back to Julia and spoke as if there had been no pause at all.

"Anyhow, Prakash Sultanpuri blew into Calcutta one day, when Helen was staying there with the Carter-Whites. She was interested in what he had to say, in his undoubted charm, in his energy. He came to Ranpore one day to see Doris and Henry. And Helen. And that was it. They fell in love.

"Of course Prakash was never going to settle down with anyone, and Helen accepted this. Arthur had gone a long time before remember, so she was used to being on her own. When Prakash was around it was a bonus; when they were together they crackled. Conversation, laughter, a love of good food, good books. They argued, discussed, played. They were truly happy. Helen had found a man to match her. And he had found a woman he found physically attractive (she was very elegant, your great-aunt, even in middle age. Not beautiful, but she had a lovely smile) and who wasn't intimidated by him."

Dorothea gave a dry little chuckle. "Prakash enjoyed life. He became a bit of a celebrity so he was away a good deal. There were concerts, exhibitions, books, invitations to Europe. He loved it all.

"And then J.J. arrived. Joy. Well-named. He made

Helen very very happy. Prakash was not interested in being a father. He was enchanted by his son, but had other fish to fry. For form's sake the Carter-Whites adopted him. He went to school in India, then university abroad (Prakash had plenty of money by then), and stayed with his mother in the holidays. It all worked very well, and I honestly think very few people knew the real state of affairs."

Julia sat still, pleased that Helen had not been so lonely after all. She'd had a more interesting, happier, more exciting life than anyone could have predicted, and J.J. was the result.

She felt a great relief.

Dorothea leaned forward.

"More tea, my dear?"

# Chapter Thirty-six

"I've something to tell you," Julia said to Hari across the table.

He lifted a glass of wine to his lips.

"Thank goodness," he said. "I've been biting my lip, bursting with curiosity."

She laughed. "Well done. And thank you. I hope you understand why I didn't talk about it. I wanted to get my head around it all first."

"It must be quite something if you were able to keep silent for – what – twenty-four hours! Go on then. Out with it! What did you find out?"

Julia told him.

"Jacaranda Lodge is a big old house. Built when there was no air-con, but it's cool. We talked on the verandah..."

"We?"

"Yes, that's what's so exciting. I met someone I never knew existed. Helen's son! My relative! He's called J.J. and guess what? His father was an Indian poet called Prakash Sultanpuri!"

"I think I've heard of him," Hari said. "He was well-known in the Forties and Fifties. Very popular in Indian high society. But I don't think he ever fraternised with the British, though. Odd that Helen and he even met."

"I know!" said Julia. "Dorothea Cartwright – you know, the headmistress Helen worked for – introduced them, and they fell in love. And all Helen's friends rallied around her to keep the relationship secret. Yah boo sucks to Evangeline."

She stopped talking for a moment.

"We've been invited to dinner tonight. J.J. said to come early – about seven – so we can have a look at some old photograph albums. I'd love to. You will come, won't you? You'll like him, I think."

Hari nodded, with an odd look on his face.

"Why are you looking like that?"

"Like what?"

"Half suspicious, half cross. I thought you'd be pleased. Dorothea said Prakash and Helen were perfect partners."

Hari shrugged.

"So there you are," he said. "Now you know. Do you need to do any more digging, do you think?"

The words were cold.

Julia frowned at him.

"Be happy for her. I am. We've spent all this time feeling sorry for poor Helen and she was actually having the time of her life. A lesson to us all. Oh, come on, what's the problem?"

"Nothing at all. I'm glad you're so relieved. The end of your quest. Time to decide..."

"Decide what?"

"What you're going to do now. Stay here? Forget about me, about your PhD?"

Hari's voice was clipped and cold.

"I thought you'd be as excited as I am," Julia said, flatly. "And as for all these decisions you're going on about, I haven't made up my mind about anything. There's a lot to think about. I need a little time."

Another shrug. He reached over, picked up his beer, and took a sip.

"Well, now you've met this bloke, you can use him to introduce you to people, so staying here might be a good idea. Which means of course that you won't want to stay working for me. I would be sorry about that. But I confess that I'd be sorry too if you decided that you've found out enough about your family, that this was an interesting little trip, and that India is now an irrelevance."

"I don't think India will ever be irrelevant to me," she said. "I feel more part of the country than I ever have. My great-aunt loved it; she was happy here. I think I could be, too."

"Here? You want to *stay* here then?"

Hari raised a cool eyebrow and she wanted to slap him.

"Hari, please stop being snooty. I don't care that you're His Excellency the very brilliant international writer whose very breath should be bottled and sold, whose every word... stop laughing."

She frowned at him.

"It's not fair. It's all happened so quickly I want to enjoy it for a little while. And I want you to enjoy it with me. Don't push me, not tonight anyway. I've found out more about Helen than I ever thought I would. I'd like to get to know her son. And I've learnt that someone in my family was brave enough to do what they wanted in the end, after putting up with all the duty crap that was forced on her. Of course I want to stay working with you. But I have something else to do now as well."

"You have a life in London, Julia. You have your PhD, and you also have a job. With me. I've come to rely on you. More than somewhat. In fact I'd – " He paused. "I would be very sorry to lose you. This trip has been a revelation. It has made me realise how lucky I was that you came to my office that day, and that we've come to India together. I don't want all this to end."

"All what?"

"All this, you obtuse idiot. Being together. Working together, of course, but – the rest too. I'd like to see if something can come out of this that makes us both happy. I'm not going to blather on about love and fidelity and foreverness. I've no idea about things like that. I just know what I want, and I want you to be with me."

She was surprised. This was not the Hari she knew. She spoke slowly, choosing her words.

"I've had a wonderful few days. I'm delighted you wanted to come to India with me to help me with the sleuthing, and believe me when I tell you that I was not expecting to end up in your bed."

"Nice though, wasn't it?" His eyes sparkled. "I'm told I'm a very good lover."

"Shhhh." She glanced round at the tables nearby but nobody seemed to have heard.

"Well, *you* didn't have any complaints. Seriously though, Julia, is there any reason why you should stay in India? Why don't you just visit every so often? Where would you live? Who do you know here? J.J. He said himself that he travels a lot. You'll be lonely. And so will I."

She didn't know what to say.

"Ah, go on Julia, make a nice young man very happy. Don't leave me in the lurch. I care about you, did I mention that?"

He leaned across and touched her hand, bringing it to his lips.

"Don't try that seduction stuff with me, Hari Dhawan." She tried to be firm. "I've seen you too often with women, and I'm not going to be one of them."

"Aha, I see. That's it. You think you're just another bit

of skirt... Honestly Julia, I've heard about women's intuition, but you're going a long way to prove to me that it isn't all it's cracked up to be. You *must* know I'm not treating you the same as I treat some fluffy little Kings Road girlie, with a flat in SW7..."

"Not any more!"

"– and a house in the country."

"Oh I've got one of those!"

"I give up. I need a drink. Waiter...Another beer please. Two – you want one? Good!"

It didn't take long. Things didn't when Hari wanted them.

Taking a sip, Julia broached a subject she'd been hesitating to mention.

"Hari, I wanted to ask you something. *If* I find out lots of interesting things about Helen, *if* I can string them into a coherent story, will you look at it? And if you like it, would you mind introducing me to your publisher, or another you think might be interested. Only if you think it any good. I don't want to compromise you, but a recommendation from you..."

She paused. His forehead was lightly wrinkled. He took a moment to answer.

"Of course I will. And if it's any good – and I shall tell you exactly what I think – I'll try to help, but I can't promise. You know how fickle the publishing world is, and that not every good writer gets a break."

"I know, but with your word behind me, it might be a little easier."

He nodded, and looked at the clock. Of course it would be easier; he would humour her, but he was sure it would all come to nothing. He changed the subject.

"We ought to think about getting ready. We're expected at seven so we only have a couple of hours – I need a shower. And so, with respect, do you! Shall we go upstairs?"

He put out a hand, and she took it, standing up. He bent his head and kissed her on the cheek, something very un-Indian, which made her heart patter. He squeezed her hand and they walked up the staircase together.

At five o'clock there was a knock at her door. She gave the mascara wand in her hand a last twirl on her eyelashes and snapped it back in its tube.

"Yes?"

The door opened, and Hari came in, bowing, with a white hibiscus flower in his hand, its petals beginning to streak with dark pink.

"Good evening, *Memsa'ab*. I'm here to abase myself. Forgive my curmudgeonly bad manners. Can we be friends again?"

She couldn't help laughing as he bent almost double.

"I was stupidly cross, and silly, and I'm sorry. Forgive me?" he asked.

He sank down on to her bed, pushing back a dark lock of hair that had fallen across his forehead. He smiled, showing even white teeth, and reached out to take her hand. Her face began to go pink, and she felt her heart beating a little faster.

"No – it's okay. Don't worry," he reassured her, squeezing her fingers. "I'm not going to bang on. I meant what I said, though. I want you to stay a part of India. And a part of my life too. I don't want you to shut all this away. Can we keep looking? Keep visiting? Together? I need someone to help me with my work, and, with respect, you'll need someone to help you with yours. And admit it, you wouldn't have enjoyed yourself half as much if I hadn't been here, would you?"

He paused and brought her hand up to his lips.

"I think I've behaved impeccably, up to now," he said, raising his head. His dark eyes met her blue ones. "Haven't I? Just a brief lapse, but I'll work on it!"

The room was still. A dog barked in the distance, a

branch tapped at the window in the slight breeze. Julia was very alert to his nearness, but she tried to keep her tone matter of fact.

"Do you mind if I don't say anything right now? Let's have a nice evening, and talk about later. You can tell me what you think about J.J. and the whole set up – there are other people coming for dinner. With luck he'll have invited some of Helen's friends."

"The ones who are still alive, at least," he said.

She giggled.

"Or perhaps we can have a séance. India's supposed to be a very spiritual place. I expect there are loads of them hanging about in the ether."

"You never know. Okay, Julia, let's try to enjoy ourselves this evening. I look forward to meeting your cousin or whatever he is, and I promise to behave impeccably. I shall be the gracious – what? Boss? Friend? Lover?"

"Can we stick with friend? With a bit of boss if people ask?" she said, with an embarrassed laugh.

"Of course," he said calmly. "Hey – it's all a bit..."

"What?" she asked, although she knew what he had been going to say.

"Well, a bit of a rerun, isn't it? Helen and Prakash. You and me. The past repeating itself."

She was silent. It had occurred to her too, and she had pushed the thought aside.

"Hmmm," she said, turning her head to look at him, her chin up.

"Hmmm indeed," he said, grinning. "Oh all right, I'll stop teasing you. But it's a bit of a coincidence, isn't it? Runs in the family, obviously. Now please come here. I want to kiss you."

He leaned very close to her now, and put his hand on her hair, looking down into her eyes. She raised her mouth to his.

Some minutes later, they moved apart, both a little breathless. Julia put up a hand to smooth her hair.

"We have some time before we need to get ready," Hari said, smiling. "And it doesn't take long to get there. Whatever shall we do now? Can you think of something really, really nice? I can."

## Chapter Thirty-seven

Peppery wood smoke mixed with warm diesel was the smell of India, Julia decided.

She'd insisted on giving Mohan an evening off, and to Hari's disdain, she'd asked the hotel receptionist to call a *tuk-tuk* to take them to Cantonments.

"Oh, stop being so stuffy. It's quick, it's cool, and I like the smells."

"Greasy curry, diesel, and dogshit. Very atmospheric."

"Indeed. You can put it in your next novel. The one about the nutty Englishwoman going back to an India she never knew. Actually, don't. That's *my* plot," she said as their *tuk-tuk* sped along through the traffic.

Hari looked out of the open side of the little yellow and black machine, buzzing along through the traffic in the dark, stabbed by the light of cars, windows, shop fronts, the kerosene lanterns illuminating stalls on the roadside.

"I won't use any of this without your permission," he told her coolly. "No, I'm being serious. I promised you I wouldn't."

She felt ashamed. "Sorry, that was unfair of me. It's a good subject, though, isn't it? Let's discuss when we get back to London."

"*If* we get back to London..."

A sharp blast on the *tuk-tuk*'s horn interrupted him, and they were thrown against each other as the driver swerved to avoid a cow standing arrogantly in the centre of the road. Julia put her hand up to Hari's shoulder and rested it there a moment. He looked down at her and smiled, without a trace of his usual irony.

"Let's enjoy this evening. I look forward to meeting your – what? Second cousin? With a removal or two?"

She nodded, slowly, and looked out across the shadowy *maidan*, trying to make out where the house was. Dark shapes were dotted with spots of yellowish light.

"It's that one there, I think."

The *tuk-tuk* slowed and the driver squinted into the darkness. After a few false turns they were by the dark iron gate, lit by the bulbs on the pillars on either side. Metal scrunched along the ground as the gate was opened by the *chowkidar*. There was a sweet scent of flowers as they walked up the path to the steps. Julia breathed it in.

"It's jasmine, night-scented jasmine. Isn't it lovely?"

The light on the verandah was bright, and through the doors they could see a dinner table beautifully laid for several guests.

J.J. appeared as they reached the top step, dressed as impeccably as before, in a red silk *kurta* and black trousers. Behind him was a handsome young man in his early twenties, with pale skin, and a sweet smile. He came forward diffidently.

"This is my – friend – Pierre. He lives in Paris, most of the time. That's where we met. We visit each other every year, here and there. Pierre, *voici* Julia, *et son copain* Hari. *Il est écrivain. Je crois que tu connais son oeuvre, non?*"

J.J. put his arm on Pierre's shoulder as he shook Julia's hand, and then Hari's.

"So you're Hari Dhawan. Welcome. It is a pleasure. I much enjoyed your last book and so did Pierre."

"It was translated very well, I thought," said Pierre, smiling charmingly, with a little bow.

"Pierre speaks very good English, as you see, but we

speak French to each other. Since I left France, I worry that I'll lose the language. Now please come and have a look at these..."

J.J. had placed four large leather-bound photo albums on a round table, and each of them drew up a chair.

"Helen was meticulous in keeping her photographs and drawings – there are both in here – very tidy. She said that it was important to keep the past in its place, and we have reason to be glad she did."

Julia opened an album, and saw, under rice paper, small square black and white photographs of little girls, with captions in Helen's handwriting beneath each one in white ink. They were held in place at two corners.

*Helen and Kate on the way to Sunday School*, said one; another had a very dark-skinned man standing beside a small carriage, a horse with a drooping head between its shafts. *Bodhi's tonga*. There were photographs of the garden, tidier than today, with strictly circular flowerbeds and neat paths. A *mali* in a dirty *lunghi* was squatting on his haunches in many of them.

"And here we have Sudham, the bearer," said J.J. "He died at a great age, having worked for the family for many years. He came with the house. And stayed with my mother. I knew him when I was tiny, and when I look at this picture I think I remember him. He was succeeded by Parag, which means pollen for some reason, who was often my partner in crime. He didn't actually encourage me when I was being naughty, but he didn't stop me either. He developed a real talent for looking the other way..."

They continued leafing through the albums. Parties, lunches, riding, school, Evangeline looking very serious, and sometimes almost smiling, but never relaxed. This was a woman who had a position to maintain.

A pretty necklace of moonstones set in gold was lying on the table.

"I wanted you to have this," J.J. said. "No, please take it.

I know my mother would have liked you to have it."

He looked at Pierre across the table, and they shared a smile.

"It was Helen's. Her father gave it to her, and she wore it often when she dressed up. Look, here, at the Monsoon Ball. I think she's with Arthur Kirkwood, your grandfather?"

Julia bent her head over the pages and saw a tall, confident man standing behind Helen and looking straight at the camera. They were both smiling, and he had his hand on her shoulder. They were in evening dress, and were clearly posing for a photographer. Another picture was of Kate. She was smaller than Helen and very pretty, with soft curly hair and large eyes; she looked at the camera, her chin raised proudly. Her left hand on Arthur's arm had a ring on the third finger. Suddenly there was a lump in Julia's throat, and her eyes filled with tears.

She felt a hand hold hers. Hari, sitting next to her, took her fingers and squeezed them lightly. He offered her his handkerchief. J.J., noticing, said nothing, and waited till she dried her eyes.

"I'm sorry," said Julia.

"Don't be," said J.J. "You've not seen any of this before. My mother could have been your grandmother, after all."

She smiled weakly. "Yes it could," she said, her voice cracking a little.

Hari gave Julia's hand another squeeze.

"Oh, for goodness sake," said Julia, with an uncertain chuckle. "I'm just a bit silly and wobbly I'll be fine in a minute. Just as your guests arrive!"

J.J. grinned.

"This is India. Some of them will, some won't. Their excuses will be imaginative and probably true, but you're right. We should be ready for them."

She passed the albums back to him, and smiled.

"Thank you. I'm so glad you have these. Perhaps I

could copy some of them before I leave?"

"Of course. Ah, here's our first guest."

## Chapter Thirty-eight

J.J.'s dinner was a great success. The Indian guests had heard that Julia was related to his mother and were curious to meet her, although their good manners kept them from being too inquisitive.

A beautiful woman in a turquoise sari arrived first, and walked gracefully up the steps, smiling broadly at her host, who introduced her to Julia and Hari.

She was soon followed by a plump gentleman in a smart dark suit and gold-rimmed glasses and an ascetic-looking man in a sleeveless woollen waistcoat who turned out to be the director of the Museum of Art. His wife Neelakshi's blue eyes matched the sparkling stones set in her dangling filigree gold earrings. A small woman with sharp features was introduced as Khalisa; she was wearing a suit that might have been Chanel.

A much older woman, in her late 70s, arrived last, and sat down in one of the large chairs, her back against the thick cushions. She had J.J.'s honey-coloured skin, and her bright eyes focused with interest on Julia, who leaned over to shake her hand.

"Auntie Joyce, this is Julia MacCleod," said J.J. "She's the grand-daughter of Kate Armstrong."

"And thus my friend Helen's great-niece. Did you know Helen?" she asked in a clear voice, with the unmistakeable intonation of the subcontinent. "No, I suppose not. That's a pity. She was my closest friend. While she was looking after that dragon of a mother, Evangeline – no you won't have known her, and for that thank your lucky stars – she was duty personified. But when Evangeline finally shuffled off this mortal coil... well, her friends could only breathe a collective sigh of relief! Come, sit here next to me. I expect you want to ask me a few questions!"

Julia obeyed.

"Please don't mince your words!" she said, smiling. "I would love to know as much as possible about my great-aunt."

"Do I look like a mincer?" asked Joyce. "I don't imagine you've come all this way to hear platitudes about your charming family. I bet you weren't expecting to meet J.J., were you? I doubt you even knew he existed! No, I thought not."

She looked sharply at Julia.

"Of course. My family, I'm sure, knew absolutely nothing about Helen's life since Arthur and Kate left Ranpore. My mother would have been happy. My father, too – he speaks highly of her, and less highly of her sister and mother."

Auntie Joyce gave something that might have been a snort.

Julia frowned slightly, and looked her full in the face.

"Auntie Joyce, I'm not like Evangeline. I really do want to know all about Helen, and I am so pleased that she met someone she loved, and had a child."

Joyce said nothing for a moment, weighing up the young woman in front of her. Then she nodded.

"Why are you so interested in Helen's life?" she asked, quietly. "How can I help?"

Julia spoke slowly, delighted that she'd found someone who might be able to explain the undercurrents in the letters she'd read.

"I'm Julia Salena Ramage MacCleod. Ramage was one of my great-aunt Helen's middle names and Salena means the moon, in Hindi, as you know. I found some letters among my mother's things when she died recently, and they made me want to know more about her life. I'm not just prying. They seemed – I'm not sure. Sad somehow. And also angry, in a very well-behaved way! Evangeline sounds – clearly was – a selfish snob."

"That, my dear, is putting it mildly," Joyce said. "She made Helen's life a misery. She stopped her marrying the man she loved, out of total self interest."

"Yes, I'm beginning to understand that. But – Helen seems to have gone along with her. Why? Why didn't she fight for Arthur – my grandfather. She comes out of it looking rather weak…"

"If you regard acceptance of duty as weakness."

"I don't, not entirely. I know that daughters did what they were told in 1930s India. And in England too, for that matter. But in the face of such wickedness, surely something could have been done? Some compromise?"

Auntie Joyce sighed. "As you say, it was a different time. You must understand that. And Kate made it her business, encouraged completely by her mother, to seduce Arthur Kirkwood. I think he comes out of it less well than anyone. Oh, he loved Helen all right, but had an eye to the main chance – his position and his career. He'd come to India to make money and have a good life, and he wasn't going to hang about once it was clear Helen wasn't going to fight her mother and sister."

"It would have been very hard for her to win, wouldn't it? From everything I learn about Evangeline, she would have fought pretty dirty," Julia said.

"Oh believe me, she did. She pushed Kate into Arthur's arms. Helen and he would have been happy together, I expect, but when it became obvious Helen didn't have the stomach for the fight, Kate fitted the bill almost as well. And when she became pregnant, the fight was well and truly over. Evangeline couldn't have been more delighted."

Julia imagined her great grandmother's satisfaction when she knew that she'd succeeded in keeping Helen with her for as long as she needed her. She could see the face in the photographs with its cold implacable smile.

"I was never invited to Jacaranda Lodge while Evangeline was living here, of course," continued Joyce. "Too Indian. Too outspoken. Didn't know my place. I worked hard to be suitable, appropriate, to behave, but I wasn't very good at it! But just because I wasn't invited to this house didn't mean I wasn't a close friend of Helen's. Once Kate was married and living far away Evangeline relaxed her iron grip on Helen. As long as she made her comfortable, nothing else mattered. We were all furious at the way she took advantage of her daughter, but anyhow, things worked out all right in the end."

"They certainly seem to have done," Julia said. She felt very happy, pleased that Helen had had good friends, and that Evangeline had not been able cause any more trouble for her.

"Just one more word from an old lady, while she has the chance," said Joyce firmly. "Helen was brave. And ultimately happy. She wasted a lot of time, though. Then Prakash appeared, and although it would have seemed impossible, it wasn't. I can't help wondering..."

She turned away to greet someone else, leaving Julia standing by herself.

I must learn from Helen's mistakes, thought Julia. What would she tell me to do, I wonder? Suddenly, the sense of her presence was very powerful. Knowing she wouldn't see anything, Julia looked round. It seemed as if the air had moved a little.

After dinner everyone went out on to the verandah again. Joyce and Julia sat down next to each other, ready to continue their conversation.

"Do you mind if I join you?" asked Hari, a cup of coffee in his hand. "May I bring you anything?"

"I'd like a glass of water please," Joyce told him. "But not before Julia has introduced us. I am an old friend of Helen's. I've very much enjoyed chewing the fat with Julia about her. I still miss her, even though she died a long time ago. People like her don't come along very often."

"Auntie Joyce, this is Hari Dhawan," Julia said swiftly. "I work for him in London, but at the moment I am off duty and he is helping me with my enquiries."

Joyce smiled and shook Hari's hand.

"Delighted," she said. "We don't often have handsome literary gentlemen visiting Ranpore. Not since Prakash Sultanpuri."

She let her words float between them. Julia filled the pause.

"I haven't had a chance to tell Hari very much about what I have learnt. But he knows that J.J. is Helen and Prakash's son. We've been visiting Ranpore together –the Club, and the school..."

"Once Julia gets a bee in her bonnet – and this is a fascinating bee, I grant you – she won't be deflected. She's very good at making me knuckle down, and I am usually very good at trying to avoid this!" Hari explained.

"It sounds as if you are made for each other then, doesn't it?" Joyce asked, without inflection. A tiny pause.

"As you say," Hari said. "We work together very well. I'm lucky to have found her – she's an admirable colleague."

Auntie Joyce smiled again, and sipped her water, putting the glass down on the table beside her. J.J. joined them a moment later.

"As I said earlier, it is a pleasure to welcome you here. Both of you." He paused. "I'm so glad you have had a chance to chat to Julia, Auntie Joyce. I've been trying to encourage her to stay here in Ranpur for a while to follow up everything she has been finding out."

Julia said nothing. She wasn't ready to make any decision yet.

"I meant what I said earlier," J.J. said firmly. "Helen's wing's empty. Pierre's only here a few months a year. I go to Paris at other times, and I've no need or desire to rent it to anyone. We like our privacy. You would have it to yourself. The old house needs someone to look after it when I'm away – the servants get lazy, for one thing!"

Joyce watched their faces. Hari's expressionless, although his lips tightened at the corners. Julia's wary, her eyes slipping sideways for a second to glance at Hari.

"I've had it painted," he went on. "There are no leaks or broken panes. The plumbing works, and I've installed air-conditioning – enough to allow sleep and reading without gasping. I've had no plans to do anything with it. Until now. Would you...?" He hesitated. "This seemed entirely sensible when I thought of it, but now I feel awkward.

Julia put out her hand and touched his forearm.

"Please, don't," she said. "It's so great to be here. To meet you. All the pieces are falling into place."

"Well, then. Please be my – our – guest. Come whenever you wish. It would be a good place to finish your paper, to do more work, or none at all. Ranpur is an interesting place, and Pierre and I'd be very happy to see you, if we are here, and to know you're using it when we are not. Think about it."

Julia, very aware of Hari, silent at her side, nodded slowly.

"I'd like to accept your offer, but I've commitments in London." She turned to look at Hari. "So I may not be able to come as often as I'd like... I can give you plenty of notice but..."

"No, no. I'll give you the keys and the telephone number, and all you'll need to do is call when you are buying your ticket so we or the servants are ready for you." J.J. looked relieved. "I'm so glad. I thought I might have offended you."

"Well that's settled then," Joyce said briskly. "It does seem a very good plan. And it means that we shall see you again, Julia. How splendid!" She clapped her hands lightly, with a broad smile.

"Yes, you certainly will. I'll come out as often as possible, finances and time permitting," said Julia.

Hari said nothing at all.

# Chapter Thirty-nine

The sky was a pale creamy gold. The sun was sneaking through the trellis of early cloud, and the air was only just beginning to pulse with warmth. This was India at its most beguiling. The dogs were still dozing in their corners, the car horns were not yet blaring.

Julia got up early and decided to go for a walk before the heat became impossible. After half an hour, she sat down on a patch of dry ground with her legs out in front of her and looked at the river, flowing thickly on its way. The water was a clayey grey, whitened occasionally with eddies of pale foam, as it made its way around a log, a branch, or something that didn't bear investigation...

Why on earth am I making such a meal of this, she asked herself? I can split my time between London and India. I can carry on helping Hari with his books and I can work on my PhD. So what's the big deal? Money isn't a problem. Or won't be after the divorce settlement comes through. What is the matter with me? Helen didn't fight for what she wanted. Surely I can learn something from her?

A voice in her head, familiar but challenging, whispered the big question. *And Hari?*

It felt as if someone beside her had spoken.

She didn't answer.

*What do you want to happen?*

Still silence.

*What's the problem?*

There was crunching on the stony ground beside her. Hari's voice broke into her thoughts.

"I've been looking for you. I went to have an early coffee and enjoy the birds, and felt like company. What's this all about?"

Hari was wearing white, and the ground was dirty. He looked at it fastidiously before sitting down beside her and dusting his cotton trousers with his long fingers.

She shrugged, sulkily.

"Okay, let's start again. Are you sitting here like a *saddhu* for the benefit of your spiritual health, or do you 'vont to be alone' to think frivolous thoughts? If you want to be Garbo, just say and I'll disappear."

She smiled, picking up a dried leaf and rubbing it with her thumb.

"I wouldn't do that. Some dog's probably peed on it. Or worse."

She dropped it with an involuntary grimace, and looked at him, a bit sheepishly. He grinned.

"Better. Stop frowning. It's such a beautiful morning. It's a shame to be gloomy."

"I'm not gloomy. There are just so many new things to take on board."

"I'd like to take a delicious fruit salad on board, with a cup of coffee, and even perhaps a pastry. Shall we?"

She ignored his offered hand.

"India is just so bloody big. Bloody everything really. Bloody unpredictable, bloody tricky, bloody happy-making."

He nodded, picking a few strands of dried grass from his spotless *kurta*, and met her eyes with a question in his own. He didn't voice it. Instead he said: "This is not something I'd do for anyone, you know. These started off white, and I want them to stay white. If you will sit on this dirty ground..."

"You didn't have to join me. I didn't ask you to."

"Well, that was a rattle that shot out of the pram, wasn't it? No, you weren't nice enough to ask me, but I was foolish enough to think you might welcome my company. I was obviously wrong. I shall try to get over it."

He stood up and looked down at her.

She bent her head, feeling clumsy, uncomfortable. Then, to her horror, she felt her eyes fill with tears. This was happening too often.

"Oh, no. Please don't cry, I was only teasing. I didn't mean to upset you. I shall leave you in peace if you would prefer it. I ..."

She put out her hand and took his, hauling herself to her feet. She held his arm, wiping away her tears with the back of her other hand. He stood beside her, teasing abandoned, waiting.

They stood together in silence, her hand on his arm.

"It's just... not what I expected," she said eventually. "I had all these ideas about my family, about what I'd find, how I'd do a bit of poking about and then life would go on as before. I didn't think about anything properly, not me, not you, not Helen. And now – blimey – I've got a relation, a house, and..."

She stopped.

"And what?" he asked her gently. "And me? And – dare I say it us? What are you going to do about us, Julia?"

Silence again.

"I think we need to talk some more, don't we?" he said. "When you're ready. No rush. We have at least – what? A couple of days till we have to go back to England. Think about it all, and let's look at it when you know what you want."

It was all so calm, so civilised. She felt her heart, which had started to beat faster, collect itself and return to its former steadiness. Hari, impatient, demanding, selfish Hari, was leaving her space to think, and she was very grateful.

*So you should be, my girl*, said the voice in her head again. *You need to make a decision. What do you want to happen? You may lose him if you dither about like this.*

The past felt very close and the future very far away. What had the man she'd met in town said to her? Things work out best when they're left alone. But she couldn't leave things up in the air for much longer. She had begun to understand what she'd interpreted as Helen's passivity, her lack of courage. Instead of being swept off her feet, her great-aunt had in fact kept them firmly on the ground, and bowed to the inevitable. Her letters made it clear that she felt empty, angry, shaken, but that duty to her mother had come first. And in the end she'd found real happiness. If only Julia could feel that she would be as successful...

Her thoughts took their own shape, swirling and settling around her. In the warm stillness of an Indian morning, nothing seemed as desperate as it had done a little while ago.

"Why are you smiling?" Hari asked gently, turning her head to his.

"I'm not sure. I feel calmer, that I understand something. I'm not sure what it is, but it doesn't matter. It'll all work out in the end."

He took her hand and held it gently. They stood together, saying nothing, watching the water. Julia sighed and laid her head against his shoulder.

## Chapter Forty

"I've been thinking."

Julia sat down opposite Hari in the cold dining room of the hotel a couple of days later. They had spent them in and around Ranpur, walking when the weather was cool enough, visiting forts and temples, shopping for silks and filigree silver and papier maché. And saying nothing about

Helen or their own future.

Hari looked at her, his lips smiling, his eyes wary.

Julia shivered, probably because the air-conditioning was humming full blast, and giving her goose pimples. Hari spoke, his tone as chill as the air.

"Jolly good. I've been waiting quite a while – rather longer than I generally wait for anything or anybody. I think I deserve some information; your decision has a direct effect on me and my plans. For one thing, I don't know whether to start looking for another assistant..."

Julia felt her heart, unexpectedly, leap. She'd not expected this so soon.

"I need someone to help me, you know that. And if you can't, then..."

She gathered herself.

"For heaven's sake, it isn't for ever," she almost snapped. "I need what? Two months? Three? Surely you can give me that. Then I can return to London and start work again – all back to normal. I've a PhD to finish for one thing..."

He looked at her angrily.

"Normal? Give me a fucking break. Normal? I've just been telling you that I want to take our – personal – relationship further, and you say we'll be getting back to normal. It's not normal, Julia. Not for me at any rate."

She couldn't believe her ears. She'd seen him be selfish, petulant and demanding to other people, but this kind of blast had never been directed at her before.

"How long are you going to hang about?" he asked her. "I need to know your plans."

"I haven't made any yet. Look, I don't want to make a huge issue about this. It would only be for a little while – what's a few months?"

"A few months 'between friends'? We're more than friends now, Julia, and I don't want all this to end. I want to be with you, to give it a go, to see where it'll take us. Don't you? I thought you did."

She wasn't sure. When she'd been in bed with him this morning, she had felt very happy, very close. It was exciting, affectionate, loving even. But she didn't dare to think beyond this time together; she'd seen Hari start relationships with other women, and knew how little they had meant to him.

"I – I'm not sure. This has been – is – lovely. I've felt very happy, but, well – I've seen you in action, remember. You're very hard to resist, at the beginning, but your interest doesn't last very long, does it? You get bored..."

"That's so unfair, Julia." He glared at her, his mouth tight. "Have I ever been indifferent to you? Stood you up? Let you down? Come on, admit it. This is different. We've got to know each other, become friends. And now there's something more. Isn't there?"

She didn't know what to say. This Hari was unfamiliar.

"Do you want a declaration?" he asked. "Okay, here's one. Make the most of it, because I don't do this very often. I've never enjoyed myself with a woman as much as I have with you. I find you interesting, attractive, sexy. You haven't ever bored me – well, not until now, when you keep avoiding a decision that affects us both. This *is* dull."

"I know. Well, I know that you are waiting for me to decide, but I don't know what to do. That's the problem, Hari. I don't know whether I should stay here and write up this story into a novel. I think it's fascinating, on all sorts of levels. But I don't know if I should stay here to write it or just take it back to England with you and try to work on it there."

Julia looked at him, her expression slightly defiant.

"I don't want you to tell me what to do. I have to decide this by myself. I know it affects you, and I am honestly not trying to be difficult about it."

He sighed, but looked less infuriated.

"Don't be so cross, please," Julia said, in a voice that

sounded more beseeching than she wanted it to. "You're making it more difficult for me, and I don't want to do the wrong thing."

He paused, and then stood up, dropping his napkin on the table.

"I think we need something to eat. I'm hungry and I bet you are too. Come on, let's get some breakfast. Decisions are easier on a full stomach."

Grateful for a bit of breathing space, Julia followed him to the breakfast bar. He was right. She was hungry. They stood side by side, waiting for their eggs to be cooked. She felt almost a physical force field around his tall figure, setting him apart. Even the man who was beating the eggs wouldn't meet his eyes.

As they walked back to the table with their plates, Hari put his arm lightly round her shoulders and kissed her cheek.

"Don't look so stricken," he said. "I'm giving you a hard time because it seems my future – our future – is out of my hands. And I don't like it! If you'd been anyone else, I would have left you to it, but..." He sat down and took a bite of his papery toast.

"But I don't want to," he continued when he had finished. "I want to be with you. I want you to come into the office and start typing and get up and make a cup of coffee, and tease me about leaving a book launch too early the night before, and take a call from some girl I took out to dinner. Not, of course" he laughed at her "that there would be any more of those if you come back to London with me."

Julia couldn't help laughing too.

"Oh Hari, you are a liar. I can't imagine you would ever be able to stick out a boring evening, with or without a young lady's company."

He grinned.

"I would try. I promise. I expect there'd be lapses, but

not in any serious sense. Listen, you annoying woman. I am telling you that I don't want to be with any pretty young thing, over dinner or anything else. Only you. There. You can't ask me to say any more than that, can you?"

Julia shook her head.

"No, I can't. Thank you. I..."

"Well I do think you could say something nice to me now," he said, sitting back in his chair and putting his chin up. "That's sort of how it works."

She couldn't help laughing.

"Okay, I'll try. I think you're the best boss I've had – not that I've had all that many. You make me laugh. You've helped me a lot with my detective work about Helen. You're very generous with your time and you make me think about things differently. And you're flattering me at the moment, and I rather like it!"

"I'm not flattering you. I'm telling you honestly how I feel," he said. "I can't tell you how I'm going to feel in a week, or a month or a year, but now I feel that if you stay in India and I go back to England without you, I shall be very sad indeed."

"I'll be sad too," said Julia, slowly. "I have felt alive and loved and happy with you. I'm worried it will all evaporate when we leave and being in London with change things. I would like to carry on working for you on your books. But perhaps not right now. It's just that... well, I don't want to lose momentum."

Hari sighed again.

"I think you've made up your mind, haven't you?" he said flatly.

"Well, while I am meeting so many people who knew Helen, and while they still want to help me, it might be a good idea to stay here a bit longer, on my own. Getting to know Ranpur so I get to know Helen better. You know that was always what I wanted to do."

"And you want to write about it. They always do. Maybe even a novel."

"Yes, maybe," she told him. "And maybe I'll ask you to read it when I've done it. Would that be a problem?"

"Not really, although I'll be suspicious of a book that keeps you away from me. But there you go. There doesn't seem anything else I can say. How long do you think you'll be here?"

"I'm not sure. A couple of months probably. Not long. I can be back at my desk almost before you know it. You can get on with writing the next one!"

Hari looked at her with an expression as bleak as a cloudy sky on a winter morning. Julia felt a wave of regret and put out a hand to touch his. He took hers and held it tightly. His palm felt cool and dry.

"It will seem a very long time without you, Julia. I feel very fed up that you aren't coming back, but I do understand. Against my better judgement I do understand. I will go back and get on with things, as you say, and then I'll see if I can come and visit, if you'll have me."

Julia smiled with relief. This was not going to be the full-blown argument she had feared.

"Thank you. Thank you very much for understanding. I need to do this, Hari. I want to look deeper and find out more. And work hard on putting the story together into something that makes sense. Helen deserves a bit of respect."

He was looking over her head out of the window, and he brought his eyes back to her face and shrugged.

"You must do what you want to do. You will, I know that. It's a new experience for me to care for someone who doesn't put me first. I expect it will be very good for my soul," he said, trying to smile.

"I'm not finding this easy either, you know," Julia told him. "I'd like nothing better than to get on the plane with you and my notes and my photos, but I know my book will be better if I write it here. I can ask if I need to check something and the smells and the sounds and the food and the birdsong will help get me in the zone!"

"Okay, I've got the picture," he said. "I'm not pleased. You can't expect me to be but you've probably made the right decision. I shall think of you, and I shall feel cross with you, and I shall mind making my own coffee. And I shall look forward to coming back. Partly to see if it's all been worth it, and partly because – well, I'm going to miss you terribly."

# INDIA
# 1939

## Chapter Forty-one

The throaty roar of the motorbikes faded in a cloud of dust. Helen stood on the bottom step, looking up at the verandah. Sudham was polishing a side table, rubbing hard; he had moved all the photographs and ornaments, and was free to buff away.

"*Sala'am*, Sudham." she trotted up the steps and when she reached the top, he stopped rubbing and stood with his arms at his side.

"*Sala'am, Memsa'ab*." He spoke in Hindi. "*Memsa'ab* Evangeline is writing letters in her room. *Memsa'ab* Kate is playing tennis at the Club. She'll be back for dinner at seven thirty."

"Thank you."

She went to her room, and had a shower. Taking the dust of the journey out of her hair made her feel lighter, cleaner, just like the happiness she felt at Arthur's proposal.

She wrapped a towel around herself, and brushed her hair, smiling at the memory. Then she thought of her mother, and felt queasy. Evangeline was unpredictable: there was no reason why she should object, but she might be tricky. She might not, of course. If anything, she'd encouraged Arthur, inviting him to dinner and putting up no objections to their meetings. Kate would be a little more difficult, but even she could not object to Helen and Arthur's closeness. Helen was the elder sister after all, and in the general scheme of things, she should marry first.

Dressed, she felt braver, and made her way out to the verandah. Her mother was there, at her table, a pen in her hand. As Helen sat down, she put the book she was reading to one side, and folded her small hands in her lap.

She said nothing. Her pale blue eyes were, as always, cool. Her face had very few wrinkles; she was very proud of her skin, to which she applied Pond's cream every night. Nothing else. She held her neck very straight, her snow-white hair piled in a bun on the top of her small head. A pair of pearl earrings and a wedding ring were her only pieces of jewellery. Her expression combined studied benevolence with patient enquiry.

Helen's heart beat faster, and her breath came stickily. She opened her mouth, and closed it again. This was not how this encounter should start.

"Mother, I've something to tell you."

It came out faster than she meant, and sounded squeaky, little-girlish.

Evangeline sat in silence, upright in her chair, her small feet in their well-polished black shoes peeping out from underneath her long black skirt. She was smiling a little, entirely in control.

"Mother, we need to talk," said Helen. She tried to keep her voice steady.

Evangeline's voice was mellow, slow, in charge.

"Of course. Kate is at the Club. She'll be back in about half an hour. What is it?"

No change of expression.

"You know I went on a picnic today?"

"Yes. You told me. With some friends."

"Mmmm. Marjorie, and Tony, and the Carters. And Arthur."

Another pause.

"It... it was really pleasant. We had delicious food, and a barbecue, and a swim, and a walk in the forest."

"Did you? Brave to swim. I'm not sure I'd have dared."

They were circling each other.

"I went for a walk in the forest with Arthur. We saw some birds, and... and we talked. He... he suggested..."

She took a breath. This was ghastly. She was stammering like a child.

Evangeline was very good at waiting.

"He suggested?" she asked, raising her eyebrows and looking at her daughter, whose cheeks were pink.

"He... He told me he's planning to leave Ranpore. He has a few job offers. In different parts of India. Parts I haven't ever been to. And he... well, Mother, he asked me to go with him."

"Did he indeed? And what did you tell him?"

"Nothing really. I said I'd have to think about it, and that of course I needed to talk to you. But – well, Mother, I'd like to go with him. As his wife."

"Oh, as his wife. That's all above board then."

Helen's heart fluttered.

"Oh Mother, does that mean you think it's possible? You wouldn't mind? I know I'm old enough to decide for myself, but I thought..."

"You thought what? That I'd prevent you? How could I do that? As you say, you're old enough to make up your own mind about your future. Your sister will be a little disappointed, and I don't think she and I'll do very well together if you leave us. But, of course, it is up to you."

Helen was disconcerted. If Evangeline had been unreasonable, and refused point blank, as she had expected, it would have been easier to fight her.

"So, may I tell him that I accept?"

"Well, of course, but I suggest you tell your sister first that that is what you have decided to do. And I think we will need to talk about what we will do if – when – you go."

Helen nodded. At least she was past the first hurdle.

"Thank you, Mother." She kissed her on the cheek, and smiled. "I'm very happy."

Evangeline smiled too.

"I'm very glad. Let's talk about it further, tonight at supper."

At supper time the three women were seated around the table in the dining room, for a change. Evangeline had told Sudham that they would not eat on the verandah, as the mosquitoes were on the warpath. Kate had returned in her tennis whites, warm and exercised, her cheeks flushed. She greeted Helen coolly, but hostilities seemed to be over.

"I'll be there in a little while. Give me time for a quick shower and a change. I came straight home off the court; the changing rooms at the Club were very busy."

Half an hour later, talking about nothing very much, they were served a light consommé. The lamp light reflected off glasses and cutlery, and candles in the centre of the table illuminated a pretty vase of flowers. It looked charming, and felt peaceful.

When the soup bowls were removed, Evangeline spoke clearly into the lamp-lit dusk: "Kate, Helen has some news."

Helen took a breath, trying not to look nervous. Again the feeling of wanting to be far away, the hole in the solar plexus, the breathless squeezing of the ribs.

Kate seemed to notice nothing.

"Arthur Kirkwood has asked me to marry him," she said at last.

The sentence crashed into the room like a rogue elephant. Kate gasped, opened her mouth, and closed it. Evangeline waited.

"What? You? But..." Kate's eyebrows snapped together. "Arthur likes me, Helen, Mother. You must see that. I, well, I know you met in Calcutta and you went on that stupid picnic but – well, you... You must know he likes me best. How *unkind* of you to push yourself in. I'm sure he was only being kind. Mother, what do *you* think about this? You told me you thought he liked me. Didn't you? Yes, that surprised you, didn't it Helen? Mother thought..."

"That will be quite enough, Kate. You're sounding like nails on a blackboard."

Helen was suddenly aware of a collusion. They were a

team, and she was on the opposite side, alone.

"What do you mean, mother thought? *What* did she think?" Her voice came from another planet. She felt sick and cold.

"You know your sister likes to be the centre of attention, Helen. No, enough, Kate…"

Evangeline raised a small hand.

"Oh!"

Kate stood up, scraping her chair on the floor, and walked out. If Helen had not felt so shocked, she would have laughed. Flounced was the perfect description of her sister's exit, chin up, nose in the air, curls bobbing. The sound of her heels faded as she clipped out, over the verandah and into the garden.

She won't last long, thought Helen. The mosquitoes will get her. She managed a smile.

"She won't last long out there," her mother said, reading Helen's mind.

Helen sat still. She'd no idea what to do.

"*Did* you tell Kate that Arthur was keen on her, mother?" she asked eventually. "Did you? Why?"

Evangeline almost looked guilty. She looked over Helen's head at the portrait of their father on the wall behind her, as if hoping he would step out of it and help the situation.

"Helen, you must know that I couldn't manage this house without you. Your father would have wanted you to stay here and help me, to look after me as I grow older. Kate doesn't have your – your organisation."

"But she thinks she can have the man I'd like to marry. And you seem to think she's right? Isn't that correct?" Her voice was still flat, with no anger, but in her head there was a bubble of disappointed rage. "I've always listened to you, mother. I've always picked up after Kate, never complained. I've managed the servants, run the house, paid the salaries… I thought it was because you wanted me to be a good wife, but it wasn't, was it? You wanted me to do it because *you* didn't want to, and you didn't think Kate was up to it. The fragrant Kate. *She* can get married, can't she? It's just me who has to stay here with you, in this stifling town, never seeing anywhere else, never doing anything different."

To her annoyance, hot tears spilled down her face.

I've done it all... my duty, my duty for nearly twenty-five years. I can hold a conversation, I don't look like the back end of Bodhi's *tonga*, I'm not a horrible person, I'd make Arthur a good wife, and – and I love him."

Evangeline made no reply. There was nothing for her to say. She did not wish her elder daughter to leave her, and she would make sure this never happened.

"Are you saying that I may not marry. Ever? This is the nineteen thirties! Do I have to be stifled here all my life? All my LIFE? With you?"

"No, Helen, of course you should marry. But surely someone here, in Ranpore would suit you better. There are plenty of men who would be delighted to marry you, and I'm sure you could have a happy life with any of them."

"Any of them? What, like a cattle market? It would suit you better, you mean, don't you, Mother? But that's the whole point. I don't *want* to marry any of them. I want to marry Arthur. He is...oh, he's clever, and amusing, and different, and above all, he doesn't want to stay here. Oh, mother, nor do I. I want to travel, if not the world, then at least India. You know Kate doesn't care. She'd be happy with someone she didn't really love, as long as they were dazzled by her, and let her do what she likes. But I *can't* marry anyone just for the sake of being married. Surely, surely you know me well enough to know that?"

Evangeline did. She let her eyes drop, and her resistance filled the room, pushing Helen's miserable indignation aside.

"Well, I'm going to marry Arthur."

Helen hated herself for sounding like a defiant child.

"I'm going to tell him the next time I see him, and I'm going to go with him wherever he needs me to go. Kate can look after you. Here in Ranpore."

Her mother put her hand on her daughter's forearm, but Helen just looked down at it. Evangeline took it away without a word.

"I'm not going to flounce out like my sister," Helen said, getting to her feet. "I'm going to walk out and sit in my room, and try to forget this evening ever happened." She tried to smile, but failed.

Evangeline looked almost sympathetic, but she'd decided long ago how things were going to be, and nothing was going to change her plans. Alone in the dining room, she raised a glass of water to her lips, and took a sip, crunching hard on bits of floating ice.

## Chapter Forty-two

Helen couldn't stop crying. She sat very stiffly, back straight in a chair, hands clenched in her lap, shaking with fury, disappointment, and a cold sickness in her stomach. A creeping certainty was confirmed. It would be a long, uncomfortable battle if she wanted to marry Arthur and taste her freedom. Her mother and sister were her enemies, and they were not to be underestimated.

Helen was in the habit of giving in to the demands of her spoilt little sister, whose determination had never failed her when she really wanted something. But did she really want Arthur? Helen couldn't be sure. Arthur had been pleasant, complimentary, appreciative to Kate – but he hadn't sought her out. He hadn't asked Kate on a picnic. He hadn't suggested she leave Ranpore with him. He had made it clear he preferred Helen, and seemed to want a wife as a companion, one for the marathon rather than the sprint. And he made Helen's heart sing. She enjoyed being in his arms on the dance floor, sharing a walk in the trees, knowing his eyes rested on her when she entered a room.

But did she have the heart for the fight? She was not used to standing up to the two women she lived with. She'd been brought up to be dutiful, well-behaved, considerate. She was educated, she read a lot, attributes encouraged by her father, but completely irrelevant to Evangeline. If anything, her mother would have preferred her to leave her books aside, and concentrate on making other people's lives (well, *her* life) more comfortable.

After several minutes, Helen's sobs quietened. She took a small lace-trimmed handkerchief from the pocket of her dress, wiped her eyes, tidied her hair, dabbed a bit of powder on her face, and opened the door to the verandah. There was nobody there.

She walked quietly into the garden, and looked up at the moon. It was very large tonight, and occasionally a bird's silhouette flew across it. The crickets buzzed, a rustling in the bushes indicated the presence of a small animal, and the night *chowkidar* sat cross-legged by the gate on his ragged mattress. Seeing her, he stood up clumsily, and straightened his *dhoti*. It was unusual for *Memsa'ab* to appear at this time, and he was used to a quick forty winks about now. She nodded at him, and walked away, leaving him to settle down again.

After a while in the night air, breathing in the heavy scents around her, and feeling soothed by the darkness, Helen went back to her room and tried to sleep. It wasn't easy. She spent much of the night staring at the ceiling and fuming.

The Armstrongs were used to the heat, and usually slept through it. Tonight, however, Helen found the warmth uncomfortable. She was angry – with her insomnia, with her family. She screwed up her eyes at her sister's selfishness, her mother's resolve, and what appeared to be their joint betrayal. It seemed that Evangeline had been encouraging Kate to set herself at Arthur, possibly to deflect him from Helen, possibly because she thought it a better outcome all round.

But she wouldn't take this lying down, Helen told herself, and smiled at the phrase. She was lying down, and so far she was taking it. But not from tomorrow. Tomorrow she would be ready for the fight. She was not giving in this time.

## Chapter Forty-three

After a breakfast which was remarkable only for its apparent normality, Helen decided to walk to Arthur's small bungalow, just half a mile away. Perhaps Doris would be there. I'd welcome a friendly face, thought Helen.

But first she needed to talk to Arthur.

She slipped quietly away while Kate was having a second cup of coffee and her mother was talking to the cook.

The gate clicked closed behind her, and she took quick strides down the grassy verge of the *murram* road. Dust soon covered her red leather shoes, and she was glad of the umbrella she'd taken to shield herself from the sun.

At Arthur's, the *chowkidar* opened the side gate, and she passed under an arch of bougainvillea into the compound.

But Arthur wasn't at home. She looked over towards the larger house a little further away, separated by a neat hibiscus hedge. The Cannons' house was smaller, less elegant, than her own, but she always felt comfortable there. She walked on across the lawn towards it, uncertain, and climbed the steps to the verandah. Mrs Cannon was there, arms spread wide to hug her. It was too much. Helen began to weep, to her embarrassment; she stood for a few moments, shoulders shaking.

"*Nimbu pani*? Tea?" asked Mrs Cannon, looking concerned. "Water? Barley water? What would you like? And whatever is the matter, dear? Come and sit here."

Her chatter gave Helen time to compose herself, and she sat thankfully back against large soft cushions.

A cold drink was brought and Helen sipped it without tasting it. Mrs Cannon frowned, disconcerted.

"Sorry! I'm so sorry," Helen stammered. "Forgive me. I've just walked here to see... I wondered if... if Arthur was here."

"Why he's just gone to pay a bill for me at the *dukaan*, but he'll be back directly. Mr Cannon is away – he's gone to Secunderabad for a few days so it is so very nice having Arthur around. And here he is now..."

Arthur, wearing khaki shorts and a loose white shirt, came swiftly up the steps.

"Helen." His face lit up. "How lovely to see you. I was going to come and visit later today and ask if you'd be free for a cycle ride." A pause as he took in the tears and blotchy cheeks.

"But whatever's the matter? Has anything happened?"

Her face told him. Mrs Cannon stood up.

"I'll leave the two of you together. I have lots to do so please excuse me Helen, Arthur."

She left them alone, and Helen sat back in her chair. She looked at Arthur and pulled a face.

"She is the kindest woman I know. I've just cried all over her shoulder."

"I wish I had been here, then you could have cried all over mine. But why? What's happened? Oh, wait. Let me guess. You've told your sister and mother that I've asked you to marry me, and the reception was – how shall I put it? Chilly?"

She sighed. "We could have made ice-cream, the air was so frosty. And then it heated up. Kate, well, Kate was livid. She had a tantrum about it and hasn't really spoken to me properly since last night. And – no, don't interrupt – my mother..." she was crying again now, "my mother has made it quite clear that she has no intention of giving her blessing to any marriage I make that takes me away from Ranpore. And she has also made it clear that if Kate wanted to marry you, she'd be happy to give her blessing. I feel so – stupid!"

The last word was little more than a loud squeak, and she took out a handkerchief.

"Well, that's no surprise. Not to me at any rate. And it should make you feel a lot better to know that I don't want to marry your sister."

He came and sat next to her and put his arms around her awkwardly.

"Look Helen, we can do this together. We need to get this sorted out. Shall I come to your mother's house? Is she there now?"

She nodded, but there was fear in her eyes.

"Kate is, too. Oh dear, I don't think... They don't want me to... I can't..."

"Come on," he said, taking her hand. "Let's go there right this minute."

They walked in silence towards Jacaranda Lodge. Helen was far less convinced than he was that all would be well. Her mother was a formidable opponent. The two women were sitting on the verandah, and stopped talking when they saw Arthur and Helen.

Evangeline smiled. Kate stared. Helen almost turned to run away, but with Arthur solidly at her side she stayed where she was.

"Good morning, Mrs Armstrong. Kate. I understand from Helen that neither of you are very happy about my recent proposal."

He paused. Kate tightened her lips and glared at her sister.

"Please sit down, Mr Kirkwood," Evangeline was gracious. "Helen, ask Sudham for some tea."

Arthur sat on the chair she indicated, and Helen rang the bell for Sudham. He came immediately, and took their order: the universal panacea. She would have preferred a stiff brandy, but anything liquid was a help.

Arthur clearly had no such problem.

He looked back at Evangeline and Kate with no embarrassment, a man who was confident all would go according to his plans.

"Helen is a young woman, Mrs Armstrong, who is free to make up her mind about her future. I know she has lived here all her life, but, I'm sure you will agree, the time has come for her to marry and have a family."

Nothing.

"You have two very attractive daughters. There seems to have been a misunderstanding of my – er – motives. I've been delighted – who would not be? – to spend time on the tennis court and dance floor with Kate, but it is Helen I'd like to spend my life with. I'm afraid I simply don't understand the problem. Is it that I'm new? That I'm not from a family you know? I assure you I've been brought up as well as your daughters, and I've a very promising future before me. My wife will lack for nothing, and I intend to make Helen happy in every way."

Evangeline frowned at Kate, who was about to speak.

"Mr Kirkwood. It seems quite clear that you do not understand the issue here, which is that we have always stuck together as a family. It is not your background, which I understand is nothing I need to disapprove of. My daughters are from Ranpore, they're safe here. Helen in particular has been brought up to stay with her family, especially as her father has now, alas, died, leaving me alone, and getting older."

"Mrs Armstrong, if I may be so bold, you're in excellent health, and living very comfortably in this house, with your servants and your friends nearby."

"Indeed, Mr Kirkwood. Thank you for those reassuring words. But this house, comfortable as it undoubtedly is, does not run itself. Helen has been in charge of everything for many years, and I rely on her absolutely. Now, if you were planning to stay in the area, that would be a different story..."

Arthur shook his head. This was going to be a long campaign, he realised. Helen looked as if she was going to faint; her face was white, her hands twisting in her lap, and he felt a twinge of irritation.

"Helen feels the same as I do, Mrs Armstrong. She has looked after everything here, as was her duty, but surely you'll allow her the chance of a future with me and ..."

"Mr Kirkwood, I am not lacking in intelligence, nor have I misunderstood what is going on. Helen, is it true that you would like to marry Mr Kirkwood, and leave your home and family to live somewhere that is likely to be very far from Ranpore?"

Helen nodded, looking more miserable than ever.

"I – I –I'd like to go with Arthur. I'd like to see more of India and perhaps other places. I feel stifled here."

"Do you love each other?"

Again Helen nodded, and looked at Arthur, who said, very slowly and clearly:

"Mrs Armstrong. I'd like to make it clear that I love Helen, I'd like to marry her, and take her with me wherever we decide to go, and that I have her assurance that she'll accept my proposal. I'm here because I do not want her to be unhappy, and because it is good manners to ask you as her mother for your blessing. Not your permission. I'd have preferred to do this more calmly and pleasantly, but what has happened has happened."

Kate spoke for the first time.

"I didn't know you were – you both were... I trusted you, Helen."

Evangeline raised her hand. She had not been spoken to in living memory as Arthur had spoken to her just now, but she lost none of her calm.

"Kate, do not let your tongue and your feelings run away with you. Helen, I think we all need to let the dust settle and think. Mr Kirkwood, this is a close family, and I must ask your understanding. Decisions cannot be made in a moment. Thank you for coming to see me."

It was a dismissal. He stood up. Bowing slightly, he went down the steps and out of the front gate, which clanged shut behind him.

Helen sat still, waiting for the sky to fall. She felt disgusted with herself, angry with her mother, upset with her inability to stand up for herself. And frightened of Kate's wrath.

"Leave Helen alone, Kate," she heard her mother say. Kate's cheeks were red, and she looked on the verge of tears, but Evangeline's force of will kept her quiet. "She has had a shock, and needs some time to calm down."

"I don't need any time. I know what I want," said Helen. The voice came from far away. "My conscience is clear. I would like to marry Arthur, and you mustn't stand in my way."

This was more like it. She felt braver, even though Kate snorted.

"Conscience. Conscience! Honestly, how can you be so hypocritical? Going off for cosy little walks in the forest, kissing under the lianas – maybe more than that..."

"Don't be vulgar, Kate. It is of little consequence what Helen may or may not have done, and I am not accusing her of anything. Would I be right, Helen?"

"Of course you're right. I don't do that sort of thing. And I've not been hypocritical, Kate, whatever you might think. I admit, Calcutta was wonderful. We talked and danced, but no more than you have ever done. Rather less, I should think."

Helen couldn't help herself, but Kate chose to ignore the last remark. Instead she said, "I'm going to see Arthur Kirkwood whether you like it or not – at the Club, or wherever. You're *not* going to marry him, Helen. You don't *deserve* him. I'm the one who'll go with him to his new posting wherever it may be..." Her voice became shrill.

"You're getting ahead of yourself, Kate. Stop this," said Evangeline firmly. "You are saying things you will regret."

She picked up a magazine, and opened it; the audience was over.

Helen slipped away to her room, and sat down on the edge of her bed. There was a sharp knock on the door, and it opened immediately. Kate walked in and faced her, shaking with fury.

"I'm going to say this just once more, Helen. You're *not* going to marry Arthur Kirkwood. *I* am. Mother knows that I should be Mrs Kirkwood, not you. You think you've got him because you're clever, you have 'conversations', you have 'opinions'. But let me tell you, a man wants a pretty wife to look after him. He doesn't want someone with their nose in some stupid book. He wants a shower, a whisky and soda, and a comfortable chair, with dinner on the table in ten minutes. Even I can do that, and what's more, I can do it beautifully. And unless you run away with him tonight, which I know you're too cowardly to do, I promise you I'll win."

She left the room as abruptly as she'd entered it, slamming the door behind her. Helen stayed exactly where she was, feeling very weary. Duty. That was the problem. All the years of doing what was expected of her made it very difficult to go against her family's wishes. So, could she do it? Could she defy her mother? If she married Arthur, would Kate ever forgive her? She would find a husband, that was not the issue, but would their relationship be damaged for ever? Was it worth the upheaval?

Kate would leave whenever she found someone she wanted to marry. And she'd go wherever she needed to. There was so much to do and so much to see. India was changing, there were opportunities for anyone who was prepared to loosen the tight reins of colonial life, and see what happened.

Helen's heart tightened. She wanted more than anything in the world to be married to Arthur, to be the mother of his children, the person he shared his life and plans with... But even as she let these thoughts crystallise, a doubt began to creep into her mind, and then it solidified into chill fear. Could she do it? She looked at her wan face in the oval dressing table mirror and listlessly picked up her hair brush. She put it down a few seconds later, very carefully, and frowned at herself. What should she do? What could she do? Could she live with herself if she left her mother alone? Kate would leave Ranpore with whomever she married, without a thought. Helen tightened her lips as she considered her future in Ranpore. The same people, the same places, the same things to do every day. An unchanging routine. Was that what she wanted?

She would tell her mother she was leaving. That was that. She stood up and straightened her shoulders. If she stuck to her guns, she thought, and with Arthur's help, she could do it. How pleased he would be! How proud of her! Yes, she had to do it now. It wouldn't be all that bad.

And then she sat down again, feeling foolish and frightened. She couldn't. Whatever Arthur said, whatever Kate might do, she couldn't face her mother and tell her she was leaving.

She couldn't face the drama, the guilt, and she quailed at the vision of a tight-lipped Evangeline and a frosty Kate at her wedding, if they came at all. The whispering among the guests, the disapproval: "Evangeline asked her to stay, but she's too selfish to think of others".

Or the alternative, leaving all she knew to marry at a sad little ceremony, in Calcutta, say, or New Delhi. She would never be able to return. And as she looked forward, she looked back over her shoulder, and her spirit failed her. With her mother's blessing, she could have taken a step into the unknown. Without it, she shivered.

She had discussed her mother's unkind inflexibility with very few – the Cannons knew, Doris and Cassandra listened and advised, but otherwise she'd kept her frustrations to herself. It was bad form to talk about such things. Her upbringing wouldn't permit it. She'd have to tell Arthur. But not right now.

Exhausted, she slipped off her shoes. She felt the cold red floor beneath her feet before she lay down and closed her eyes.

Sleep was elusive. She couldn't lie still. Thoughts came and went. Happy images of a contented life, far from Ranpore, with Arthur and children and a house of her own. How she wanted a family, to live with someone who encouraged her to talk about what she had read, what she thought. Someone with whom she could travel – around India, and even possibly to England one day.

Then came uncomfortable visions of Evangeline, unforgiving, the house huge around her. And Kate, married, heedless, coming and going as she wished.

The butterflies in her stomach flew up and swirled, then settled a moment, gathering themselves before fluttering off again.

She couldn't do it.

It wasn't fair, it wasn't right, but it was how she'd been brought up. One day a woman would not have to give up her chance of happiness to stay at home and do what was expected of her.

Arthur couldn't marry Kate. Could he? She couldn't

bear the thought. Her sister was pretty, she was not intentionally unkind, or even stupid, and she wanted to be married more than anything else, to a man she thought worthy of her. But she was a flirt, she was not interested in reading or discussion, or any of the things people thought odd about Helen, which Arthur clearly liked.

Perhaps Kate was more realistic about men than she was. Perhaps what a man really wanted was a cosy wife, the mother of his children, who ran the house efficiently, helped him in his career, entertaining, smiling, dealing with staff.... Well, whoever married Kate would soon be disappointed on the housekeeping front. Helen almost smiled. And then it faded as she looked down the dark corridor of the future, with its shadows of loneliness and a solitary old age.

## Chapter Forty-four

Kate Armstrong didn't mean to be selfish. It wasn't her fault. She'd been encouraged to think she was at the centre of everything by the people around her, and she had no reason not to believe them. Her mother let her win the clashes between them that didn't matter, so she felt important and they got along fine.

The older men in Ranpore spoiled and flattered her, squeezing her cheek and paying clunky compliments. The younger men were fair game. Kate twinkled and flirted and turned away, calling them to her side when she felt they had suffered enough.

She taught at Sunday School and took the younger girls for music at the High School. She enjoyed singing and the piano, and the compliments she received about her skill.

She loved her older sister. She admired her education, her efficiency, her elegance. But she was hardly competition. Until now. Arthur Kirkwood was hers by right. Everybody in Ranpore knew that. Except him, it seemed. Kate found it hard to believe he preferred Helen to herself, and decided that he would have to be shown how wrong he was.

She dressed carefully, in her tennis whites, and she applied powder and a pink lipstick that made her mouth look full and soft.

She took the *tonga* to the Club and told Bodhi to come back in an hour. It was the time when offices closed, and dusty, hot and tired men came for a shower and a game of tennis followed by a drink at the long mahogany bar.

The tennis courts were in use when Kate arrived, but one couple stopped when they saw her.

"Great! Kate, my wife says I'm cheating. Find a partner and come and play doubles with us – it may save our marriage."

Martin Hammond was bluff and smiling, eager to please as ever.

"He's the world's worst loser, and is prepared to lie his head off about balls in or out, I warn you," called his wife, Deirdre. "But do come and play. Look, here's Arthur – come on Arthur, we need a fourth."

Kate looked down to hide her expression of triumph. This was going well. The gods were smiling. He couldn't refuse without looking churlish and soon they were on the court together.

The game was well matched, and they all enjoyed it, and Kate and Arthur won in three sets. Her lobs disconcerted her opponents, and her smashes won them points. She felt Arthur's approval, and knew that for a moment he'd forgotten her sister.

Better and better, she thought.

"Well done, you two. See you at the bar in twenty?"

Kate nodded, and walked off the court with Arthur, who tipped the ballboy with a small coin.

"Would you like a drink?" he asked her, coolly, keeping his distance.

"A glass of barley water would be lovely. Thank you."

"The sun's over the yard arm," said Cornelius Clandon, as they came into the bar. Clandon was usually found sitting on one of the high bar stools, a glass of something golden and Scottish in front of him. He disdained ice or water.

"Only when I'm feeling a bit weak, m'dear," he had told Kate one day. "Fish fornicate in it, as WD Griffiths would say."

His pale eyes always ran over her, making no secret of his admiration. "An old widower like me needs a pick me up every so often," he had told her the first time they met, "and my goodness, girl, you do pick an old man up!"

"Come and sit next to me," he said to her now, "and tell me all the exciting things you've been getting up to. How is your mama? I must drop in and see her one of these days."

Kate climbed up beside him, her tanned thighs covered to just above the knee.

"Only for a second, Cornelius. It's nearly six o'clock, and I've to go and change or they'll throw me out, won't you, Achad?"

The barman, wiping a glass with a spotless cloth, smiled neutrally.

"You know the rules, *Memsa'ab*," he said, in his light voice, sending a quick glance up to the clock.

"I'd better go and change. I'll be back in a few minutes."

She slipped off the bar stool and went to change. Her tennis shoes squeaked on the wooden floor. Cornelius took another sip. Arthur, beside him, raised his hand, and nodded to Achad, indicating a refill for them both.

"Thanks, old boy. It should be on me, in devout gratitude for the attention and proximity of your lovely partner. Although I thought you were keener on her sister, the gracious Helen."

Arthur turned his glass in his hands. He looked up at Cornelius, whose face was for once entirely serious.

"Hmmm. You're right. But I'm not sure things are going to work out."

He looked at the old man, whose wrinkled brown face behind a raised glass told him nothing.

Nobody knew how Cornelius managed to know so much about what was going on, but if ever anyone bothered to check his observations they usually found them accurate. He missed nothing.

"Cornelius, to tell the truth, I've no idea what to do. I could have sworn everything was going to go our way. How could it not? Helen is an adult, and I believe she cares about me. As I care about her. But she doesn't stand up to her mother, and her sister makes her quiver like a leaf."

"Evangeline Armstrong is a formidable enemy, my boy. A pretty formidable friend too, if the truth be known. I'm not sure how I've managed to remain in her good books. She's never lost a battle yet. Helen is like her father, however, so you may be lucky. He knew how to handle Evangeline."

Cornelius looked up at a photograph of a group of men in tennis whites over the bar.

"There he is. In the middle. A terrific serve and the only person who could make Evangeline listen to any reason but her own. He loved Helen a great deal. Kate was very young and I'm not sure he did much more than read her bedtime stories."

"Was he a friend of yours?"

"Close enough for him to ask me to be Helen's godfather. And she makes me proud. Kate, now. That's a different kettle of fish. She has her mother's conviction that if she wants something it must be right.

"But you're a man on the move, aren't you? Looking

for the right wife. I know you're keener on Helen – I would be myself – but either of them would do for a coming man. Why have a fight about it?"

Arthur looked at Cornelius, whose expression gave nothing away. He took another sip of his drink as Kate slid gracefully on to a vacant stool beside them.

"Ah here she is! How delightful you look," Cornelius exclaimed.

She smelled of lily of the valley, and her skin, fresh from the shower, was gleaming. Her curls were brushed and soft, and as she climbed up on the tall bar chair, her floral dress of soft cream lawn fell in folds to mid calf.

"Oh, thank you, Arthur," she said sweetly, taking the drink Arthur had ordered for her. "Just what I need. That was a good game."

"Of tennis?" enquired Cornelius blandly.

"Mmm. Arthur plays much better than I do, but we managed to keep our end up."

She smiled at them both, then looked into her drink as if the secrets of the world were to be found among the ice cubes.

Cornelius turned to Achad to ask him to add his guests to his table.

"I hope you'll both join me for something to eat? Is your mother expecting you home, Kate? In which case, let me send someone with a chit to tell her I've forced you to keep an old man company."

"Thank you, Cornelius," said Arthur, "but…"

"Arthur, I shall only have to sit and chew my way through a course or two, with nobody to talk to."

He raised his voice.

"And if you have that bloody *murghi masala* again, Achad, old chap, I shall go into the kitchen and force the cook to eat it, every drop. Every dried-up piece of ancient bird, every shrivelled cardamom seed. You get the picture?"

Achad grinned.

"Yes *Sa'ab*, I'll tell him. I think he has made a curry with lamb tonight. And mulligatawny soup."

"Thank the gods. At least he can't mess up a *rogan ghosh*. Shall we drink up and move to our table, my friends?"

"My mother is expecting me," Kate told him. "And you know how she hates surprises!"

"A chit from me will do the trick, m'dear. We can't let Mr Kirkwood spend his time with just an old fogey. What a pity Helen isn't here too? But she can dine with your mother. That should keep Evangeline happy. Achad, pen and paper please."

## Chapter Forty-five

Arthur accompanied Kate home in Bodhi's *tonga* after dinner and coffee. Ranpore was hardly a den of Thugs, but you never knew. He waited until she was on the verandah, and the *chowkidar* had closed the gate, before he turned and walked off to the Cannons' guest cottage.

The night was full of noises, and shadows slid about as trees were nudged by a languid breeze, hot and heavy. A child's cry came from someone's servants' quarters, and the peaty smell of smoke. The moon tonight was a tiny sliver in the darkest blue sky, there were silver clouds, and a hint of rain.

Arthur's mind was whirling.

He had, a little guiltily, enjoyed his dinner at the Club. Cornelius was absolutely right about Kate and Helen, and of course he hoped Evangeline would come round. But there was no doubt Kate knew how to make herself a charming companion, although the sisters weren't as interchangeable as Cornelius had implied. Kate lacked the little extra something that made him excited about Helen

– she wasn't as amusing, for one thing – but she was easy on the eye, smelt delicious and was born to flirt with men. Cornelius responded with ironic gallantry, and had watched Arthur's reaction.

"Easy does it, old chap," he said, when Kate left them briefly for a visit to the Powder Room. "Steady the Buffs. You're in the eye of a storm here, and you need your wits about you."

Arthur sighed. "I know. I know that. She's nothing on Helen." He paused. "But I don't think Evangeline would put any obstacles in the way if I decided that Kate was the easier proposition."

"You're right. Evangeline ain't going to let Helen go without a battle – she's far too reliant on her. Kate, on the other hand, is by no means indispensible to her. Which is something you might do well to bear in mind. She's a determined little soldier, though. And used to getting her own way."

"*Touché.*"

Arthur raised his glass, and touched his forehead in mock salute.

"Takes one to know one, my boy. Why do you think I'm not married? Not interested in arguments. And certainly not in changing my habits. Are you?"

Arthur was about to reply, but Kate arrived in a cloud of lily of the valley. She sat down, a wide smile on her face.

"You seem very cheery, Kate," Cornelius said.

"Am I not always, Cornelius? I try to be good company – without burying my head in a book or being preoccupied or sulky. It's always better that way, don't you think?"

*

Kate appeared at breakfast smiling sweetly. Helen sat opposite her mother, pale, and tight about the eyes. She

251

had woken just as the dawn began to seep into the sky, and had found it impossible to still her thoughts. No good telling herself that every worry worsens in the still watches of the night, and that all would be better when dawn broke. It wouldn't. And it wasn't.

Her mother was in good humour. She'd heard Kate return at about ten-thirty, after Helen had gone to bed. The expression on her daughter's face told her that the evening gone well, and she left the subject alone.

"Mango, Helen?" said Evangeline, passing the plate of sliced golden fruit. Helen took one sliver.

"Only one, Helen? Don't waste it – mid-season fruit are so delicious."

Helen shook her head and picked up a fork listlessly.

"Mother, I shall be playing tennis again this evening. At the Club. We had an excellent game yesterday, and dinner with Cornelius was delightful," said Kate.

"Cornelius is always good company. Please give him my best wishes and tell him that I'd be very pleased if he would pass by one day soon. In fact, we could ask him for dinner tonight. You could ask Arthur Kirkwood, too, if you see him."

"If I see him I certainly will." Kate looked so pleased with herself that Helen wanted to hit her. This wouldn't do, she decided. It couldn't go on.

"I think I'll come and play too, Kate. We could play ladies doubles if you like."

"That seems a good idea. I think I'll go about four o'clock and perhaps stay for tea?"

"No problem at all. Enjoy yourselves," said Evangeline serenely. "As long as Helen tells the the cook that there may be four of us."

Helen wanted to throw her spoon at Kate, but she controlled herself, forced a smile, and stood up.

"I'll talk to the cook," she said, quietly, trying not to mind that, as usual, it had not occurred to her sister that she should offer to do anything at all.

"Let's order the *tonga* for 3.30 then," Kate said. "I'll be ready."

I bet you will, Helen thought.

"Good," she said. "So will I."

## Chapter Forty-six

That afternoon, Helen's tennis had verve, accuracy and a vicious slice. Arthur was her partner, and they made short work of Kate and Ronnie Layland, a young man with a lisp and a mean lob. But not mean enough. Helen's returns shot about the court, just out of reach of her opponents. Her serves zipped on to the white line, fast and furious. Her volleys were murderous, her drop shots wicked.

Kate was not happy. Her intention had been to show Arthur what a graceful and clever player she was, and she was counting on Ronnie (usually such a reliable partner) to support her and show her off to her best advantage. He did his best, but Arthur and Helen were unbeatable. He rose to the challenge, and they won the match 6–1, 6–0.

"Thank you, Ronnie, Kate," said Helen, slipping her racquet into its wooden press, and tightening up the screws.

"Well played you two," said Ronnie, rather missing the point. Helen was looking very fine today, her eyes sparkling, her cheeks flushed, breathing harder than usual.

"See you inside," she said, leaving the three of them on the court as she strode off and up the flight of curving white stairs. She looks like an Amazon, thought Arthur, as he watched her go. Kate looked merely annoyed. They were proving a bit complicated, the Armstrong sisters, but he had every confidence that everything would turn out for the best. And for him, at present, the best was Helen.

\*

There were eight for supper that evening at Jacaranda Lodge. The dining table had had a leaf inserted and was now an oval. Evangeline sat at its head, the low light of candles and side lamps making her small diamond drops sparkle. Archibald Cunningham from St Xavier's was on her right, with Helen between him and Cornelius. Cassandra was next, and Kate sat between Arthur and Ronnie; she was making the most of it, working hard to sparkle.

As usual, Kate was charmingly hospitable to everyone, while Helen told an amusing story about Speech Day, which made everyone laugh.

At one point Arthur touched Helen's foot under the table, and she withdrew hers quickly. She told another story, about the portly San sister at school, who had got herself stuck in the door of the small children's Wendy House, and had to be pushed and pulled out, "like Pooh, when he was stuck in the rabbit hole," she ended, amid laughter.

"Good girl," said Cornelius, taking a sip of his cold beer, which he, like many, preferred to drink with his meals. "Has battle commenced?" he asked. "I should say you were a little bit ahead."

Helen frowned at him, and then her face relaxed.

"Yes, I suppose it has," she murmured. "I may be ahead for now, Cornelius, but I wouldn't bet on staying there!"

Arthur was flattered – it was quite clear they were fencing for his attention. Cornelius kept the conversation light, contributing a reminiscence or a joke, or a compliment when one was needed. He felt that Helen needed his support this evening, and he was generous with his enthusiasm for her tennis, her household management, her tales...

"Excellent beef, Helen," he said. "Well done. I saw you

at the bazaar today, and I think you did very well. I try to buy good meat from the stalls, but even when I send the cook, it turns out stringy. I suppose it could be the cooking though, in which case I congratulate you further."

Evangeline bridled somewhat – she preferred the myth of her own excellent housekeeping to be maintained in company, and congratulations to be addressed to her.

Cassandra and Cornelius observed the skirmishes while chatting politely to each other about trivialities. Soon it was clear that Cornelius found her unexpectedly interesting. Keen as the next man on a pretty woman, Cornelius had initially dismissed Cassandra as a frump, but it did not take long for him to decide that she made up for her plainness with a quick wit and a sense of humour.

Arthur let himself enjoy the pleasant feeling of being fought over. He thought he deserved a rest from the turbulent undercurrents in the Armstrong family. He had asked Helen to marry him, she had said she would, but then he had entered the treacherous waters of Evangeline's strong will. What more could he do? He had done his best, and now he was ready to get on with the next stage. I've done the decent thing, I've been up front and clear, he thought. I'd love to make an honest woman of Helen, but this is...

"Arthur, would you mind passing the salt?" Evangeline cut through his thoughts.

Cornelius's eyes flicked from one to the other. The use of the Christian name seemed innocuous, but he knew it indicated a shift in the power struggle. You had to hand it to the old girl, he thought. Arthur would find it much harder now to fight his corner without appearing petulant or ungrateful.

The plates were cleared, the pudding served, the glasses replenished. Then Evangeline cut through the gentle hum of chatter and tapped her glass with her fork. The chime silenced everyone.

"Thank you Cornelius, Ronnie, Arthur, Archibald, Cassandra, for coming to dinner at such short notice. It is always a pleasure to see old friends and new ones. I sincerely hope that you will continue to feel free to come and visit us three women at Jacaranda Lodge whenever you wish. We are very lucky to have such excellent company, and we are always here. That's all. Thank you. Let's go on to the verandah and have coffee."

She stood up and walked out of the room, followed obediently by Ronnie, and the urbane Archibald, looking at his watch. Helen stayed where she was, a tiny gesture of defiance (this wasn't all that difficult, she said to herself, rather enjoying it). Cassandra and Cornelius, realising their presence was not wanted, stood up immediately and went out to find a sofa where they could carry on their conversation. Cassandra collected her clutchbag and her shawl, and as she did so, gave Helen a quick glance. It said very clearly "Get on with it."

Kate hovered, unwilling to leave Helen with Arthur.

"Kate," called Evangeline. "Will you pour the coffee please?"

She left the room to sit next to Ronnie, who looked as if it were Christmas.

Arthur's expression combined discomfort, exasperation, and hope.

"Helen, I..."

She looked at him directly, her eyes challenging. She took a cigarette from the wooden box on a small table and lit it with the heavy silver lighter next to it.

"Are things any further on?" he asked. "Are we any nearer? Your mother must have got the message by now."

She inhaled deeply and bought herself some time by exhaling a cloud of smoke.

"I'm doing my best. But my mother doesn't change her mind easily. She doesn't want me to leave Ranpore and will do everything she can to stop me. I do what she tells me, you see. It's what I've been taught – Mother is always right. Mother mustn't be defied. I know you find this hard to believe. Men are so lucky, but women, especially women like me, don't have the same choice."

He nodded. "I understand, of course. But in my experience mothers are usually very keen for their daughters to get married to a man who is of good character and so on... like me."

He smiled. She did not.

"Character is not the issue. She knows what she wants and what she wants is me, here. If I marry, it must be to someone in Ranpore so that I can still be within calling distance. I can't see that changing. Kate has never been expected to..."

She stopped. Her voice became bitter.

"Kate is not someone my mother relies on. They're too alike. Kate can't see any point of view except her own. I, unfortunately, see too many."

"The only point of view at the moment is ours, surely, Helen? It's our future. Not Evangeline's "

"Well, it's her future too. She wants to live comfortably and be looked after. It is rare for people in Ranpore to leave, you know. Life is comfortable, safe, we all know each other. It doesn't feel like an outpost of Empire, but Empire itself."

He frowned. He was sensing a change in her mood. Arthur Kirkwood's focus was determined, not to say narrow. Handsome enough to please, intelligent enough to convince, failure was a new experience.

"Empire spreads wider than this, Helen. I want to see more than just this part of India. I may not even stay in this country, after a few years. There's the Middle East, Australia, Malaysia. What's to stop us seeing as much as we want to, while we're young? Come with me. I'll work for a few years, and then we can travel and see what jobs there are on other continents. Think about it, Helen. Can't you see what a life we would have?"

Her eyes filled with tears.

"Oh God!" she dashed them away with the back of her hand and pressed her wrist to her forehead.

"I'd love to see everything, everywhere. With you. I'd absolutely love it. But..." she made a decision. Her voice hardened "I really don't think I can."

Silence. The clock on the mantelshelf chimed the half hour. A low chatter came from the verandah on the other side of the double doors, and when the chimes subsided, the seconds tick-tick-ticked.

It felt to Helen as if life was dripping away like the wax from the candles on the table. Arthur got to his feet and looked down at her. She felt very small in her chair.

"You don't love me at all, do you?" he said coldly.

Helen gasped.

"That is really, really unkind of you. I love you, and I could love you more if we were given the chance."

"Take the chance. Take the chance, Helen. For goodness sake, there's no need to throw it away. Why can't you just say yes?"

She looked at him miserably.

"I've no idea. I really don't know. But I find I can't."

He looked at her with hardly any expression. She noticed a little scar on his top lip she'd not seen before, and wondered, inconsequentially, where and how he had got it.

He opened the doors and walked out, leaving her sitting very still and alone at the table, her face in shadow, her shoulders lit by a single lamp.

"Mrs Armstrong, Evangeline," she heard him say, all politeness and charm. "Thank you for a delicious dinner."

"You're very welcome, Arthur. Come and join us for coffee. There is a *tonga* at the gate for Cornelius, but I'm sure he'll stay for a Scotch. It is only just nine o'clock."

"In that case, the night is still young."

Helen in the other room winced at the cliché and waited.

"How would it be if you all came to *my* verandah for a change, and took a glass with me?" said Arthur. "Or we could drop into the Club? May I tempt you?"

Helen strained to hear the response. Surely her mother would refuse. It was not her custom to go out after supper.

"I think I'll have to decline, Arthur. I'm an old woman and I retire early. But Kate might like to join you – at the Club, I think, not your quarters. And Cornelius?"

"I'm of your generation, my dear, and I'll also decline the offer. Thank you. Another time perhaps? My bed calls me. May I offer you a lift, Cassandra? I'm passing Auchterlony. But perhaps Helen …"

Kate, who was walking out to change her shoes, turned back irritably and spoke in a high, clipped voice:

"Oh, I don't think Helen would like to come. She doesn't go out after dinner either. She prefers a good book or an intelligent conversation."

Helen walked out to the verandah.

"I would indeed like to come," she said. "But I'd be intruding. I think it better if I stayed here, with, as you say, a good book. I hope you both have a very pleasant evening."

Cornelius frowned and said nothing. Cassandra, who had stood up to accept Cornelius' offer, sat down again, and lifted her coffee cup to her lips.

Cassandra looked at Arthur, willing him to argue, to include Helen, to insist, but instead he answered: "I'm sorry you feel that way. It would, of course, be good to have you with us, but if you prefer to stay here, that is up to you. You must – as with everything – make up your own mind."

Everyone looked at Helen, who smiled, her eyes flat.

"I have. And so have you. I wish you every happiness."

Kate's eyes were bright, triumphant. She'd won. Arthur

was as good as hers. She did not see the regret in his eyes, and ignored the misery in Helen's.

"Very well then," he said, after a few seconds, accepting the inevitable. "Let's go, Kate. Goodnight everyone. Thank you for a delightful evening Evangeline, Helen. "

"Take the *tonga* and send it back for me," said Cornelius. "You don't mind if Cassandra and I spend a few more minutes with you, do you, Helen? We won't be keeping you up?"

"Not at all. I'll pour you another whisky, Cornelius. More coffee, Cassandra?"

Arthur and Kate left for the Club, Evangeline for her bedroom, and soon only the three of them sat on the verandah.

"What are you doing, you silly girl?" Cassandra snapped.

Helen inhaled deeply on a cigarette.

"What does it look like? I can't win this one, Cassandra. Not against the two of them."

"You could, you know," murmured Cornelius, looking down into his glass. "You have your allies, Helen. You may not believe it, but there are plenty of people who'd be very happy to see you married to someone worthy of you. My only problem is, I have to confess, that after tonight I'm not at all sure that's Arthur."

Helen nodded bleakly.

"It's my fault, not his," she said. "I just can't do it."

And that was it.

Helen could have changed her future that evening. If she'd accepted Arthur's proposal, and stood up to Kate and Evangeline, she would have begun a life away from her mother and away from Ranpore. Instead, she made sure she was going nowhere.

## Chapter Forty-seven

In the following days and weeks, Helen's heart was heavy; her spirit, usually wry, generous and good-humoured, became flat. She managed the house, went on with her work at school, and watched as Kate and Arthur grew closer. Sometimes she caught his eye, but both would instantly look away, or turn to talk to someone else.

Doris saw all this and felt very sad for her friend. She and Cassandra had formed a tacit Supporters Club. They watched Arthur and Kate together, and apart. He was handsome and preoccupied, busy at his job in Ranpore, and looked like a man with a mission.

Kate seemed very happy and prettier than ever. She proudly wore Arthur's mother's Victorian ring, its diamond flanked by two sapphires. He had brought it with him "in case I met someone I wanted to give it to," he'd told her.

Arthur was an ambitious man, itching to get settled into work and married life, and expecting to rise through the ranks, his wife at his side. He didn't spend time on introspection. His attraction to Helen had been instant, and he had quickly decided to do something about it. The obstacles had been unexpected, but he simply did not understand why Helen couldn't get her own way. He wanted to move on to the next stage of his life and although he thought Evangeline's bullying despicable, he resented what he saw as Helen's lack of backbone. Surely if she really loved him she would have fought harder?

He was looking around for the next step, and it did not take him long to accept an engineer's job at Tindharia Tea Estate. The next step was Assistant Manager, and, if all went well, a move as Manager to the big house on the hill. He was given a month's notice to start, and Kate and he filled that time with fun and games that livened up life for her in Ranpore Cantonments as never before. They spent a great deal of time together, rarely alone.

He dined at Jacaranda Lodge, she had supper with him at the Club, and Arthur organised various outings and picnics, with or without friends. There was always something planned. Doris, watching from the sidelines, wondered how Kate would like it when she and Arthur were alone together on a remote tea estate. A family would occupy her, of course, but Doris felt angry at that thought. It shouldn't be Kate's family, it should be Helen's.

Kate gave no sign that she'd considered this. She, too, was impatient. She wanted to become Mrs Kirkwood without delay, and pressed Evangeline to set the wedding date as early as could be.

Evangeline had resisted, as only she knew how, but three weeks after Arthur had left Ranpore she'd relented, to Helen's surprise. She gave no explanation, but suddenly the big day was to take place in a few months' time.

If anyone raised an eyebrow Evangeline would answer: "He is such an energetic young man. Going places. They're young and there is no reason they should not start their new life. I've always brought my children up to know that they're a part of a family, so I've no doubt I'll see her as often as she can arrange it. There seems no reason for any delay. Life will go on."

Life did. Kate glowed with triumph – and something else. A softening around the edges which everyone put down to happiness, proof that she was doing the right thing. People began to look forward to the celebration.

Arthur was expected back in Ranpore a week before his wedding day, which gave Kate time to collect all the equipment necessary to start married life in what was going to be a comfortable but remote part of Bengalnent. They would move to Tindharia together as soon as the formalities were over, and their possessions and wedding presents would be sent on ahead.

Of course, Kate and Evangeline turned to Helen to help them organise the day, and Helen, as always, got on with it. There were discussions about bridesmaids, about seating, about the service and the hymns. Helen planned and prioritised, organised the menu, the flowers, the dressmaker. Doris and Cassandra noticed she was losing weight: her normally sturdy body was becoming bony, her cheeks more hollow, her clothes looser.

Dorothea, at the school, had asked if she felt all right.

"Absolutely, thank you. Never better," Helen told her, brisk and efficient as always. But she no longer had the gleam in her eye that made her company so comfortable and amusing.

One day, in the midst of all the lists, Doris said to her, firmly:

"Helen, stop a moment. I need to talk to you. No, don't look shifty. Everything's under control, and we can take an hour off to chat. Come on..."

She took her friend off with her to her house and made her sit down on the verandah with a cold drink and a soft cushion behind her back.

"Now, Helen Armstrong. This has got to stop. I know you very well indeed and you are not happy. You should be choosing the silk for *your* wedding dress, the seed pearls for *your* veil. You shouldn't be working yourself to a frazzle, organising a perfect day for your sister, who simply does not deserve to marry the man you love."

For a moment Helen looked as if she would cry. Then she collected herself and answered lightly, "I don't love Arthur, Doris. I couldn't, could I? Or I'd be devastated. And I'm not. I'm a more fickle person than people think."

Doris glared at her.

"Don't give me all that nonsense. I can see you are–"

"What, quieter? That's true. Things are changing and I'm getting used to the idea. Unhappy? I'm not. I've accepted that I'm staying here, in the comfort and familiarity of my old home, with my old friends. I'm very lucky to have you, for one. Cassandra, for another. Sometimes it's best to let wounds heal over, without picking at them. I'm an inveterate picker and it's not helpful."

She took out a piece of paper from her handbag. "Now, shall we have Brahms or Bach?

## Chapter Forty-eight

Time sped by. The wedding day drew nearer, Kate looked prettier every day, her smooth skin blooming softly. Helen saw to everything, Arthur would be back a week before the wedding day, the whole of Ranpore would see them make their vows and then they would be gone. Life would return to normal.

On her way back from her weekly trip to the bazaar, Helen stopped at the post office, as usual. She bought a stamp for a letter from Kate to Arthur, and picked up the post for Jacaranda Lodge from the man behind the chicken wire screen at the dusty counter. There were two dreary-looking brown envelopes for her mother and an aerogramme for her, the address typed.

She opened it in the *tonga* on the way home.

"*My dear Helen,*" it began, innocuously. She turned over the page to see Arthur's signature. Her carefully-cultivated *sang froid* deserted her. She felt relieved that she was alone. Biting her lip, she looked over towards the dusty horizon. Sunshine lit the tops of the trees, and brought out their vivid greens and yellows. The monsoon had finished three weeks earlier and splashed the world with colour; the paddy was growing in wide flat emerald stretches on either side of the road and the jacaranda trees were hazy with their blue grey flowers. Helen seemed suddenly to be looking down from somewhere far away. She surprised herself by thinking that the harvest this year would be a good one, the thought neutrally, and then returned to the pale blue paper in her hand.

*My dear Helen,*

*I had to write this letter before I return in two weeks' time. The wedding is arranged, Kate is wearing my mother's ring and we are going to be man and wife – very far away from Ranpore.*

*I'm not good at writing letters like this – Kate, if you were to ask her, would tell you that.*

*I want to say – before I make my vows – that we could have done very well together. That is now past. I accept that you feel you cannot marry me, and I also accept my responsibilities towards your sister. I know she doesn't love me, not deeply, and if I've a fear, it's that we may bore each other before long. I'd wish that it had not turned out this way, but things have taken their course.*

*Kate will be a good wife and a good mother, I know. She can charm people, she's pretty, and above all, she wants to be married. I'm sure most marriages work perfectly well along those lines. For a moment, I thought that you and I could have a greater connection, but that is not to be.*

*I have thought about writing this letter to you many times and have hesitated because I know I should not, but if you change your mind before our wedding day, please tell me. It won't be easy to disentangle, but better now than later. I want you, Helen. I always have and I probably always will. I wish we had not got ourselves into this sticky mess. But you give me any sign, any at all, that you would come away with me and be my wife, I'm prepared to face the music. Even if everyone thinks I'm a cad.*

*But I'm not hopeful – I know your sense of duty better than that – so, unless I hear to the contrary, I must, with a heavy heart, accept your decision.*

*I send you my greatest admiration and best wishes for your future.*

*With my love, Arthur*

Helen sat as still as she could in the jolting *tonga*. She wanted more than anything to run away with him, to pack a small bag and meet him at the airport. Her thoughts were incoherent, full of hopes and happiness and fear.

And she knew he was right – Kate wanted to be married, to anyone suitable. He was new and glamorous and thus appealing, but he was, after all, not unique. Only to Helen. She felt warm and loved and happy when she was with him. It was indeed a caddish thing to do. How could she consider his proposition for a second? How could he have made it? Could she do this? A dark terror descended immediately. Impossible. How could she face Evangeline? Kate? The whole of Ranpore? And herself?

*But you will be gone*, said a voice in her head.

*Yes, but you will never be able to come back*, said another.

*So what*? her imp wanted to know.

I can't. I can't hurt my family...

*But they've never minded very much about hurting you.*

This went on for some time, until she'd a headache and was no clearer about what she ought to do. She needed to talk to someone. Not a close friend, who would take her side. That ruled Doris out. Someone who would not be shocked at her heretical thoughts, but someone who knew her well, and understood the situation. Cornelius.

"To Acacia Avenue, Number 27," she told Bodhi.

He nodded. "Clandon *Sahib*. Yes, *Memsa'ab*."

It was not long before she was sitting very straight, clutching a glass of cold water, her face pinched and pale.

Cornelius had not looked surprised to see her. After dropping a light kiss on her dry cheek, he had invited her to sit inside instead of on the verandah.

"I think we need to be private, don't we, my dear?"

Once she was comfortable, she looked at him, and held out the letter, which by now was damp and crumpled.

Cornelius took his half-moon glasses off his forehead.

"Well?" he asked, folding it in half when he had read it. The room was very quiet.

"Cornelius, you were my father's oldest and best friend." Helen was almost whispering. "I'm apparently very much his daughter, more than Kate. So people tell me. You have known me all my life, you know my mother, you know me better than anyone else could."

Cornelius nodded slowly, still saying nothing, his spectacles balanced on his head.

"And I know your mother very well indeed too. It seems to me she's the most influential person in this whole dilemma. You, on the other hand, are the most important. We are discussing your life here. The rest of your life. What do you want, Helen?"

She looked at him miserably.

"I – I – I want to be happy, but I want everyone else to be happy, too. Does that sound stupid?"

"No, of course not. Very laudable, if a little naïve."

"I know. Someone has to be disappointed, don't they?"

He sat back in his chair, and tapped his wrinkled brown fingers on its wooden arm.

"Why should that be you?"

"Because – my mother expects... And it would upset Kate terribly. Humiliate her. How can I do that, just because..."

He waited.

"Because?"

"Because I want to leave Ranpore and have a *life*. A *life*, Cornelius. Not just be married. I can't bear the idea of checking if the tablecloths at Jacaranda Lodge are starched, and crocheting into the evenings, and occasionally organising a correct dinner...I just can't. Not on my own."

"You won't be on your own. Your mother will be very much in evidence."

Helen nodded glumly.

"I know. She has made it very clear that I'm expected –

by father, too – to look after everything here."

"Your father, Helen Armstrong, was a fair and warm-hearted man. I admired him very much, and I'm certain that he would never have drawn up a life sentence for you of this kind. He would have hoped that someone would care for Evangeline if he were not here to do it, but I don't think he'd have expected you to give up a life you want."

"That's the whole point, Cornelius. *Do* I want it? Enough? Am I being blinded by novelty, the fact that Arthur wants *me*, instead of Kate? Do I want to marry him, or do I want to marry him to get away?"

"Well, that's something only you can decide. You can use me as a sounding board – and your friends Doris and the delightful Cassandra – but I can't tell you what to do. Except to remind you that life lasts a very long time!"

## Chapter Forty-nine

Helen went home soon afterwards. She thought of all the reasons why she could not go back on what she'd decided, mostly because she would find it so hard to go against her family, but Cornelius had given her food for thought. Life was a long time, and could she bear to spend it as her mother's sidekick until she died?

She read the crumpled letter again, and put it carefully away in her handbag.

At home, Kate and Evangeline were sitting opposite each other on the verandah; preoccupied with their own talk, neither asked where she'd been. Kate was looking discontented, and rather pale, and her mother had the expression she wore when she'd laid down some law or other. Bland, unchanging, immovable.

Kate suddenly stood up and walked very fast towards her bedroom. She returned ten minutes later, and sat down again in the seat she'd left.

"Is everything all right?" Helen asked. "You look a bit uncomfortable. Here, here are some letters. One from Arthur for you, Kate, and a couple for you, mother."

She placed them on the table, and Kate snatched up hers. Her mother left the other two where they were, and frowned at Kate, who had ripped open the envelope.

She read the first lines, and then looked at Helen.

"Uncomfortable? No. Why do you ask? What makes you think so?

"Nothing really. You look a bit pale."

"Kate has been overdoing it, Helen," said her mother slowly and clearly. "She is overexcited – Arthur is returning in a few weeks, and she's looking forward to seeing him. And there are still bits and pieces to do."

Helen nodded, knowing that any arrangements were going to fall to her.

"Don't worry, Kate. It'll be fine. Everything is going smoothly, and if not, well, we can manage."

"Oh, everything is going smoothly, except that I feel tired and a bit queasy and I'm missing my husband to be, and mother won't let me go and spend time with him. It would make me so much happier, and I don't see why I can't go."

It was an odd demand. Kate was no adventurer. The journey by train would take several days, and it had been decided that there was no need for her to travel. Arthur would come back for her, and they would leave together, with a comfortable hotel room booked on the way, and a car to meet them at the railway station for the five-hour drive to Tindharia on roads ravaged by the recent monsoon.

Helen didn't know what to say.

Kate stared crossly at her mother, who tightened her lips and sighed.

"There is no reason for you to waste your time and tire yourself out by going to see Arthur. The roads are terrible, you can't get there by train, he's busy, and won't welcome distraction. Leave him to get settled, and then when you get there, you can work on making everything as comfortable as you know how. Men appreciate being left alone, Kate, when they have work to do. As much as they appreciate coming home to a welcoming atmosphere and a pretty wife."

"And a..." Kate stopped.

Her mother frowned at Kate and rang the bell beside her. Helen, puzzled, looked from one to the other. What had Kate meant to say, and why had her mother cut her off? She felt once more the force of the two of them joined against her.

"*Chai*, Sudham, please." Evangeline turned back to Helen. "Is there anything that still needs attending to? I had planned to go to the Club for Bridge tonight. Would you like to come with me?"

"I'd prefer to stay here, Mother. I'm tired. Kate and I could have supper here and go to bed early."

Evangeline looked as though she was going to demand her company, but thought better of it, and nodded.

"Then I shall go alone. I'm sure the Cannons or the Cornwallises will bring me home. Sudham," she called, "please order Bodhi to be here at seven this evening."

## Chapter Fifty

Helen was not looking forward to an evening at home with her sister. They had, up till now, managed to avoid one, but tonight, Evangeline's departure had left them together.

Evangeline climbed laboriously into the *tonga*, settling down on the gaudy cushions with much sighing and smoothing of her skirt. She was wearing her usual black and resembled Queen Victoria at her jubilee. Helen wondered if she would wave a regal hand as the *tonga* drew away; she rather hoped she would, but was disappointed.

The sisters made a pretence of reading quietly on the verandah. Helen flicked open the crumpled pages of an old *Vogue*. The model on the cover was reclining, rather stiffly, on a white sandy beach, her hat beside her. The caption inside described her *"two-piece beach suit in West Indian colours"*. Helen wished she could join her. She looked at the word *Vogue* carelessly outlined with rope in the sand, and wondered what it would be like to lie semi-clad in the sunshine without risking sunstroke, or the interested glances of the crowd that would gather should she ever dare to try.

"Everything seems to be going very well." Kate's voice was tight and deliberately light.

Her sister nodded. "Yes. I don't want to jinx it, but I think we have most things covered. About a hundred guests, church booked, flowers, food, music, tents... It'll be a glamorous and warm-hearted affair."

Helen spoke pleasantly. Anyone watching would have thought they didn't know each other very well.

There was a silence.

Then they both spoke at once, and fell silent again.

"Helen..."

"Kate..."

"You first," said Helen.

"I wanted to say – I'm very sorry if I've made you sad about Arthur. But you were never going to marry him, were you?"

Sad? Was that the word? The word for the scooped out emptiness that Helen carried around with her every day? The word that covered the resentment, almost hatred, that she felt for her mother and sister?

"Not sad exactly," she said slowly. "I'm not sure I'd have dared to marry him. But I did want to."

Kate looked guilty, and began to bluster.

"Well, Arthur thinks you didn't really want to. He says

that you left the field free for anyone, and he says that he's very pleased it's me."

"Well, if that's what he says..."

Helen thought of the letter and kept quiet. She'd thought of little else for two days: of course she wanted to be with Arthur. Of course she wanted to leave Ranpore – but the obstacles remained the same.

She sat up straighter. Opened her mouth. She needed to speak now, to tell her sister that she couldn't go on with the charade. That Arthur was waiting and the wedding would just have to ...

"Helen, I've something to say."

"Me too – but go on. You first."

The air felt thick and turbulent, as if the oxygen had been sucked out of it.

Kate blushed.

"Well – before Arthur left, we... I..."

Helen felt the cold water in her veins turn to ice.

"I... We..." Kate was having trouble continuing. Suddenly Helen lost her temper.

"Oh, for Heaven's sake," she snapped. "What the hell are you trying to say? Let me guess. You and Arthur went to bed together? You're no longer a virgin? Well, that's a surprise! Actually, the only surprise is that you waited so long – or perhaps you didn't? You were always pretty keen on..."

Kate stared. The spiteful words coming out of her sister's mouth were so unexpected and out of character. Helen was going to continue, feeling that she had to stop whatever Kate was going to tell her. She knew she would not want to hear it.

Suddenly Helen felt absolutely certain. She knew what Kate was trying to tell her, and she knew she didn't want to hear it. She felt a distaste and a cold dislike of her sister, and spoke without softening her words.

"You're going to have a baby, aren't you, Kate? Mother

knows and Arthur knows. Of course. That's why Arthur agreed to marry you so quickly, and why Mother agreed to move the date of the wedding. Oh, how stupid of me!"

Kate's eyes filled with tears, embarrassment, shame and triumph mingling in her face. They spilled, and made her look soft and very young indeed, as if she'd been caught stealing a *paisa* from her mother's purse. She sobbed, looking at Helen, her bottom lip quivering. Helen noticed that, as usual, her nose didn't go red and she didn't sniff.

But she remained unmoved. Her sister sobbed in front of her, and she watched impassively as her tears ran down her pale cheeks. Eventually she relented, took out her handkerchief and passed it to her.

"Wipe your eyes, Kate. It's not the end of the world. At least you're getting married. And you're leaving Ranpore, to have a family. And Mother doesn't seem to think it the worst thing in the world. You'll be far away when you start to show and your dress will fit you perfectly on your wedding day."

"I didn't mean to, Helen. I really, truly didn't. It was just..."

"Please. I don't want to hear about it. When were you going to tell me? Were you going to tell me at all?"

Kate nodded. "I wanted to. But mother said..."

There it was again. The complicity, the ganging up. She couldn't stop herself.

"You're the most selfish, unkind sister anyone could have," Helen cried. "I thought we were close, that you loved me, that you of all people would never be so unkind as to steal, yes, *steal*, someone I ..."

"I didn't steal him. I didn't! Mother agrees. She says you couldn't love him, or you would fight for him, and whatever she thinks wouldn't matter."

"Oh, don't be so naïve. She's encouraged you to nip in under the fence, like a jackal stealing chickens. And that's what you've done, Kate. You *have* stolen Arthur, and I don't think I can ever forgive you, either of you. But..."

"Stop it, Helen. Stop it. This isn't you speaking. You don't love him. You can't. Mother says so, Arthur says so, I think so. And anyway, even if you did, it's too late. Yes. I'm pregnant. I've written to Arthur to tell him."

Of course she had. Of course Evangeline had encouraged her to marry quickly and leave before there was any scandal. Kate and Evangeline would always stick together, and Helen – useful, reliable, duty-bound Helen – would always be different, left out, but always *there*.

And now she'd no choice. She would always be there, and Kate would have Arthur and Arthur's baby.

Kate was looking at her pleadingly.

"Be pleased. Please be pleased. I really want you to be pleased for me."

Helen nodded, and stood up. Her pale face was very serious.

She looked at her sister for five seconds.

"I wish you all well. How could I not? I'll help you as much as I can with your wedding, and then you will leave, and I'll be here, a maiden aunt, a maiden sister, a spinster," she said bitterly. "I've no choice – unless someone else I might care for turns up, to stay. But that is not very likely. Arthur was a breath of fresh air, and air moves on."

She angrily wiped at her eyes with a handkerchief she took out from her sleeve, her mouth puckering up, trying very hard not to cry: "I only have one request. That you never ever lie to me again. Never, never, never..."

"It wasn't a lie. I never lied."

"Okay. Lying by omission. Which in my book is just the same. I cannot bear it. Do you want my permission to marry Arthur? Is that what you're asking? Well, you can have it, for what it's worth. And I'll try to forget that your child could have been mine."

Helen walked away very carefully, picking up her

handbag from beside the chair. She went slowly down the steps into the garden; a blast of heartless, violent heat made the perspiration pop out on her forehead and her top lip.

She went to the flowerbed full of scarlet canna lilies and frothy blood-red hibiscus flowers. The evening sun gave dark shadows, and a breeze made the flower heads shiver on their stems. A hornet buzzed past.

She walked over to the bonfire the *mali* had lit the previous evening to get rid of the stems and branches he had pruned. It was still hot, its core glowing red.

She took the letter out of her bag, folded it and tore it into tiny pieces. They fluttered down into the embers, flared and in a moment shrivelled into dusty ash.

## Chapter Fifty-one

On the night before the wedding, Helen checked everything one last time. Cassandra and Doris had helped her make sure the food, the drinks, the flowers, the table settings, the seating plan were all in order.

"First the champagne, Achad, and then light cold drinks," Helen said gently. "*Nimbu pani* and iced water for the ladies, and beer for the gentlemen. People should arrive after the service at – what? Half past one? So lunch at a quarter past two. Please make sure that there is a mixture of curries, and plenty of fresh tomato chutney. Ice cream for pudding, and of course the wedding cake. You have that?"

"In the cold room, *Memsa'ab*. And all the drink is on ice. Don't worry."

"I know, I know, Achad, you have done all this many times, but my mother would be mortified if anything went wrong, and *Memsa'ab* Kate – well, it's her big day."

He nodded. Said nothing. She caught a tiny glimpse of

something in his eyes that could have been sympathy, or respect. She looked away at once, and moved towards the top table set with starched damask and crisp thick napkins, and Evangeline's own knives and forks.

"I hardly ever get a chance to use the silver," her mother had said. "And I can't think of a better time. And the crystal vases – they're perfect, with the *épergne*, and the table runners. Helen, you must make sure to have them laid out carefully."

"Yes, mother. All will be lovely, I promise. We'll give Kate the send-off she deserves."

Her mother gave her a quick glance, but found nothing in Helen's expression to take issue with, so returned to the list in her hand.

"Transport. We have the loan of Henry's car. Kind of him. It has been cleaned, of course?"

She'd the grace to look a little embarrassed as Helen raised an eyebrow.

"Just try and stop Abdul showing off his motor to its best advantage, Mother. He has been shining and buffing and polishing every ten minutes since he heard we were using it. You and I are being dropped at the Club first, after the service, and then Kate and Arthur will come on in style. Bodhi'll be there to help with transport – he, too, has been decorating his wagon. It's bedecked with tassels and flowers. Rather beautiful."

She grinned, and enjoyed her mother's grimace.

"Well, there aren't many motors to go round, so we will have to be grateful," Evangeline said, sighing.

"Indeed."

Helen was well aware that the next day was Evangeline's moment of glory, and although she accepted her role, she'd a tiny, wicked wish to upset the apple cart.

She squashed it. She would not let the wedding guests locate any fly in the ointment. Everything would go off as smoothly as she could arrange it; it was a matter of pride.

*

On the day Arthur Kirkwood married Kate Armstrong the weather was the same as it always was in November – warm, sunny, clear. The rains had washed away the dust that had collected over the summer months, and now the air felt fresh and the landscape new and clean.

Helen joined her mother for breakfast on the verandah, relishing the peace of the morning. It didn't last long. As Helen poured herself a cup of coffee, Kate appeared, flushed and agitated.

"Helen, could you come and help me please. I've tried to do my hair, but it won't stay right. I wanted to get ready in good time. Could you please come and see what you can do with it."

Putting down her napkin and accepting the inevitable, Helen stood up.

"Of course, Kate. Let's get you looking beautiful! Please excuse us, Mother."

Evangeline smiled.

"Of course. Every bride is excited on her wedding day. Off you go."

In her bedroom, Kate looked at herself sideways in the mirror.

"Oh, Helen, I hope everything is going to be all right. I hope my dress is going to look pretty. Should I have chosen lace? Is satin going to be too hot?"

Helen laughed.

"It's a bit late to change your mind now, you silly thing! Stop fretting. You'll look absolutely lovely!"

Kate met her sister's eyes in the mirror.

"Nobody knows about this…" looking down at her smooth stomach, "…and I hope Arthur isn't just marrying me because of it. He does love me, don't you think?"

Helen looked coolly at Kate.

"You should know that, Kate, if anyone does. You are

going to be the mother of his child. He's taking you away to start a new life with him. You're going to spend a lot of time together, so he must think that he wants to do that."

Helen suddenly looked serious.

"I shouldn't ask, I know, but – do *you* love *him*, Kate?"

She couldn't help herself.

Kate didn't answer for a moment. She smoothed her sleeve and adjusted a curl of hair. She put the palms of both her hands on the dressing table in front of her and took a deep breath.

"I know you think I stole him from you. I probably did. I expect he would prefer to have you walking down the aisle today, but there you are. It's me. I'm having the baby, and you're staying here. I'm not sure what I'm going to, and I don't know Arthur very well at all. Or if we have much in common. Do you think you do?"

Helen wanted to scream: *Of course I do. Of course I understand him. I love him. I want to make him happy, to make sure he's comfortable, to look after him, but also to talk together and read books and go for walks and watch the birds.*

Kate watched the emotions that crossed her sister's face, but said nothing.

Helen turned briefly away to look out of the window and then turned back.

"I'm sure everything will work out for the best," she said levelly. "Now, come on, finishing touches, best foot forward. In a little while you must greet the servants who are waiting to wish you well."

*

Helen arrived at the church at ten to meet Doris and Cassandra and check that everything was as it should be. Doris wore pale turquoise blue, which highlighted the warm honey of her skin and her glossy dark hair. She looked very elegant beside her plump and smiling friend, who had decided on sprigged cotton, mostly pink and mauve, which clashed with her complexion. It didn't matter – she, like Doris, was putting her best face forward.

Helen looked every inch the elegant maiden sister of the bride. She wore soft grey, with a pretty pink and cream corsage of fern and flowers, and a necklace of moonstones set in gold. From her ears dangled small moonstone drops, and Doris put up a hand to touch them.

"They were my grandmother's," Helen said. "I never met her, but mother gave them to me this morning. I was touched."

"Really? Sounds like bribery and corruption to me. But you look lovely, Helen, really stylish. Everyone will be looking at you!"

Helen shook her head.

"No, they won't, or if they do, they'll just be checking whether I mind about Kate and Arthur. Kate looks absolutely ravishing in satin and lace, with a mass of flowers. Really, she's shining with happiness and..."

"...Triumph?" asked her friend, sweetly. Cassandra said nothing but couldn't help a little nod of agreement.

"Listen you two, I need a bit of help here. This really doesn't help. There is nothing I can do, and I'm not going to be pitied."

"That's lucky, because pity ain't what I'm feeling at present," said Cassandra sharply. "Fury, yes. A frustration at this ridiculous situation, perhaps... oh, all right, all right. I'll stop. As long as you know that I know what is really going on, and that I wish things were different."

Doris became efficient and crisp.

"What's there to do? Nothing, I imagine. You have Achad and his troops, Henry's motor is at the ready, the church is full of flowers, the vicar knows his stuff, and all you have to do now is get through today with a smile on your face. I'm right beside you."

"And I," said Cassandra clearly. "Right here."

# Chapter Fifty-two

"Well," said Doris, as the three women sat watching the bride and groom walk among the tables, bending over to talk to the guests. "You've done a grand job, Helen. Everything looks wonderful. It's gone off without a hitch. They'll be off soon, and we'll stay here in Ranpore. We must be sure to enjoy ourselves – and show – er – people that we don't miss them one little bit."

By now the noise in the room was high, as champagne toasts had been drunk, and the gentlemen were settling in to some whisky. Cheeks were flushed, the hot air stirred only a little by the overhead fans. Ladies were using fans of their own to cool their faces. Even Evangeline had relaxed and was laughing with Leonora Cornwallis and even Dorothea Cartwright.

Helen decided that she could come off duty. When Kate and Arthur appeared at her elbow, she stood up and gave Kate a hug. Over her head she met Arthur's eyes.

"I wish you both the greatest happiness," she said. "I hope you know that."

She would have said more, but Dudley came up behind Arthur and clapped him on the back.

"Well done, old man. You're a lucky dog. The prettiest girl in Ranpore. Or rather, one of the two prettiest."

He bowed clumsily to Helen, and knocked over a glass of water. Cassandra immediately produced a thick napkin, and patted the wet fabric; a bearer sent by the vigilant Achad removed the cloth from her hand, and spread another to take its place. It had been a welcome distraction.

"No harm done," Arthur said firmly. "Thank you Dudley. If you'll excuse me I need to talk to Mr and Mrs Cannon over there. They're waving at me. Kate, I'll be back in a second."

"Oh, do go over. If you don't mind I won't come, too. I've smiled till my face aches. I just want to sit down here and rest for a moment. Come here, Dudley. Sit down beside me."

Helen, her cheeks flushed, walked out on to the balcony outside for some air. She looked out across the tennis courts below, the polo field, into the distance towards the river, thinking about the times she'd been here before, to play or to dance, to celebrate the visit of a grandee or to listen to a talk, or to choir practice. She wondered what she was going to do now?

"Hello, Helen."

She wasn't surprised to hear the deep Welsh voice. She felt a twinge of guilt, a sense of the inevitable, and turned to face him, two feet away, holding a glass of iced water.

"I thought you'd like this. Kate is talking to her friends, and enjoying herself, so I took a moment."

Helen frowned.

"You should be inside with Kate. You're marrying her, and extending our family. A very good idea."

She'd used up her good humour, and her voice was tired.

"What are you going to do, Helen? When Kate is gone?"

"Oh, I expect I'll carry on as I've always done. My mother will get older, I'll have a little more time to myself, I'll continue to watch birds, do a bit of painting, reading, supervise gardening. Cassandra and Doris will be here, and we'll get along famously." And then the dam burst. "Oh, hell! Why did you come here and make a mess of my life? I hate you. I wish I'd never met you."

"You still do care for me, then?"

"Oh, for goodness sake, why ask me that – now? You've just made some promises in a church, you're going to be a father, although nobody knows that yet. You and Kate are married, for God's sake. Married. I'm a maiden sister, and soon to be a maiden aunt. I..."

He looked into her eyes. Neither spoke. He was near enough to smell her scent, and for a moment he felt like taking her in his arms.

Instinctively, she turned her head away.

"This is ridiculous. Where's Kate? My mother?"

Tears again! They trickled down, smudging her eye makeup. He offered her his handkerchief, and her mascara left a sooty mark on the starched white cotton.

"I had better go back," he said, taking it from her and tucking it into his top pocket.

His shoes creaked on the polished red stone as he walked back in through the French windows. She picked up the glass she'd placed on the top of the low, whitewashed wall, and followed him.

Kate watched them both, her face blank, hard to read. She met Helen's eyes defiantly. There was possession, determination, knowledge in her stare. She'd won. She was now Mrs Arthur Kirkwood, and she knew that however much her husband and sister might regret it, there was no going back. The message to them both was very clear.

He's mine, and I'm not letting him go.

# INDIA
# 2006

# Chapter Fifty-three

*Email:*

*Dear Julia*

*I'm sending this email from the Imperial Hotel in Delhi to let you know that I'm in India.*

*A couple of things. One, I've just been told by Aaron Rabinowitz at Cranleigh & Millford that they have, in principle, accepted the manuscript of your Indian book: not quite a novel, not quite non-fiction – sounds interesting. And I'm impressed that you have placed it so efficiently, without my help. Makes me feel a little redundant, but I wish you well.*

*Which brings me to my second point.*

*I've never minded leaving a woman, so I assumed life would go on as normal, without you. But you matter more than that, I now realise.*

*I miss you, Julia. As an assistant – that goes without saying. As a friend, certainly. And as a lover, of course. More than the rest.*

*So – I'd like to try to make things better between us. My father asked me to come to India with him to have a look at one of his businesses, but I'll finish this in a few days, and then take about a week off. Please reply to this email if you a)are prepared to see me and b)where you'd like me to stay. I'll arrange my travel and accommodation around your preference.*

*There is unfinished business between us, Julia, and I'd like to clear that up.*

*I hope we can at least be friends.*

*With love*

*Hari*

# Chapter Fifty-four

*Email:*

*Dear Hari*

*Thank you for your email.*

*As you're in India, it seems churlish not to invite you to stay!*
*J.J. and Pierre are in Paris for a few months but he has told me*
*that I'm welcome to use the house as I wish, and as you know*
*there are plenty of spare bedrooms. Let me know when you're*
*planning to get here, and I'll meet you. The train is perfectly*
*comfortable, but I expect you'll want to fly? Either way, let me*
*know.*
*Julia*

Julia pressed 'Send' quickly. She'd avoided replying to him for most of the morning. His email had been a surprise, not altogether unwelcome. Unsettling certainly.

She had returned to London a week after he had left her in India to sort out her flat and her belongings, to check on the progress of her divorce, and to confirm with Annie that her PhD was progressing alongside her other writing. She had seen Hari, but their meeting had been stilted. Since then, over the following six months, she had visited Ranpore twice, spending a month at Jacaranda Lodge, writing and researching. Then she had decided to come for longer and it had not taken her long to settle into her new life.

She started writing in the cool of the morning, by seven, and stopped for breakfast at half past eight. Clutching a cup of coffee (she'd made sure to bring stocks of her favourite coffee beans with her), she would go to the room she used as her office, where the air-conditioner whirred to keep her and the laptop comfortable. She worked for a few hours more, stopping for lunch and an hour's rest, and then continued until the bearer lit the mosquito coils on the verandah.

And now this simple existence, enlivened sometimes by an invitation to dinner, to Bridge at the Club, to an exhibition, by an occasional visitor, a sightseeing trip to a nearby fort, or further to Lucknow or Calcutta, was going to be interrupted. Hari's personality took up a great deal of space. He expected attention, and usually got it. Did she have this attention to spare?

"You're looking into the distance. Does this mean you're inventing something interesting, or just that you're letting your brain have a rest?"

It was Auntie Joyce, the old friend of Helen's she'd met at J.J.'s party. She had become a friend and often dropped in for an hour or so.

"How lovely to see you," Julia cried. "I'm delighted! Come and sit down. Sireet! Could you bring us–"

She looked enquiringly at Auntie Joyce.

"*Nimbu pani*? Yes, that would be good. Two please."

Sireet inclined his head and disappeared, returning a few minutes later with a laden tray.

"Just here, thanks. On this table."

The Lloyd Loom chair creaked as Auntie Joyce sat down on its rosebud-printed cushion.

"Do you need to put any of your shopping into the fridge?" asked Julia. "Or should Sireet tell your taxi to take it home? Then he can come back for you – how about sharing a sandwich with me? Nothing special, but it's nearly lunchtime."

Auntie Joyce nodded, and the arrangements were made. They settled down comfortably and Joyce looked hard at Julia.

"I feel, for some reason I can't really put my finger on, that you are a bit distracted," she said, gently. "Is this right? Or am I just a silly old woman with too much imagination?"

Julia tried to answer, but her voice let her down. It cracked, and in a moment she was in tears.

Joyce waited, her expression benign.

"I've been so happy here, Auntie. Quiet and getting on with my work, and learning so much about my family and India, and really feeling settled, and then I got an email. Today. From Hari Dhawan. Do you remember him?"

"That very glamorous gentleman who was here the first night we met? And then, rather suddenly, was not?"

There was nothing wrong with Auntie Joyce's memory. Or her instincts. She waited, smiling, leaving Julia to fill the silence.

"That's him. He... I... We...had an understanding."

"That, my dear, was obvious. We were all surprised he left. And now he's coming back?"

Julia nodded, wiping her nose with a tissue.

"We had unfinished business, he says."

"Is he right?"

"I suppose so. He left in a bit of a – fury, I suppose. I had put my foot down about staying here, and he wanted me to carry on working for him. He's coming on Saturday. I hope it'll be okay. I'm sort of looking forward to seeing him, a bit nervous and a bit resentful. I've things to do. I want to keep writing, now one book's been accepted, and finish my PhD and I – well, I'm sick and tired of other people interfering with my life."

She shrugged and bit her lip.

"Rather like Helen, I suppose," said Joyce, matter-of-factly. "And look what happened to her."

Before Julia could reply, Sireet announced that lunch was ready. The two women followed him into the dining room, and sat opposite each other in the middle of the old table, laid with blue and white china on a lace cloth.

"This is rather like it was when Helen was here, you know. Evangeline was a stickler for a pretty table setting, and Sudham obviously passed it on to Sireet."

She spoke in Hindi to the bearer, who nodded as he replied. Julia's Hindi was up to only a sketchy understanding of their conversation, so she was grateful to have it translated for her.

"He says he's Sudham's son, and that *his* son is also being trained to take over. Sudham retired when he was seventy-five, and that was forty years ago."

"Gosh, you got a lot of information very quickly!"

Joyce grinned.

"It helps being an old lady who has been around for ever. I expect one of my servants comes from Sireet's family – everyone is connected to everyone else in the servant fraternity, the good servants anyway. They're proud of their craft, and pass it on. The bad ones don't last, or get jobs with the incomers and those who aren't used to having staff. They learn pretty fast, though, after they realise how often their foodstuffs need to be replaced."

After lunch, Julia poured tea into almost transparent cups. They sipped in silence.

"Oh, Auntie Joyce, what shall I do? I've enjoyed being on my own, without anyone to answer to. I've been free, writing when I wanted, staying in or going out. I've felt grown-up for the first time, in charge of my life. It's been great. But Hari makes me wobble. He…"

"This seems like an awful lot of fuss – for what? A short visit, a few days. Everyone will know that he's here the moment he arrives, so you had better bite the bullet and have a dinner or a party to show him off. Take the wind out of their sails, so to speak."

Julia looked at her.

"I… It's just that – well, I did like him. I did once think we might… but he's very used to doing whatever he likes, and to being allowed to get away with murder…"

Joyce giggled. "Hark, I hear the echoes of a distant time."

"What? What do you mean?"

"Just that your great-aunt Helen once said something very similar to me about Prakash. Handsome and demanding. Here one moment, gone the next. And I don't think fidelity was one of his strong suits either. But Helen was nothing if not realistic. She knew that she couldn't change him, and soon enough that she didn't particularly want to. She let things be and enjoyed her friends and her son. This is a happy house, and I know you enjoy it. Let it work its magic!"

Julia grinned. "Okay, Auntie Joyce. Let's think about who we're going to invite. How about Saturday dinner? Sireet and the cook can do that on auto-pilot. Hold on, I'll get a sheet of paper."

## Chapter Fifty-five

Julia arrived at Ranpur station far too early. As if to call her bluff, Hari had decided to take the train. She smiled at the decision – he would have much preferred a First Class flight!

Abdul, Joy's driver, dropped her under the arches at the station entrance, and then parked the car under the bright green leaves of a spreading *neem* tree. She walked into the station, picking her way through a throng of people. The signs told her that Indian Railways were the "Lifeline to the Nation", and that the train from Delhi would be on Platform Two in twenty-five minutes, so she sat on a hard wooden bench, varnished in bright orange, to wait.

Hari would be in a luxury train, she was sure. He did not like discomfort. She wondered how he would enjoy his "Tea Kit" (six rupees), or his "Evening Tea" (forty-five rupees) – not much, probably. He was never charmed by noise and crowds. She smiled at the memory of trips they had made together!

"It's nice to see you smiling," said a familiar voice.

Hari. Tall, elegant, well-groomed – exactly as he always was. Without thinking, she stood up and took his outstretched hands. He squeezed her fingers.

"That's a lovely welcome. I thought you might still be feeling a bit frosty."

They walked out into the forecourt; Abdul had spotted

the arrival of the big Delhi train, and was waiting just outside, ignoring the angry shouts of taxi drivers.

"Good afternoon, *Sahib*! Welcome!"

He held the back door open for Hari, and then ran round to the other side to do the same for Julia. A minute later, the car was nosing its way through the traffic and on to the busy road.

"Not far to Jacaranda Lodge," she told Hari. "Do you remember?"

"Not in detail, but I knew it wasn't a long drive from the station. How are you? You look great."

"Thank you. So do you."

The conversation was stiff, polite. They had to re-establish a connection, gloss over awkwardness. Hari sat back in his seat, looking out of the window. This gave her a chance to look at his profile; his lips were tight, his bearing tense. Mine too, she thought.

Five minutes later they were outside Jacaranda Lodge, and the *chowkidar* was taking Hari's aluminium suitcase up the front steps. Sireet collected it and led it on its wheels down the long verandah to the largest guest bedroom.

"Your room's called the Blue Room – for obvious reasons. It used to be Evangeline's. It probably hasn't changed much since her day, except now there's air-conditioning. There's still a fan, if you'd prefer."

"Was Gandhi skinny? I'm not a fan of fans." He grinned. "See what I did there? No, if there's an air conditioner going, I'll take it!"

She nodded, remembering very well. They were uncomfortable for a moment, not sure what to say. He quickly broke the silence.

"I'm sure I shall be very comfortable. I shall try not to offend the shade of Evangeline, who is probably turning in her grave at having her venerable furniture slept on by a tinted gentleman, but I expect she has had plenty of time to get used to the idea."

Only Hari could tread the creaking ice of racism so casually, without causing or taking offence. She nodded, and he walked past her and into the bedroom, leaving her standing on the red stone floor. She turned and walked back to the sitting room calling to Sireet.

"Please bring tea, and is there any cake? I asked the cook to make one. And scones, too, please. And *nimbu pani* too. We will have it on the verandah."

Twenty minutes later Hari joined her, wearing a white *kurta,* his hair wet from his shower. He looked at his ease, and this made her feel more relaxed. They spoke of many things: his parents, his sister, his writing.

"Which has not been flowing as easily as usual. I wondered when that would happen – it seems almost inevitable after all the books I've written. I'm not a never-ending stream, it seems. You have to be very happy, or very untroubled, I find, to write well and continuously. I haven't been either for a while."

She didn't ask why. There was bound to be a moment when they would have to mention the elephant in the room, but she wasn't ready for it yet. Conversation remained social, superficial. He made her laugh, telling her stories about London life. He mentioned a girlfriend occasionally, and she found that each time he did so her stomach clenched. She hoped nothing showed on her face.

"And you, Julia? How have things been, since our last rather difficult meeting in London?"

"Oh, pretty good." Her voice sounded high and brittle. "I've moved out of my flat, Freddie is getting close to seeing the colour of his investors' money, or so he says. We had dinner together a couple of times in London. He was okay. The usual. Lots of snide remarks, lots of questions. He doesn't change."

"Including the question about when are you coming back to him, I expect."

She caught a twinge of something – jealousy?

Annoyance? At her? At Freddie?

"Don't look like that," Hari said firmly. "He's a manipulative shit, as we all know. Likes to stir up a lot of nonsense."

Nonsense. That's what it was, she thought. Freddie liked a lot of nonsense, in his glitzy, moneyed, razzmatazz world, where the noughts increased exponentially in bank accounts when things went well, and evaporated if they didn't – until the next time.

"He hasn't been difficult about my settlement, at any rate. I thought he might be, but so far so good."

"That's good. I'm glad you've been able to be independent. Write your book, do your research. And I'm honestly pleased it's been accepted for publication by C&M. Aaron is no fool, and only takes on something he really likes or feels will sell. Well done. And I apologise for not helping."

Here it was. She blushed, feeling acutely uncomfortable.

"No, no, it's okay. I managed," she said, quickly.

"You certainly did, no thanks to me. I was just extremely cross, and very worried that what has happened would happen."

She took a deep breath.

"Hari, you will always be fine. We had a lovely time together for a while – no, don't grin like that, it makes me feel wriggly – it was a lovely time, but it wasn't the right time. Not for me. I had just got away from Freddie, and was setting up a life for myself. The letters I found took up a lot of my attention. I..."

"It's okay, Julia. It's okay. Water under the bridge. May I have another cup of tea? And then I'd like to move gently on to a gin and tonic. Are we eating in or may I take you out for dinner?"

"I thought we could have an early supper in, and go out tomorrow? What are your plans? Do you have anything you particularly want to do while you're here?"

He grinned again.

"Julia, my plans, such as they are, include getting to know you again. Shall we do a bit of sightseeing? There's that fort we never made it to last time? Massacreghat, too – that will bring up all sorts of interesting questions, for me at any rate."

"Sounds good to me. I've been there, but I'm happy to go again. I can get Abdul to take us, Sireet can run up a picnic, and while we are out, we can get him to drop off invitations to a buffet supper I thought I would have on Saturday? Not a huge group – how about twenty? Would you like that?"

"You have already collected twenty people you know well enough to invite for an evening? Well done! I'm not sure I could do that in London..."

"Well, you could, but you'd probably leave them half way through, like you did that time when you invited Whatsername, the agent you thought you might move to. You decided she was boring after twenty minutes, so smiled dazzlingly, forced lots of champagne on the poor woman and then disappeared. Leaving me to lie for you. She wasn't thrilled. I was a very poor substitute!"

They both laughed. Soon, the light had changed to dusk, and Sireet brought out two gin and tonics, ice clinking deliciously in the tall glasses.

After supper, sitting out on the verandah with their coffee, Julia gave Hari some white cards.

"Here. Make yourself useful. Please write addresses on this lot. It would help Abdul tomorrow. I'll do the other half, and it'll be done in no time."

"Very good, miss," said Hari, and got down to business. His writing was flamboyantly large with italic flourishes.

"This is very formal," he said. "I rather like it. Well, what now? Another drink, and then I shall turn into the Blue Room for the night. That's right, isn't it?"

His expression was hard to read.

"Yes. Please call Sireet if you need anything. He'll be here a bit longer, and there's the night *chowkidar* if you need something urgently – as long as it isn't too complicated! This isn't the Ajmer Palace!"

She could have bitten off her tongue as she said this. Instead her cheeks turned red, and she couldn't meet his eyes as he answered.

"No, it isn't. But it might be one day!"

There was nothing she could trust herself to say. She was annoyed with herself for moving off neutral territory. She wasn't ready for the verbal swordplay Hari liked so much, and now who knew what she'd started?

"Good night," she said, crisply, "I hope you'll be comfortable."

He stood up and gave her a little bow.

"I'm sure I shall," he said, smiling. "Sleep well."

## Chapter Fifty-six

The next two days were spent, as Hari had said, getting to know each other again. They soon fell into a comfortable routine.

Breakfast was about eight. They met each other at the round verandah table, saying little, enjoying the sound of birdsong, and the steady splash of water on the flowers from the *mali's* hosepipe. It was a lovely time of day, before the sun was high in the sky and the heat became almost unbearable. Now, butterflies flickered from flower to flower, and dragonflies filtered the sunshine through their iridescent wings.

"Well, my dear," Hari said on the third day. "This is cosy. Sireet is getting used to us being together. Are you?"

She looked up sharply from the paper she was reading.

"Oh dear, have I said something I shouldn't?" he said.

"But we are getting on so well, quite like an old married couple."

"From what I've learnt of marriage, Hari, I'd prefer to say, like a pair of old friends."

"Whatever you prefer, Julia," he said blandly, and returned to his reading.

She read the first paragraph of an article three times before she put the paper down.

"What shall we do today? We have our party this evening, but Sireet has it in hand, so it could be time for a bit of gentle sightseeing? The Orchid Palace, on the hill just above Ranpur? Fifteenth-century origins, lots of beautiful marble and mirrors. I've only been once and I didn't get to see the harem, which I've been told is the best bit."

Before long they were being driven up the hill, passing elephants, decorated with paint and silky pennants, their whiskered eyes sad and soulful, as they slowly carried howdahs of squealing tourists up to the Palace.

"Ugh," said Julia. "I hate it. It is so humiliating for them, and the *mahouts* poke great pointed sticks into them to make them walk. How can tourists be so insensitive?"

"Not everyone understands what's going on, Julia. And anyhow, everyone has to eat. A tip from one of those Americans will feed a *mahout*'s family for a week, or more."

He never encouraged sentimentality. She put her reaction to one side and looked out of the window at the valley below her. A crenellated wall followed the road up to the sprawling stone building that squatted on the hill top. The sun was heating the air like a gas burner under a kettle and she was grateful for the air-conditioning. Leaving the car, she and Hari walked slowly across the paved forecourt and paid their entrance fee to a small woman in a *shalwar khameez*. A pair of Americans, wearing baggy blue shorts and T-shirts with some words on the front, pushed their Tilley hats back on their heads and looked about them.

"This way Brian, it says here. This way to the *Hairem*. It's supposed to be stupendous. What do you think?" said the woman, reading from the guidebook in her hand.

"A large cold beer would be stupendous, that's what I think," muttered Brian, mopping his red face with a large handkerchief. "Okay. Let's do it. Then let's find a café." The two of them disappeared through the archway.

Julia grinned at Hari, who she knew had enjoyed the little scene as much as she had.

They spent a delightful afternoon, laughing, taking in the mosaics and the carvings and the views across the valley through windows fringed with lacy carved marble. They stopped for a cold drink in the café at a table under a white sunshade. Uncomfortable memories had been erased, if only temporarily, and there seemed no reason to think about the future in this limpid, sun-soaked afternoon.

"Good lord, is that the time?" Julia exclaimed. "Four-thirty already. We need to get back. Thank you for coming with me. I really enjoyed it."

Hari turned to look at her. He took a moment to speak.

"It is – nearly – always a pleasure to be with you, Julia. It's been great. And I haven't moaned about the heat once."

"No you haven't," she said. "For which I'm profoundly grateful. It must have been a real struggle to restrain yourself."

"You have absolutely no idea," he said. "Come on, let's go."

He held out his hand to help her up, and they walked together to the exit, sidestepping a child's pushchair, and avoiding a round bed with a cactus in the middle of it.

It took hardly a moment to hail a taxi, which took them swiftly down the hill to the main road, and turned towards Cantonments.

"Right, let me check with Sireet about the

preparations," Julia said, as they walked through the gate ten minutes later. "You'll probably want to freshen up. I do too. See you here at six?"

All was in hand, of course. Flowers had been brought in from the garden and were arranged in vases, small canapés were laid out on plates, glasses on trays. The fans moved briskly to dissuade the flies, and bright red Mansion Polish had been applied to the floor, which shone.

Julia and Hari were on the verandah in plenty of time, and enjoyed a glass of cold white wine together before their guests arrived.

"I want to say something," she said suddenly.

"You always do," he sighed.

"Everyone will think that we – well – that we are... you know, together. And..."

"What? And what, Julia? Are we together? Or aren't we? Is it a little early to decide? I'm not pressing you, but I didn't come here just for the sightseeing."

She nodded, looking at him with a small frown between her brows.

"I know. I'm not trying to avoid a conversation, but I don't want to rush things either. And you know how people jump to conclusions..."

"They do. Especially here in India. I promise I won't say anything controversial. Look, I think your first guest is here."

Not sure whether to be irritated or relieved, Julia welcomed Auntie Joyce who was wearing a purple silk sari with a gold trim.

"You remember Hari, don't you, Auntie Joyce?"

"Of course. How very good to see you again."

And so the evening began. Guests arrived, were greeted and introduced to Hari, who made himself agreeable to everyone.

Julia made it as clear as she could that he was a friend

who was visiting, and leaving in a couple of days. Everyone was politely interested: Subayah, the businesswoman; Khalisa, the gallery owner; Sahanj, the doctor; Samirvir, the director of the Museum of Art, and his wife Neelakshi; Amina, the painter. Julia had invited Dorothea; Abdul the driver collected her, and took her home half an hour later. It had not been a long stay, but she'd been delighted to come. She and Joyce decided between them that it was quite like old times!

By ten-thirty, the last person had gone home.

"Shall we stay out here on the verandah for a bit?" Julia asked. "Let me bring you a drink. What would you like?"

"A whisky and water would be lovely," he said, watching her with warmth in his eyes.

As she reached for the bottle of Johnny Walker, Julia unexpectedly felt embarrassed and clumsy.

"Thank you," he said softly, as she passed him his glass. He patted the chair next to him.

"Come and sit down here, Julia. Now listen. We've got to mention the war. Haven't we? Let's get it out into the open. Do you think we have a chance of making this work? As I remember we rather enjoyed it last time, and I have to say that I've not enjoyed not having you around."

He put out his hand and touched her arm, leaving his neatly-manicured fingers on her smooth tanned skin.

"You... I...I'm not coming back to live in England all the time," she said. "That's what we came to blows about last time. I'm happy here, for the moment."

"But your visa must be a bit of an issue, no? Surely you can't keep coming back to stay for any length of time?"

"I've a research visa and so far there seems no problem, for a year or two at any rate. After that I shall have to think..."

"Well, there are ways, I'm sure. Especially if you're toing and froing."

"I shall be," she said, slowly. "I like being in England,

but I like it here too."

The silence was very busy.

"I could help with the visa, of course," he said.

"How? I didn't realize your contacts extended to the government, or at least the Ministry of Immigration or whatever."

"If you're the *wife* of an Indian citizen..."

Julia's face went white and her heart jumped in a very unsettling way. Hari waited impassively, saying nothing.

"Wife?" she said foolishly. "Yours?"

"Well, unless you think my father might divorce his wife, or perhaps you could see yourself marrying your cousin...although his partner Pierre might have something to say about that. And you have to admit that it wouldn't be as much fun, would it?"

She shook her head slowly, thinking hard. Then she looked into his eyes.

"This is hardly the proposal of marriage a young girl hopes for, but I admit, it has its pluses," she said, and began to laugh.

He still had his hand on her arm, and his fingers pressed her skin. She turned towards him, and he raised his hand to her cheek.

"Dear Julia. Very dear Julia. It wasn't the proposal I expected to make either, but it does seem to be the right time and place."

Very slowly, he moved his head to hers, and they kissed gently in the shadowy candlelight.

"This feels very odd," she told him when she could speak. "And yet..."

"Shhhhh," he said, and kissed her again. Then, "I've missed you, Julia. I didn't want to – I thought you were an irritating, stubborn woman who had got too big for her boots and I admit I wanted you to come a cropper with your book. But I missed you. Some girlfriends were prettier, some more – er – adventurous, but they didn't feel right. You do. That's it. I can't promise that everything will be plain sailing, but you know that. Come on, at last, let's go to bed. We deserve it."

She stood up, blew out the last two candles, and took his hand in the darkness. They walked together across the verandah, past the narcotic sweetness of the moonflowers, and opened the door to her room.

## Chapter Fifty-seven

"I'll call you when I get to London," Hari said, his mouth against Julia's hair on the back seat of the car.

"That'll be lovely. And I'll be back in about three weeks."

"Good. I'll miss you. While Abdul is negotiating the traffic, come here. I want to kiss you."

It was rush hour. There were cars everywhere, motorcycles carrying families of four or more, bony cows sauntering down the centre of the road. Horns blared, people shouted, vehicles avoided dogs by veering to right or left with no warning.

Abdul wound down his window and shouted to another driver, a man he seemed to know.

"He's asking if there's traffic on the back road to the airport," Hari told her. "I hope there isn't because at this rate I'll miss the plane."

Abdul jerked the wheel to direct the car through a tiny gap, past a clot of traffic. Ignoring the racket around him, he put his foot down on a short stretch of empty road. It wasn't for long. The traffic came together again, forcing him to slow down. A man on the roadside squatted incuriously on his haunches, looking at the traffic, chewing betel nut. Julia sat in the crook of Hari's arm, resting her head on his shoulder, feeling very happy. Abdul moved off again and the car began to gather speed.

Suddenly, with no warning, a van shot out from a side road. There was a squeal of brakes, a thud of crumpling metal, the shouts of other drivers as car hit car. Abdul looked over his shoulder and saw Julia slumped on the back seat, glass splinters from the smashed window in her lap. Hari had been thrown on to floor, and was lying there, very still, folded into the footwell.

Julia was still holding his hand, and she bent over to see if he was conscious. Blood was pulsing darkly from his half open mouth and his eyes were closed, their lashes occasionally flickering on the pale brown cheek.

Everything seemed to be happening in slow motion. She could hear the tinny wail of a baby, and saw a group of bus passengers standing, shocked, on the side of the road. Police sirens added to the hubbub; suddenly there were men in uniform shouting, pointing, ordering people to move off the road. Ambulances arrived, their blue lights flashing. Julia watched, stunned, as two policemen climbed over the folded bonnet of their car and started wrenching at the doors. Abdul's door opened with a screech of metal, and a minute or two later, the back door on Julia's side. One by one, they were dragged from the wreckage, Julia and Abdul first, then Hari, his limbs loose and nerveless, head lolling, the front of his *kurta* crimson with his blood.

He was laid on a stretcher, his body covered in a blanket and strapped down, a neck brace wedged into place. Julia watched, wanting to help, but knowing there was nothing she could do except stay by his side, follow the stretcher to the ambulance and climb in beside him.

As one white-coated paramedic attached a drip to a blood-smeared hand and another plunged and emptied a syringe into Hari's upper arm, the doors of the ambulance slammed shut. Its siren wailed as the driver wove his way through the crowds, lurching from side to side, gathering speed as the road opened up before them. Tears poured down Julia's cheeks, leaving her lips sticky with salt and

Hari's blood. She leaned over Hari and whispered:

"Don't die, Hari. Don't die. It'll be all right. I'm here. Don't die," staring at his closed eyes, praying for a flicker, a moment of recognition, even a smile.

But there was none.

At the Ranpur Memorial Hospital, Julia was shown to a cramped, curtained cubicle while Hari was wheeled away. She sat down thankfully on the bed. Chai was brought, and tissues to wipe away her tears, which kept falling, and cool damp cloths to clean away the sticky, drying blood on her hands and face.

Suddenly her teeth began to chatter. A doctor was summoned – how young he is, she thought inconsequentially, how handsome – and she felt a prick in her arm before swimming into sleep.

Julia awoke on a bed in a small white room. The curtains had been drawn and she was covered by a crisp white sheet and a blanket. She was still dressed and felt hot, so she flung it off, and swung her feet tentatively to the floor. Something wasn't right, she thought, and then remembered the noise, the blood, the screams. Her head began to spin and a moment later, a nurse came in.

"Miss MacCleod. Miss MacCleod. Don't rush, don't hurry yourself. The doctor wants to see you. Please hold on. I'll call him."

Julia turned her head slowly to look at her, saying nothing, waiting. When the doctor appeared, she wondered why he was looking so concerned. She soon found out.

"I'm so sorry, Miss MacCleod," he said. "So sorry. The van driver. He didn't care about the traffic. He just wanted to get going. It was a bad accident – very bad. Cars crashed and yours was crushed – a terrible pile-up. But you are okay, I think. Just a few scratches from broken glass. And your driver too. He was not hurt at all, I am pleased to say. A very lucky man…".

The doctor spoke so quickly that it was hard for Julia to get a word in. She held up a hand and waved it weakly to stop him. She asked in a whisper: "And Hari? Mr Dhawan?"

The doctor's face fell.

"I am afraid...afraid that Mr Dhawan was not so fortunate..."

Julia whimpered, shook her head. It couldn't be true...It couldn't be... He couldn't be dead, not now...

"Your companion in the car, Mr Dhawan, was indeed very badly hurt. His chest wound was deep and he lost a great deal of blood... And it took some time to get him to hospital..."

Julia began to sob, her shoulders heaving.

"...So we have operated without delay and he is seeming stable. Critical, but stable. So now he has been transferred to intensive care..."

The words took a moment to register, for Julia to understand. So he wasn't dead... he wasn't dead... There was still a chance.

"Oh please don't let him die...Please say he won't die. He won't, will he?"

The doctor tipped his head, his lips not quite forming a smile of reassurance.

"We will do our best, of course. But you must understand that the prognosis..."

"Stop. Don't say it. Just do whatever you can. Can I stay? Can I see him?"

"I think you need to rest, Miss MacCleod. To go home and have something to eat."

She shook her head sharply.

"It would do you good," the doctor continued steadily. "There's nothing you can do here. As I said, your friend is in intensive care – heavily sedated. You should go home. Come back tomorrow – we'll know a bit more then."

Julia looked at him blankly. She pushed her hair off

her forehead with the back of her hand, and wiped her cheeks with her fingertips. A nurse offered her a tissue. She took it, turning it over and over in her fingers, folding it over. She thought of Hari, cradling her in his arm on the back seat of the car, until she heard the doctor's voice again, a soft murmur, from a long way away.

"You shouldn't be alone," he was saying. "There's a lady waiting for you. She asked me to tell you her name is Joyce."

Auntie Joyce was waiting outside. She took Julia's hand and led her to a waiting taxi, with Abdul sitting beside the driver. He had on a clean white shirt, but there were still bloodstains on his trousers. They drove to Jacaranda Lodge, and Julia, still sleepwalking, went up the stairs, with Joyce beside her. Sireet was waiting, his face a mask. In her room nothing had changed. The sheets had been turned down as always, there were fresh flowers in a small vase on the bedside table beside a Thermos flask of iced water and an empty upturned glass. The fan was turning overhead, and the air-con was on – the room felt cool and peaceful.

"Here, Julia. Drink this," said Joyce. "A nice cup of tea."

Julia smiled at the familiar phrase, put her lips to the cup and sipped.

"Lie down. Come on, shoes off. That's the ticket. I'll wait here, and when you have gone off, I'll go and sleep next door. I hope you don't mind. I've brought some clothes. I'll stay as long as you need me."

Joyce helped to get her comfortable, arranging the pillows, gently brushing a curl of hair from her brow, smiling kindly.

"What shall I do now, Auntie Joyce? If he dies?" Julia asked in a whisper. "Everything was going to be lovely... and now... And now..."

"Don't think about it, Julia dear. I'm so sorry this has happened, my darling girl, but there is everything to hope for; Hari is young, he is strong, and he is still alive..."

Julia smiled weakly. A bird twittered outside the window, and the fan blades hummed softly overhead.

"That's better. Look, there's nothing we can do at the moment, so let's not waste time thinking the worst," said Joyce gently but firmly. "The Ranpur Memorial is a very good hospital, and. he's a very good doctor. They will do their best, and you never know..."

Julia put her cup down, leaned back against her pillows and closed her eyes.

"Thank you," she whispered, but tears still trickled down her cheeks. Eventually they stopped. Her breathing calmed. Joyce waited, then put down the hand she'd been holding, and wiped Julia's face with a small starched handkerchief. Her face was inexpressibly sad.

## Chapter Fifty-eight

When Julia awoke, her bedroom was the same. A ceiling fan turning slowly. The sounds of birds. Water splashing lightly in the garden, and early morning sun playing through the curtains across a polished wood floor. She could smell flowers and dust and wood smoke. Just another morning. She sat up in her bed, and then she remembered.

The crash. The blood...Hari.

Someone – Joyce, she supposed – had undressed her, made her comfortable, but she couldn't remember. And had put a cup of tea beside her bed. She picked it up and sipped it. Still warm. She felt cold, flat, a little nauseous. The tea helped.

Hari, she thought. Hari. Are you still with us?

Julia pushed the sheet back and got out of bed. Her feet met the cool wooden floor, and she slipped first one foot, and then the other, into her leather slippers. The timeless smell of polish and ironed bedclothes was soothing. Helen would have recognised the scent of fresh air and starch.

Suddenly it felt as if she was no longer alone in the room. The sensation was so strong that she looked around, expecting to see someone.

"Aunt Helen," she whispered, feeling foolish. "Is it you?"

Nothing. Of course.

But for some reason she couldn't quite identify, she continued talking. As if Helen really were there with her. "We aren't very lucky, are we, you and me? First you lost first Arthur, and then Prakash. And now, here I am, and maybe I've lost someone too. It feels terrible."

But through it all, Julia thought, her great-aunt had kept her dignity, and lived as she wished. People remembered her with enormous affection, so there must have been a great strength, a self-belief, a courage there. Julia needed a bit of that. If Hari didn't make it, she'd need to decide what to do with the rest of her life. She sat very still, there on the edge of her bed, listening to her breathing, to the fan, to the water, the birdsong.

The room felt very calm, and she took comfort from its stillness, its familiarity, and from that odd sense that Helen was somehow close by. She went to the dressing table, sat down, and checked her reflection. Her eyes were red, of course, but she felt different. Less vulnerable, less isolated. The comforting sensation of another presence faded. Now there was just her, and Hari. And whatever the future held.

When she was dressed Julia left her room and, squinting in the sunshine, followed the sounds of voices to the verandah. Auntie Joyce was talking quietly to Sireet, who saw her first, acknowledging her with a brief bow before turning for the kitchen.

"I know you'll not want much," Joyce said, "but I've asked Sireet to bring tea and toast and an egg. Can I encourage you to have a little?"

Julia smiled. "You are a dear person, Auntie Joyce. Thank you so much. I'll try. And if the hospital hasn't called by the time I've finished my breakfast, I'll call them."

When it came, Julia made an effort to eat the boiled egg. She managed most of it, and some of the buttered soldiers, but it was a struggle. Pushing away her plate, she smiled at Joyce.

"Thank you. That does feel better. Now I'm going to the phone."

She dialled the numbers and watched the dial rewind each time. It took several rings for someone to pick up the phone at the other end.

"Hello. Memorial Hospital?"

Julia, her heart beating fast, gave her name, and said she was calling about Hari Dhawan.

"Could you hold on, please. I'll see if the doctor is available."

The neutral voice was replaced by some irritating music. Then a man's voice came on the line.

"Miss MacCleod. This is Doctor Choudhury. Thank you for calling. Mr Dhawan is comfortable. Not yet out of danger, of course, but I am pleased to report that his condition is no longer critical."

Julia tried to speak, without success. All she could manage was a sort of squawking gasp.

"Miss MacCleod?"

"Yes," she whispered eventually.

"Please be assured that we are doing our best for your friend. There is still some way to go, but at this stage I see no reason not to be hopeful."

"You think he'll be all right," she asked, the blood beating in her ears. "That he'll recover?"

"I am not in the business of prophecy, Miss MacCleod. And I will not underestimate the gravity of his condition.

The metal in his chest may have missed his heart but there has been considerable bleeding and tissue damage. There is no doubt that it will be a long haul... But he is young and he is strong. At this early stage, we will just have to wait and see."

"Can I come in and see him?"

"If you want to visit, please do. But he is still heavily sedated, and will not be aware of your presence. In a few more days, perhaps, there will be some improvement."

All she could say was "Thank you. Thank you so much," before putting the receiver down slowly. It felt as if she had been holding her breath for several minutes, so she stood there taking gulps of air to steady herself before going back to the verandah and Auntie Joyce.

## Chapter Fifty-nine

It was eleven days before Hari Dhawan was discharged from Ranpur Memorial Hospital and returned to Jacaranda Lodge, sitting in a wheelchair that was carried up the verandah steps by Sireet and the *mali*.

It was here, on the verandah, that Hari spent most of his time, resting amid the birdsong and the dragonflies and the bougainvillea, which seemed to Julia suddenly brighter and more prolific. He was still quite weak, and drowsy from the medication, but day by day his strength and colour improved. At the end of the first week, the wheelchair was returned to the hospital and a walking stick took its place. By the end of the second week his dressings had been removed, and he'd started to put on a little weight. He was now able to get out of a chair without Julia or Sireet having to help him.

Each morning after breakfast he sat with a book or a pile of newspapers beside him, a cup of tea on the table and his spectacles on the end of his nose. And in the afternoon, with their arms linked, he and Julia made their way around the garden, stopping every now and then to sit on chairs or benches strategically placed around the grounds by Sireet and the *chowkidar*.

After the first few days Joyce discreetly left them to it, and went back home, dropping in every now and again – for lunch or for dinner – to check that all was well. And it was. They settled easily into each other's company, taking everything very slowly. Each had developed a healthy respect for time and serenity, and they began to enjoy it together.

One morning, Hari folded up the newspaper he was reading and put it to one side. He picked up his teacup, sipped, and put it down with the clink of china. Julia looked up.

"Yes? Is anything the matter?" asked Julia, looking up from her book.

He smiled at her. "We need to mention the war, you know."

She smiled gently. "There's been no war. It's been lovely. Do you think we can manage this for ever?"

"I doubt it, don't you? When I get stronger I'll probably be much less amenable."

They sat in silence until Julia spoke.

"So what are we going to do? You aren't going to stay here for ever, are you? And I want to spend time in India and do my writing and settle in. That wouldn't work for you would it?"

"It might."

She looked at him, eyebrows raised.

"Not all year," he said. "But how about we split our time? We could both write here, and enjoy the time after the monsoon, just as we have done for the last few weeks. And, if and when you want to, we could spend some time back in London. That would work very well for me."

She said nothing.

He waited.

"I don't want to be in your shadow," she said at last. "I want to have my own writing, and my own life. And you may not like that...?"

"Then I'll just have to learn to like it, won't I? At least, I'll try to like it. I'll try very hard. That's all I can promise. We may argue, we may clash about space and so on, but I promise I will try. I don't want to have to have another accident to understand what is important."

Julia blinked hard.

"Don't cry, my love. It was a joke. Sorry. I didn't mean..."

"It's fine. I'm being silly. You're right. It is important, and yes, let's give it a go. But I have conditions."

"Here we go..."

She tried to order her thoughts. It was important to set down some ground rules.

"I must know that I can come and go as I wish," she began. "And you are not to nag me if my plans don't fit in with yours. No, don't argue. I know exactly what you're like."

"Okay, okay. I know I'm not perfect. But I promise I'll try."

"It's just... I am not going to be bullied by you."

Hari stood up carefully, and reached for his stick resting against the wall beside him. Walking unevenly over to her, he bent his head and kissed her on the lips, stroking her cheek.

"There will be no bullying, you have my word. Just one more thing."

She looked enquiringly at him. Did he want her to fetch something? His pills? A drink? Something to eat?

It was none of these.

"I would go down on one knee," he began, with a soft, uncertain smile. "But even for you I can't do that right now. Instead, let me just ask... Julia MacCleod, you difficult, opinionated and often very irritating woman, will you marry me?"

Silence.

She looked past him into the garden. India, she thought. This is it. I'm home. A new life is beginning, here and in England, and with the man I love. Could anything be better?

"That's good. I'm glad you're smiling! I'll take that as a 'yes' then."

Hari put his hand on her hair and combed his fingers through her dark curls. She looked up at him, and her smile broadened.

"Yes," she said. "Yes, I will. Marry you. I will. I'm sure we'll argue and sulk and disagree about most things, but not about what matters. And I don't want to have all this fuss again. You have to promise – no more car accidents!" She put her hand on his and brought it to her lips.

A car horn sounded harshly in the distance. A dog barked. Water from the garden tap drummed into the *mali's* tin watering can. And there was the sound of footsteps behind them.

"Hello, you two. Oh... I'm so sorry... Am I interrupting?"

"Auntie Joyce, you are the most discreet of people," said Hari happily. "You could never interrupt. But you can be the first to kiss the woman I'm going to marry!"

His words stopped the old lady in her tracks. The next moment she flung her arms around him, and then Julia, hugging them both tight.

Hari called for Sireet to bring champagne, and Joyce flopped down in her favourite chair.

There's a lesson here, thought Julia, looking at them both, her head spinning. A lesson Helen had taught her.

*When something feels right, believe that it is.*

It was as if someone had actually spoken, as if someone had whispered in her ear. She looked around. This time she did not expect to see anyone, but she recognised a familiar warmth. A feeling of approval, love, comfort. She took a deep breath and watched them for a moment, two people who cared for her. And another thought came to her:

*Don't forget. Your happiness depends on you.*

Thank you, Helen. I won't. I've come too far for that.

**I would like to thank**

David, Jacquie, Sarah, and Sophie
for asking the right questions,
and making me answer them...

Paul Fulton at refreshingwords.co.uk
for his patience and formatting knowledge.

# ABOUT THE AUTHOR

Sylvia's family has had connections with India
since the East India Company.
She grew up on a tea estate in Bangladesh,
and was taught by her parents
until she came to school in England.
Sylvia has worked in London for *Vogue,
Country Homes and Interiors*
and *London Portrait*,
and as a freelance
for many national newspapers.
*The Jacaranda Letters* is her first book.
Her second, *Feverfall*,
is based on her years in Africa.
It will be published in 2018.